RAVEN

From the Caribbean's sultry rain forests to England's gracious country estates, over the Atlantic's stormy waters to America's vast frontier came the black-haired voluptuous beauty known as Raven. A plantation heiress turned pirate, she becomes the first of the dazzling Paxton women . . .

YELLOW ROSE

The one small bit of beauty in a Pennsylvania town, torn from the earth to take root in distant Texas where the family fortunes lay. YELLOW ROSE, the story of the pioneer spitfire, Elizabeth Michaelson and lean, hard-riding True Paxton, is a prairie-fire saga of love and the war for independence in the raw new West . . .

And Then,
PAXTON PRIDE

The tempestuous novel of ravishing Karen Hampton and Vance Paxton—an elegant, city-bred woman, a proud, unyielding man, a love welded by passion and wedded to the brawling new turf of TEXAS!

*Books by Shana Carrol
from Jove*

PAXTON PRIDE
RAVEN
YELLOW ROSE

YELLOW ROSE

Shana Carrol

A JOVE BOOK

YELLOW ROSE

A Jove book / published by arrangement with
the author

PRINTING HISTORY
Jove edition / April 1982

ISBN: 0-515-05557-3

Jove books are published by Jove Publications, Inc., 200 Madison Avenue,
New York, N.Y. 10016. The words ''A JOVE BOOK'' and the ''J'' with
sunburst are trademarks belonging to Jove Publications, Inc.

PRINTED IN THE UNITED STATES OF AMERICA

PROLOGUE

"We might as well be eating in a tomb," Carl Michaelson said.

It was a solemn, quiet night, the last to be spent in this house in which they had lived for twenty-two years. But that was, to Carl, a source of joy. He glanced at Hester, his wife, who stared at the unappetizing mass on her plate, all that remained of the year's turnip crop, now gone long before winter. For two years drought had dried the garden, left the well shallow and the grass short and brown with no hope of a hay crop. For three years blight had cursed both corn and wheat. The larger farms with better soil and deeper wells were more able to ride out ill fortune; the small ones bore the blunt of the misery. It was a small sop to Carl's pride that he had held out longer than many others.

Hester swallowed with difficulty and put her fork down in disgust. Carl often wondered where the pretty girl he had courted and married had gone. But then, she was a city girl, a doctor's daughter with a decent if not abundant dowry. Somehow, she had never learned. After twenty-two years, she was still unused to the hardships of a farm life.

Carl hadn't minded the first years. The weather had been good then, the soil still strong. His father and mother were alive and helped work the land and care for the two daughters who eventually came. Hester was bright and vivacious and, if she considered working in the sun anathema, she did keep the house clean and good food on the table, and enjoyed raising her daughters.

Something had changed, though. When and how, he wasn't sure. As his mother and father aged, she failed to take up the slack. She laughed less often and openly began to yearn for the city again. By the end of another ten years, she had forgotten how to laugh, had become thin and gaunt and gray. Now her lips were permanently set in a grim line, and trembled before the frequent sighs that drove him nearly to distraction.

Had he laughed once? Of course. Plowing, sowing, reaping, thrashing. Watching his daughters, Lottie and Elizabeth, grow through childhood had been a joy. And if they hadn't married yet . . . Surreptitiously, he inspected Lottie. Twenty years old, fair-haired and buxom, she had come close to marriage twice within the past two years, only to be left waiting at the altar when the question of other men in her life arose. Her reputation had suffered accordingly, and he had had to keep a close eye on her. The last batch of rumors he'd nipped in the bud with a stout left hook that took the measure of Elisha Rueben down at Meade's Tavern.

And then there was Elizabeth, sitting to his right where his son would have sat had Hester given him one. At least seventeen-year-old Elizabeth didn't consider leaving this godforsaken place to be the end of the world. And for one member of the family to agree with him was better than none, Carl thought, grateful for small favors. Elizabeth was golden-haired, with eyes like the first blush of green in spring. Cursing himself for his lack of self-control, he had watched her more than once down at the creek. The first time, three years ago, had been an accident. She was scrawny then, slow to develop, with a bare hint of breasts poking from her chest. But then she had bloomed and her breasts had grown high and round and firm. Her legs had thickened, and the shadow near their tops . . .

Carl forced himself to eat, to swallow the pasty mess Hester called supper. He never should have seen his daughter that first time, should have walked away from the temptation the Lord put in his way. Watching her made him think things no man should ever think about a daughter. If Hester had only loved him more . . . "I said, we might as well be eating in a tomb."

"You needn't shout," Hester scolded dully. "If we are lost in our misery, so be it. There is only one remedy, and that you refuse to take."

"My mind is made up, Hester. We'll be gone by noon tomorrow."

"But not to Philadelphia or anywhere else civilized."

He had told her a thousand times that he knew no way to

make a living in a city. "The new land is paid for. So are the supplies, and our wagon and passage."

"You could sell them to someone else. There are others who would be glad to go."

"Very well, Hester," he said between clenched teeth. "Have it your way. I don't *want* to sell them to anyone else. Does that satisfy you?"

Hester's smile was maddening. "Not in the least, but that was my point nevertheless."

"Which you yourself have made until I'm sick of it." Carl's voice rose in anger he found less and less able to control. "My God, woman, will I have to listen to this all the way to Texas?"

"I did not ask to travel to that godforsaken place. A man reaps what he sows."

Carl's knuckles were white and the fork bent in his hand. "I sowed neither blight nor drought, but am forced to reap the bile you spout. You twist the meaning of the Lord's Word, wife. Do not let me hear you do so again at my table!"

Hester's face colored and her eyes glinted with righteous indignation. "I don't think the girls need to listen to this," she said in a tight and trembling voice. "Will you leave the table, please?" she asked, glancing at each in turn.

"Stay seated!" Carl thundered.

"My, how you have changed," Hester clucked, knowing that her oh so reasonable tone enraged him.

Carl's fist slammed into the table. "Do you think it is easy for me?" he asked, almost choking with frustration and rage. "Do you? I look out my window and see brown corn and black wheat. I see a dead garden and a land of rocks and empty promise. What do you know of the land or what it takes to bring life out of it? You couldn't even make me a son!"

Hester's face turned white and her lips pursed. "It is my duty to accompany you 'whither thou goest,' " she said in a dry husk of a whisper. "So I shall, for I made that pledge before God on our wedding day. I keep my vow. But you, husband—" The word a curse, the way she said it. "—promised to care for and honor me, and you have broken that vow." She rose majestically, scarcely aware that her chair tipped over and fell behind her. "You have broken your word to me and to your daughters!'' she screamed and, spinning, ran into the pantry and slammed the door behind her.

"Wife!" Carl roared, following her and stopping as he heard the bolt slam closed. "Wife!"

Lottie looked at Elizabeth and rolled her eyes.

"Hester! Open this door!" He struck the door twice with the side of his fist, gave up and staggered back to the table. His forehead was beaded with perspiration, as if every fiber of his strength were required to keep him under control. "I'm sorry, you girls. I mean . . . Daaamnnn!" he bellowed like a beast in pain, and beat his fist into the table top.

A cup bounced out of a saucer, rolled, and crashed to the floor. The broken pieces crunched under Carl's boots as he stalked across the room. A second later the front door crashed open and he was gone, out into the night.

Lottie looked around the kitchen. "It's not even ours anymore," she said with a shrug. Dropping her fork, she picked up a piece of gingerbread and began chewing it slowly.

Her appetite destroyed, Elizabeth pushed away from the table.

"Where you going?" Lottie asked, not really caring.

"I don't know. Just out, I guess."

"Better stay away from him until he calms down."

"I know." *Oh, how well, but not for Lottie's reasons.* "I will."

The old house. It breathed around her as she walked through it. Granddaddy and Mamaw had built it years ago around the turn of the century when Carl was a boy. Sometimes she felt as though they still lived in it, Elizabeth thought, as she walked down the hall past the living room. If she listened, she could hear Mamaw rocking in her downstairs bedroom, could smell Granddaddy's pipe as the smoke wafted in from the front porch. Quietly—needing quiet after yet another dose of rancor—she closed the door behind her and sat on the top step.

The night was clear, hot, and dry, as every night had been for the past month and a half. Not a breath of wind stirred the trees. Leaving. Her last night on the porch, in the house, on the farm where she grew up. Whatever the future brought, there was no turning back, as she had known on that night a month earlier when, his face flushed with excitement, her father had returned from Philadelphia to present Hester with the deed to more than two thousand acres of what he described as prime Texas land. Shocked, her face bloodless, Hester listened as he explained that he had paid for the land with their savings, his and Hester's meager inheritances, and the title to their farm. All their debts were paid, and there was enough money left to secure passage down the Mississippi and buy food for the journey and supplies once they reached their new home. For the first time in months, Elizabeth remembered, he had smiled and joked.

She had found his rare excitement contagious, had quickly shared it. And on that night she had been poignantly reminded of the way her father used to be, even three or four years ago, when Granddaddy and Mamaw were still alive. Father had yet to get religion then, didn't fall into the black rages under whose influence he changed from the warm and loving father she had known and became the frightening stranger who watched and touched her when her mother was out of sight.

Texas, she hoped, was the answer. Somehow, if they started over, things would be the way they were before. The land would be fruitful and her father tender and caring as she remembered him when she was younger. He wanted that, too, she could tell. She could see it in his face during his most anguished moments. No matter how great his rage, how deep his frustration, how tormented his mind, he did not want to be the man he had become, and fought against the demons that seethed inside him. If she could just tell him that, she thought, just tell him that she loved him, then their lives would change. This night of all nights, he needed to hear that he was loved, for as hopeful as he was, the leaving was as hard on him as it was on Hester. A man didn't live all his life on one hundred and sixty acres of land and then, one day, abruptly pick up and move a thousand miles without feeling upset. If she could just tell him. . . .

He was alone in the night. Alone, angry, perhaps afraid, although he would never admit to fear. She wanted to go to him, feared letting herself near him, yet found herself rising and walking down the steps. She knew where he would be. Rounding the house, she passed the barn and struck out across the north fifty where the black wheat crunched drily underfoot. There on the crest of the hill where the four fences met, she saw him silhouetted against the starscape, standing on the stump.

Closer, Elizabeth could see the stump itself. Almost five

feet in diameter, the remains of the massive elm plunged into the moat her father had dug around it. The outer roots had been hacked and burned in two, but the inner and tap roots remained. Carl had tried to dig it out. He had set fire to it, he had used black powder on it. And he had all but ruined a team of stout mules trying to pull it out.

"I thought you were your mother," he said as Elizabeth stopped outside the moat. "Thought maybe she'd slipped out to tell me she really didn't mind and that she wanted to go." He laughed bitterly. "You'd think I'd know better, after all this time."

"I want to go, Father."

Carl chuckled, more warmly now. "Maybe I should have married you. But then we might have had Hester. Ahhh. What am I saying? I must be as mad as your mother thinks."

"Mad with dreams, maybe. There's nothing wrong with that."

"You're always defending me."

"You're my father."

Carl held out his hand. "Come on up. You can see the whole farm from here."

"I know," Elizabeth said, stiffening.

A heartbeat. Two, three, four. "Why do you hesitate?" Carl asked, his voice becoming flat and ominous when she didn't move.

"It's dark. I don't want to turn my ankle," Elizabeth lied.

"You know what this stump is?" Carl asked. He sat, felt for a firm foothold in the dark moat, and stepped across to stand at Elizabeth's side. "Failure. *My* failure. I tried my best to uproot it from this field, but it beat me."

Elizabeth shied at the touch of his hand on her arm. "Maybe it belongs here," she suggested, making herself stand still.

"The devil you say!"

"Don't you see?" she asked, hoping she'd found a way to free him from his misery. "It belongs here, and we do not. There is no shame in that."

The stump. The implacable damned stump, soft in the starlight but hard as iron and stubborn as time itself. Carl stared at it, remembered the day lightning had felled the tree it held, remembered the long hours of cutting and splitting and hauling, and the half a winter's stack of firewood it had made. That was gone these thirteen years, but the stump remained. So maybe it did belong and he didn't. That was it! Had been all along. A message from the Lord that he hadn't understood. "I like that, Beth," he said, embracing her. She smelled slightly of gingerbread, the treat she had baked for their final meal. "I like it. Yes, it suits me well."

The Lord had spoken. Ecstatic, he bent down and kissed Elizabeth's forehead. She tasted good and he wanted another kiss. If only Hester would love him! A wife should love her husband. Love and succor him, give him pleasure as the Lord had decreed. Not drive him in temptation's way, send him lusting into another woman's arms, send his blood racing with unholy desire.

"Father." Elizabeth tried to push him away, clenched her teeth to keep from screaming. "Father, Father, please! . . ."

A dimly heard voice. The clouds parted, and he saw himself as though on a height. In his arms was his own daughter, tense, rigid as a board, near tears with fright. "Get back to the house," he said, pushing her away from him lest his arousal betray him further. "You'll be needing your sleep. We've a long day tomorrow."

Elizabeth had felt his rising heat. Her face red with shame, she was torn between revulsion and the deepest sympathy. Rationally, she knew the fault was not hers. At the same time, deep inside, she blamed herself. At least, this time, he had refrained from touching her. "Father?"

"Go on, I say!"

Elizabeth whirled, and ran back across the blackened wheat toward the beckoning sanctuary of the amber-lit house that was no longer theirs.

Alone, Carl looked down at himself and clenched his fists as he willed the symbol of his unholy lust away. At last, his face a mask of pain and perplexity, he squatted, grabbed one of the cut roots, and began to pull. The muscles in his hard arms and back stood out. His teeth clenched. Where mules and gunpowder and fire and shovels had failed, he tried to heave the stump from its earthly grip. His lips curled back. His back straightened, his shoulders creaked. A silent scream tore his throat. And then his fingers slipped free and he flew backward to land in the dusty black wheat.

Some time later he sat up and crawled back to the stump, leaned across the moat and let his forehead rest against the wind and fire-smoothed wood. "Stay, then," he gasped. "Stay."

And acknowledging his defeat, he curled his body around the sharp roots and went to sleep.

Elizabeth watched her reflection shimmer and tremble in the still water. So many memories in a simple moss-encrusted oak bucket. The depths held secrets she had told to no one else. Secret hopes and secret hates. Ambitions better left unspoken. Wishes normally reserved for the first star of evening. Joy and sorrow. A girl's life, from the day she could walk and first looked into her own eyes . . .

I could take the bucket. No one would know.

She sighed and remembered her father's words. The wagon was more than full enough. They had already packed everything they needed. All else was to be left behind. Even a plain bucket that weighed so little, yet was deep enough to hold all the memories that made life worthwhile. Mamaw's lined face beside hers, so young and innocent. Granddaddy's, too, more than once. Mamaw had smiled and hugged her. Granddaddy had looked serious as she explained to him how the little girl was really her. His eyes twinkled, though. She remembered that.

But such silliness! She was leaving many other, more important things behind. Not that many of her personal possessions remained. Even her precious books—Shakespeare, Fenimore Cooper, the poetry of Pope, her entire legacy from Granddaddy, who had been her teacher—all had been sold by her father. As had Lottie's dresses, all but two.

Elizabeth dashed illusion with a dipper and lifted a final cup of clean, sweet well water to her lips. The well was near the house. The window was open. She could hear her parents arguing. It amazed her that though the matter had been long resolved, her mother still pleaded and argued on the very morning of their departure.

"Disaster," Hester moaned plaintively, as she had almost daily for the past month. Then a quiet of sorts, that aggravated Carl even more, followed by a heart-rending sigh. The sigh had proven to be a formidable weapon where argument had failed. Sighing at breakfast and at lunch, sighing at the supper table. Sighs in the morning and at night, as she walked and as she lay stiffly in bed. The sighs had almost won her point, but Carl had only to step to the door and stare across the rocky, barren fields where his father had year after year coaxed crops from the merciless soil, had only to look at the brown, rustlike stains on the corn, the black blight that killed the wheat, had only to see his failure spread before him, had only to consider the sky too long devoid of rain, had only to plumb the damning depths of self-recrimination and guilt for failing, had only to *look* to feel his resolve return. Another place waited. Another land, another chance was what he sought. He would not be denied.

The front door slammed. "Whoa, mule, whoa! Easy, now." Her father's voice sounded as empty as the house they were leaving, as full as the packed wagon that waited at the front steps. Elizabeth peeked around the corner of the house and saw her sister Lottie emerge from the barn and run toward the well. "Good thing Father didn't catch you with that Ephraim Rueben," Elizabeth said.

Lottie was slightly heavier in build than Elizabeth. Her hair was a deep corn yellow and lacked the luster of her younger sister's, but her full figure and daring lips more than made up the difference. "I was just saying goodbye," she explained, wiping her mouth and glancing apprehensively toward the open window.

"A long goodbye."

"Mind your own business, Miss Snoopy Nose. Anyways, what would you know about such things?" Her point made, Lottie turned on her heel and, her gingham dress swirling, flounced into the house.

Elizabeth searched for a suitable retort, but as usual stood in tongue-tied silence. At seventeen, she had grown into a beautiful yet solitary-natured girl given to introspection and a yearning for sincerity as opposed to the games of mutual deception engaged in by Lottie and the boys who came calling. Lottie was the popular one. She was glib and sociable, never alone, went to all the parties, and even had the Rueben brothers fighting over her favors. She was right, too. No boys had called to say goodbye to Elizabeth. There was nobody to whom she wished to say goodbye.

Elizabeth left the well to walk toward the edge of the field where the mixed grove of lilacs and dogwoods formed a canopy of limbs and leaves over the wrought-iron fenced enclosure where Mamaw and Granddaddy Michaelson slept. The gate creaked closed behind her and Elizabeth knelt between the headstones, not to pray, for it would have embarrassed her to do so, but to talk to them as she always had.

"I guess there isn't much to say," she began, brushing a

tiny cobweb from her grandmother's headstone. "Just that we're leaving. Really leaving, and not coming back." She brushed away what few leaves and twigs had fallen on the cut grass covering the graves. "I'll miss you, Mamaw, Granddaddy. But Rita Hedges said she'd see to the tending, keep the weeds down and everything. I told her how you hated weeds, Mamaw."

"What are you doing, daughter?"

Her cheeks flushing, Elizabeth twisted around and looked over her shoulder to see her father towering over her.

"Who are you talking to?"

"Mamaw and Granddaddy," she said. "I was just saying goodbye."

Carl Michaelson held out his hand. Elizabeth took it and let him help her to her feet. "They're dead, daughter. They can't hear you."

"Yes, they can," she said, pulling her hand out of his and stepping away from him. He didn't like being contradicted, and she was a little afraid of his reaction. Still, he seemed in a relatively good mood. . . . "I know they can, Father."

Carl smiled ruefully, glanced at the house, the loaded wagon, and Hester sitting in morose and sullen silence on the seat. "I hope not," he chuckled. "Otherwise your Granddaddy would be wondering just what kind of a son he raised. Can't keep a woman in line. Can't raise a decent crop. And Ma would be saying, 'I told you so.' " He sighed, rubbed a hand across his jaw. "Well, nothing to be done about it now. It's all over with, and time to leave. Come with me, Beth."

His large-boned frame sagging with weariness and defeat, Carl led the way to the fence in back of the house. Elizabeth looked over her shoulder and silently whispered a final goodbye to the grove and the grave markers shaded there. "I won't forget you, Mamaw, Granddaddy. I promise"

Patterns of light played across the land. Rainless clouds shaped like short, squat puffs of cotton drifted in a slow parade across the steel blue summer sky. Carl was sweating by the time he reached the gate and the roses growing there. The day before he had selected the shoots he wanted, and now removed a pair of stout clippers from his pocket kneeled by the bush, and began to clip the stems a foot from the ground. "We will take them with us," he said dully. "They'll be a link. It's the least I can do for your mother."

The shovel, now. "We won't dig deep. Just enough to keep the roots moist."

His features were soft, and he was the father Elizabeth knew of old as he dug a careful circle around the trimmed bush and lifted it from the ground. The roses had been handed down from generation to generation of Michaelsons. Originally carried to the new world during the early birthing of the nation, the roses bound this family through the long dim corridor of time and across the wide spaces that separated its various branches. Her father had grown up with those roses, and after his own father died, had cared for the bushes more carefully than he had the failing crops that patched his fields. The roses brought out in him a depth of tenderness rarely seen in recent years, for it was only as he trimmed and plucked and watered and weeded that he seemed at peace with himself. Now, as she helped him wrap the balled roots in burlap, the fear and pain of leaving eased. The bond would not be broken. Mamaw and Granddaddy would not be forgotten. The chain of yellow roses they carried with them held the comfort of continuity, and the life force within the moist roots waited patiently to throw new stems and buds and blossoms that, in their strength and beauty, would defy death and time.

"It will be your duty to water the roots, to keep them alive," Carl said, rising and handing her the burlap bundle. "I trust you with this, Elizabeth. Your sister is busy mourning the loss of her clothes and friends. Your mother has contested my every step. But you . . . I think you understand."

"I do, Father. I do," Elizabeth replied, cradling the roses as if they were a child to be protected and nurtured.

Carl touched her shoulders and pulled her to him, gently kissed her forehead, and held her close. "Good," he said. His breath was warm on her face and Elizabeth was relieved when he let her go. "It is time, then. Tarrying serves no purpose."

Together, they walked away from the fence where, before the day was done, the cut bush would have begun to wither. Carl paused at the well, drank a dipperful of water, then grabbed the wooden bucket and smashed it against the rock wall of the well. "I am done with ye," he shouted to the barren fields, as if they heard or cared. "Bestow thy grand blessing on another!"

Wild-eyed, jaws clenched and hands balled into fists, he

turned to look one last time upon the land that had defeated him, and then stalked to the wagon.

"You'll kill yourself," Hester said as he climbed in beside her. "And all of us. You can't do everything by yourself."

Carl unwrapped the reins from the brake and shoved the handle forward. "I wouldn't have to do it by myself if you'd given me a son." He snatched the whip from its socket and swung it over the mules. "Git up, mules."

Elizabeth climbed into the wagon as it lurched forward and took her place in the back beside Lottie, whose face suddenly contorted. "We're going," Lottie sobbed. "We'll never see it again. Never, never."

Elizabeth cradled the cuttings and turned so she could see out the back. The old stone house, the barren garden, the barn, stark and leaning, were framed in the canvas opening.

"I miss it already," Lottie said, straining valiantly to keep from crying outright. "Well?"

On the front seat, Hester sighed and Carl hunched his shoulders as if wounded.

"Well, say something!" Lottie hissed. "Isn't it awful?"

Elizabeth watched the clouds tumble, watched the sunlight glint off the weathervane on the peaked barn roof, and the grove where the sweet dreams of innocence and childhood rested with the dogwood and the lilacs and the graves. "No," she whispered, her voice choked with emotion. "It isn't awful at all."

Slowly, the wagon rounded the curve at the foot of the hill and, as if it were a picture being wiped clean from a slate, their home disappeared. Elizabeth lay back and closed her eyes to picture the miles ahead and the new land that awaited them. "It's wonderful," she said dreamily. "It's all new, and marvelous, and wonderful."

PART ONE

Leavetaking

Chapter I

The serrated line of molten sunlight touched his hair first, then crept across his forehead. When it hit his left eye, True Paxton woke and looked around. Before him, covering the lowlands as far as the shimmering beach, the Brandborough Fair lay spread like a multicolored quilt set out to dry. There was little activity at three in the afternoon, for it was then that the heat-dazed crowds sought shade and relief from the humid, still air. True calculated another hour at least before the return of the ocean breezes. Only then, when whitecaps roiled and tossed in the Atlantic and the tent canvases started to pop and snap, would the pace begin to pick up again.

The cottonwood in which True sat was a massive old tree, one that had stood there as long as he could remember. For the moment he perched motionless, one with the tree. His sandy-blond hair almost matched the light leaking around the edges of the leaves. Partially by birth and partially by sun, the deep bronze of his skin approximated the color of the bark. His eyebrows were incongruously dark arches over eyes so light blue they appeared almost white. High, sharply defined cheekbones, a narrow if somewhat bent nose and tapered jaw gave his face a not unpleasantly triangular look. Lower, his neck, shoulders, and chest were hardened by work, knotted with muscles that even in repose reminded one of the strength of the limb against which he rested. But the time for rest was over. Groggy, True grabbed for a limb over his head and heaved himself to his feet. Sweat ran down his temples, dampened the fringes of his hair, streamed from his armpits. Late August was a hell of a time to hold a fair, but the old traditions took a long time to die out. The year was 1834, and the Brandborough Fair had been held every year for the last fifty, starting when Brandborough was but a hamlet of twenty-seven souls, not counting bondsmen and slaves. The years had wrought many changes at the same time they were so firmly bonding traditions. True remembered his first trip to the fair as a five year old excited over the prospect of new discoveries. He hadn't missed a single year in the seventeen that had followed. Nor had he lost the sense of excitement, not even, he thought with a wry grin, after the grueling ride that had brought him here this year. Stocking feet cool on the rough bark, he padded down the limb, jumped lightly to the slatted roof of the stables, to the top rung of the ancient wooden corral, and then to the ground.

The stables were quiet, sweet with the smell of horses and hay. A half dozen paces inside the shade, listless and lazy after a day of rest, a huge hammerheaded roan stallion whisked his long, flowing tail at the flies that plagued him, and waited out the afternoon. True walked to the horsetrough, scooped bitingly chilly water, and doused his head and chest. "You're hot too, I guess," he said, rubbing the excess water from his belly with his hands.

The roan stallion shook its massive head and nickered softly. True wet the animal's nose, grabbed the outthrust tongue briefly. "Cool off soon, Firetail," he said reassuringly. "Relax. Heat'll bother her just as much as it does you. You'll be fine. Here." He dipped a bucket in the trough and set it in front of the horse. "Last you'll get before the race. Drink it up and we'll take a walk. Get the kinks out."

It wasn't the best day in the world for a race. Only five days earlier, in Charleston, they had run against a New York horse and a surprisingly fast mule that must have had lightning for a sire. The heat had been brutal there, too, and Firetail had had to work hard enough that True felt it wise to rest him and ride the pack horse for the next two days. One thing had led to another. Two days out of Charleston, Joseph's horse picked up a limp and they were forced to lose a day. Consequently, they had arrived at Brandborough sometime after midnight the night before, which stole the day of rest they always tried to give Firetail before a race. Then to compound matters, neither Tom Gunn Paxton, True and Joseph and Andrew's father, nor Adriana, his wife, nor anyone else of the house, could be found. None of the boys knew what had happened until that morning when one of the hands showed up with the news that Temper, Firetail's sire, was ailing and Tom Gunn Paxton didn't want to leave his prize stud's sire. And besides, a visitor had showed up at Solitary, the Paxton homestead. "So just win and get on home, he says," the messenger reported. "Your pa's expectin' you no later than noon tomorrow, Maggie Hansa or no," he added with a knowing leer directed specifically to Joseph.

True wasn't sure about Maggie Hansa and her girls, but the admonition to win was more easily given than followed. Talking low, holding the tension well in rein, he began the routine that preceded every race. He'd checked Firetail's shoes early that morning, but did so again. He took out the blanket, light saddle, and tack he'd use for the race, inspected them all, and relocked them in the special carrying chest he'd made for them. He gave the horse a brief, brisk rubdown. By the time he'd finished, Firetail had had his fill of water and was beginning to react to the routine. "Easy, boy," True crooned. He smoothed the workout blanket across Firetail's back and threw on the heavy saddle made for everyday riding. These preparations always fascinated him. It was as if horse and man were one creature, each feeding off the other's anticipation of what was to come. True tried to hide the tension that slowly built in him but knew he was unsuccessful, for the horse picked it up, magnified and passed it back to his master. As Firetail's tail switched faster, True's fingers drummed on the nearest piece of wood. As True found he was unable to sit still, Firetail punished the floor with his hooves. Firetail's ears perked forward, and his nostrils flared. True's senses were keyed to a fever pitch. Only in the last moments before the race, as if they had planned it that way from the start, would a calm settle over both of them, only to shatter in a burst of energy that was as explosive as the report of the starter's pistol.

The ritual had become almost second nature over the past two and a half months. During that time, True, his brothers Joseph and Andrew, and Firetail, the roan stallion, had traveled from town to town up and down the state. Learning quickly who had the fastest horse and who the next fastest, one of them would challenge the latter to a race. True then let Firetail win, but only by the slimmest of margins, just enough to pique the sporting blood of those who had truly swift animals, and then they would repeat the whole process. So far, as the Paxtons' money belts attested, they had been remarkably successful, but the strain on horse and man was great. True was glad this was the last time they were running, at least for the year.

The first tentative stirrings of wind had started to float in from the Atlantic by the time True was finished and led Firetail out of the stable. Walking the animal around the core of the fairgrounds, he headed for the beach and the course they would run in another hour and a half. The crowds had started to build again. Barkers rubbing heat-drugged, sleepy eyes began desultory pitches that would build in fervor as the temperature dropped. Boys and girls tested their legs and lungs in mad scurrying dashes from booth to booth and tent to tent. Farmers stretched, popped their backs, looked knowingly at the sky, and nodded sagely. The word that True and his animal had appeared spread quickly, and the careful men who made it their business to know about horses stationed themselves where they could see how the stallion moved before they placed their final bets.

True could feel their eyes on him as he swung into the saddle at the starting line. He'd seen a half score of them at other fairs. There had been only one or two at first, but their number had grown quickly during the last two weeks. He didn't like them, but was aware that their bets stimulated the locals' antagonism to Firetail, and so indirectly helped the Paxtons' cause. In any case, their own self-interest necessitated their keeping Firetail's great speed a secret, so no harm was done.

The professional gamblers were another increment of the building tension. True held the reins lightly and let Firetail break into a trot as he guided him over the marked course. As they neared the great oak that marked the mile, True let him run for a few hundred yards, then reined him in for the turn and swung wide in order not to dig holes in the sand. When next he came that way, Firetail would know what he had to do, and the following rider would be forced to swing a little wide if he didn't want to endanger his mount's fetlocks at the precise moment they were the most stressed.

A mass of bunched and quivering muscles, Firetail was becoming harder and harder to hold in. Breaking, wheeling, prancing, he worked his way along the mile back to the start and finish line where True swung down for the walk back to the stables. The level of activity had increased dramatically, for the temperature had dropped a good ten degrees in the last half hour. The smell of candy and fried food filled the air.

Babies squawled, mothers shouted, children ran laughing underfoot, men argued and debated. An organ grinder's monkey solicited pennies from children and, with a comical grimace, dutifully bit each one before placing it in the cup he carried. Off to one side, a dozen men drove marked posts into the ground and weighed hundredweight boxes of stones for the horse-pulling contest scheduled to start right after the big race between Firetail and Tory, Mose Nolan's Virginia-bred mare that was the pride of the county.

Tory was a fine-looking mare, True had to admit as he led Firetail into his stall and stripped off his saddle. Lithe and trim, she looked even more so in contrast to the pair of huge Percherons in the open stall next to her. Looks were deceptive though. Experience had taught that more than once. True stripped off the sweat-soggy saddle blanket, opened the traveling case, and took out Firetail's racing togs. "Easy, boy, easy," he whispered as the stallion crowded him toward the rails.

"How is he?" a voice asked.

True turned and saw his older brother, Joseph. "He'll run."

Not given to accepting such pronouncements on faith alone, Joseph inspected Firetail himself. Lightly complected, his broad face was friendly-looking and heavily freckled. Thinning dark brown hair hung below his shoulders. Six feet four inches in height and broader by far in the shoulders than True, he was more often than not taken by strangers as a good-natured, shambling country bumpkin who lacked the wits to fend for himself. The truth of the matter, that Joseph was a shrewd judge of both men and horses, and used others' mistaken impressions of him to good advantage, was a secret he took great pains to protect from outsiders. Another horse expert would not have been fooled, of course, if he were given the chance to observe Joseph's eyes as he studied Firetail, or his hands as they quickly searched the stallion for fever or swelling. "Looks like it," he announced a short moment later, stepping back from the horse. "Only a couple hundred dollars left to go. I'll have it all down on him by the time you start. Luck," he finished laconically, melting into the crowd.

Twenty minutes remained. True tightened the cinch, checked out reins, bit, and halter. A row of boys watched as he pulled off his heavy work boots and shoved his feet into the light racing boots he'd ordered specially made from Charlotte. A clean shirt, fresh white lawn with bloused sleeves and leather laces at the neck, completed his outfit. The only thing left to do was go out and win the race.

Mose Nolan and his mare still hadn't left the stable. True let one of the boys swing open the stall door for him, another hand him his hat. The hat was a touch of genius. An English racing hat, it drew ridicule from rustic onlookers and helped foster the illusion that True was as much an idiot as his horse was too ungainly to outrun even a Percheron. "There he is!" a voice shouted from the crowd.

"That's him, right enough," another chimed in gleefully. "Oo-oo! And look at that hat! Bet his daddy ain't seen that."

"Hey, Paxton! I seen that so-called stud of yours race. Barely nosed ahead of Gierson's nag up Charleston way. He'll not do as well against Nolan's mare. Nolan whipped Gierson's by better'n a length."

True waved a hand toward the man who had spoken, one among a group standing on a wagon. They mistook his confident smile for a sheepish grin. Long, gangly, and awkward-looking in the clothes that hid his hard, trim muscles, he tucked a sandy curl beneath his cap, and continued on his way.

The crowd closed in behind him. Through it, moving with a grace that belied his bulk, Joseph angled away from his brother and wove through the crush. Five years older than True, Joseph had learned little more in his twenty-seven years than the lust for a tidy profit and the value of having the odds in his favor no matter what the situation. "Well, then, Mr. Miles," he announced, as he reached the farmer's wagon. "If you are indeed so confident of Mose Nolan's stock, perhaps you would care to join the wagering." He tugged on the brim of his hat and stared up at them. "Or it is true what I hear," he went on drily, "that you're all gut and bluster when it comes to the manly exercise of wagering and showing something more than an open mouth?"

Cameron Miles's friends, two other farmers cut from the same cloth, guffawed and slapped their companion on the back. "Joseph's got you there, Cameron," one said.

Around the wagon, those who had laughed at True's expense now turned on the red-faced Miles. "That's right. He's called your number."

"Show him, Cameron. Play your money—"

"If his wife will let him!" someone interjected, drawing good-natured laughter.

"—and make him pay. She won't mind that too much, will she?"

"All right!" Miles growled. The sight of his purse stilled them. "And who'll stand with me? Any of you? Who'll drink with me tonight on winnings from these high and mighty Paxtons?"

The farmers looked sullenly at one another, then grudgingly began to dig into their pockets. Good old bad-tempered Cameron Miles, Joseph thought to himself as he led the way to the speakers' stand near the starting line. Barley Hamilton, the mayor of Brandborough, was in the middle of a speech extolling the wonders of South Carolina, denouncing the policies of Andrew Jackson and the Congress that had passed the Force Act, coercing the states into paying revenues that all law-abiding, God-fearing South Carolinians knew were nothing more than taxation without representation. Joseph and the farmers edged around to the side of the platform where Judge Chaney was trying to stay awake. The judge did not hold with horse racing, much less gambling, but agreed to hold their bets anyway after a stern, whispered reproach.

Men had raced horses at the Brandborough Fair for years. Scheduled or scratch, there was never a lack of either contestants or spectators. The big race of the year, though, had been held for the last twenty-odd years at five o'clock on Saturday afternoon, and woe betide the politician who delayed the proceedings by so much as a minute. Mayor Hamilton's face was as crimson as the side of his fist, with which he rhythmically beat the podium. At last, with but ten minutes to go before five, he heeded his wife's frantic gestures and swung in tone from vituperation to patriotic fervor and launched into a final, rousing exhortation for a return to the good old days. With the change, the audience began to come alive again because they knew he was winding down and it was nearly time for the race to begin.

This year's contest was even more special than usual. For the first time in over a decade, a locally owned horse was considered fast enough to go head-to-head with a Paxton animal and, furthermore, given a good chance to win. Nothing could have delighted the townsfolk more. Brandborough had been founded by Paxtons, and the proud, aloof clan that descended from those forbears still ran it. The Paxtons, so it was said, were as easy to dislike as to like, for although they were generous, no man could remember that generosity not being repaid in multiples. With interests in shipping, horse raising, tobacco, and cotton, not to speak of the more than thirty votes they controlled either directly or indirectly, the Paxton presence was impossible to ignore. Watching a Paxton horse being outrun in the big event of the year would be balm to many a sore soul, even more so if the exchange of hard currency were involved.

All three Paxton brothers were aware of the animosity, and each reacted differently. True, in a way he couldn't quite define, sympathized with the townfolk; Andrew didn't really care one way or the other; and Joseph responded with a vindictive desire for revenge. That he might lose everything he'd won in the past two and a half months didn't occur to him as he bulled his way through the crowd in order to join Andrew. The two brothers, half-brothers really, for Joseph's mother had died some years before True and Andrew were born, were a study in contrasts. At seventeen, ten years younger than Joseph, Andrew was a good half a foot shorter. Where Joseph was broad, Andrew was slim as a cable and just as tough and wiry. Where Joseph was fair of skin and dark of hair, Andrew was darker, bronzed like True, and boasted wavy blond hair. Where Joseph gave the impression of plodding stolidity, Andrew exuded energy and appeared, even at rest, to be in motion.

Andrew was perched on the top of a pile of boulders at the water's edge. "Well, little brother," Joseph said, noting that the full course could be seen from their vantage point. "Looks like you've found the best view at the fair."

"The truth is, I had to pay half a dozen kids a dollar for it," Andrew admitted. "Thought it was worth it, though. Have a seat."

Using Andrew's shoulder for support, Joseph eased himself down, then jumped to his feet with a sharp yelp as the sun-heated rock blistered the seat of his pants.

"Takes getting used to," Andrew snickered.

"Like seeing your new bride take out her glass eye," Joseph growled, trying to figure out how Andrew could endure sitting on what felt like a red-hot blacksmith's forge. "Aha!" A triangle of dark leather poked out from underneath Andrew. Joseph reached down, grabbed Andrew by one arm and a leg, and lifted him into the air. "What have we here?" he asked, using his foot to pull the leather saddlebag Andrew had been sitting on out from under him.

"Put me down, you dumb ox."

"Not so dumb I haven't found something to sit on." He set Andrew down and quickly expropriated the saddlebag for himself. "Not very generous of you, little brother."

Andrew almost fell off the boulder, caught his balance at the last second, and burned his hand on the rock in the process. "Hey!" he yelled. "That was my idea."

"And a good one." Joseph wriggled around until he was comfortable. "Should have thought of it myself."

"Damn it, Joseph!"

"Wish me no ill will, Andrew. Tell you what," he went on expansively, "I am in a mood to be generous. Suppose you accompany me to Maggie Hansa's after the race. I'll see to it that she gives you something more important to worry about."

"Unfold that saddle bag so two can sit, and we have a deal," Andrew agreed.

Joseph produced a flask, uncorked it and drank before offering it to Andrew. "You do drive a bargain, little brother."

The bourbon took away Andrew's breath and brought tears to his eyes. He reached up to tuck his hair behind his ears and carefully fit his hat more firmly into place, and in the process wiped his eyes. "Had a pretty good teacher," he wheezed, returning the flask.

"That's what big brothers are for," Joseph said. He stuffed the flask into his hip pocket, and failed to make room for Andrew on the saddlebag. A smattering of applause reached them from the crowd surrounding the speakers' platform. " 'Bout five, don't you think? He look ready to go?"

Resigned to contenting himself with a minor victory, of sorts, Andrew sighed and looked out over the crowd.

True was easy to spot with his white shirt and silly hat, not to speak of the great strawberry roan. Next to him, Firetail looked bored as the applause died down and the mayor accepted his plaudits. *The calm before the storm*, True thought, stroking the animal's muzzle. *It's time to get on with it.*

The sun, still high in the sky, hung like a glob of white-hot steel. To the east, the Atlantic spilled creamy froth on the white sand. Beyond, the limitless blue of the ocean merged with the darker hues of the eastern sky. Farther down the beach, a hundred or so yards inland, the Christian Ladies

Auxiliary was busy setting up tables, unloading platters of cakes and pies from a flatbed wagon, and tending the fires burning under the huge cauldrons and grills where, later, crabs would be boiled and fish and oysters fried.

True breathed deeply, letting the sea breeze fill his lungs. His earlier nervousness had dissipated, and with the ensuing calm he was able to view, as from a distance, the course, the horses, and himself. As for the course, he'd seldom seen better. Staked out on hard-packed sand, it ran along the edge of the Atlantic where the shore road nipped at the beach, bent inland around a shallow cove, circled the massive live oak at the edge of the swamp, and returned to the starting line.

The two horses could not be assessed so easily. That Firetail was eager to run, there was no doubt. But Tory was too, and although True had not seen her in action, she did look fast. As much as Firetail liked to win, he could be in a losing race. One never knew. Nolan was no fool. He certainly couldn't be totally ignorant of Firetail's prowess, and perhaps he knew something that True didn't. More to the point, a horse could slip, lose its footing, pull a muscle or tear a tendon. Both animals were subject to the same vagaries, though, so there was no sense worrying about that. The third and final factor was himself. He and Joseph and Andrew had been traveling for two and a half months, and he was tired of it. The ordeal of travel and racing that had brought them back to where they had begun had engendered a listlessness that True couldn't seem to shake. The truth was that, aside from all the money involved, he didn't really care any more. He'd feel differently once away from the starting line and in the heat of the race, but the feeling would be temporary at best. Outside of those few minutes with the wind in his face and the sound of Firetail's hooves drumming in his ears, True was indifferent. Although the attitude bothered him deeply, for a man ought to care, it was all the same to True Paxton whether he won or lost.

"Ugliest creature I've ever seen," Mose Nolan sniffed, breaking into True's thoughts. He led his lithe mare, brown as sandy loam in a just plowed field, to the starting line, and turned to grin at True. "You sure his daddy wasn't one of them damn gators back in the swamp? That head alone ought to weigh him down."

It was true that Firetail had an unusually large head, that his legs were knobby and thick as tree limbs. His chest was too heavy, he stood too tall, and carried too much weight in his withers. But there was one other thing about the stallion that did not show. Pure, sweet, and simple, he liked to run fast.

What True had seen in the gangly colt three years earlier he never was able to say, but when his dam had died in the swampland around Solitary, True had taken him as his own, named him Firetail, and raised him. He had fed him, trained him, nursed him though sickness, and seen him grow strong and healthy, if not exactly picturesque. Like his sire, Firetail could be mean and irascible, and had a temper so unpredictable that only True might approach him without being wary of a nip or sudden kick. As he grew, though, it became evident that Firetail's liabilities were also his advantages. The too-wide chest housed huge lungs. His height let him cover a distance in incredible, yard-eating strides. His legs, so heavily muscled as to look misshapen, were more than capable of sustaining his bulk and giving him great speed. Only his oversized and overweight head remained a detriment, and that he overcame with pure pride and the will to win. All in all, as Joseph had been first to note, Firetail was one hopelessly homely animal that no one in his right mind would breed, but he could be made to show a tidy profit. At Mose Nolan's expense, True thought, hiding his anger with a good-natured smile.

"Are you ready, gentlemen?" the mayor called. "If you'll take your places, please."

Amusement rippled through the crowd as True mounted and guided Firetail to the starting line. "Maybe young Paxton ought to be allowed a few extry minutes to show that loghead which leg to start off on," someone called.

"Or just to figure out which end is fore and which is aft," another yelled, adding to the merriment.

Tory pranced to the starting line and took her place next to Firetail beneath the brightly colored banner that had been stretched between two posts. "You sure you have him pointed in the right direction?" Nolan asked, smirking.

"You going to race or talk?" True snapped, dropping all pretense of affability.

Nolan colored. "Ain't no call—"

"Get ready, gentlemen!" the mayor called, interrupting. Nolan shut up. Tory seemed to tense. True leaned forward in the saddle, felt Firetail's muscles bunch beneath him. The mayor lifted a flintlock pistol, checked the pan, then pointed the weapon up and out to sea. The crowd hushed.

"Get set . . ."

The mayor squeezed the trigger. Released, the flint snapped forward and struck the frizzen. Sparks ignited the powder in the pan and flashed down into the charge in the barrel. The pistol shot flame and a cloud of black powder smoke into the air. At the sound, both horses leaped forward.

Tory took a quick lead. Lighter than Firetail, she shot from the line and showed him her heels. Behind her, his eyes wild, Firetail thundered in her wake. "Go!" True shouted, the adrenaline surging through him as he leaned forward to become one with the horse. "Go!"

What they had was a by God first class horse race! The crowd spread along the course roared its approval. The Paxton horse was coming on strong, but Tory was holding her own. No one doubted she would win, and oh, the thought of pockets crammed full of Paxton money was as sweet as the smell of victory

At least for the first half mile.

"What's happening?" Joseph said, jumping to his feet. The roan picked up steam, began to close the gap. "What's he doing?" he asked no one in particular. "Too soon!" he shouted vainly. "Too soon!"

At five hundred yards, Tory was ahead by two lengths. At a thousand, less than one. At fifteen hundred, when they disappeared behind the tall sea grass at the head of the cove, by no more than a nose. And when they reappeared, Firetail was in the lead.

"What the hell!" Joseph screamed. Andrew stared dumbfounded. It wasn't part of the plan. True was supposed to let Nolan have the lead, then pull forward at the last minute to eke out a victory. Any other way, their odds on the next race would be diminished.

True had other notions. He drove his bootheels into Firetail's flanks. "Come on!" he whispered, knowing the wind whipped his voice away, yet knowing too that Firetail would sense his urgency. Winning or losing hadn't mattered much to him only minutes earlier. Not until Mose Nolan smiled and joked once too often, until the crowd of Brandborough's citizens had laughed once too often, until the starting gun, as it had the horses, had set his emotions loose to race wildly. Heedless, he swept the English racing cap off his head and let it fly away. Enough of silliness and cleverness! He had choked on Joseph's scheme for the last time. To be taken as a fool in a dozen other cities and towns was onerous enough, but could be lived with so long as they won. To be the laughingstock of Brandborough was intolerable under any conditions. No man had dared mock or deride a Paxton for the last hundred years, and True was damned if they would start with him, no matter what the cost in future winnings.

Blue water to his right, green trees to his left, ivory sand beneath him. How did the oak tree rise out of the ground just ahead? Magic? A mile so soon? True tugged on the reins, guided with his knees, felt his mount slow and lean, then come out of the turn and accelerate to full speed. A blur to his left was Nolan and Tory, just beginning to slow for the turn. "Move!" True yelled. "Run, you sonofabitch, run!"

Whatever thoughts reside in an animal's head no one knows, but it is said that some animals love winning. For the first time, free to run as fast as determination and muscle and sinew could carry them, Firetail bounded forward. His mane whipped True's cheeks, left them burning as if stung by a thousand needles. His hooves pounded the earth. Ears back, neck stretched, forelegs reaching, his whole body appeared an elongated blur, an exact symbol of pure swiftness and nobility of motion.

Four lengths became five. "Run, run, run!" True breathed, energy flowing from his fingertips into the reins, into the horse itself.

Five became six. "No!" Joseph shouted.

Six became an incredible seven lengths' lead. Firetail's nostrils flared and his chest heaved.

Seven became eight and eight became nine. "Why?" Joseph screamed, kicking the saddlebag. "Why?"

The banner blurred overhead as Firetail streaked past the finish line. Tory, a sure winner, followed an ignominious eleven lengths behind. Some few of the spectators whooped their delight. More, all those who had bet against the Paxtons and their ungainly roan stallion, stood in stunned silence. Nolan passed through the sullen crowd and savagely reined his mare to a dead halt. A hundred yards ahead of him, shedding grace as a snake does its skin, Firetail was slowing to an awkward, shambling trot before turning to walk back up the beach. Tory was breathing heavily and needed to walk, but when Nolan let her, she moved with an economy of effort and a fluid grace that made the loss all the more unbearable. A thousand-dollar weariness weighting his shoulders, Nolan slumped in the saddle. He didn't want to face True, wanted less to face the accusing stares that waited for him back at the finish line. That left only one direction. Slowly, he turned Tory to the right and rode through the fairgrounds. A short stop at the stables and he'd head home. It would be a long, lonely ride, but at least he could nurse his humiliation in private.

Feeling better than he had for the last month, True rode back through the crowd to the pile of boulders where his brothers waited for him. Andrew looked perplexed. Joseph stared in slack-jawed disbelief. "What's the matter, Joseph?" True asked. "You look like you just lost your best friend."

Joseph's mouth snapped shut and his shoulders hunched dangerously.

"Your best friend's wife, then?"

"Do you know what you just did?" Joseph groaned in a strangled voice.

"Yup," True said, all innocence. He patted Firetail on the neck and, obviously pleased with himself, grinned hugely. "I won."

Chapter II

Thomas Gunn Paxton had been a privateer during the War of 1812, and still looked the part. Tall and rangy, his raffish good looks were marred only by the patch covering the scar that cut across his blinded left eye and lent him a devilishly cruel appearance that his frequent, merry smiles did little to mitigate. At fifty-one, he looked fit to venture to sea again, and in truth, there were times when the seafaring blood of his great-grandparents, the pirates Jason and Marie, stirred his soul and left him yearning for a deck beneath his feet once more.

Such thoughts were not on his mind this August morning as he stood on the bedroom balcony that overlooked the drive leading to Solitary. Behind him the door closed, as Adriana entered to dress after the morning ritual of getting the household started. Thomas had met and wooed Adriana and taken her from the French Quarter in New Orleans to be his wife after the death of his first spouse, and he hadn't regretted a single moment of their twenty-four years together. "You are shameless," Adriana said, walking to his side and placing her hand on his where it rested on the balcony railing. "Only a shameless man stands naked where all the world can see him."

"It's my house," Thomas growled, stretching in the morning sun. "Nobody has to look." He glanced sideways at her. "Well?"

Adriana shook her head. "No word," she said, "except that they were seen at the fair yesterday morning, which you knew already." Her longing the equal of her husband's, she looked down the road for her sons.

"Hunh," Thomas grunted. "Is Hogjaw awake?"

"I don't know. Vestal says he slept outside under a tree

29

last night, with the excuse that roofs make him restless. We have such a friend.''

''A good friend,'' Thomas added.

''Yes.''

He turned and pulled her to him. ''Did you know,'' he asked, his voice deepening, ''that I dreamt last night of the first time I saw you dance? It was real as real can be. My blood was boiling and my throat was as dry as last year's kindling when I went to talk to you.''

''And did you continue this dream to see what happened next?'' she asked coyly, looking up at him.

''Well . . .'' Thomas grinned impishly. ''My memory sort of dims, but I *think* . . .'' He frowned in mock concentration. ''No, that was—''

''*Mon Dieu!* I am insulted, and by a brigand!'' Adriana's green eyes flashed and her fingers clawed at him as Thomas ducked inside.

''Now, now,'' he said laughing and putting a chair between them.

Adriana's cheeks colored and her auburn hair whipped wildly about her face. Thomas caught her and, still laughing, wrapped his arms around her and kissed her until she stopped struggling. ''That was a horrid thing to say,'' Adriana whispered in his ear.

''I was teasing you. What came next was . . .'' The sentence unfinished, Thomas carried her to the broad, white expanse of bed that dominated their room. A moment later, her gown swept away, their bodies joined in a union of sultry motion and driving energy that rose to a peak and, while they held one another close, only slowly subsided.

''No woman need fear time,'' Adriana said at last, reaching up to touch Thomas's cheek, ''as long as her husband makes love to her in the morning.''

''You will never need to fear time, then,'' Thomas said. He rolled off her and, one hand on her stomach, lay watching her. ''You are too beautiful not to make love to in the morning.''

Adriana curled onto her side, molded her body to his, and parted her hair to let him kiss the back of her neck. ''You did remember,'' she purred, drowsy from the exertion.

''Always,'' he said, shutting his eyes against the sunlight that gradually filled the room.

''They'll be here today,'' Adriana said. ''This morning.''

Thomas did not ask how she knew, for his wife was of the gypsies, and there were secrets he could never share. He nodded in simple acceptance. It was good to have his wife at his side. It would be good to have his sons home.

Solitary.

The swamp guarded it. Water brooded over by a dense forest of cypress gleamed to every side. To pass through, one had to keep to the path.

Solitary hadn't always been so far away from the Atlantic. Not until the first rumblings of the war for independence did Jason Behan Paxton, Thomas's father, move back into the deep woods and lay the foundation for the great house. That was ancient history, though, of no importance to the roan hammerhead stallion who plodded through the swamp with unerring accuracy. In the distance, a stone curlew piped insistently. True rode with his hands crossed on the pommel of the saddle. His mind wandered. Joseph was whistling out of tune. Behind him, his mouth pinched and his shoulders tight, Andrew studied the swamp. He had no love for this part of the journey, for he had been lost here once as a child, and had wandered for two nights and a day before Vestal found him. Andrew could remember the nights as vividly as if they were only yesterday.

Mosquito hawks of all colors, bottlefly blue, bright red, irridescent green, and jet black, flashed in and out of the sunlight. The water turned from green to red to dark brown. A water moccasin parted the brackish scum with its head, leaving a long V wake that caught a cypress limb. A heron stood one-knee deep, peering into the water. When he moved, his beak stabbed the water and emerged with wiggling silver fish which he tossed expertly into the air, caught, and swallowed. Then he stood motionless again. Above him, spiders hung suspended on glistening lifelines dangling from vines and limbs and leaves. So many eight-legged puppets performing the tiny choreography that nature had instilled in them, they toiled mindlessly through the stillness. Ever so slowly, the brown muck shelved and rose out of the cypress to become a meadow clear of cover for a good three hundred yards before it ended in a line of oak forest.

To come to Solitary, it was necessary to pass the graves where three generations of Paxtons lay. Many markers dotted the lush, vine-shrouded glade. As always, True sought out two in particular, for they were inscribed with the names of those who had brought their name and sunk their roots into the new land. Jason Brand Paxton and Marie Ravenne Paxton. They had been pirates before forsaking their wandering, plundering ways. A diary kept by Grandmother Marie—as Thomas, True's father, referred to her—had recounted their adventures at sea and chronicled the first years of their new life in South Carolina. The diary was moldering now, but where it was incomplete or illegible, tales told to children and the children of their children had left an indelible record to be carried in the hearts and minds of the Paxtons.

They were stories True treasured, perhaps more so than his brothers. He often had imagined himself as Jason Brand Paxton, facing the raw wilderness with no more than a gun, a cutlass, and courage. Instead, almost a hundred years later, there were a warehouse and office in Charleston, and a small fleet of four Paxton ships plied the world's oceans. In addition, there was property in Brandborough and the surrounding countryside, horses, crops, and the home plantation with Solitary at its center. All of this was easily inventoried and assigned a value in dollars and cents. What was less tangible was the Paxton name itself, and what it meant to those spirited men and women who had, over the years, carried it with pride and upheld its honor.

"True!" Andrew called from horseback. "You ready?"

"Come on, True," Joseph added. "Hell, you peppered me this far with a burr in your blanket to get home, so what's doused your fires? Damned sure can't be common sense."

"Just daydreaming, I guess," True said, shoving his boot into the stirrup and mounting Firetail. "It's hard to ride by this place without stopping."

Andrew watched True as he slowly wheeled Firetail and started down the trail. True had a quiet, contemplative streak that Andrew didn't understand, and often wondered about. "What is it, True?" he asked as his older brother caught up with him.

"It's as if they talk to me."

"They're dead," Andrew said, his skin prickling.

"Are they?" True asked, half smiling as he urged Firetail into a canter. "Sometimes I wonder."

The expanse of clear ground after the ominous darkness of the swamp was more than Firetail could bear. Frisky, smelling home, he tossed his head and bolted across the meadow, followed in short order by Joseph's and Andrew's horses.

"Jesus! Doesn't he ever get enough?" Joseph called, reining in beside True.

"Nope," True said. He slapped the stallion's neck and grinned boyishly. "Be glad he doesn't."

"Be glad you don't have to ride like that with a hangover."

"Not my fault. He's just feeling his oats. Been gone a long while."

"Are we gonna talk or ride?" Andrew asked. "I smell something cooking."

True and Joseph sniffed the air. "A pig!" Joseph whispered, his mouth watering. "A double eagle says Vestal's put on a whole pig!"

"A lousy bet," True said, lifting one foot and booting Joseph's horse on the rump. "Lead the way, big brother. Age before beauty."

"Let's go, then!"

Only one mile left! With a wild cry in their hearts, the sons of Thomas Gunn Paxton galloped up the broad winding path that cut clearly through the forest. Branches looped with thick brown vines left shadowed patterns on the dark red earth. Clods of rich dirt flew from beneath their horse's hooves as they neared the final gentle curve at whose end stood the massive hewn ornamental fence posts that announced the entry to Solitary.

Solitary! True restrained Firetail, reined him in while his brothers raced ahead. He had never been gone so long, and the idea of returning home had taken on meanings beyond all proportion. Now, for the moment, he sat in stunned silence as the expected surge of emotion failed to materialize. He was glad to be there, of course, but in a quiet, contemplative way that left him feeling he'd been gone no longer than overnight.

Nothing had changed. The great, whitewashed two-story house sat on a flattened terrace and was surrounded by magnolias, catalpas, chestnuts, and the twin white oaks whose trunk-sized main branches together spanned almost two hundred feet of lawn. A circular drive led to the front entrance that was set under a pillared portico and flanked to either side by a deep, shadowed veranda that ran the width of the house. White board fences ran up either side of the main drive and delineated twin paddocks where mares grazed peacefully while their colts frisked about them. Behind the show paddocks, a

large two-acre garden lay to the west of the house, and a wide
lawn complete with a gazebo and tables and chairs lay to the
east. To the rear, stretching north and west, True could
picture the hay fields and fenced meadows and horse barns
where the Paxton thoroughbreds were raised and trained.
Further to the east, where the land sloped down again along
the back creek, two full sections would be green with corn
and cotton and tobacco.

True nudged Firetail with the heels of his boots and started
the roan slowly up the drive toward the house. To his right, a
mare looked up at him briefly. He could hear the dull thud of
an axe at work behind the house, and from the edges of the
fields where the black peoples' cabins lay, the muffled voice
of John Preacher exhorting his charges in their Sunday morning service. True was halfway up the circular drive in front of
the house when he caught a glimpse of Lavinia, the housekeeper, emerging from her cottage and going into the garden.
Smiling secretly, he turned off the drive and quietly guided
Firetail through the garden gate.

Lavinia had been brought to Solitary as a child and had
lived all the rest of her nearly sixty years there without
traveling more than ten miles from the front door. At one
time, long ago, she had been slim and saucy and desirable.
Now, her proportions were massive, and accentuated by a
bright yellow blouse and skirt and an equally bright red
embroidered apron and head kerchief. "Vestal!" she called,
turning and raising a hand to shoo away the horse she heard
coming up behind her. "You git that colt outa my gard . . .
Oh, Lawd!" she exclaimed when she saw who it really was.
"It's True! Mr. True come home!" Her face lit by a broad
smile, Lavinia trampled radishes and greens and carrots and
onions as she ran across the rows toward True and, barely
allowing him to dismount, enveloped him in flesh and gingham and garden smells and the honest aroma of cornmeal.

He was home at last. Finally, once and for all, he was
home. Grinning like an idiot and swallowing the hot lump in
his throat, True extricated himself from the black woman's
grasp and held her at arm's length. "Easy, Lavinia," he
laughed. "You're gonna squash me before I get a chance to
say hello."

"Lawd, Lawd." Lavinia's head bobbed up and down and
her eyes glistened with happy tears. "You a sight, boy. And
if you wants to say hello, you'd best hurry, 'cause I'se sure

gonna hug you a . . .'' She stopped mid-word, and her smile turned to a mock glare. "Now, see here, Mr. True. You give a old lady a fearsome start riding up secret like that. Why just yesterday one of Vestal's colts got loose and trolleeploded my garden something awful.''

"Trolleeploded, huh?" True muttered, amused.

Lavinia indicated a staggered row of broken plants. "Something awful,'' she repeated, already dismissing the subject and going on to another. She looked around and behind True. "Where's Mr. Joseph and young Andrew?"

"Probably with Father and Mother by now. And wondering what's become of me."

The black woman tilted her head and inspected True from the feet up. "Well, I hope they're fitter lookin' than you. You boys have breakfast yet, or just ride straight in?"

"Just coffee."

"Coffee ain't breakfast. What you been eatin' the past two months, anyhow?"

"Our own cooking, mostly."

"It shows." Lavinia clucked in disapproval and shoved True toward the horse. "Skinny as you has got, I'd best warm up some cornbread and gravy. And fry up a mess of them catfish Vestal brought in this morning, too."

"You cook 'em, I'll eat 'em,'' True said, grinning.

Lavinia was already on her way to the kitchen. "You git, and say hello to your mama and papa. I'll be along in three shakes."

Cornbread and gravy and fresh catfish. A man couldn't get any further home than that, True thought, mounting and riding to the front of the house in time to interrupt Vestal untying Joseph's and Andrew's geldings. "Welcome back, Mr. True," the black man said, as unconcerned as if True had just returned from a night in town.

"Thank you, Vestal." True jumped down, ducked under Firetail's head, and shook Vestal's hand in greeting. "It's good to *be* home. How's Temper? We heard he was ailing."

"That horse! Drove a splinter into his right rear hoof by kicking the wall out of his stall. Your daddy had to cut it out, and the hoof got infected. I think we got it stopped, though. Durn fool animal."

"Sounds like him. Joseph and Andrew inside?"

"Yes, sir." Vestal's worn and troubled face broke into a smile. "Andrew ain't growed any. Not that I could see."

"He's trying to," True said. "You doing all right?"

"Fair as can be. I got me two colts to attend to. Bony little girls, but not near as ugly as ol' Firetail, here. He win anything?"

"Never beaten when it counted. Nobody even came close to him, unless I held him back."

Vestal nodded. "I could tell he was the one for you, Mr. True, 'cause you was the onliest one who had the patience to work with him. Well—" He took the stallion's reins and patted him affectionately on the neck. "I'll give him some oats and a rubdown. How're things in town?"

"Not that you give a damn."

"Not that I do," Vestal chuckled, and sauntered off around the corner of the house.

True ran lightly up the steps and into the foyer.

"The last of my wayward sprigs!" Thomas called from the front parlor. "What kept you?"

"Hello, Father," True said, stepping through the door. "I stopped to say hello to Lavinia." Adriana, her forty years resting easily on her willowy frame, flew to her son and kissed him on the cheek. "Hello, Mother."

Adriana could be in a roomful of people and still make the one with whom she spoke feel as if he were the only one within hearing. "I missed you, my firstborn," she said, touching his cheek.

"We've only been gone a few weeks."

"Almost three months, you mean. You are too much like your father, with no concern for time."

"Hah!" Joseph snorted. "You wouldn't have thought that, to see him this morning."

"Don't listen to him," True laughed. His left arm still around Adriana, he gripped Thomas's hand in greeting.

"You're home now, and that's all that matters. Joseph tells me you fared well."

"Did he tell you how well?" True asked, unstrapping his money belt and handing it to his father.

Thomas was beaming. "Six thousand dollars," he said, proud of his sons. "You know how old I was before I saw my first six thousand?"

"Five thousand, nine hundred and fifty-six, to be exact," True corrected. "Won fair and square, too. Take back what you said?"

"He already has," Andrew said, referring to Thomas's

prediction when Firetail was a colt that he wouldn't amount to a hill of beans. "Don't make him say so twice."

"Now there's a son a father can dote on," Thomas laughed. "Eating crow once in a morning is enough for any man."

"Eating," Joseph broke in. "Now there's a subject I could talk about more. What about that pig we smelled?"

"Vestal started the fire a half hour after we heard you were in Brandborough," Thomas said. "We put the pig on about sundown last night. It'll be ready by suppertime."

Andrew groaned. "I hope we don't have to wait that long for something to eat."

"You haven't had breakfast yet?" Adriana asked. She took Andrew by the hand, started to lead him out of the room. "Come with me. We'll see what there is. Lavinia ought to have—"

"I already talked to her," True interrupted. "She's cooking right now, unless I miss my guess."

"I'm game, whatever it is," Joseph said, following his stepmother and Andrew out of the parlor.

Thomas and True were left alone. Neither spoke for a moment, just looked at the other. "It's good to see you, son," Thomas said at last. "Good to have you home. We both missed you."

"And I you," True admitted, adding with a characteristic grin, "It was one hell of a time, though. That horse does love to run. He's every bit the animal his sire is. More, maybe. They may turn out ugly as sin, but his babies ought to be runners, father."

"Yes. Well . . ." Thomas cleared his throat, moved to one of the front windows, and stared out. "We'll see, of course."

"What's that supposed to mean?" True asked sharply.

"Mean?" Thomas asked a little too jovially. "Why, nothing, of course, except that you never can tell what a horse— Damn! I forgot all about our guest. Wait 'til you see who's cooking the pig. No," he said, stopping True before he could ask, and taking him by the arm to lead him out the door. "No questions. It's a surprise."

Something strange was going on, but what, True couldn't guess. Curious, he accompanied his father down the hall past the long, spacious dining room and through the central gallery/work room that separated the front of the house from the winter kitchen at the rear. The smell of roasting pork intensified as they hurried out the back door onto the rear veranda and started across the lawn toward the grove of mulberry bushes, where an entire hog was sizzling on a spit. Suddenly, from behind the thick trunk of the catalpa tree where True had played as a child, a massive form moved like lightning, swept him up in arms as hard as tree limbs, and tossed him into the air. He hit the ground tumbling, but before he could roll free, his attacker pinned him face to the ground with a foot on the back of his neck.

True tried to push himself up, but lay still when he felt fingers twine through his hair and saw fifteen inches of double-edged, razor-sharp steel pointed at his throat. "If I was a Comanche," a rasping voice said, "you'd be a true dead man and this ol' Arkansas Toothpick'd be claimin' another scalp."

"Hogjaw?" True asked in a choked voice.

The fingers loosed their grip, the knife disappeared. "Less'n you was made of the same stuff as me, of course," the voice continued. "Git up, ya scamp. It ain't perlite to lay down when ya got company."

True rolled onto his back and looked up with affection at the ugliest man he'd ever seen. "Hogjaw!" he said, incredulous. "God*damn!* Hogjaw!"

"Hogjaw? Is that any way to talk?" He looked more a monster than a man, for he had been scalped years before by Indians. Unfortunately, the homesteader who replaced the missing skin with a piece of tanned pig leather had badly miscalculated the lay of Hogjaw's face, which sagged hopelessly as a result. His brows hung low over two black gleaming eyes. His nose was a wadded lump of meat. His cheeks hung like wattles on either side of his jawbone, and wiggled as he spoke. "Mr. Leakey to you, younker," he said, pronouncing the name "Lake-ee." Whirling, he let out a howl and hurled the knife, which hit the cooking pig with a sickening *thwock,* and sank haft deep.

"When'd you get here?" True asked, grabbing the mountain man's offered hand and pulling himself to his feet.

Hogjaw didn't answer, merely stared out from under his sagging brow. "Ye've growed, boy," he said. "Learn anything since I last saw you?"

True grinned, pulled his own Arkansas Toothpick from its sheath, and sent it whirring into the pig, barely an inch from Hogjaw's. "That, if nothing else," he said.

Hogjaw nodded approvingly. "Knew I'd gave it to the right person," he said gravely. "It ain't a weapon for just anyone, but I see it fits you, by God."

"It's Leakey! Hogjaw Leakey!" Andrew shouted, running from the house.

"Another one!" Hogjaw roared, shoving True aside and planting his feet firmly. Andrew, as he had five years earlier when the mountain man had last appeared at Solitary ducked his shoulder, drove full force into Hogjaw's belly and bounced off, almost knocking himself unconscious in the process. Hogjaw roared with laughter. "You'll have to wait another five years before that'll work, lad." He thumped his chest and belly with a fist the size of a small ham. At fifty-three he was still as hard and strong as a man twenty years his junior. "And be lucky if it does then. By God, Tom!" he exclaimed as Joseph crossed the lawn toward him. "Do the Paxtons never run out of sons?"

"Hello, Hogjaw," Joseph said, extending his hand. "Long time."

Hogjaw's yellowed teeth showed behind his lips as they curled back in what he thought was a grin. His and Joseph's hands met and their fingers interlocked in a test of strength. The blood drained from their knuckles, which turned a milky white. Their forearms bulged. Suddenly, Joseph howled and tried to pull away. Hogjaw gave his hand an extra squeeze, and let him loose. "Not yet, Joseph. Not yet."

Joseph frowned, but even he couldn't keep a sour face for too long around the mountain man.

"Appears I should have waited another year or two," Hogjaw said, looking at the three and sadly shaking his head. "I'm beginnin' to wonder if they can take the guff. What the hell you been feedin' them, Tom? They're pale as mother's milk and soft as corn mush."

"Who the hell asked for your opinion?" Joseph asked, bridling.

"We'll do," Andrew added, equally defensive.

"Oh, my oh my. Temper like a grizz at an empty hive." The mountain man focused on True. "And what have you to say, younker?"

True took his time answering. "Nothing," he finally said, his eyes darting from Hogjaw to Thomas and back again. "Until I figure out what you two are cooking up. Besides a pig, that is."

"Ah, True lad." Hogjaw's eyes twinkled and his cheek flaps bobbed up and down. "I knew you had a head on your shoulders. Always wait to get riled until you have a good reason. Makes it hard to tell if your craw's full of goosefeathers or sand. We'll see, though, one of these fine days."

"Which tells me nothing," True said.

"No it doesn't, does it?" Hogjaw said, turning and walking toward the pit. "First things first, though, says I," he shot over his shoulder. "A homecoming first, and then we'll talk."

"About what?" Andrew asked, following him a few steps.

"Leaving," came the guttural reply as the buckskin-clad figure trudged off.

"Leaving?" Andrew looked at his father. "Leaving for where? What's he talking about?"

"Ah, he's just been in the woods too damn long," Joseph said.

"Maybe," Thomas agreed, moving to join Hogjaw, "but like the man says, first things first. You'll find out soon enough."

True folded his arms and blotted out Andrew and Joseph's conversation. Bird and insect sounds, the smell of smoke and cooking pork. His father serious and, in retrospect, soft-spoken. Hogjaw Leakey, hard as granite and nimble as a mountain goat, plucking the knives from the pig, tossing True's to him, and licking the grease from his before sheathing it. Leaving. The word had a sound and feel to it that matched the air of expectancy that, happy as he was to be at Solitary once again, prickled the hairs at the back of his neck and raised goose bumps on his arms. Turning, he looked back to the house where his mother stood framed in an upper story window. Leaving. She knew. She always knew. And was beginning, he could tell by the cast of her shoulders and the tilt of her head, to say goodbye.

Chapter III

"Think of it! Deserts dry as bone and lonely as the grave. Swamps so deep no white man has ever seen their innards. Mile upon mile of low mountains covered with mighty cedars that tower to skies so clear and blue they must be the color of God's eyes. Coastal marshes flat as a table and brimming with ducks and geese. Why, a man can bring down vittles for a week with a single load of buckshot. And plains. Plains, I say, vast as a mighty ocean, so broad and wide a man can travel across them 'til his guts quiver and still not reach the end. Not like these tame little meadows you got here," Hogjaw rhapsodized. The firelight glowed in his eyes and the shadows played a danse macabre on his sagging face.

"The *Llano Estacado,* the Staked Plains in English, are still closed to the white man, but there are others. Plains that roll gently and rumble to the sound of Lord Buffalo. Buffalo, aye! Millions of 'em, and the best eatin' a man might ever know in a lifetime. Buffalo hump is mother's milk, and the tongue—" His eyes closed as he remembered "—is ambrosia."

In the darkness outside the net-enclosed gazebo where they sat, fireflies hovered suspended in space like tiny floating lanterns, and a multitude of insect songs filled the heavy, warm night air. Inside, around the table, Joseph pretended indifference and Andrew gnawed thoughtfully on a pork rib while True sat with closed eyes and pictured the awesome world Hogjaw had conjured. Thomas nudged Adriana, who leaned across his chest and refilled his clay mug with the cider he kept for special occasions. "All that is very good, Hogjaw," she said, topping off his mug too. "But our home is here."

"I'm not talkin' about you or Thomas," the mountain man said, spitting out a chunk of gristle and reaching for his mug.

"I'm talkin' about these here boys and about raw beginnin's for 'em. I'm talkin' about land made holy by distance and a kingdom beggin' for the souls hearty enough to wrest it from Mother Nature, the old whore—beggin' your pardon." He touched his fingers to the cap he wore to conceal the piece of pigskin sewn into his scalp.

Adriana acknowledged his apology with a nod. "I know," she said, a hint of sadness in her voice. "I understand. There have always been such places, and young men—and the young at heart—" she amended with a sweet smile, "have always flown to them." She rose to awkward silence, leaned over and kissed Thomas on the cheek. "I will miss my sons," she whispered, to everyone's surprise, and hurriedly left.

"It's harder on the womenfolk," Hogjaw finally said, nodding sagely. "They feel the leavin' worse than men."

The playing shadows made their faces look as serious as the conversation had become. "I wouldn't count on that," Thomas said.

"If Texas is so wonderful," Joseph asked, "why'd you come back here?"

"To see your pa," Hogjaw answered without hesitation. "Man like me runs across a good deal of humankind, but counts his friends on the fingers of one hand. You know how long I've known that man acrost the table?"

"I've heard," Joseph said.

"Since 1795," Hogjaw went on, paying Joseph no attention. "We was younkers, no more than fourteen when we run off to sea together. Why, hell, we seen more of this world in ten years than the three of you could draw a map of. Places so far distant it'd make your head swim. We fought pirates—fought *with* 'em, too—and was shipwrecked together. Hell, I stood up for him the day he married your mother, Joseph, a woman I loved too." He sighed, shook his head dolefully. "But she had an eye for him, by God. I never did stop bein' his friend, though, and never stopped owin' him either, for as many times as I saved his life, he saved mine once more."

"Well, now," Thomas demurred, reddening.

"It's the truth, damn it Thomas. And if I don't repay you personal, well . . ." He sputtered, searched for words. "Well, hell! I'd hate to think this was the last time in my life I was gonna see a Paxton."

"The last time?" True asked in the silence that followed his outburst.

"By this hand, True lad." The mountain man's voice dropped, and he seemed to be looking into a distance only he could visualize. "I ain't gettin' any younger. How many more times do you think I can make this trek? No, it's not long, says I, that these old bones'll move a mite too slow and a Injun lance will put an end to Hogjaw Leakey." His gaze turned to True and his voice returned from that far place. "Mind you, I carry nor remorse nor grudge. Bloodthirsty heathens that Injuns be, they're a kinder fate than old age, for at least a man knows he's dyin' and don't totter off like a babe." The folds in Hogjaw's cheeks rearranged themselves into a grin as he called for the cider jug and filled his mug. "God, but this is as silken a snake poison as ever bit me!"

True had heard Hogjaw spin poetic tales of the far sides of mountains before, but never had he known him to reveal so deep an introspective streak. Mulling over the older man's words, he pondered what he'd heard of Texas—that it was part of Mexico and that land-hungry settlers from the States were buying immense tracts of land with the expectation of taming the savage wilderness. Hogjaw was the first person True knew personally who had actually been there. He took a sip of cider, felt the world shift beneath his feet, and knew he'd had enough to drink.

"Tom Gunn Paxton," Hogjaw went on, his voice ringing, "the land calls to me. Land, wealth, adventure enough for a dozen lifetimes. I got to go back, and go back I will, for Texas is a fever burnin' beneath my skin." He paused and leaned across the table to stare into Thomas's eyes. "I ask you now, old friend. Will you give your sons your blessing to go with me?"

Thomas returned the mountain man's stare for a long moment. Deep in his heart he knew this moment had been due for some time, and now that it had come, he found himself resisting it as he had promised he wouldn't, for had he not left home too, as all young men must? He turned to his youngest. "Well, Andrew?"

"I'm game," Andrew said, the excitement rising in him.

"And you, Joseph?" Thomas asked. "Your brother, Jason, would be happy to see you in Charleston to help manage Paxton Shipping."

Joseph stiffened, but kept his temper. For years, his father had held up his twin brother as an example to him. "Jason is a good businessman. I'd never be anything but a subordinate to him and you know it." He leaned his elbows on the table, and for one so gruff his voice was strangely gentle. "I'm twenty-seven, Father, and if Hogjaw has seen the look of far places in your eyes, I've seen the look of disappointment at having a son who's done naught but shamble through life." No sign of emotion escaped his face, but his eyes narrowed as if he were looking at something far, far away and indistinct. "You're always telling me I should make something of myself. Well, this is what I've been waiting for. This is my chance. I can feel it in my bones and it's a blessing for all of us. Neither you nor Jason will have to be embarrassed by me any longer."

True bridled at the way Joseph adressed his father. The tension between the two had increased the older Joseph had become and the more responsibility his twin, Jason Brand Paxton, had assumed in the family businesses. Still, not all the blame could be laid at Joseph's doorstep. The fault was Thomas's too, for he refused to acknowledge that the wild streak that had pushed him to sea as a young man ran strongly in Joseph. And the fact that Jason, unlike his namesake, was suited more to desks and order forms and weights and bank balances shouldn't be held against Joseph.

"What about you, True?" Thomas said, refusing to rise to Joseph's anger and turning to his first-born by Adriana, and the one she would miss the most.

"Texas," True said, savoring the word. He looked up at Hogjaw, and back to his father. An irrepressible grin lit his face. The air seemed charged with electricity, as during a storm. "Texas," he repeated, not wanting to hurt Thomas's feelings, and yet already feeling Firetail beneath him and the long road unfolding ahead of him. "It has a ring to it, father. With your blessing, I'll follow Hogjaw."

His sons watched him. Joseph's face was an indistinct blur in the shadow cast by Hogjaw. Impatient in his youth, Andrew leaned forward expectantly. Motionless, his head silhouetted by the red glow from the fire pit behind him, True waited.

And Thomas Gunn Paxton said a single word.

"Go."

Chapter IV

On Monday morning, the eighth of September, 1834, two weeks and a day after True had arrived home, he prepared to ride away forever. The sun rose in the normal manner, the birds sang as always. The mares suckled their foals in the front paddocks, and the smell of fresh coffee permeated the great house that was Solitary. True had been up and dressed since the first stars began to fade. In the early morning stillness, he had walked the paths he'd explored in childhood, looked in for the last time on Temper, and then busied himself helping to load Fritz, the huge, dappled gray jack mule that would carry their gear. When all was ready, and as a final, sentimental gesture, he climbed the catalpa tree in the side yard and perched on the limb where he'd spent so many hours as a boy.

They all gathered for breakfast in the large dining room where Lavinia had stacked the table with enough food to keep a small army alive for a month. The atmosphere was confusing at best. Bright chatter one moment was followed by strained silences which no one knew how to break gracefully, and throughout, Hogjaw and his charges stuffed themselves in order not to hurt Lavinia's feelings. When the clock struck eight, they all pushed back their plates and left to go about their final chores, as if they had heard a mysterious signal that had to be obeyed.

In truth, everything had been ready for some hours. The packs had been loaded with spare clothes and extra boots, powder and shot, food, pots and pans, a half dozen bottles of whiskey for trading along the way, and a minimum of personal effects, all easily accessible in order of their importance. True, Joseph, and Andrew had each selected a Kentucky rifle and flintlock pistol from Solitary's stock of arms. These they would carry on their horses, along with a carefully honed knife and hand ax, their bedrolls, and their share of the money they had won racing Firetail.

True slipped out the side door. He could still feel the warmth of Lavinia's parting embrace, still see her ebony, tear-stained face contort with grief as she started to sob and ran back into the kitchen. Joseph and Andrew were standing by the horses and watching Thomas busily making last-minute adjustments to ropes and cinches. "Well?" True said. "We ready?"

Thomas's face reddened. He hadn't needed to lift a finger, but hadn't been able to help himself. "You say goodbye to your mother yet?" he asked, his voice gravelly.

"I was, ah, gonna save that . . ."

"She's waiting inside for you."

"Yes, sir." Every other aspect of leaving was tempered by the excitement of the adventure ahead. This moment, though, was one True dreaded. The front steps seemed too high to climb. His feet dragged. She was in the parlor, her back to him as she sat on the sofa. True paused in the doorway. "Mother," he said.

Her auburn hair hung to her shoulders, which stiffened at the sound of his voice. The brightly colored print dress was more festive than any he could remember her wearing. She turned slowly and waited for him to join her, then reached out as if to draw him to her, but instead encircled his neck with a chain and amulet. The amulet was of pounded gold filagree, shaped into finely worked brambles clustered about a tree.

"First-born of my flesh," she whispered. Tears appeared at the corners of her eyes and spilled down her cheeks. "Your father gave this to me when we married. It has been in his family for generations, and passes from the first-born son to his wife, and so on. There are those who would say your brother Jason should have it, but it is mine to bestow and I choose you. You are my first-born. The blood of pirates and of gypsies flows in your veins. You will wear the charm."

True started to speak, but Adriana pressed her fingers to his lips and shook her head no. "Loneliness for the mother who bore him, loneliness for Adriana," she said in a wistful singsong. "I love you, my son, so I won't lie to you. You won't be back. None of you will return. I have seen it in the flame of the candle and in the lay of the cards. Trouble lies ahead, flesh of my flesh. Great deeds, death for some, life for others. And for you?'' The faintest of smiles played fleetingly across her face. "As the tree rises from the brambles, so shall you overcome adversity."

"I don't have to go, Mother," True said, faltering.

Adriana stood and cupped True's face in her hands. "Yes you do, my first-born. More than any of the others, perhaps. I do not know this Texas that Hogjaw speaks of, but I can see in your eyes that it calls you. And it is written, somewhere, that you must go. As I love you, I would not hold you back."

True rose, leaned forward to accept her kiss on his cheek and feel her arms around him for the last time. "Part of me will always be here with you, Mother," he said, his eyes misting.

"I know, my son. And my love will be with you all your days." She pushed away from him, held him at arm's length. Her smile was forced, a smile to belie the pain in her heart. She patted his arm. "Your brothers will be anxious. . . ."

True tucked the amulet inside his shirt. The metal was cold against his skin, but it warmed quickly. He leaned down and kissed his mother's cheek. She tasted of tears.

The heat outside was oppressive though the hour was still early. Joseph and Andrew, already mounted, waited patiently. Their father stood between their horses, holding Firetail's reins. Hogjaw did not like departures, and was waiting down by the gate at the end of the meadow. Thomas and the mountain man had parted with no more than a perfunctory wave of the hand. At first, True had not understood such a casual farewell between close friends, but in that moment when he faced his father, he did. There really was nothing to say. Any attempt to express the bond between them would have been banal. Adequate words simply didn't exist. True's and Thomas's hands met, and through that grip flowed twenty-two years of love, of a little boy's tears and of his laughter, of a father's hopes and dreams, of quick anger and chastisement and forgiving, of lessons small and large, of gifts and sharings, of the quiet moments when, hand in hand, they had walked across meadows, and through forests, and down shaded and bright lanes that brought them to the moment of parting, but from which they would never be parted. It was that way, and it was enough. When their hands fell apart, True mounted and, with his brothers leading the way, turned his horse down the path.

Hogjaw watched them approach. When they drew even

with him, he lifted a battered bugle to his lips and blew a blast that drove the herons from the marsh into the air and echoed over the meadows, causing the field hands to stare around in terror and the animals in the forest to turn and listen. "Come along, you Paxtons," he said. "And don't look back, mind you, for him that does begins a habit that's hard to break."

Joseph gave a derisive snort. Andrew chuckled and urged his horse into the lead. True pressed his hand against the amulet beneath his shirt. Together, they rode from Solitary.

And none of them turned back for a last look.

PART TWO

Chapter V

October 10, 1834

"You ought not to go," Elizabeth Michaelson cautioned soberly. "You know what Mr. Jones said."

Lottie raised her eyes to the cloud-filled heavens, which rumbled a warning of their own. "Mr. Jones is as staid and stuffy as Pa," she replied peevishly. "If we must go to Texas, where I'll probaby never see pretty lights or hear music or go to dances again, I intend to have some fun while the opportunity presents itself. Honestly, Elizabeth! How can you be such a stick-in-the-mud?"

Elizabeth's back stiffened. Thaddeus Jones, the wagon master they had met the day before, had spent a half hour warning his new charges that Natchez must be the limit of their excursions, and that the thin line of bordellos and taverns clinging to the banks of the Mississippi at the base of the Natchez Bluffs was to be avoided at all costs. In the first place, it was physically dangerous, for when the Mississippi uncoiled and flexed its muscles in awesome muddy majesty and roared above the banks like the Apocalypse itself, it carried off the pineboard buildings and bullied the patrons inside them into watery graves. More importantly, the short strip called Natchez Under the Hill was a den of gamblers, shady women, and thieves, where no decent person could or would be found. It existed, and was barely condoned by Natchez's more proper elders, because it provided an outlet for the roisterers and carousers who passed through on their way west, and in the process kept them from the streets of Natchez itself. That Elizabeth had taken the warning seriously while Lottie had not was a fair indication of the difference in temperament between the two sisters. "Papa wouldn't like to hear you talk like way," Elizabeth said. "He asked around. It's a place of sin and damnation."

"Old folks always say that fun is dangerous and sinful," Lottie sniffed. She pulled her cleanest dress over her head and patted the bodice smooth against her swelling bosom before turning to the mirror.

Elizabeth compared Lottie's abundant figure to her own trimmer, firm physique, and quickly donned a clean workshirt. "You still ought not to go," she repeated, tucking the shirt-tail into her trousers. "There's so much to do here."

"Oh, certainly!" Lottie pinched her cheeks to bring out the color and set to work on her hair. "Like being ogled by Dennis and Mackenzie Campbell, as if we were a pair of brood mares trotted out for them to play stud to. Well, no thank you."

"Not so loud," Elizabeth shushed.

Lottie's hair hung in a cascade over her shoulders. She pinned it up over her ears to keep it away from her face and once again regarded herself in the mirror. "Really, Elizabeth," she said with a tinkling laugh. "No one can hear. They're all out by the fire." She adjusted a pin, arranged a curl just so. "Anyway, you carry on too much. Natchez Under the Hill! Why, the very name is exciting. And I intend to be a part of it, even if it is only for a little while."

"But it will be dark in a while. And it looks like rain. What will I tell Papa? He'll expect you at table."

"Well, I won't be there is all." Lottie pulled aside the rear flap and checked to see if anyone was watching. "You can tell him I'm sick or something. That it's my time," she said, gathering her skirts and stepping over the rear gate. "Unless—" She leaned back into the dimness. "—you want to go with me."

"You know I can't do that," Elizabeth whispered, shocked.

"Why not?" Lottie asked. "You'd be real pretty if you gave yourself half a chance. Why not get out of that men's homespun and put on a dress and come along? It's time you had a man, and don't tell me you haven't thought about it."

"Of course I haven't."

"Oh, pooh. You're lying." She pulled her cape from the top of the trunk and threw it over her arm. "It only hurts for a minute, and that's little enough to pay for all the fun you'll have afterwards."

Elizabeth's face burned with anger. "You can't be satisfied, can you?'' she snapped. "We left behind trouble in Pennsylvania, with those Rueben boys fighting over you. Now you want to disobey Papa and see what new strays you can bed with here. By the time we reach Texas you'll no doubt have the Campbell boys at each other's throats as well. And you'll keep on until you get pregnant or someone gets hurt, and all because you have to have your fun.''

"That's right!" Lottie retorted angrily. "You sound just like Papa. Well, all I have to say, Miss Prissy, is that you'd better not tell." She jumped down from the wagon, then poked her head over the gate for a final, parting shot. "Maybe time will make you understand and trim your high and holier-than-thou ways, Elizabeth Michaelson. I certainly hope so!"

The flap dropped in Elizabeth's face. Not sure of what to do, she leaned back against the cedar-lined trunk where the clothes were kept. The wagon was neatly arranged with household necessities packed inside and farming implements, sacks of seed, and water barrels rigged to the exterior. The niceties of life, chairs and tables, beds; wardrobes, tubs, and the like would have to be purchased in San Antonio or built from what trees they found on their land, for the mules could pull only so much weight. The most important item of all was the parchment signed by Cirilio Medina and cosigned by an official of the Bustamente regime in Mexico City. Elizabeth crawled forward, removed a heavily waxed leather pouch from the special compartment under the driver's seat, and opened it. The document inside was penned in Spanish and bore the seal of the government of Mexico. Similar to others secreted in each settler's wagon, it stated that for a sum of money already received, the government recognized the transfer of title of one thousand hectares or, in more familiar terms, two thousand, four hundred and seventy-one acres, from Medina to one Carl Michaelson and his heirs, forever in perpetuity.

Elizabeth had never seen or held such an important piece of paper. It represented sacrifice and a dream of independence and wealth—and more, perhaps, Elizabeth thought, wishing she understood better what drove her father so. He had talked to her often when she was younger, divulged to her his secrets as he carried her about on his shoulders. That had been a long time ago, though, and she could remember little of what he had said. In those days, he had been a laughing, light-hearted man, solicitous of his wife and considerate of his children. But the changes in him over the past three or four years had tinged her devotion for him with fear. Nor was she the only one affected. Lottie hadn't always been insolent and rebellious. Their mother had not always been so wan and pinched of face. "I used to love him so," she had told Elizabeth in an unguarded moment one night no more than a year before they left Pennsylvania. If there were only some way, Elizabeth thought, that she could help. If she could exorcise the devils that plagued her father, restore her mother's love for him, dissuade Lottie from her licentious ways, perhaps they could be a happy family again.

"Lottie! Elizabeth! Dinner time!"

Elizabeth shuddered, returned the document to its pouch and hiding place, and began to pull on her shoes.

"Lottie! Elizabeth!" Her mother's voice, frail and high-pitched, trembled with exhaustion despite an uneventful voyage by steamboat down the Mississippi to the rendezvous at Natchez with Mr. Jones. Each day it had become more evident that she had no desire to lead a pioneer existence, and that she accompanied her husband only because her religious convictions were stronger than the temptation to desert him and remain behind.

Elizabeth hurriedly finished with her shoes. "Coming, Mother," she called, reaching for a bit of ribbon to tie back her tumbling, golden hair. Thunder rumbled in the distance and rolled over the waiting landscape. Elizabeth snatched one of her father's broad-brimmed floppy hats and then reconsidered. Next to returning to the East, Hester's most ardent desire was that her daughters marry well, and though she despaired of their ever doing so in Texas, she was resolved to see that they did nothing to minimize the chances should an eligible gentleman come along. There was no sense in forcing a confrontation. Sighing, Elizabeth put down the hat and decided to go bareheaded. Hester would no doubt find fault with her appearance anyway, but there was nothing to be done.

They were all gathered about a makeshift table constructed of a wood plank salvaged from the river and stretched across two tree stumps. Reverend Kania cleared his throat, smiled at his wife, Mila, and held his arms outstretched in blessing over his flock as he looked from one to another of them and named them in his mind. Resolute Carl Michaelson, middle-aged, desperate for a new beginning, and his wife, Hester, head bowed, her hands fluttering at her apron strings. Nels Matlan, a thin, wiry young man of thirty and his pretty wife, Eustacia, like her husband a teacher, and their son, eight-year-old Tommy. Stocky, stalwart Scott Campbell, another farmer, his dutiful spouse Joan, a handsome, robust woman, and their four children, two older boys molded in their father's image and two younger girls in their mother's. Kevin Thatche, a lad of sixteen and Mildred, his fifteen-year-old bride, pregnant, hopeful, and not a little worried. Childless, middle-aged Jack Kemper and his wife, Helen, storekeepers with illusions of a sprawling empire, and strangely secretive as to the origin of the money they had used to buy their land, even though no questions had been asked. And himself, the Reverend Buckland Kania, graying in his fifty-second year on earth, with a wife twenty years his junior who loved him and inspired him to lead one more flock to the Lord's pastures. Only the Michaelson girls were missing, and they would be along soon, for he could see Elizabeth coming down the path from where the wagons were parked.

And one other, too, the Reverend added, noticing Thaddeus Jones standing at the edge of the clearing and staring hungrily at the communal stewpot. "Will you join us, Mr. Jones?" he called, delaying the blessing. "After all, you will be our shepherd in the wilderness, so to speak."

Jones, a black man of indeterminate age and narrow build, dressed in homespun britches and a shirt that appeared too small for him, doffed his slouch hat and stepped into the circle. "The vittles do smell good. Never quite thought of myself as a shepherd, but I'd be proud to join you. It's a long road ahead we'll share." He nodded to each of the ladies and muttered, "Ma'am . . . ma'am," as he passed them and took a place at the end of the table.

"Almighty Father . . ." Kenia paused to wait for Elizabeth to take her place between her mother and father.

"Dressing like a boy," Hester whispered loud enough for all to hear. "Oh, Beth what am I ever . . . And where's your sister?"

"Back at the wagon," Elizabeth lied, feeling herself blush.

"Ahem," Kania said, pointedly clearing his throat. "If we are ready?" He spread his arms again. "Almighty Father, under whose protection we—"

"I *got* to go, Ma," little Tommy Matlan blurted, unable to

help himself. "If I don't get to the bushes real quick, I'll wet my britches."

"Godda!—" The Reverend caught himself, checked his temper, and hurried on. "Almighty Father, bless this food and those who partake of it. Amen!" he said, running the words together as he rushed through the prayer.

Nels Matlan waved to his son and Tommy darted toward the riverbank. "Sorry, Reverend," the teacher said.

An exasperated Kania sat and helped himself to a bowl of stew. Mila, his wife, looked away so he wouldn't see her smile. "Nothing to be sorry about, Nels," the preacher said, spearing a chunk of meat with one hand and reaching for the cornbread with the other. His good humor restored, he grinned around a mouthful of beef. "Nature will have its way."

"Isn't Lottie coming down to eat with us?" asked Dennis, the eldest of Scott Campbell's sons.

"No," Elizabeth said, taking a wedge of cornbread from the platter as it was passed. Lottie had flirted outrageously with Dennis and Mackenzie on the riverboat. Both of the young men were nice enough, Elizabeth supposed, but if they expected the same coquettishness from her, they were sadly mistaken. "She's not feeling well," she added, averting her eyes from them.

Young Mildred Thatche's face mirrored her own worries for herself. She placed a protective hand across her swollen abdomen. "I hope it isn't serious," she said, smiling wanly at her husband as he ladled food into her bowl, took some for himself, and passed the pot.

"Can't be too sick," Little Ruthie Campbell spoke up before being nudged into silence by her sister, Dianne.

"What is that supposed to mean, young lady?" Carl Michaelson asked, frowning.

Everyone was looking at her. Ruthie, concentrating on her stew, pushed a piece of carrot around. "Nothing, Mr. Michaelson," she finally said.

"Ruthie." Scott Campbell's voice was a rumbling warning. "If you know something, best speak it out or I'll be having to take a strap to you for carrying on so."

Ruthie's face went beet red. "I didn't mean no harm, Pa. It's just that me and Dianne heard Lottie talking today about seeing the sights. I mean," she added, stammering, "those down by the river."

"You mean Natchez Under the Hill?" Carl asked, staring at Elizabeth, who kept her head lowered.

"Tsk, tsk." Helen Kemper clucked her disapproval loud enough for all to hear.

"Oh, dear God!" Hester whispered.

"I think that's what she said," Ruthie replied, wishing she hadn't been so anxious to join the conversation.

Thaddeus Jones came to his feet and leaned across the table toward her. "Think won't do, little girl," he growled. "Now you remember straight and fast."

Tears were running down Ruthie's face. "She said them words," she sobbed. "Na . . . Na . . . Nachez Under the Hill."

"Damn!" Jones cursed, stepping over the bench and jamming his hat on his head. "The rest of you stay here. I don't want any more trouble than we got already."

Hester's eyes widened, and one hand fluttered to her mouth. Carl rose slowly, a figure of wrath, and faced the company. "You'll excuse us, Reverend Kania." He turned to his daughter. "I should like to speak to you alone, Elizabeth," he said, stepping over the bench and walking away from the table.

A frightened Hester followed Elizabeth toward the wagons. Jack Hemper stood and called after them, "Be glad to help any way I can, Carl," but Carl did not answer. Kemper looked around at the others and when his wife placed a restraining hand on his wrist, sat again. Reverend Kania glanced at Mila, who shook her head no. The meal resumed in uncomfortable silence, broken only by Ruthie's sniffles.

Elizabeth counted the steps to their wagon. The exercise, mindless as it was, kept the fear at bay, at least until she rounded the wagon and found her father waiting for her. "Have you lied to me, daughter?" he asked, his cheeks red and his scalp flushed beneath the thinning gray hair.

"Now, Carl. I'm sure the girl . . ." A look from her husband, and Hester's voice faltered, and failed.

His hands moved to his waist and began to remove the thick leather belt he wore. "Daughter?"

"Yes, sir," Elizabeth admitted, unable to keep her eyes from that terrible instrument that now swung free in her father's hands.

"She did go to Natchez Under the Hill against my instructions?"

"Yes, sir," Elizabeth whispered.

"And you condoned her transgression!" came the thundering accusation.

"No! I told her—"

"Silence! You share her guilt, and to it have added your own!" His face contorted with rage. "Woe to the rebellious children that add sin to sin, saith the Lord." His voice lowered menacingly. "Prepare yourself, daughter."

Her fingers fumbling at the fastenings, Elizabeth unbuttoned her shirt as her father walked around her and stopped behind her. She knew what was coming, what was expected of her. She had been punished before. Her shirt dropped and caught at her waist. Hester's lower lip was trembling. Elizabeth looked away from her.

"You have no place here, wife," Carl rumbled.

Hester stumbled around the wagon and weeping, collapsed on a barrel.

"I have brought this family with my sweat and blood to the promise of a new land."

Elizabeth caught up her shirt and covered her breasts as she saw her father step to one side and plant his feet.

"I will not be disobeyed."

Doubled, the leather snapped as it swung back, and then hissed through the air like a snake and struck her naked back. The shock rocked her forward. Searing pain ripped across her back. Elizabeth bit her lip to keep from crying out, and stood her ground.

"I will not be lied to!"

Again, the sharp snap, this hiss, the strike, and excruciating agony.

"I will not be made mock of!"

Snap . . . strike. Angry welts now rose on creamy white flesh.

"Nor be shamed by Jezebels!"

Snap . . . strike. Strike. Strike. Strike . . .

The pain was overpowering, she could not bear it any longer. Her shirt, forgotten, fluttered to the ground. Half naked, gasping for breath, Elizabeth staggered to the wagon and braced herself against the wooden frame with both hands. Suddenly, her father was close behind her. "It's wrong to lie, Beth. Wrong, wrong! We have come too far to be divided by deceit." His hands touched her waist, slid around her and up to cup her breasts. "I'm sorry," he whispered softly, his voice husky. "I'm sorry, Beth. Sweet Beth." His weight pressed her against the wagon and his fingers kneaded her breasts. "You didn't mean to lie, but a lie must be punished. You understand, don't you?"

"No!" Elizabeth gasped, struggling against his touch.

"You have to say you understand. I love you, Beth!"

Choking with horror, Elizabeth found the strength to push him from her, then twisted and tripped, sprawling, into the dirt. "No!" she hissed, crawling away from him. "No!"

Carl stood slumped, his hands hanging lifelessly at his sides. As if stunned by a blow, he stared dully at her. Slowly, sense returned and reason replaced passion. At last, awakening fully from what he thought must have been a dream, he shook his head and squared his shoulders. "Get thee covered, Jezebel," he snapped, turning his back on her. "It is a sin to be naked in thy father's sight!"

Her back was a sheet of flame. "Oh, God!" Elizabeth moaned, shamed. "Oh, God, God . . . Why, Father?"

"We will speak no more of this," Carl answered in a hollow voice. He replaced the belt, slid the lid off the barrel fastened to the side of the wagon, and poured a dipperful of water over his head. "See that you do not tempt me further," he ordered by way of a final admonition, and stalked off toward the road to Natchez Under the Hill.

Elizabeth lay without moving for long moments, then at last struggled to her feet and climbed inside the wagon. There, exhausted by pain, she collapsed again on a pallet Hester had spread for herself.

"I have some oil. It will take away the sting," Hester said, climbing into the wagon. "Move over. It's in that trunk."

"You saw!" Elizabeth said bitterly. "You saw what happened and said nothing."

Hester took her daughter's arm and helped her to a sitting position. "It's right here somewhere," she said, rummaging through the trunk. "It was the last batch your grandmother made."

Elizabeth pounded her fist on the pallet. "You saw!" she shouted. "Why didn't you stop him?"

"I have no control," Hester said in a tight, strained voice. "The Lord made the husband the head of the household. As a dutiful wife I have no right to question his judgment."

"You questioned plenty before we left." Elizabeth couldn't stop the hateful words. "You questioned and nagged and made life miserable for all of us every foot of the way here, but when it comes to a beating, and worse, you—''

"I never wanted to leave." Hester looked far older than her forty-five years. Her hands trembled and she gazed into the jar as if the murky depths therein held the past she so mourned. "I was frightened. We had such a lovely home. Your father worked hard and our farm was flourishing. My flowers . . . Oh, my lovely flowers. All gone . . ."

"We were dying there," Elizabeth said, cutting off her mother's wistful monologue. "The land was dead from drought and the crops had failed for the past two years, ever since Mamaw and Granddaddy died."

A mad light glimmered in Hester's eyes. "Our home was lovely, I say! We were respected. I told him this would end badly. I told I would not be his wife if he took me away from my home!"

"You call that being dutiful?" Elizabeth asked in a voice heavy with sarcasm.

Hester poured some of the oil into her hand before she answered. "He meant no harm," she said at last, moving behind Elizabeth and gently applying the balm. "You're his daughter. It was for your own good."

Anger gave way to despair in the face of such warped logic. "He tried to have me, Mother, don't you see?" she said, wincing as Hester's hands touched the welts on her back. Twisting, she showed her mother the growing dark spots on her breasts where Carl had mauled her. "This wasn't punishment!"

"No," Hester agreed. She blinked, refused to look at Elizabeth's breasts. "He was trying to comfort you, dear. Now turn around again like a good girl."

Elizabeth obeyed, crossed her arms on her knees and rested her forehead on her wrists. Her breasts ached, her back was on fire, and pain stabbed at her head behind her eyes. "Comfort?" she said sarcastically. "Well, just so you'll know, it wasn't the first time he's tried to 'comfort' me."

"That's a terrible thing to say!"

"It's true. He's touched me before. Too often to be innocent. But this was the worst. And so help me Almighty Creator, its the last time. I swear to you, I will not be touched by him again!"

Hester's hand shook so badly she had to replace the cover on the bottle. "I won't hear such talk," she said. "You are his daughter, and . . . I . . ." She gasped for air, tried to go on. " . . . won't . . ."

"I'm telling the truth, Mother," Elizabeth said, frightened by the look on Hester's face.

"Truth? Truth?" Hester rocked back and forth on her heels and her eyes blazed madly. "The truth is you tempted him!"

"That's not so," Elizabeth whispered.

"And that is how you repay him for all the years he has cared for you! He never meant you harm. He loves you!" Her voice rising, she stood and, back bent under the canvas roof, hovered like some dark bird of prey over her daughter. "Why are you so terrible to him? Do you hate him that much?"

Elizabeth stared in horror. She had known her mother was distraught, but these were the signs of madness, and the thought terrified her. Fighting to remain calm, she reached with one hand for her shirt and at tne same time got to her knees and retreated toward the front of the wagon. "Now, Mother," she said, the voice of reason in the face of distress. "I love him. He's my father and I love him." Desperate, she sought the words to soothe her mother's troubled spirits. "I love you too, Mother. Here." She smiled and patted the blankets. "Why don't you lie down. I'll rub your temples. You know how much you like to have your temples rubbed."

Instead, Hester whirled, climbed down from the wagon, and disappeared. Elizabeth hurriedly buttoned her shirt and started to follow, only to find that her mother had stopped a few paces away. Small and lonely, she stood and stared at the broad, sluggish ribbon of muddy water that divided the continent for hundreds of undulating miles. "Mississippi!" Elizabeth heard her say. "Louisiana!" She spat the words as if they were a poison she was ridding from her system. And last, hands clenched into fists and held raised: "Texas!"

Overhead, storm clouds gathered in quarreling numbers. Lightning cursed the lowering western sky. Hester's hands dropped to her sides and her shoulders slumped. "We were so happy," she said in a tiny little voice so filled with sadness that Elizabeth almost wept to hear it. "We were so happy once."

Chapter VI

Rain drove the settlers from the supper table and sent them streaming up from the river toward the shelter of their tents and canvas-covered wagons. A blanket wrapped around her shoulders, Elizabeth huddled in the Michaelson wagon. Behind her, stretched out on the pallet, an exhausted Hester lay without moving. Rain dripped from the trees, plop plopped in heavy droplets onto the canvas top, slid down the sloping sides to puddle underneath the wagonbed. Drip drip drip. Counting, counting, trying to sleep, to forget the aches and pains and fears. *One thousand and twenty-one, one thousand and twenty-two, one thousand and twenty-three*. Like counting the stars in hopeless, numbing, tiring, sleepless tedium.

Elizabeth, watching her mother, wondered if she was pretending to be asleep so she wouldn't have to face her daughter. She needn't have worried, Elizabeth thought dully. Hester could have said anything she wanted. Her dutiful daughter had no stomach for another scene. Elizabeth would be a good girl. Elizabeth would be what her father wanted her to be, as long as he did not touch her again. Elizabeth loved her father. Elizabeth hated her father. And how was Elizabeth to explain that to a woman like Hester who, carried a thousand miles from a home she had never wanted to leave, teetered precariously on the edge of hysteria?

Hester stirred and moaned in her sleep. Feeling a stab of pity, Elizabeth reached to pull the cover over her. The lantern she had lit earlier burned low, a dim light that did little to alleviate the darkness. Outside, the rain drummed down harder and a rising wind pressed the arched canvas to the ribs that held it erect. Yawning, Elizabeth wrapped the blanket more tightly about her and wondered what time it was. It felt as if her father had been gone for hours. Her back stung and she shifted her position. High overhead, thunder prowled the invisible sky like a wild beast stalking its prey. And on earth, something could be seen on the path, moving in a sudden flash of lightning.

Quickly, Elizabeth pulled on her father's hat, grabbed the lantern and a rain tarpaulin, and stepped out. "Lottie?" she called. "Father?"

"Beth? It's me, Beth," Lottie answered. "And Mr. Jones."

Dark shapes loomed out of the rain, slipping and stumbling through the mud. Elizabeth hurried to them and threw the tarp over them.

"You told," Lottie gasped. "Curse you, you told."

"Father made me," Elizabeth explained. "Where's . . ." She held up the lantern. A bedraggled Jones stared back at her. "Where's Father?" she asked.

"Still there, far as I know," Jones said, obviously disgusted with the whole soggy affair. "That road's pure mud."

"I was just dancing," Lottie whined. "I wasn't doing anything wrong." She wiped a muddy wrist across her face. "Just dancing, that's all. Holton wanted to go out back, but I wouldn't let him, and then Father found us."

"Where is he?" Elizabeth asked.

"He was awful! Why did you have to tell? It's all your fault."

Rain ran down her back, soaked into her shoes, beat on her hat. Elizabeth thought she would go mad. *"Where is he?"* she screamed. "For the love of God, where—"

"I don't know."

"You don't know?" A bolt of lightning struck nearby. All three cringed and moved closer to the wagon. "What do you mean you don't know?"

"They began to fight. I was so frightened I just ran, and then he—" She gestured to Jones. "—found me and took me away. I don't know. I don't know."

Furious, Elizabeth turned her wrath on the wagon train leader. "You didn't help him?" she screeched, pounding the black man's chest with her fist. "You just left him—"

"That'll be enough, miss," Jones interrupted, catching her wrist and restraining her as easily as if she were a child. "Señor Medina hired me to take you people to Texas, not fight your unnecessary fights. If your pa wants to fight, he does so without me."

"But you could have at least gone to see—"

"I'm a black man and this is the east side of the river, miss. Once we cross the Sabine into Texas it's another story. But east of the Sabine?" He shook his head. "You got to understand how it is, miss. If I walked into any one of them places, I'd have the chance of a rattlesnake in front of a herd of buffalo."

"But—"

Jones was losing patience. "No buts, durn it. Now, you take your sister inside that wagon and both of you get some dry clothes on." He stepped out from under the tarp and saw that it was firmly wrapped around the two girls. "I'm gonna go and do the same, and have me a cup of coffee. Another hour, when this lets up, you come and tell me if he ain't back yet, and I'll take the chance and go scout around. But not until, you hear? Can't nobody do nothin' in this rain."

"But you can't—"

"I can, miss!" Jones grabbed Elizabeth's shoulder and turned her around so that she faced the wagon. "Now do as I say 'for I get ired. There's nothin' you can do."

He sloshed off. In a moment, the sound of his footsteps had faded. "Where did you leave him?" Elizabeth asked, restraining Lottie when she started toward the wagon.

"Mr. Jones said—"

Elizabeth's hand lashed out and caught Lottie's dress at the shoulder. "So help me, Lottie, I'll tear this dress off you and you'll only have one left. Now where did you leave him?"

The lantern was held close to her face, the glass almost touching her cheek. Lottie shrank back. "I don't know," she said, frightened. "A place. A dance hall, I guess. It was big, with two stories and lots of people. . . ." She stumbled when Elizabeth let her go, handed her the lantern, and ripped the tarp from around her shoulders. "Don't do it, Beth! It's horrible there. I'll tell Mr. Jones that—"

"You'll tell Mr. Jones nothing for at least an hour!" Elizabeth hissed. She wrapped the tarp around herself and snatched the lantern from Lottie's hand. "Now go to the wagon. Mother's asleep. If she wakes up, tell her I've gone after Father and that I'll be back in a little while. Do you understand me?"

Tired and drenched to the skin, Lottie nodded dumbly and trudged through the mud to the wagon. Elizabeth pulled the hat down over her ears and, with the lantern held low to light the way, disappeared into the gap in the trees.

The path to town was lined with oak trees and yellow pine, eerily moss-hung and menacingly spiny against the devilish glow of the lightning. Here and there along the trail, betrayed to Elizabeth by a crack of light or the barking of a dog, humble lodgings lay nestled in the heavy woods. When Thaddeus Jones had first instructed the settlers to stay away from Natchez Under the Hill, he had described the path to town. They would know when they were nearing Natchez when the path suddenly became a road at the end of a low, whitewashed picket fence that surrounded a country estate. Shortly thereafter the road branched, the left fork leading to Natchez itself, the right to its iniquitous companion. Elizabeth found the picket fence as expected and, a hundred yards farther along, a great two-story house that was brightly lit against the night. Short paces later, the road branched as Jones had said it would. "This has to be it," she mumbled, pausing momentarily and squinting through the rain. Ahead she could see lights that marked the outskirts of Natchez proper. To her right she could hear the Mississippi running in darkness. With a deep breath, she turned and entered the narrow, tree-overhung path that, she discovered soon enough, sloped down precipitously. She slipped and slid, caught at branches for support, once stepped off the path itself and found herself knee deep in what must have been a ditch. Thunder crashed on every side. Lightning cast grasping shadows of lurking monsters. The lantern barely lit the few feet of path in front of her and, quite suddenly and surprisingly, revealed a sheer red clay and mud wall that was the base of the bluff under which lay Natchez Under the Hill.

The Mississippi roared in her ears, drowning out all other sounds. Dim outlines of squat buildings, shot through with myriad holes that leaked warm lantern light, marched in irregular formation ahead of her. Elizabeth approached one and saw that the windows were covered with clapboard shutters to keep out the rain. She pressed close to a peephole and peered inside where a conglomeration of unsavory-looking individuals danced with chunkily built, painted harlots who spun and bobbed in approximate time to an out-of-tune piano. Cigar and pipesmoke hovered over the whirling assembly, giving it the appearance of a scene from the nether world her father was so quick to describe on each occasion of her or Lottie's slightest misdeed.

Lottie had described a large, two-story dance hall filled with lots of people. Elizabeth leaned against the wall, wiped the water from her face, and looked up just as a flash of lightning revealed a half dozen or so buildings to her right and a single two-story structure. "As good a place to start as any," she said aloud, more to bolster her spirits than to be heard.

A boardwalk constructed by some mad inebriate angled out from the tavern and passed in front of two or three other buildings before becoming indistinguishable from the mud that filled the street. Elizabeth scraped some of the mud off her shoes and struck out along the boardwalk. The rain was coming fitfully now. Driven off the river by hard gusts, it whipped the edges of the tarpaulin she wore. A sign creaked overhead. KARANKAWA KATIE, it said. From inside, a loud crash and a flurry of curses, shouts, shrieks, and a single shot sent her scurrying away. The next building was completely dark and smelled of smoke and charred wood. Just beyond it, the sound of a violent struggle came from an alley. Elizabeth paused, then almost ran before she heard what sounded like her father's voice. Her heart beating wildly, she jumped off the boardwalk, nearly tripped on a half-sunken beam, caught hold of a post for balance, and entered the alley where two shadowy figures were rolling in the mud.

"Stop!" Elizabeth shouted.

The man on top glanced up, but kept pummeling his victim.

"I have a gun!" she warned, raising her arm and hoping the lie sounded convincing.

The man struggled to his feet, waving his hands in front of his face. "Damn!" he cursed, and stumbled off down the alley to disappear among a tumble of barrels and crates.

Elizabeth ran to the downed man and crouched by him. "Father," she said, turning him over and rolling him out of a puddle. "It's me, Father. Elizabeth."

Lightning flared, revealed heavy-set features covered with a sheen of offal and mud. An arm encircled Elizabeth's neck and yanked her down to be kissed by a hideous, foul-smelling mouth. Horrified, Elizabeth struggled free with such force her momentum propelled her against the wall of the burned-out tavern. Barely able to keep from screaming, she watched as the figure approached. "I've been called a lot of things, honey, but never a father."

It was a woman! Elizabeth's stomach churned and she tried to wipe the taste from her mouth.

The woman shook her head, spraying Elizabeth with the

foul-smelling mud, and stuck her face under the torrent of
water running off the roof. Grabbing Elizabeth's wrist, she
raised the lantern to see Elizabeth better, and in so doing
revealed her own face, pox-marked and bruised. "So it's a
sweet innocent thing that's chased away my bucko. Well, I'll
not hold it against you, dearie. Still, you'd best get back
where you belong. This is no night for a young thing like you
to be out."

The woman lurched away in search of her lost bucko,
leaving Elizabeth to feel her way back to the boardwalk, from
where she saw she would have to descend once more into the
mud in order to reach the two-story building. The raw, acrid
taste of vomit burned in her throat; the taste of the woman in
the alley lingered on her lips. Blinded by tears of revulsion,
she stumbled out into the muddy street and into the path of a
team of horses.

"Lawd!" A voice exclaimed.

Elizabeth screamed, and fell back as the horses reared over
her and the driver fought to bring them under control. The
mud was cold and deep. Elizabeth's hands sank to the wrists.
The lantern hissed and, as the hot glass snapped with a
crackling sound, went out. Above her, another lantern dangled from a thin arm.

"Mistuh," the reedy voice went on angrily. "Ah'se sorry,
but you run right in front of— Oh, Lawdy, Lawdy. Don't that
beat all. You ain't no mistuh at all!"

Utterly defeated, drenched to the bone and covered with
mud, Elizabeth realized how totally helpless she was. She
didn't have the courage to search every building, brothel,
tavern, shed, and alley in the hell in which she found herself;
she would have to find the town constable and ask him to
help locate her father. "Please," she said, struggling to her
feet and leaning wearily against the wagon. "Please help me.
I'm looking . . . that is, I have to find the constable. Can
you take me to him? It's important. Please help me."

The black driver studied her suspiciously. She was not a
woman from the district, for he knew all of them by sight.
Moreover, this was little more than a girl, and lost at that.
"Ah'll help you, miss," he finally said, glancing around
nervously in case anyone should see him in the presence of a
white woman, no matter what the circumstances. "Ah'm on
mah way to find ol' Cap'n Martin myself. Reckon you kin
come along if'n you a mind. But you'll have to ride in back,

'cause Ah could git me in a pow'ful lot of trouble was you sittin' up here with me an' all. 'Course,'' he added, jerking his head toward the back of the wagon, ''you might not wanta ride there 'cause of what Ah'm takin' to the Cap'n, but that's up ta you.''

"I don't care,'' Elizabeth said, her voice thick with exhaustion and anxiety. She climbed onto the step and into the rear. "Just as long as we find him, I don't care.''

"Jest watch yer step, Miss. And mind you stick close to the side. They's a tool box there you can set on, an' not git touched by—''

Too late. Lightning arced across the sky and the horses shied. Off balance, Elizabeth fell over the edge and onto something soft and clammy, then sucked in her breath and jerked away from a cold, damp hand that pressed against her.

The driver fought the plunging horses with one hand, and held the lantern so the girl could see better with the other. "Whoa, Bess, whoa, Blue,'' he hollered. "You all right, miss? You sick?''

Elizabeth crouched on hands and knees and stared at the mud-crusted apparition lying on the floor in front of her. The skull was partly flattened, and oozed a grayish-white material. The rain, as it cleansed the blood from the bloodless face, fell into the lifeless eyes that stared past her and into eternity. The scream started in her stomach, and tore free from her throat.

"Ma'am? Miss?'' the old man stuttered. "Ah tried to warn you.''

A rising scream of anguish was his only answer. Worried, the driver clucked to the team and applied the whip. He wanted to be shucked of his load and the crazy woman as quick as quick was. Being scared of a dead man was one thing, he didn't blame her for that, but this durn girl was carryin' on like she was kin.

Chapter VII

Carl Michaelson had always wanted a son, a son his wife had been unable to produce. Carl Michaelson loved his wife in the ways an upright man is taught to love his wife, by providing for her and caring for her. At one time he had loved her passionately, too, but that was a love that somehow faded through the years. He had never known, nor had he bothered to ask himself, why. Carl Michaelson would have said, if asked, that he loved his eldest daughter. Perhaps he did, because he gave his life for her, in a manner of speaking. No man who knew Carl would have said, either to his face or behind his back, that it was his own honor, not Lottie's, that he was defending. The thought occurred to some, but it was a thought best kept secret even to those who thought it. Carl Michaelson had been heard to say that he loved his youngest daughter, that she was as nearly a son as a daughter could be. He did not realize that he had unintentionally shaped Elizabeth's personality, nor that she, in return, had spent most of her life trying to be a son as well as a daughter. Later, when her body changed, he found that in spite of himself he loved her in a different, forbidden way that, no matter how hard he tried to deny it, plagued him during his sleeping and waking hours alike. The love drove him to the brink of madness, and to the Lord Jesus Christ and His Father, the Almighty God of the Universe, in whom lay salvation and peace. This Lord and this God, whom he had loved, through a fear he failed to recognize, were the twin forces that drove his restless feet westward. There, he dimly perceived, he would find rest through travail and an unending struggle for survival.

Now Carl Michaelson lay dead in a pine box. He was dressed in a black suit and his hands were folded across his stomach. The mud and blood had been cleansed from his face, and a large white bandage hid the gaping hole in his head. He did not look particularly at peace, only pale and tired and weary beyond belief, ready, almost, to descend into the earth from whence he had come.

At nine o'clock on the morning of Saturday, October 11, 1834, the last of the band of settlers filed past and gazed mournfully down on the remains. Two minutes later, Alton Babcock, owner and proprietor of Babcock's Funeral Parlor, drove into place the four nails that held the lid, and led the way through the double doors to the waiting hearse. A half hour later, the assembly gathered around an open grave in the Natchez cemetery where the rising waters of the Mississippi would not exhume Carl and add further humiliation to his untimely demise.

The Reverend Buckland Kania read all the necessary words from the Bible, then improvised a eulogy. He had known Carl Michaelson only during the trip from Pennsylvania and had soon discovered that the farmer's religion involved a strict, intensely private relationship with God, one that felt little need for the brotherhood of a religious community. But he sought words of comfort for the man's family.

The balm of words became a drone, a buzz. Hester sat in a chair provided for her and wept softly. Lottie, her eyes puffy and her cheeks pale, stood slightly bowed forward, much like a tree in a windstorm. Elizabeth stood at her mother's side and stared at the pine box as if her gaze could penetrate the wood and see within it the man she had called Father.

Their friends were close at hand. Joan Campbell had not left Hester's side since the arrival of the horrible news. Scott Campbell and his sons had carried the body to the funeral parlor in Natchez and had made all the arrangements. Pregnant Mildred Thatche sniffed back tears. Her husband Kevin, suddenly older than his sixteen years, held her hand and tried not to show that he was more concerned for the life blossoming within his wife than he was for a dead man in a wooden box. Heads prayerfully bowed, the Matlans stood with Jack Kemper, whose wife, Helen, glared reproachfully at Lottie and Elizabeth. Lips pursed, her head slowly wagging from side to side, she was an austere figure who, because no one else had had the temerity to do so, had taken upon herself the task of passing judgment on those who were to blame for a righteous man's death. Mila Kania and Thaddeus Jones stood apart at the rear.

He is dead, and that is that. No matter how hard she tried, Elizabeth could not see through the layer of wood that separated her from her father.

He is dead, but if he had a son, his killing would not go unavenged. The pine was transparent compared to that impenetrable though invisible barrier between death and life.

He is dead. The last moment I spent with him his arms were around me and his hands held me. I hated and feared him then, and was ashamed for him. I swore my own father would never touch me again. But transparency or opacity had nothing to do with the dead and those they left behind. Memory existed outside those physical attributes, and the good memories were as easily recalled as the bad. *We labored together in the garden and in the fields. His praise lightened my heart with pride. If he was sometimes weak and overbearing, he was often noble and strong and tender. Oh, God, please let me remember him as he, and You, would want me to remember him.*

"Lord, Heavenly King, Almighty and Triumphant God! As You taught us to live in Your likeness, teach us to face the loss of our brother, friend, loving husband, and beloved parent in the hope of rising again, reunited at the last judgment in Thy merciful sight and gentle grace. In Your name, Who discerns all and loves all. Amen."

Buckland Kania lowered his hands, bent down and took a fistful of dirt, the red dirt that was so foreign-looking, so different from the dark brown Pennsylvania soil they all knew, and sprinkled it onto the coffin. The small assemblage responded, "Amen," as one, and brought closer together by their loss, filed by the grave and repeated the final gesture.

"I told him. I told him, I told him, I told him," Hester chanted, and suddenly leaned over and vomited.

Joan Campbell and Lottie rushed to support her. The men backed away and, embarrassed, averted their eyes.

"You see how it is," Thaddeus Jones said, striding forward and standing at one end of the grave. His eyes were bloodshot, accentuated by the bold contrast of his ebony skin. One hand rested on the pistol he wore in his belt. "Death ain't never pretty, especially when it comes like this. You'll probably see more of it before you reach San Antone. A lot depends on if we meet the Comanche or not, but even more depends on how much common sense—"

"Mr. Jones!" Reverend Kania blurted. "This is hardly the time or place."

"Have you no regard for common decency, man?" an incensed Nels Matlan added.

Jones's eyes lingered on Kania's, then shifted to Matlan's, and finally dropped to the wooden box sprinkled with red dirt. "As much as any of you," he finally said. His voice was deep and sad, but forceful. As he spoke, he looked at each of the settlers in turn. "Maybe more. Maybe, too, this is the only time what I say will sink in deep. I told you we weren't out for no Sunday stroll, but you wouldn't believe me. Now you know what I meant. We're on the fringe of the law here—" He waved one arm to indicate the emptiness across the Mississippi. "—and it'll get worse the farther we go. Now, I'm paid to see you to San Antone, which is a long way off through some mean and tryin' country. Whether we get there kickin' or die crow bait along the way is a matter of me doin' my job right and you listenin' to what I say. Just so you'll know, if trouble comes unbidden, Injun or otherwise, I'll stand in front of you and be the first to meet it. But if any other man of you wants to make trouble on his own . . ." He paused, and the hand that had pointed west now pointed to the remains of Carl Michaelson. " . . . he meets it best he can, for it's the women and children I'll worry about."

"I think that that will be enough," Elizabeth broke in, not bothering to hide her anger. "I'm sure we are all deeply touched by your concern, such as it is." Wheeling, she took her mother's arm and, with Lottie, led her away from the open grave and toward the waiting carriages.

"I guess you can start now," Jones said to Babcock's helpers. "You can tell Babcock I want to see that stone Miz Michaelson paid for when I come back through, too."

The drift of the settlers toward the carriages speeded up as the first shovelful of dirt thudded hollowly on the coffin lid. Mackenzie and Dennis Campbell, their red hair bright in the sun, hurried to catch up with the Michaelsons. "If you or your ma needs anything, Lottie," Mackenzie said, speaking for them both, "you just—"

"We don't," Elizabeth snapped, then immediately regretting her tone added, "I'm sorry, Mackenzie. You and Dennis and your father have done more than enough. We're just a. little . . . just upset, right now."

Both young men nodded in reply and rejoined their mother

and father for the mile-long trip back to camp. The day was hot and terribly muggy after the previous night's downpour. The sky, clear and blue, contradicted the dark mood of the settlers. Each family went its own way when they arrived in camp, the men to tend stock and the women to prepare the noon meal. The small children, Tommy and Ruthie and Dianne, were herded out of earshot so that their laughter, as they played, wouldn't disturb Hester and her girls.

At the Michaelson wagon, Hester lay limply while Elizabeth changed into her work clothes and got the fire going under the coffee pot. Lottie set the small table Kevin Thatche had fixed for them that morning.

"Ladies."

Startled, all three looked up to see Thaddeus Jones. Elizabeth added a final stick to the fire, rose and stood between him and her mother. "Ah, how nice," she said, bitterly sarcastic. "It's Mr. Jones." Hands on hips, she leaned across the fire. "Why don't you just leave us alone. You've said enough for one day."

"Yes, ma'am." Jones, looking embarrassed, removed his hat but stood his ground. "I'm sorry about that, miss, and about your pa, too, but what I said had to be said. Coffee smells right drinksome."

"It's not hot yet, but help yourself."

"Thank you." Uncharacteristically awkward, Jones took a cup from the end of the rod that held the pot over the fire, tipped some coffee into it, and sat back on his heels. "I talked to the captain."

"The captain?" Elizabeth asked.

"Captain Martin. The constable, sort of."

Hester looked up expectantly. Lottie took a step forward. Elizabeth's face hardened. "I trust he's arrested my father's murderer."

"Well . . ." Jones looked into his coffee, the only safe place he could think of. "Not exactly."

"Not exactly!"

"There were witnesses," Jones said, hurrying now that he'd managed to broach the subject. "They say it was a fair fight, and one that Mr. Michaelson started. Now, give me a chance," he said, standing and holding up a hand to cut off Elizabeth before she started. "Even your sister told it that way. He started it with the wrong man, is all. Holton Bagget's got him a reputation as a roisterer and knuckle dancer. Your pa took a broken bottle to him and Bagget picked up a three-legged stool.'' He shrugged. ''It was a poor choice of weapon on behalf of your pa. I'm sorry, but that's the way it is. The law's on Bagget's side. He can't be touched.''

''I can't believe that,'' Lottie said, her face white. ''This is justice?''

''I reckon so,'' Jones said, scratching his head. ''I warned you. Warned you all.''

Lottie flushed, helped her mother to her feet.

''I . . . uh . . .'' The wagon master replaced his hat, took a sip of coffee, and looked at each of the three women before going on. ''That is, it makes everything especially uncomfortable seein' as I already told Bagget last week that he could ride along with us. He's headin' west, and I figured the extra gun would come in handy.''

''You invited that murderer! . . .'' Shaking, lips tight, her face older by far than a seventeen year old's, Elizabeth fought for words.

''Now calm yourself, miss. That was before the killin', so I can't be held—''

''And now?'' Lottie asked for them all.

''Well . . .'' Jones was an easygoing man, one who avoided trouble whenever possible, and confrontations with angry, riled women were high on his list of trouble. Careful not to put out the fire, he poured the dregs of his coffee around the edge of the shallow pit before answering. ''I can't see it makes any difference, to be truthful, 'cause there ain't gonna be no unescorted womenfolk in the train. Which is to say,'' he mumbled, before coming right out with it, ''you ain't goin'.''

''What?'' Elizabeth asked, incredulous.

''That was agreed on a long time ago, miss. 'Fore I took this job.''

''But . . . but . . .'' Elizabeth looked helplessly at Lottie, back to the wagon master. ''But Father never said . . . Why weren't we told? That's not fair! You can't—''

''What your pa told you and what he didn't tell you ain't none of my business. That was the agreement, an' Medina told them all. You see, you got to understand. There's nothin' more dangerous and troublesome than unattached womenfolk in a wagon train. It's a fair far journey to Texas that can make folks sort of crazy. They do things, think things they might not do or think at home. Young pretties with no pa to keep a

rein on 'em are just too plain fiercesome and tribulatin'.'' He
tried a conciliatory smile, but it failed miserably. "Like I
said, no reflection on you personally, but that's the way it is.
I'm sorry."

"But we own land there," Lottie said, near tears.

"Yes, ma'am, you do. Maybe you can sell the land to
someone here," Jones suggested, putting the cup on its hook,
and backing away from the fire. "I'm sorry."

"Oh, God, will you stop saying how sorry you are?"
Elizabeth shouted. She followed him, beating her thighs with
her fists. "You're *not* sorry! If you'd just helped when it
mattered!"

"Beth!" Hester called. "It's for the best."

"No it's not!" Elizabeth screamed, whirling on her mother. "Don't you realize—"

"Your mama's right, miss. The matter's closed. Unescorted
women is bad luck and plenty of it. Plenty."

"Beth!" Hester repeated more sternly, taking strength from
the hope that she might return home after all. "We can have
Mr. Jones speak to Sênor Medina. I am sure he will return
our money when he learns what's happened. We'll buy a
small house somewhere back East and—"

"No!" Elizabeth said. "No no no no no no! We've left the
East. That part of our life's over. The only home we own is
out West in Texas. We *own* it, Mother. It's waiting for us.
We can't deny Father's dream. Not now."

"Your *father's* dream," Hester said, rising and striding
toward Elizabeth. "Not mine, do you hear. Not mine!" All
the rancor and ill-will that had festered in her for months now
spilled out. "Your father is dead and I am the head of this
family. You are my daughter, not the man you dress to be,
and you will do as I say. We shall follow Mr. Jones's advice,
and that is that!"

Elizabeth felt caught in a trap. On one side, the implacable
wagon train master, on the other, her mother, willful and
vindictive. "Lottie?" she said, pleading for support.

"I . . ." Lottie twisted her bodice string around one index
finger, and stared at it as if it were a fortune teller's device
that, in its spirals, held the secrets of her future. "Father's
dead," she finally said in a tiny voice. "It's not our decision
to make."

"Oh, no?" Shoulders squared, anger and determination
sparking in her eyes, Elizabeth faced each of them. "Well, I

think it is, and I—we—whether any of you like it or not, are going to Texas. One way or another, we *are* going!'' Unable to stay in their presence without saying something she knew she would regret later, she turned and ran for the sanctuary of the trees. ''You can count on it!'' she shouted over her shoulder.

''Beth?'' Hester called after her. ''Beth! You come back here immediately!''

Jones cleared his throat. ''I, uh . . . I reckon I'll be goin','' he said, unused to family squabbles and wanting nothing more than to escape. ''Let you work it out for yourselves. Best way. I'll see what I can do about findin' someone to buy your grant and wagon and all.'' He tipped his hat to Hester and Lottie in turn. ''Ma'am. Miss.''

The two women watched him leave. ''Beth?'' Hester called again before returning to her seat and twisted thoughts. ''It's no good, Beth. We're going back to Pennsylvania.''

Huddled alone in the damp shade beneath the still-dripping broad leaves of a magnolia, Elizabeth heard but didn't respond. They weren't going back, of that she was sure. One way or another, they would press on to Texas as her father had wanted. Of more importance was the man named Holton Bagget. *Damn the murderer! Damn the thief who stole my father's life and dream.*

''He can't be touched,'' Jones had said.

And with that recollection, the anger, rekindled, burned anew. ''I wouldn't be too sure about that, Mr. Jones,'' she said, rising abruptly and striding toward the clearing. ''Not too sure at all.''

Chapter VIII

Ponder's Crossing. If a man wanted a drink, a good time, and a reasonable chance not to regret it later with infection, if a man wanted to hear news of the trail west and who was where and why in the howling wilderness, if a man wanted a touch of civilized damnation before beginning a lonely journey to follow the setting sun, he went to Ponder's Crossing.

On that noon in October, with the clouds coming down the Mississippi on the north wind that had cleared out the previous night's storm, Ponder's Crossing was quiet, if a lack of drinking, cussing, and fighting could be called quiet. More than a dozen men were strewn about the hall in various attitudes of dissipation and snoring off the excesses of the previous night. The Vikings in this Mississippi Valhalla were a singular lot. Big Nose Castor lay stretched across two tables, honking and whistling as he breathed. Antlers Stoner lay crumpled in a corner by the piano. Crease Anthony lay with his head on the great pillowy gut of Frank "Savory" Dill, which wasn't all that good an idea except that Crease was unconscious and his nose was out of order anyway due to an overdose of unholy spirits. Holton Bagget was there, too. One of the two men standing up at that hour, he was a mustachioed, swaggering young man with red-rimmed eyes and a fresh cut through the dark brown kidney-shaped birthmark on his right cheek. Holton had had a long hard night followed by a restless morning. About ready to sleep at last, he quaffed a mug of Luke Ponder's house beer, fondly referred to as River Rat, and stared at the delightfully lewd painting hanging over the mahogony bar.

Luke Ponder, Hon. Prop., according to the sign that hung over the door outside, looked up from his account books.

" 'Nother?" he asked automatically as the empty mug hit the bar.

"One," Holton answered, shifting his gaze to the reflection of a lanky man about his age who sat on the outside balcony overlooking the river. Holton leaned his elbows on the bar and jabbed a thumb in the newcomer's direction. "He one of them farmers from that goddamn wagon train Jones is takin' out?"

Luke's deft twist of the wrist sent the full mug right where Holton could pick it up without moving. "No," he said. "He's with Leakey."

"Hogjaw?"

"Who else? I guess you didn't hear him come in, bein' up in town with the Cap'n an' all."

Holton spit in disgust. "Man can't get any sleep at all, the way it's gettin' around here. Too damn much law, anyways. Hogjaw still as ugly?"

"You still afraid to call him that to his face?"

"I ain't afraid of no man."

Luke sniggered. " 'Ceptin' Leakey."

"What the hell you trying to say, you old bastard?" Holton snapped.

"That you're smarter than you look." Luke Ponder grinned. "I'm payin' you a compliment, boy. I'm sayin' you ain't no fool."

"Ahhh . . ." Holton picked up the mug, took a swallow of beer and made a face. "When it don't taste good, I need sleep. You got any rooms left?"

Luke ran a mental tally, shook his head no. "They're all bein' used."

"What about Jodie?"

"Her too," the bar owner muttered, returning to the task of taking inventory, a routine to which he adhered every midday.

A cooling breeze drifted in through the open doors facing the river. Holton stepped over Crease Anthony and walked outside. Built over the slow brown waters of the Mississippi, the balcony provided a place for men to stack their rifles and gear or, for the occasionally reflective sort, a point from which to contemplate the queen of rivers. Holton demonstrated two further uses. Leaning on the railing, he urinated in the river, and then, after a perfunctory search among the assorted packs, arranged a bed for himself along the back wall. Soon he was snoring as industriously as the men inside.

True's chair was tilted back on its hind legs. His heels were propped on the balcony railing and his hat was pulled down over his eyes. He had been dozing lightly and, with the intrusion, sighed over the loss of his solitude and pushed up his hat so he could see. The air was balmy enough, but with an edge of crispness that presaged fall. New clouds, dark and heavy, hid the noon sun. From time to time, a beam of light like a gilded saber plunged into the river before the brooding gray clouds could gather and snap the blade at the hilt. Then the world would be somber and still again. Below, a raft carrying two boys and a black man drifted by. Embarked on a grand adventure that would last until supper time at least, the boys shouted and waved to True while the man, concerned for the smaller one's safety, tried simultaneously to steer the raft and to grab hold of his charge's belt loop.

True watched the boys into the distance, extended his legs, and rocked back and forth. The journey from Solitary had been, in the main, uneventful. They had traveled through dense forest for the most part, with little more than occasional vistas from high points to give them a sense of direction or of the passing miles. They had eaten their own cooking, and grown bored with it. They had wished for any other voice to relieve the boredom, for they had only their own tales and complaints for distraction and entertainment. They had hoped to make Natchez the night before, but the storm had forced them to a halt three miles out of town where they camped under a makeshift shelter in the lee of a huge old magnolia and, wet and disgusted, listened to Hogjaw describe Ponder's Crossing as the wildest place east of the Green River Rendezvous up in Sioux territory. The next morning, Joseph and Andrew just naturally had to see for themselves, so all four had headed straight for Natchez Under the Hill.

To True's way of thinking, they had seen a few worse places, and many better. Home sweet home, as Hogjaw affectionately if sarcastically called the thin strip of weather-beaten buildings connected by a sea of mud, was still going strong an hour after daybreak. Hogjaw left immediately, saying he had to attend to business. Andrew disappeared just as rapidly with a statuesque mulattress to an upstairs room. Joseph downed two shots of rye and picked out a woman almost as fast, lingering only long enough to rib True for rebuffing the advances of a well-endowed whore named Mouse. True was content with two mugs of River Rat, which he took to the balcony where he could watch the sprawling, twisting expanse of water unravel toward the horizon. Shortly thereafter, with Ponder's Crossing finally winding down and emptying behind him, he watched a fleet of keelboats poling past, working their way upriver close to shore. A hard life, Hogjaw had remarked once during the long miles, and one often ended prematurely by a knife or gun or the river itself. Not the sort he'd like to lead, going up and down and up and down and never getting anywhere a man could call home. It looked like a fair assessment, True thought. Dirty and unkempt, shoulder and thigh muscles bulging under thin homespun as they trudged the deck with their long poles, the keelboaters presented a picture of drudgery patterned after Sisyphus, the Greek who was doomed for eternity to push the same rock up the small hill over and over again.

Half a continent lay behind him, another half in front. The keelboaters went up and down, up and down. Everything changed, nothing changed, not least the river that, even as its face was altered by the changing light, remained eternally the same. People too were little different. They came and went, worked and lazed, hoped and despaired, laughed and wept. Some wore fine linen, others drab homespun. Some lived in fine houses, others in hovels. Some drank and caroused and copulated without a care in the world, and he, True Paxton, thoroughly melancholy by this time, sat alone on a balcony and listened to men snore and delved into his soul and tried to forget his mother's disturbing farewell and prediction that he would never return. Half a continent behind him and half before. It was one hell of a way to spend a day.

Luke Ponder shook his head and spat into the nearest spittoon. "A mite too serious," he muttered to himself, keeping an eye on True and wondering where Leakey had found him. "But then, there's some that say men of a serious nature are destined to accomplish much."

He broke open a new keg of River Rat and tasted it, made a mental note to let the next batch age another day or two before using it. " 'Course, they also tend to be a trifle shortlived," he went on in the interminable conversation he held with himself when no one was about. "The man to bet money on, though, is the brother, Joseph. Now there's one to move mountains." Ponder counted the bottles of rye, checked them against the head barkeeper's tally sheet. "He's bold and he's strong, and there ain't a timid bone in his body, from the looks of him. Yessir, Luke, that Hogjaw knows how to pick 'em.''

A shrill whistle muted by distance interrupted his train of thought and reminded him that it was Saturday and that the sidewheeler from Vicksburg was due to dock before very long. He glanced at the clock in the center of the bar and told himself to shut up and get on with the counting so he could hie it back home before the place started waking up and got took with the usual Saturday fever. Ought to just sell the damn thing, he thought. The widow he'd married was wealthy enough to support them both in her fine house in town, and with what Ponder's Crossing would bring they could live like real gentry. He slid a stack of gold American coins into the bag, made a note on his tally sheet, and started separating the Mexican coins from the French ones. But he wouldn't sell, he knew, even if his wife did worry about losing another husband. "You're too old for that place," she said. "Dangerous men go there." Dangerous men, faugh! What did she know about dangerous men? He was the one who'd handled every brand of man, these last thirty years, and made Ponder's Crossing the busiest place north of New Orleans and south of Vicksburg. Built it with his own hands, he had. It was in his blood. Wasn't dangerous, so long as he limited his visits to the middle of the day, and let the head keep run the place at night. Hell, today it was dead as a whorehouse at Christmas. Luke Ponder slid the pesos into a small bag, tied it, and dropped them into a leather saddlebag. Too bad, in a way, he thought wistfully. Sometimes, he plumb missed the excitement.

"If I was you," the trapper said to the fairskinned lad who had awakened him from a whiskey-induced nap, "and I was lookin' for just about anyone, the place I'd begin askin' at is Ponder's Crossin' over there. Nary a soul comes into Natchez Under the Hill without stoppin' to sample ol' Luke's whiskey and pay respect to his darlin' doves." The trapper smacked his lips. His smile was a blend of the beatific and the Mephistophelean. "Got a colored gal there by the name of Mouse," he said in a dreamy voice. "No dove ever cooed so sweet. She'll leave your feathers all aruffled so it takes a coon's age afore they straighten down."

"I'm not a bird fancier, sir. It is a man named Holton Bagget I seek."

"Holton Bagget, eh? Well, seek and you shall find," the old man said with a cackle. "Go and you shall come, buy and you shall sell, drink and you shall by God drink some more."

Elizabeth waited, but anything else the trapper might have wanted to say came out as a combination of wheezes and grunts as he fell back to sleep. She felt to make sure her hair wasn't hanging out from under her hat, tucked in her shirt, and adjusted the bulge at her side. Natchez Under the Hill looked even more dismal by day than she remembered, but only, she told herself, because she hadn't been able to see much the night before. The tension built in her as she picked her way across the mud bath they called a street and paused outside the two-story dance hall and saloon. THE CROSSING, LUKE PONDER HON. PROP., said the sign swinging over her head. Elizabeth looked past it and wondered if God was watching her from somewhere beyond the slate gray roof of clouds. *You certainly didn't disapprove of Father's murder or else You would have stopped it. Unless You weren't watching at all. Unless You just don't care. Unless Carl Michaelson simply wasn't important enough with all the rest of the world to worry about.* And if her father wasn't, then neither was Holton Bagget, Elizabeth thought defiantly, and plunged through the door.

The wide, surprisingly spacious room strewn with tables and the forms of sleeping men smelled of tobacco, raw whiskey, sticky sweet rum, stale beer, and sweat. The lofty roof was supported by round white columns of wood. Chandeliers of tarnished brass swayed to and fro in a breeze that, given a year, might have sucked away the stagnant aroma of the human condition. A man behind the bar appeared to be the only person awake. He was busily polishing a gold-framed mirror that hung side by side with a painting of a voluptuous naked woman who was copulating quite happily with a creature part man and part goat. Blushing despite herself, Elizabeth walked to the long heavy bar lined with rows of shot glasses and mugs. "Excuse me," she said, pointedly clearing her throat and trying to sound masculine.

Luke Ponder leaned over so he could see her in the mirror and continued polishing. "Your pa know you're here, sonny? If it's a breaking-in you want, all the girls are spoken for. Reckon the Widow Tater will take you on if you've a bottle handy. Just try the Lamplight Saloon. Ask—"

"You don't understand," Elizabeth said, somewhat taken aback.

"Yeah. I don't blame you, come to think of it. The thought of Widow Tater sets me ascratchin' too. I'll tell you what. Wait upstairs in the hall, and when one of the doors opens and a man comes out, you go right in before the gal gets settled down. Just say I told you to tell her to go on and break you in."

"But I'm not—"

"Just put your dollar in the bottle at the end of the bar and go on up. Ain't nothin' to be scared of."

Elizabeth's face was beet red. "I'm not looking for a . . . breaking-in, sir," she said heatedly. "I seek a man by the name of Holton Bagget, and was told to ask here."

"Up to you," Luke said with a shrug. He jerked a thumb over his shoulder. "Out there."

Elizabeth turned to see a balcony where a man sat with his legs propped on the railing. She nodded to Luke Ponder's back and, a hollow feeling forming in the pit of her stomach, walked across the room toward the open double doors. Her hand closed around the pistol she had taken from the wagon after the funeral. She checked the frizzen to make sure enough powder remained in the pan to fire the weapon. She cocked the flint. To her left, a man snored and growled in his sleep, and in the process almost lost his life, for Elizabeth was nervous enough to wheel and level the gun at him before recovering her senses and going on to the door.

The man in the chair wore his hat low over his forehead as he gazed out over the river. Sandy-colored curls stuck out from under his hat at the rear of his head. His face in profile was seriously handsome, its lines as clear-cut and chiseled as a statue's. Her heart seemed to skip a beat as she studied him. *So this is what my father's murderer looks like! How strange! I had assumed he would look evil, but he is—*

A snore behind her took her by surprise. Elizabeth glanced over her shoulder to spy a second man asleep among the packs that lined the outside wall. Confused, unsure of which was her quarry, she dropped the pistol to her side.

"Can I help you, lad?" the man in the chair asked. He had caught her motion out of the corner of his eye.

"Are you Holton Bagget?"

"No. Should I be?"

"Only in Hell," Elizabeth said, wheeling, raising the pistol, and aiming at the sleeping man.

True's reaction was instantaneous. He lunged from the chair and knocked her arm upright just as the gun spat flame and fired. The .55 caliber lead ball flew through the open doors and into the dance hall, where it struck the spiny brass arm of a chandelier and ricocheted across the room to carve a smidgeon of flesh off the top of Luke Ponder's left ear before burrowing into his mirror image. A spider web of cracks streaked to the gilded border of the frame.

"Sheeiiiitttt!" Luke howled, dropping behind the bar.

On the balcony, Holton awoke with a start to see two men struggling over him. Rolling instinctively out of the way, he sprang to his feet just as one of the men lost his hat and golden hair spilled past his shoulders. "Goddamn!" he cursed. "It's a girl!"

True let go of her as if burned, and stepped back in surprise.

Her eyes ablaze with fury, Elizabeth's wrath turned on True. "He killed my father, and you . . . you . . . stopped me, you . . . you . . ."

"What do you mean, killed your . . . Oh," Holton said, remembering the night before and deciding the woman had to be one of the settlers camped upriver. "Now look here, miss," he said, trying to explain. "If that was your daddy, he come at me first."

"Murderer!" Elizabeth hissed.

"Murderer?" Holton squawked, outraged. Hell, the father coming at him face-to-face was one thing, but the daughter trying to shoot him in his sleep was quite another. "The little bitch tried to murder me!" he said to True. "She goddamn tried to murder me!"

"If justice is murder, so be it," Elizabeth spat. Tears streaking her cheeks, she glared at Holton Bagget and then, as if he shared the guilt, at True. "I hope you both burn in Hell!" she added, spinning on her heel and stalking out past the bleary-eyed onlookers.

"Oh, my ear. My ear. Shit!" a voice wailed from behind the bar.

"Stop her, Crease," Holton shouted, grabbing a rifle and starting after her. "Somebody stop her!"

The striking beauty of the girl and her obvious hatred of Holton Bagget, whoever he was and whatever he'd done, prompted True to interfere. "There's no need," he said, stepping in front of Holton and catching the rifle by the stock.

"Get the hell out of my way, farmer," Holton snarled.

"I said, there's no need," True repeated softly.

"And I said back off, you scrawny . . ." Holton dropped his right elbow and, aiming for True's groin, slashed upward with the rifle butt.

It was a routine True had practiced with his father and both his brothers. Hands locked firmly on the rifle, he leaned back and, with three quick steps sideways and backwards, swung his attacker in a circle, then let go the rifle. Unable to stop himself, Holton tripped over True's outstretched foot, crashed through the balcony railing, and plummeted fifteen feet straight down into the Mississippi.

"My ear! Oh, Jesus, it's plumb shot by God off!" Luke Ponder wailed. His wife was right. The hell with the afternoons!

Crease Anthony, Savory Dill, and Big Nose Castor formed a ragged line and started walking toward the doorway to the balcony. "I think you maybe made a mistake there," Crease grunted a wide, toothless grin slowly spreading over his face. "Holton was a partner of mine."

True unsheathed his Arkansas Toothpick, took a step to his left, and stood ready. The three men paused. Savory reached up to scratch his head. When his hand came back down, it held the knife he kept sheathed at the back of his neck. Big Nose chuckled and pulled his own Arkansas Toothpick out of his boot. "It's you against the three of us," he grunted, clearly enjoying the prospect of carving up True. Then suddenly, he ducked out of the way as another shot rang out and a brass chandelier crashed to the floor in front of him.

A form landed feet first on the bar, dropped down beside Luke Ponder, and, after reaching below the bar, straightened with a blunderbuss in his hands. The gun was more than a century old but, as Crease, Savory, and Big Nose knew from experience, it was still in excellent working condition. The three men froze, and in the silence, their quickly dropped knives thudded to the floor.

"Very good, gentlemen," Andrew said, flashing a wicked grin at the men he held at gunpoint.

Joseph hurried down the stairway, and stopped at the bottom to button his trousers and buckle his belt. His shirt was open and fresh bite marks showed on his collarbone. It had been his accuracy that had brought down the chandelier.

"Sorry, boys," he said, careful to stay outside the blunderbuss's spread. "Two steps backward away from those knives, if you will."

True had busied himself gathering their gear, and now waited for Joseph to button his shirt before handing him his rifle. "It's loaded," he said. "The balcony's clear, so our backs are safe."

"Damn it, True!" Joseph exploded. The two brothers slowly circled Crease, Savory, and Big Nose, working their way around toward the front door. "Why the hell are you so determined to ruin my love life?"

True kept an eye on the front half of the room while Joseph watched the back half. "Just circumstance, Joseph. Who knows? Maybe the angels are watching out for you."

"I wish to Hell they'd look the other way if they are," the eldest Paxton growled. "Andrew, we have your warbag! Let's go."

Luke Ponder stood up and noticed the fractured mirror for the first time. "Oh, Lord! My mirror! My chandelier. My ear!"

"We'll be leaving now, Mr. Ponder," Andrew said politely, edging down the bar but keeping the blunderbuss ready.

"Leave? Get the bloody hell out!" Ponder roared, his hand clamped tightly over the ruined tip of his ear.

True headed for the door to check the street and, to his surprise, saw Hogjaw standing in the shadows just inside the entrance. "A lot of help you were," he fumed, storming past.

Andrew followed True and Hogjaw out the door. Joseph was the last to leave. They hurried around the corner, gathered their horses, mounted, and galloped away through a gap created by two teetertotter buildings. Once clear of Natchez Under the Hill, Hogjaw slowed and motioned for the brothers to rein in. "You mind tellin' me just what the hell's goin' on?" he asked. "I thought the idea was to have us a time."

"We did," True said. "Just wore out our welcome, is all."

"We, hell," Joseph said, pointing at True. "He, you mean."

"And we just sort of joined in to make it unanimous," Andrew added with a laugh, secretly relieved to be out of the clutches of the athletic mulattress.

"Most of us, that is," Joseph said, sliding his ill humor from True to Hogjaw. "You weren't any help at all."

The mountain man shrugged. "I wanted to see if it still held, is all."

"If what still held?" Joseph asked, suspicious of being baited.

"Trouble with one Paxton is trouble with 'em all." His jowl flaps jiggled as he nodded in approval. "Hell, Joseph, you didn't need me. The three of you are no different from your daddy and his brothers. Full of bear spit and brimfire even with your pants down."

Joseph colored, snapped off a curse in Hogjaw's general direction, and urged his horse on ahead.

"What was all that about, True?" Andrew asked. "I mean, since you ruined our fun, I think we have a right to know."

"The lad has a point, bucko," Hogjaw said. "For a quiet, peaceable sort, you sure do have a way of riling folks. I swear, but you'd prompt a sparrow to grow porcupine quills."

"It wasn't my fault," True said. "It was the girl's."

Andrew blinked uncomprehendingly. "What girl?"

"I think she was going to shoot me, but then decided to shoot that fellow Bagget instead."

"Holton Bagget?" Hogjaw asked, recognizing the name.

"Who in thunder is Holton Bagget?" Andrew asked, exasperated.

"The man I threw in the river," True explained blandly, unable to take his mind off the girl. Her golden hair and ivory skin, her soft lips and bold, blue eyes flashing fire and ice, were still as vivid as if she were standing next to him.

Hogjaw scratched the leather patch that held his scalp together. His eyebrows bobbed up and down. "I had me a drink with an old friend by the name of Thaddeus Jones this mornin'," he said, peering at True. "I think I'm beginning to understand."

"And I think I'll ride with Joseph," Andrew replied, throwing up his arms in disgust. "Some year when you two decide to make sense, let me know."

True waited for Hogjaw to enlighten him further, but the mountain man waved him aside. "I'll let Jones explain it," he said, nudging his horse's flanks and following Andrew.

"Who's Thaddeus Jones?" True asked, catching up.

"You'll see. He's waiting for us in camp. Wanted to talk to us, and what he has to say I figure you and your brothers ought to hear together.'' He fixed True in a wily stare. ''Tossed Bagget in the Muddy, huh?'' The disfigured face crinkled with humor, then flopped around like wet wash on a line when Hogjaw leaned back and roared with laughter.

True looked away. Despite his affection for the mountain man, Leakey was, sometimes, just too gruesome to watch.

Chapter IX

On the whole, Thaddeus Jones decided he'd rather deal with Comanches. At least they were predictable. Feeling sorry for himself, he lit a pipe and worked on getting up his courage to approach the Michaelson wagon. His back was up against the wall and he knew it. He couldn't in good conscience simply strand the Michaelsons, and yet every randy dandy bucko in the territory would be sniffing around and cooking up trouble if he took those women along without a man to ride herd over them. The fact that Elizabeth impressed him as one girl capable of handling just about any trouble didn't make any difference. The problem was, she was equally adept at starting it. So much so that Captain Martin had sent orders the night before to keep her and the rest of the Texas-bound families out of Natchez unless he, Thaddeus, personally accompanied them, and then only on business.

There were no simple solutions. Jones had worked like a dog since the burial the morning before. First, he heard from Scott Campbell that his sons, Dennis and Mackenzie, had offered to marry the girls, but both sisters had declined. When Jones went to them and told them that they could travel with him if they were married, he was sent packing. Lottie he could understand. Talk was she preferred more than one suitor around. Elizabeth, though, ought to have been grateful. Few men sought a girl with a temper like that. She was spinster-bound for sure even if there was a pretty kind of way about her beneath all those men's clothes. Next, with marriage no longer a possibility, he went to town and rounded up a local banker after church and talked him into purchasing the Michaelson wagon, supplies, and deed for a reasonable sum. Back at camp, Hester had been more than willing, but when Elizabeth dumped a bucket of water on the banker's head, he flew into a rage and stamped back to town. If Jones's next ploy didn't work, he had no idea of what he'd do.

"Well? We paying a visit or not?" True said from behind him.

Thaddeus treated the younger man to a jaundiced look. "Always the young with coals 'neath their bootheels, always the old who get burnt. Don't rush me, boy. My name ain't exactly a tuneful harmonizing melody to some folks over that way. In fact, I'd say it sounds more like a rock dropped in soft mud, at least as far as one little gal is concerned."

"You afraid of a bunch of women?" Joseph asked.

"Not a bunch. Just one, mainly. And another that just may set her sights on you, when she sees you. Fella your size don't come along too often."

"Suits me," Joseph said, grinning lasciviously.

" 'Course," Jones snorted, "havin' all your teeth does help." He looked up questioningly at Joseph. "You *do* still have 'em all, don't you?"

Across the fire, Andrew chuckled.

Joseph glared at him. "Something funny?" He growled.

"No," Andrew said quickly, taking a prudent step away from his older brother and changing the subject. "I wish Hogjaw was here. You still think we ought to do it before he comes back?"

"Damnation, yes," Jones said, aghast. "That's the whole point of it. Mentionin' him will be enough. Them ladies catch sight of that flop-faced tree bark he calls good looks, and they won't agree to nothin' but runnin' for their guns." His head bobbed up and down. "Not that I'd blame 'em. By golly, long as I've known him, I still 'preciate a few minutes warnin' afore runnin' into the cuss."

"If we're planning on staying here all morning," True broke in laconically. "I'll build up the fire and make some coffee."

"All right," Jones said, grunting as he rose to his feet. "Follow me."

Elizabeth sliced the bacon, arranged the strips in the skillet. She filled a tea ball with coarse, black loose leaf tea mixed with dry cherry bark and rose hips and, as Mamaw used to do every morning, dropped it into the tea kettle and added boiling water. Lottie was seated on a nearby log combing her hair. Her calico dress billowed out around her, cheerfully patterned with tiny blue flowers in contrast to the black armband she wore. She hadn't yet tied the ribbons of her bodice, and her breasts swelled dangerously over the fabric. It was mid-morning. All three had slept late after an argumentative evening and a restless night. The bacon was nearly done and the tea had been set aside to steep before Hester emerged from the wagon and walked to the fire where she stood over Elizabeth. "I want to talk to you," she said, her face sour with disapproval of her daughter's attire.

Elizabeth looked up briefly in acknowledgment of her mother's presence and went back to the bacon.

"Talking to Beth is like talking to this log," Lottie offered, patting the wood beneath her. "I've tried, but she's so almighty wise and wonderful that she won't listen to reason."

"That's because you give all the wrong reasons," Elizabeth said. "Father wouldn't have listened to them."

"You are not your father," Hester snapped, once again angry enough to assert herself. "Your father is dead. I am the head of this family and we will do as I say."

The bacon was curling at the edges. Elizabeth flipped it piece by piece to let the raw sides brown. "I'm going to Texas," she finally said. Studiously polite in an effort to ameliorate her intransigence, she poured a cup of tea and handed it to her mother. "The land is part mine, the wagon and supplies are part mine. And my part is for Texas."

"And what about the part that belongs to me?" Lottie asked.

"Both of you stop it!" Hester said, all too quickly reduced to pleading in the face of their bickering.

"No, Mother. The rest are leaving tomorrow. We have to settle this now." Hands on hips, Elizabeth left the fire and walked to Lottie. "You tell me, Lottie. Do you have a better idea? What else is there to do? Cross half a continent and end up in Philadelphia in the dead of winter, *if* we can get there, and then try to find some miserable job to wear *us* out? Or maybe stay here and join your friends in Natchez Under the Hill?"

"You have no call to talk to me like that," Lottie said primly, concentrating on her hair.

Elizabeth was in no mood to be put off. "I'm waiting. What do we do? Where do we go? And with what?"

"I don't know!" Lottie hissed, slamming down her brush. "You tell me. You're the one who got us in this mess. No one will buy our holdings, thanks to you. We can't stay here, we can't go back. We certainly can't go on alone, and Mr. Jones won't take us along with the others, unless—'' She stopped abruptly, and hurriedly began tying her bodice laces, having looked beyond Elizabeth to see Jones and a trio of young men heading in their general direction. ''Unless he's had a change of heart,'' she added.

Hester followed Lottie's gaze, and nervously smoothed the front of her dress. ''Perhaps found someone else to buy the wagon and land grant,'' she added hopefully. ''Now Elizabeth, you stay away from that kettle!''

Thaddeus Jones doffed his hat and kept his distance from the glowering younger daughter of Hester Michaelson. ''Mornin' all,'' he said.

''Good morning, Mr. Jones,'' Lottie said, smiling at the three men accompanying him.

''Like you to meet Joseph Paxton . . .''

''Ma'am,'' Joseph said, tipping his hat to Hester.

''His brother, Andrew, here . . .''

Andrew's smile took in all three women. ''Ladies . . .''

''And that's True.''

Surprised, True was staring at Elizabeth. ''Ah, my pleasure,'' he said quickly, his face turning red. ''I'm sure.''

Hester summoned a motherly smile. ''It's so nice to meet you, gentlemen. My name is Hester Michaelson and these are my daughters, Lottie and Elizabeth.''

Lottie nodded coyly. Elizabeth glared at True.

''Well! Now that everybody knows each other . . .'' Jones rubbed his hands together and took a deep breath. ''It seems like the Paxtons here just might be able to help you ladies out of your predicament.''

''How wonderful!'' Hester exclaimed, her expression brightening. ''I certainly hope so, don't you, girls?''

''How?'' Elizabeth asked flatly.

Jones held up a warning hand. ''Now don't jump to no conclusions, Mrs. Michaelson. And you, Miss Elizabeth, back off from that kettle and keep your hands clear of that skillet. It ain't what you think, neither, so hear me out.''

Elizabeth hesitated, but replaced the kettle. Lottie flashed a winsome smile that might have been intended for Andrew or Joseph or True. Hester set down her cup of tea and waited expectantly.

''We all know you are between a rock and a hard place,''

Jones went on by way of preamble, "and since that's partly my fault and I'm mightily concerned, I been tryin' to do somethin' about it." Pleased with himself, he allowed himself a smile and plunged on. "Now, it just so happens that I run into a good friend a' mine yesterday, an older gentleman by the name of Ho . . ." His mind raced for a name, any name. "That is, Mr. *Howard* Leakey."

"Mr. Jones, will you come to the point of all this," Elizabeth said.

"Yes, ma'am." Jones scratched his ear, then his nose. "Well, it turns out that Ho—Howard, that is," he amended, emphasizing the name again so the boys would be sure to get it right, "a perfect gentlemen of a man I might add, and his nephews here, the Paxtons, is on their way to Texas, too. Between us, we figured it would be a good idea if they threw in with our bunch. It was right about then that I told Howard about your, uh, predicament, and asked if he'd be willin' to help out."

"How?" Elizabeth broke in again, immediately suspicious.

"I'm gettin' to it. Now, uh . . . Howard is willin' to take on the responsibility for you three ladies if you'll abide by his directions in every way, and if the boys here is willin' to take on the work, and if a fair deal can be arranged. I told him that from what I'd heard in camp, you Michaelsons bought twice as much land as any other family with us, and he allowed as if there might be room to bargain with that land."

"The land isn't for sale," Elizabeth said, shushing Hester.

"We aren't talking about all of it, Miss Michaelson," True said, stepping forward. "Uncle Howard—" He sneaked a look at Joseph who was stepping on Andrew's foot to keep him from snickering. "—has deed to one parcel of land already. We don't even know if we're going to like your land, so for now we'll just pay you five percent of your original cost as an option on half of it. On the journey, then, we'll act just like parters. You'll be under our protection. We'll see to your stock and wagon, do all the hard work, and in repayment take our meals at your fire, there not being a decent cook among the four of us. Once we reach San Antonio, we'll look at the land. If we like it, we divide the grant to our equal benefit, sharing the choice sites, water and such.

"But I thought you, that is . . ." Her hopes dashed once again, Hester was on the verge of tears.

"We do not need protection," Elizabeth replied defiantly, though with a sinking heart, for she knew better. "Especially from the friends of Holton Bagget."

Lottie's face turned red.

"That's not fair, Miss," True said. "The only time I ever laid eyes on him was yesterday afternoon. I don't know him at all."

"But he knows True," Jones said, facing Elizabeth and speaking to her alone. "The lad here dunked him in the river, so I'm told, when Bagget tried to follow a certain young lady into the street and cause her some harm. Make no mistake, girl, you may be leaving the civilized world behind you, but there are still rules. Not as many as back East, maybe, but held close to nonetheless. Now, harsh I may sound, but the truth is your father was killed in a fair fight that he started, so the rules say the man who killed him bears no fault. On the other hand, them same rules don't hold with shootin' a man in his sleep. That's called murder, and a noose waits the guilty party, be it man or woman."

Elizabeth looked as if she'd been slapped.

"My God! That's what you were doing with Father's pistol yesterday afternoon when . . ." The blood drained from Lottie's face as she pictured her sister hanged, and only herself and her mother to carry on. "Elizabeth, you didn't!"

"Unfortunately, no," Elizabeth snapped, turning on her heel and walking away from the group.

Hester's eyes darted nervously from one to another. "Whatever are you talking about?" she asked weakly.

"It's nothing, Mother." Lottie hurried to Hester and helped her sit before she collapsed. Falsely cheerful, she took her mother's hands and gently chafed them. "You see, it will work out. Why, the Paxtons and their Mr. Leakey are practically our salvation." Her animated chatter was meant to bolster her own misgivings as much as to allay Hester's fears. "Such a good idea after all! We have so few choices as it is, and when you think about it, whatever would we do with over two thousand acres? Why, that's over three square miles!"

"But . . ."

"We're talking about survival, Mama." Gone for the moment was the flirtatious girl who took nothing seriously but her own pleasure. In her place, now that the stakes were high enough, was an intensely practical woman. "Elizabeth was right. We can't go back. In no time the ground will be frozen, and how would we make it through winter? We can't stay in Natchez either and we certainly can't risk life and limb on some foolish venture alone in the wilderness.''

Hester's voice was tiny, like a child's. ''I don't want to go.''

''You have to, Mother,'' Lottie said firmly. ''And be glad it's worked out so well in the end. There's really nothing to fear, believe me. Not with Mr. Jones and Mr. Leakey and the Paxtons to protect us.'' She glanced at Joseph. ''I'm certain we'll be safe, and even enjoy ourselves if we only will.''

They could not hear the river, and paid no attention to the singing birds and the laughter of the children in the next camp over. Hester's soft weeping was the only sound, one against which the embarrassed men had no defense except to look away. At last, Jones stepped forward and cleared his throat. ''You'll have to decide, Mrs. Michaelson,'' he said gently. ''We have to know now whether you and your girls will be going with us.''

''I . . . I . . .'' Tears ran down Hester's cheeks and, untouched, fell to the ground. ''I suppose there is no alternative,'' she finally said in a voice deadened by the realization that she had lost and would not, no matter how greatly she wanted to, go home again. Stiffly, she rose and faced Jones. ''We accept your offer. And now, if you'll excuse me?'' Her back painfully rigid, as if the vertebrae would snap if she let them bend, Hester walked to the wagon and climbed in.

''Mother's very distressed, I'm afraid,'' Lottie said, rising, ''but I can't imagine she'll stay that way forever. In any case—'' She shrugged and, the immediate crisis past, shed her seriousness as one would a cape that had grown too warm for the weather. ''—I can't *stand* being so morose on such a beautiful day. After all, we're going on an adventure together, aren't we?'' Her smile was dazzling as she offered her hand to Joseph. ''I hope you don't look so serious all the time, Mr. Paxton. Have you had breakfast?''

It was impossible to remain glum. A slow smile warmed Joseph's face. ''Yes ma'am. I'll have coffee if there's some ready, though. And you can call me Joseph.''

In her element, Lottie had come to life. ''I would like that, Joseph,'' she said. Her hair floated behind her head as she turned from one brother to the next. ''And I'll call you Andrew, and you? . . . Oh, yes. True. What a funny name.''

Her laughter, bright and clear, told him it was a perfectly lovely name as well. "Will you have coffee with us, True?"

"Yes, ma'am," True said, looking in the direction Elizabeth had taken.

Normalcy returned to the clearing. Joseph added wood to the fire. Lottie bustled about getting cups and directing Andrew to fill the pot with fresh water. "Well?" True asked Jones.

The wagon train master looked dubious, as if he didn't trust the radical shift of moods from tears to laughter. "I hope it works," he said.

"Me too," True agreed. He glanced away from the clearing to where Elizabeth stood at the edge of the forest. "Not sure what to think about her, though."

Jones grinned. Of the three Paxtons, True had impressed him the most from the start. And now, as Joseph and Andrew bustled to Lottie's beck and call, True impressed him again with his obvious choice of the quieter, less voluptuous but seemingly far stronger Elizabeth. "Be a good idea," the black man said with a nod in Elizabeth's direction, "if you was to set her at ease a little. If you've a mind to."

True didn't need convincing. The sound of Lottie's laughter at his back, he walked to Elizabeth and stood at her side. "Miss Michaelson . . . Elizabeth, that is," he began lamely, aware of her anger and wanting badly to defuse it. ". . . your mother and sister have agreed to our arrangment. I thought maybe I ought to hear your feelings on the matter."

They could see through a gap in the trees to the broad expanse of the Mississippi. "I wanted to go to Texas," Elizabeth finally said. "Now I know I will. I suppose that's what counts."

"Yes, ma'am." She was just a girl, but he called her "ma'am" and wondered about that. "About the land. Like I said, we may not want it. Even if we do, a thousand acres is plenty for three women, and the cash'll come in handy."

Her pale eyes glistening, Elizabeth looked up at him. "It doesn't matter. Mother and Lottie own two-thirds of everything. Once we're in Texas, my share will go along with theirs."

True hooked his thumbs in his belt. A large blue green beetle crawled along the ground in front of his foot. He nudged it with his toe, watched it flip over and kick helplessly, then nudged it again to turn it back over, and watched it scurry off. "I'm sorry about your father, Elizabeth," he said.

Confused and angry, hating her own stubbornness, Elizabeth neither replied nor looked at him, though she could feel his comforting presence at her side. It was an enticing sensation. Overhead, a breeze soughing through the trees whispered to her, but she could not understand what it said. Not then. Not right then.

Chapter X

Monday morning before first light, the secret sounds of night were interrupted by the low murmur of men's voices, the neigh and snort of mules and horses, and the jangle of harness. Woven through these masculine, equine notes, were the softer, sweeter tones of women at work clanking pots and closing trunks. Little arpeggios of nervous laughter and excitement rose above the small and flickering fires. The rich smell of frying fish and crusty gold cornbread and thick, black coffee played a somber counterpoint to the melody of people on the move, westering.

This was no idle jaunt to be lightly undertaken. As the men gathered around the fires and their voices stilled, you could see that in their faces, and the faces of their women as well. They possessed pieces of paper that said they owned land, and their own stock pulled their own wagons loaded with their own goods, yet they sensed that these material goods were in the main ephemeral. All they really owned were their lives and their reputations, both of which were at stake as they struck out anew. There were dangerous miles ahead, where peril awaited them, formless peril except to men like Thaddeus Jones and Hogjaw Leakey, who had ridden and driven and even walked these trails before.

Withal, an undercurrent of heady excitement ran strong among the settlers. An eagerness to be on the way, to feel the wheels moving beneath them, to contend with whatever rose to impede their way, and to taste the triumph of adventure met head on. Theirs was a sense of mission and of history that surpassed their own puny individual desires and goals. They were the vanguard of civilization determined to wrest a vast section of a continent from the ungodly heathen, then transform it into a lush paradise by virtue of their bravery and tenacity and hard work. Danger was their meat, adversity their bread, hardship their drink. They would feast, and on that invigorating diet, grow lean and hard and strong. And they would prevail.

Thaddeus Jones and Hogjaw Leakey knew it wasn't that simple. Somber now as the black of night grayed and the land began to stir and wake, the two men hunkered across the fire from each other and finished the water moccasin steaks they'd fried the night before. Somewhere off in the woods a crow called reveille. "Well?" Jones said, looking around as if to check the bird's timing.

"Reckon," Hogjaw grunted.

Coffee dregs were poured on fire. Cups rinsed, pot emptied, dried, tied to saddle. Urine hissed onto coals then covered with dirt and stomped down evenly. A final check before yet another leavetaking. They were men accustomed to living off the land, taking their substance from it. They preferred coexistence with nature, a symbiotic relationship in which they disturbed as little as possible while passing through unnoticed, but knew the chances of doing so, especially with a wagon train in tow, were slim. The land and what lived on it could turn against them in many ways, so they were prepared to defend themselves with an economy that contrasted sharply with the settlers' loaded wagons. Blanket, slicker, and duster. Two knives and a tomahawk. A rifle and two pistols. Shot, powder, flint. Two loosely coiled ropes. Pot, frypan, cup. A foodbag containing a pound of coffee, a pound of rock candy, ten pounds of flour, ten more of beans, and a small bag of salt. An extra pair of socks. A needle. A bar of lye soap. And a bottle of whiskey. A man who knew how, traveled light.

"Well, Mama, here we go again. Up and at 'em, girl." Hogjaw swung aboard the scrawny mule and nodded to Jones. "See you at the landin', Blackie."

Blackie was a nickname that Jones accepted from few men. He waited for Hogjaw to ride off, then mounted and sat quietly, relishing his last moments of solitude. Once he joined the settlers, they would be his responsibility until they arrived in San Antonio some two months later. It was one hell of a way to make a living. But at least Hogjaw was along. There'd be one person to talk to. "You ready, horse?" he said.

The thick-chested, mud-dappled gray gelding pricked up his ears and shook his head.

"Me neither," Jones said. "But somebody's gotta get

them greenhorns to Texas, and we already been paid, so let's go.''

They looked just like the last batch he'd escorted and the one before that, Jones thought, pulling to a halt at the edge of the clearing. The six wagons were drawn up in a rough semicircle headed by the Kanias. All trailed an extra horse or mule, three a milk cow as well. The Paxtons and the Campbell boys rode horses, the rest sat stiffly erect in their wagons. Their faces, pale and featureless in the gray light, looked to the West. No one spoke, for each was busy with secret thoughts. They had left behind home and livelihood. They had crossed Pennsylvania and Ohio. They had rafted and steamboated down a thousand miles of river. And still they hadn't left civilization. Now they were about to, and their apprehension was apparent.

The wagon train master watched their faces turn as one to him when he entered the clearing. ''Mornin', folks. Y'all fixin' to go somewhere?'' he asked, trying to break the tension.

Someone laughed and Jones felt better. It was a good group, he thought. Green but willing, ready on their own without his having to prod them. Starting at the rear, he rode slowly along the line, checking the wagons, stock and gear. ''Mornin', Nels, Mrs. Matlan.'' An experienced eye could discern nothing out of order. ''Where's Tommy?''

''Over here, Mr. Jones,'' the boy called.

Andrew Paxton cantered up. ''Ridin' with me, Mr. Jones.''

Jones grunted his approval, moved up the line with a word for everyone, and stopped at the Michaelson wagon. Elizabeth was driving, Hester sat between her daughters. Joseph and True rode to right and left. ''You all right, Mrs. Michaelson?''

Hester nodded, barely.

''You know how to handle them mules, Elizabeth?''

''Of course,'' came the curt reply.

Jones decided that then was as good a time as any to find out how capable she was. ''Keep a close eye,'' he told True, and moved on.

''Well, Reverend, you're first in line. I guess we're ready.''

''Not quite, Mr. Jones,'' Kania said, rising and turning to face the other wagons. ''We will pray before we leave.''

The men removed their hats. All bowed their heads. Firetail snorted and whinnied, but no one paid attention.

"Almighty Father, Thou who watcheth over us, we Thy servants bow our heads in praise and supplication. As we venture forth, we humbly beg the strength that comes from knowing Thee. We ask that Thy love enfold us and Thy power protect us. And as Thou leadeth us to the new land we seek, help us to keep Thy name before us in all matters and to magnify Thy name to Thy greater glory.

"Thou art our God, Oh God. We have no other.

"We haste this prayer in Thy name, and in the name of Thine only son, Jesus Christ, the risen lamb and our Redeemer. Amen."

"Amen," twenty-two voices murmured reverently.

Jones gave them an extra five seconds and then clamped his hat on his head to signal it was time to replace prayer with practicality. "Boat's waitin', folks," he called. "Let's say goodbye to this place. Wagonnnsss—" Durned if it still didn't give him goosebumps, he thought. "—ho!"

The stock was fresh, the trail to the riverbank hard-packed and easily negotiated. The sun was just showing over the flat land behind them when the wagons pulled to a stop at the ferry landing. "Captain will oversee the loading," Jones called after handing over the prearranged fee to a short, stubby man with one sound leg and the other of wood. "His name is Jorunn Maland, if you've any questions. Let's not waste time."

Hogjaw was waiting off to one side. "That it?" Jones asked, riding to him and gesturing to a wagon already waiting on the shallow draft ferry.

"Yup. Two hundred pounds of seed corn, five hundred pounds of oats, a hundred seed and the rest for eatin' along the way, an' six tubs of grease," Hogjaw said. "The mules ain't the best in the world, but they'll do. Oh, yeah. And I picked up a half dozen extra water barrels, though I doubt we'll need them this time of year."

Jones nodded in approval and watched the loading. The Kanias went first, followed by Jack Kemper and his shrewish wife, Helen, who had made no effort to hide her displeasure with the Michaelson girls and the four male companions that had joined them. Next, Scott Campbell guided his team onto the ferry on foot while Dennis and Mackenzie helped the Thatches.

"Would you like me to drive them aboard?" True asked Elizabeth, next in line.

"I can manage," Elizabeth replied stiffly, determined not to give an inch.

"Whatever you say." He gestured to the team. "That off mule looks a little spooked. Keep his head up and use your whip if he balks."

Hester looked worried. "Are you sure—"

"Mother," Elizabeth snapped in warning.

"Get that damned ugly horse aboard," the captain yelled at True. "All the way forward with him. And you, miss," he went on as True followed orders. "Time's a'wastin'."

The mules started forward at the flick of the reins, walked surefootedly down the path and onto the gangplank at the same time Holton Bagget and one of his cronies appeared from behind and darted past them. Startled, the off mule shied and backed sideways. The reins went slack and the team lost its lead. Elizabeth grabbed for the brake and jerked it toward her, but not before the right front wheel was half off the edge of the gangplack.

Hester screamed. Elizabeth froze, one hand on the brake handle, the other holding the reins. The wagon creaked backward a half inch. Suddenly, a buckskin-clad figure astride a scrawny, nimblefooted jenny appeared alongside the frightened team. The man reached out, caught the lead mule's reins, and literally hauled it back from the edge. Bellowing a curse at the team, he turned in the saddle and gave Elizabeth, Lottie, and Hester a glimpse of his hellish face. "Push off the brake, damn it! Let it go!"

Just aboard the ferry, not daring to run down the gangplank to help for fear of frightening the mules even more, the captain froze in place. Someone screamed. Elizabeth's hand wouldn't move. The fall into the river wasn't far, but far enough to ruin the wagon and half their belongings, not to speak of what would happen to the three of them. Terrified, she did nothing.

"The brake, goddamnit, girl, the brake! Shove it forward! Now!"

The man's urgency, the wild look on his horrifying face, cut through the fog of her fear. As quickly as panic had seized her, Elizabeth regained self-control and relesed the brake. The wagon jerked another half inch backward but then stopped and, with the man firmly gripping the lead mule's harness, rolled forward uneventfully onto the ferry.

Hester was sobbing, Lottie staring wide-eyed at the water.

The crisis over, Elizabeth started to shake. Beyond their monstrous-looking benefactor, who had dismounted quickly and was tying the mules to a ring set in the deck, a furious True was working his way aft on foot. Captain Maland, no less furious, was cursing at Baggett and Crease for endangering his passengers.

"Shut up, Maland. No harm done," Baggett said, leering at the shaken women. "Nice timing, Leakey. Tell that little gal that the next time she'd better think twice before shootin' at a sleepin' man."

"Ain't gonna be no next time, Baggett," Hogjaw said, crossing the space between them in four easy strides.

"I know. 'Cause the next time I'm gonna . . . Hey! What're ya'? . . ."

Hogjaw ducked under Baggett's horse's neck. Baggett reached for his rifle, but then grabbed his saddle horn as Hogjaw ripped his foot from the stirrup with his left hand and slammed him in the back with his right.

"Godda—" Baggett squawked as the mountain man lifted him bodily from the saddle and held him in the air, face up and helpless as a bug, then took three more steps and pitched him over the side and into the water.

"Crease?" Hogjaw said, his eyes small and dangerous as he turned to Baggett's partner.

For one second, Crease looked as if he might try to fight, but he quickly reconsidered and dropped his rifle. "Okay, Leakey, okay. Hell with it. I'm goin'," he said, and leaped from his horse into the Mississippi. Seconds later, covered with mud, he and Baggett stood side by side in the shallows.

Hogjaw bent double laughing. The skin on his jaws jiggled up and down alarmingly. He pulled off his hat and slapped it against his thigh. The hair around his jaggedly stitched leather skull flap flailed out. "Your gear will be waitin' on the other side, boys," he yelled gleefully. "Gaw Dee, but I ain't seen two wetter rooster chicks since cuss all!"

The last wagon came clattering aboard and the crew raised the gangplank and began casting off. Captain Maland disappeared into the pilot house, leaving behind him a string of orders. "Everything under control?" True asked, at Elizabeth's side.

"I think so," Elizabeth said, forgetting her hostility for the moment.

A shrill whistle piped over the din of anxious horses and

mules and the exclamations of the settlers. Unnoticed by Elizabeth, the great side-wheel paddles began to turn and the ferry edged away from the landing. "Who is that?" she asked, pointing at Hogjaw.

Remembering their ploy, True colored. "Well," he began, embarrassed. "That's, uh, well . . . He's your new . . . what you might call, uh . . . Actually, he's . . . Uncle Howard Leakey!" He laughed nervously and added helpfully, "We call him Hogjaw."

Elizabeth stared dumbstruck.

Lottie gasped and stifled a scream.

Hester put her hands over her face. "Oh . . . my . . . God!" she groaned.

Chapter XI

There were trails across Louisiana, to be sure. Rough trails, but trails blazed and cut and rutted. There were dark places where the ground was soggy the year round, and ferries across rivers and fords across creeks. Always there were trees and mosquitoes. October was their only friend, for the mosquitoes would have been much worse and the flies nearly unbearable save for the cooling weather.

They learned how to address one another in the morning before they were fully awake and the long hard day lay ahead. They learned how not to tread on frayed tempers when the afternoon came spinning to a close and the bone weariness was descending upon them. They learned what comments played havoc with civility and what jokes eased the inevitable tension. On Sundays they rested, and gave thanks to the Lord before turning to the more mudane matters of patching harness and greasing wheels and caring for hooves and repairing torn clothes and cooking. And, blissfully when possible, finding a spot simply to lie down and gaze up through the trees to the sky, and sleep.

None of them knew it, but they did not travel alone. A flame, a candle in a darkened room, a song softly sung—a gypsy song, a lullaby—accompanied them. From a distance, Adriana watched.

Auburn hair hiding her face, she sat in solitude. On the table in front of her, a deck of cards, a candle, a needle. Silently, she dripped a puddle of wax on the middle of the table, pricked her finger with the needle, and allowed a single crimson drop of blood to stain the cooling wax. Then, as the red dot glared upward, she placed the cards just so, fashioned them just so in a spiral radiating from the waxen island. Her hands manipulated the cards, but fate decreed the order in which they lay. When the spiral was complete, she placed her hands upon the cards and closed her eyes. Outside, an October wind rattled the windows and summoned her spirit.

Night, day. Day, night. Past, present. Present, past.

Find him find him find him.

And then the chill. Always the chill as the power and spirit lifted her from herself and drew her into the vision.

She followed him—them—across Carolina, Georgia, Alabama, Mississippi. She heard the names and faces of the rivers and towns and hamlets. She smelled the dust of the road and the wet of the rain, watched green leaves become autumnal in the slow evolution of the year, in the tilting of the sphere, in the changing. She rode with him across the Father of the Waters and under the canopy of the forest.

Always was she drawn to the image of brambles clustered about a tree, a tree that earth never knew, that never existed but in the imagination. The amulet of gold worn by her first-born was her talisman. An amulet of gold floating on her consciousness, and bright in a shuttered room of Solitary.

As Adriana promised, she did not leave True's side.

You won't be back. None of you will return. I have seen it in the flame of the candle and in the lay of the cards. Trouble lies ahead, flesh of my flesh. Great deeds, death for some, life for others. And for you? . . . The faintest of smiles played fleetingly across her face. *As the tree rises from the brambles, so shall you overcome adversity.*

Chapter XII

"Heave!" called the ferryman, leaning into the hawser. The inch-thick spliced hemp line fixed to the upstream side of the narrow plank raft ran through pulleys attached to trees on either bank of the river. The first half of the trip across was always the easier, for then the ferry ran slightly downstream as the current formed the hawser into a long, flattened U. The second half, when the ferry canted upstream against the current, was the harder. "Heave!" the man repeated. His sons, muscles bulging as the boat inched across the Sabine, hauled with him.

The Kania and Michaelson wagons were the first to cross. Positioned just slightly upstream of the center line of the ferry, they shared the ride with the Paxtons and Hogjaw Leakey who, once they landed, would add their effort to that of those on the eastern shore. Buckland Kania read from Psalms while Mila held the team steady. Behind her, Elizabeth kept the reins carefully entwined in her tapered fingers, experience gained in the crossing of the Mississippi and half a dozen lesser rivers in the last two and a half weeks.

The Sabine was special. Elizabeth and all the other settlers had felt it when they first set eyes on Gain's Ferry and looked across to the river's western bank which marked the beginning of Texas. Once there, they would be in a foreign land, would be immigrants as their forebears had been not too many years ago. The wagon bobbed and creaked as Lottie stepped down. "Where are you going?" Elizabeth asked.

Lottie nodded toward the front of the ferry in response, gripped the side rail for support, and squeezed between it and the Kanias' wagon. Elizabeth craned her neck. Through the open wagon ahead of her, she could see past Mila and Buckland to where Andrew and Joseph stood at the squared prow. As she watched, Lottie appeared at Joseph's side, and Joseph's hand stole to the small of her back. A moment later, partially blocked by Mila, True moved into sight at Lottie's right side. Elizabeth arched her eyebrows, then looked away as an inexplicable pang of jealousy struck her. *I should have expected as much,* she thought, as much surprised by the jealousy as by True's apparent interest in Lottie.

He's nothing to me. Not really. Just like all men who, like bees, gather to the ripest flower.

And Lottie had made no bones about being ripe.

Still, Elizabeth was forced to look at herself, and in so doing, make comparisons. Her nails were short and ragged. One was black where she had pinched it while replacing the lid to a water barrel. Lottie's were longer and smooth. Her hair looked mousy, she knew, for she had spent much of her time caring for Hester and little on herself. Lottie's shone with a rich luster: she brushed it at least a hundred strokes each day while Elizabeth was driving. She dressed like a man in baggy trousers and an ill-fitting workshirt. Lottie always looked feminine and desirable.

Why was she so perverse? True had tried to be friendly, had offered to drive, to help in every way, and she had declined. And now, illogically, she seethed with jealousy when in all candor, she had no right whatsoever to complain.

Sighing, she watched the approaching shoreline, then glanced back to check on her mother. Each passing day, each unraveling mile, had added to Hester's distress. Her husband was dead, the provider was gone. She was incapable of facing the frightening prospects of the world into which she was heading. Unable to accept reality, she had withdrawn deeper and deeper into a self-spun cocoon of loneliness and apathy. Elizabeth had searched for the right words, the magic phrase that would bring Hester to life again, but so far had failed. All that was left to her was fear, and hope. "Mother?" she said, leaning back into the wagon. "Mother?"

"Texas, miss," a voice at her side said.

Elizabeth straightened to see Hogjaw's horrid, friendly face smiling at her. She had long ago gotten over the shock of learning the identity of the fourth member of the Paxton party and, much to Lottie's inability to understand, had even taken a liking to the mountain man. "I know," she said, glad for the interruption. "I hope it's not as dull as Louisiana."

"So it's excitement you want, eh?" Hogjaw said with a laugh. "Well, gal, Texas has a way of twisting a person's wish. Sort of like the Great Spirit. Sometimes you find out that what you asked for ain't really what you wanted when it shows up on your doorstep. I recollect one time out here I got so lonely I made the mistake of sendin' up my prayer smoke just for the sight of a two-legged critter like me. And damn and by golly if not more than a day later a whole party of Comanche come off a ridge and lifted my hair and left me for dead." He shook his head, made a clucking sound. "Well, when I come to, I stumbled around for I don't know how long an' finally run into some Quakers who sewed my head together as best they could. I don't know to this day which hurt more—gettin' my hair lifted or patched back on. But I'll tell you what. I sure plumb had my fill of folks for a while. An' learned to be a sight more careful 'bout my wishin', too."

As horrible as the story was, Elizabeth laughed.

Hogjaw leaned over in his saddle and winked. "Real pretty smile," he said. "Ought to show it more often. Mighty becomin'."

Ahead of them, Buckland Kania started a new psalm. "O God, Thou art my God; early will I see Thee: my soul thirsteth for Thee, my flesh longeth for Thee in a dry and thirsty land, where no water is; to see Thy power and Thy glory, so as I have seen Thee in the sanctuary. . . ."

And at that moment, the ferry jerked sharply, scraped the river bottom, and ground to a stop. Hogjaw let out a war whoop, kicked his mule in the sides and urged her forward. True, Joseph, and Andrew answered with howls of their own and, as one, grabbed the hinged ramp and flipped it into the water. "Best sit down, Reverend," Andrew yelled, "and get that team movin'!"

Joseph helped Lottie back to her wagon and stood by to help lead the team off. Hogjaw went ahead and splashed into the water to check the bottom and the clearing where the first two teams would await the others. Unable to restrain himself, True jumped aboard Firetail and, with an exuberant whoop, rode him off the deck and through the shallows. Water exploded in his wake. Clods of wet sand flew from Firetail's hooves. There was work to be done, but True didn't care. They had come this far! They had reached Texas!

The western shore of the Sabine was sandy. Fifteen or twenty feet inland, thick-boled, towering pine trees walled out the distance. True raced Firetail along the winding shore, leaped him over fallen tree trunks, roared through the shallows, and waved his hat to the settlers still on the opposite bank. Then suddenly, as he went around a sharp bend, he found himself alone and reined Firetail to a stop.

The forest lay hushed and brooding to his left. Hard by his right, the river slid stealthily past. He sat in a pool of silence and in total isolation, poised between the known and unknown. Beneath his shirt, the amulet he wore felt hot against his skin. Stretching to the east, the October sky was pure and blue as sapphire. Only slowly, as his ears became accustomed to the quiet, did he become aware of the soft sounds that meant he was not alone, that this was not an enchanted place where all life was held in suspension. His saddle creaked softly as he leaned back. Firetail breathed rhythmically. Somewhere, a small animal made dry scurrying sounds through the underbrush. A fish flopped out of the water. Far off, a woodpecker rapped against a rotten tree. And his own heartbeat, felt more than heard, whispered to him from his temples.

Texas. A new land, a new life.

The muted sound of a shout floated upriver, brought him back to reality.

"But not alone," he said aloud to Firetail. The whole earth was alive and vibrant, pulsing beneath him. There was nothing he couldn't do. No thing was denied him. He was as strong as a giant, capable of great feats. The sensation was startling and exhilarating, one he had never encountered. New though it was, it gave him added strength and confidence. And strangely enough, peace, for he saw his direction laid out before him. Elizabeth would fight him as she had from the day they had first met, but the end was preordained. Never in his life had he been more sure of anything. Laughing with pure joy, he turned Firetail's head and started back toward the landing. "She doesn't know it yet," he whispered in Firetail's ear as the great horse thundered through the shallows and around the bend, "but not alone."

"First camp in Texas!" Scott Campbell exclaimed. The chunky, lantern-jawed farmer handed a tin cupful of whiskey to Kevin Thatche. "Which means your little one will be a native, by God. The only real Texan among us. And that's something worth toastin'."

Kevin laughed nervously, held up his cup, and clanked it against Scott's before drinking.

"And best you quit frettin' about that child, my lad. It's a waste of time and energy, I can tell you from experience. The first is no worse than the fourth. It only seems so. In any case, there's nothing better to still a quaking stomach than fine Scotch whiskey."

Kevin drank and made a face. It felt as if the whiskey were eating through the walls of his stomach. "It ain't my quakin' stomach I'm worried about. It's Millie's, and what may drop before we reach San Antonio," he replied, trying his best to manufacture humor where none was felt.

Nels Matlan and Mackenzie Campbell entered the circle of light. Each carried a pistol that he was busily cleaning. The clean-cut, bespectacled, one-time schoolteacher looked incongruous with a gun in his hands.

"That's the third weapon I've seen you with tonight, teacher," Scott said to Matlan. "And now my own son is following your suit and tending to a weapon I saw to myself but a week ago."

"Mr. Leakey and Mr. Jones said we couldn't be too careful, Pa," Mackenzie replied.

"And seeing as that barn-sized lunker who calls himself Joseph Paxton has made off with Lottie Michaelson, you and Dennis have nothing better to do, I suppose," Scott observed dryly. "Well, maybe so. If Leakey and Jones say so, it's fine with me." He poured a cupful of whiskey and offered it to Matlan. "But you, now, Nels. I thought you were a teacher, not a soldier."

"Not according to Leakey," Matlan said, accepting the drink. "Thanks." He gestured around the circle with the cup, then drank it off in one gulp. "God!" he croaked, paling.

"Every man's a soldier in the howling wilderness," Scott said, mimicking Hogjaw. "Well, maybe so, maybe not. Maybe he's just exaggerating to keep us on our toes, and things won't be as bad as he says. Hell, I haven't fired a weapon in anger since the war, and even then I had to work it up some to bloody those pretty British jackets."

"Say what you will, Pa," Mackenzie blurted enthusiastically. "Whatever happens, I'll be ready. I hope we do have a run in with the Comanches."

"And I hope I'm upwind of you at the time," Thaddeus Jones said, emerging from the darkness. "I heard my first

Comanche war whoop when I was just about your age. And as cocksure, too. By golly, but it left my britches sour for a week.''

Mackenzie's cheeks turned red to match his hair. "Laugh if you want," he said. "We'll see what happens when the shooting starts. One thing you can bet on. I won't run."

"Neither did I," Jones replied. He crabbed his legs, pulled out the seat of his britches, and duck-walked around the fire. "I couldn't."

The men roared with laughter. Jones held out a cup for his share of the whiskey Scott had promised everyone to celebrate their arrival in Texas. "Cheers, gents," he said. "We're closer than we were when we started. Always an upliftin' feeling, crossin' that river."

Coming from rural Pennsylvania, none of the men around the fire had ever had much to do with black people until they reached the Mississippi. Mostly they had been told that blacks were naturally inferior to whites, and that slavery, though onerous, was a condition that fit them well. That being the case, learning that their wagon train master was a black man had been a surprise that they hadn't quite known how to handle. Many hours had been spent discussing the matter and there had even been a secret vote taken before the wagon train left Natchez to determine if they wanted a black man leading them. Jones had won—who else was there, after all?—but the questions still lingered. Only now, after nearly three weeks of travel and seeing a man like Leakey accept Jones's leadership, had they begun to feel at ease with him. "Tell us, Mr. Jones," Nels said. The rest of the men quieted, as if they knew what was coming. "We been curious how you . . . That is, how come a, well, a—"

"How does a black man from slave stock come to be a wagon master?" Jones chuckled. "Don't worry, Matlan. No offense taken. You're not the first to wonder, nor will you be the last. My father was a slave in what's now Louisiana back when it still belonged to Spain. If you think this is wild now, it was a far sight wilder then when they had an insurrection, razed that plantation, and headed this same way." Thoughtful, he paused and sipped his whiskey. "I was borned not too far from here, and like your babe to come—" He nodded in Thatche's direction. "—that made me a Mexican citizen.

"Well, my folks got away with it, and made it all the way to San Antonio where my daddy took up workin' for Medina's daddy. I grew up with his family and learned to speak better Mex than most whites. Even got me a Mex wife, now, an' four little ones to boot, all livin' in the old señor's house down in Santa Catarina, where I'll probably go after I get you folks to your land.''

"Fascinating,'' Matlan said, thoroughly intrigued.

"Calls for another round,'' Scott added enthusiastically. He held the bottle to the light before refilling Jones's cup. "Still plenty left, but let's take it easy. Leakey and the Paxtons haven't had theirs yet.''

Mackenzie grunted. ''What do you make of them Paxtons?'' he asked, obviously put out by the attention Lottie had been receiving.

"Well,'' Jones began, not wanting to blow too hard on a smoldering fire, ''they do their share. I ain't seen 'em shirk a job yet. An' Hogjaw says they'll do.''

"Leakey?'' Kevin Thatche asked. It was said that if a pregnant woman looked too often at a disfigured face, her child would be born with a similar disfigurement. Consequently, both he and Mildred were afraid of the mountain man and bore the man a certain animosity. ''You take his word?''

"That's the way it is out here, son-o. You know a man or you don't.''

"Still—''

"Still nothin',''Jones snapped. ''Let me tell you about Hogjaw, but don't you call him that, for—no offense meant—you're not man enough yet to do so. Why, the first time I seen him he'd just got his new pate, and the top of his head was so swole up with infection he couldn't put on a hat. Even so, he went chargin' through a Comanche war party like it was a bunch of Sunday School teachers on a picnic. That was back in twenty-two, as I recall.''

His voice droned on, a low murmur barely heard at the Matlan wagon where the women were gathered about the weekly sewing. Socks, shirts, skirts, and blouses lay piled about on split logs to keep them off the damp ground. Most of the work had been completed, except for some wagon covers, not a one of which had failed to sustain at least one rip. They were just starting on the worst, the Kanias'. Joan Campbell and Eustacia Matlan took the largest tear where a tree limb had fallen through the canvas cover. Mildred Thatche and Helen Kemper took smaller holes and set to work. Still not finished with the lapel on Buckland's frock coat, Mila sat good-naturedly to one side, licked the blood off her left ring finger, and tried again. She'd had little practice at the womanly art of sewing, but was determinedly learning to become adept in order to better know and work with her husband's flock.

"Oh!" Mildred Thatche exclaimed, catching her breath. The fifteen year old came from a large family and was right at home with needle and thread.

"Did he kick?" Mila asked.

Mildred nodded. "I still don't understand how you can be so sure it's a boy, though."

"I have learned," Mila said with a bright laugh, "to trust Joan's judgment in such matters."

"It has to be a boy," Joan said, threading a new piece of waxed cotton through her needle. "My own two kicked just that way. Dennis and Mackenzie. Such a time they gave me. And still do." She chuckled with the memory. "The girls, now, were content to lie quietly. So comfortable. But boys? Oh, me. Always anxious to leave before their time."

"Joan is right," Eustacia chimed in, adjusting her brown hair, tightly drawn into a bun that Joan had helped pin in place. "Tommy was just like that. All the energy of a storm. I was exhausted when I had him, and I've been tired ever since."

"One simply has to learn, is all," Joan said with an emphatic shake of her head.

Mildred waited. "Well, what?" she finally asked, exasperated. "Learn what?"

Joan's eyes twinkled merrily. "Why, to sleep standing up, dear."

Laughter floated above the dull white cloud of canvas. Outside the light, Elizabeth paused on her way back from watering the roses she was carefully nurturing and checking on Hester, then turned and walked quietly away. She was filled with a restless energy that no sewing or idle banter could discharge. She passed the wagon Hogjaw had bought in Natchez. Jack Kemper, down with a bad back after trying to push his wagon out of a mudhole without help, was asleep and snoring in his wagon. The least sociable of the group, Elizabeth thought, immediately adding herself to that short list as she sneaked away to be alone. One more fire lay ahead, and that was her own, where Lottie and Joseph sat talking languidly. Silently, Elizabeth detoured around them and headed for the river.

Alone.

Ah, there was a word she had thought much on. She resisted the idea, but maybe it was better to be like Lottie and seek out warm caresses and muttered endearments, no matter how insincere they were. To feel arms warm in the dark, to experience release, to yearn and be fulfilled. To toy with words and play the game of smiles and teases. But oh, by all that was holy, she had neither the strength nor desire nor urge to be anything more than what she was and who she was.

The unavoidable problem, then, came racing to mind. Who was she? Who was Elizabeth Michaelson?

A woman, a girl: she who had come in the place of a son. She stared down at her clothes. Work clothes, they were. Men's clothes. So? They adapted well to the myriad daily tasks. Someone had to do those jobs, after all, and she was damned if she'd let any of the Paxtons rise to the role. She was willing to let them be responsible for what she couldn't physically accomplish, and equally willing to cook for them as agreed upon, but no more. Their alliance was one of convenience only, and should never go beyond that. And for one single unforgivable reason: True Paxton had prevented her from avenging her father's death.

But the argument was assailable, as well she knew. The past three weeks had tempered her grief and anger with understanding. The incontrovertible truth was that True had probably saved her life. Then why did she resent him so, with his bold bronzed face and unkempt, wind-curled hair and pale azure eyes set in that serious face? Why did she turn her back on him, answer him grudgingly if at all, refuse even his thanks at the end of each meal? Why did she find it so uncommonly difficult just to be civil? True hadn't sought her out, after all. He had simply been nearby during her moment of foolishness. Fortune, not he, had thrown them together. It was childish to blame him for all her troubles.

Nor was there anyone else to blame, she thought, emerging from the trees and finding herself on a bluff overlooking the river. Not her father, though temptation was great, or her mother or sister or even herself. Nudged hither and yon by unseen and unforeseeable forces, events unfolded willy-nilly. People were people, met and interacted according to rules so complex as to be incomprehensible. As well to blame the wind for bending the tree or the cat for eating the robin. Exhaling softly and overcome by the enormity of life, Elizabeth leaned against the trunk of a lightning-blasted tree and, in the same instant, realized she shared her solitude with another. True Paxton had preceded her to this very spot and stood but a few feet from her. The sigh froze on her lips. She forced herself to look straight ahead across the river, and to ignore him. *See. The moon is nearly full.* A gentle breeze tugged at her hair. *That cloud churning through Cassiopeia looks remarkably like a tiny dog.* The long grass rustled underfoot. *I wish I'd put on one of my dresses. The yellow one, I think.* She caught herself and frowned. *Now why should I think a thing-like that? For him? Really . . .*

Suddenly the night turned emerald. Startled, Elizabeth looked up to see a glob of green fire arc across the sky like a miniature sun racing to violent extinction. She cried out involuntarily and, in the lingering afterglow of the shooting star, found herself in True's arms. Frightened by his touch, yet somehow not wanting him to let her go, she tilted her head and tried to say his name, only to be stopped as his lips met hers. *Impossible. Impossible!* Her breasts crushed against his chest. Her arms rose of their own volition to wrap around him. Her fingers dug into the bunched muscles beneath his shirt. Her soul, soaring, searched among the stars. Far, far below, the tiny world hung suspended and motionless in space. Elizabeth fought for control, surrendered, fought again, and thought she must have won, for the kiss had ended and True was looking down at her intently.

"Elizabeth," he said.

Her brow furrowed. Her father had held her that way, crushed her to him, and frightened her. In True's arms, she had felt no fear. And yet . . . and yet . . . Puzzled, she looked at his lips. Her name sounded different, coming from them. As if she'd never heard it before, as if she were, perhaps, dreaming. Dazed, confused, she stepped away from him and leaned against the trunk for support. But the world whispered that it could not wait for her; nature commanded birds to fly, clouds to sail, waters to sing on their way to the sea, time to unreel as it sadly must. Two people on the raw free heights of a bewildering journey. The kiss had ended moments before. Blushing, Elizabeth lowered her face. And angry, too, though at him or herself she could not tell. She folded her arms across her chest, walked away from him along the bluff, turned around and came back. She searched for words but could find none, imagined a mocking smile on his face, and spun around to leave.

"Elizabeth," True said again. She paused on the fringe of the trees as his voice drifted to her. "I am going to marry you. Within five minutes of the first moment I saw you, I knew I would. You did too, didn't you."

No, she wanted to say. Her mouth opened but her tongue stuck to the roof of her mouth. The denial died unspoken. Instead, she walked into the forest and, once out of his sight, began to run.

True watched her disappear, and after a moment moved to the edge of the bluff and sat with his legs dangling over the edge. The words had poured from him. He had been unable to control what he felt and had bluntly broached a subject that probably needed tenderness and finesse.

That was foolish, he thought, worrying. After all, what did he know of Elizabeth Michaelson? That her hair was like spun gold. That her lips were warm and full. That her body had betrayed the same urgency as his. That her eyes . . . Enough. He knew enough. More than enough. Being with her was right. She eased the loneliness in him at the same time she aroused his hunger. It was only a question of time.

Suddenly, with a joy that was impossible to contain, he was laughing. She had looked so surprised! So totally surprised. Blunt honesty had its strong points after all. And as for tenderness, Elizabeth Michaelson would soon learn that one True Paxton had plenty of that to share.

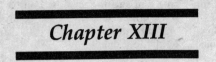

Chapter XIII

Distance growing out of distance and becoming . . . distance.

And the trees, the pines and the wind that stirred the branches with an everlasting soughing, dangled the branches, lifted the branches, waved the branches. And the sunlight streaming down in columns touched by Midas, radiant columns intersecting spaces and shadows with endless regularity, repeating themselves again and again.

It was the trees that drove her mad.

It was the whispering silence, too.

And memory . . . sunlight . . . distance . . . wind . . .

Her mind populated the passing wilderness with demons of fear and uncertainty.

"Hester."

Someone said the name to her. It sounded vaguely familiar.

"Mother."

Familiar, too. Was she Hester? Or Mother? Or neither? Were they perhaps commands? Be Hester? Be Mother?

She thought not. Madness was safer. There were no dead husbands in madness. There were no uncertainties in madness. There was no wilderness in madness, no theft of all the old and dear things.

Madness was simple, madness was safe.

She would search for madness, find madness. Be mad, stay mad.

Stay mad . . . where it was safe.

A hundred miles? More? They had crossed the Sabine on the thirtieth of October, rested three days later on Sunday, and now, on the following Saturday afternoon, the eighth of November, they plodded toward the campsite where Jones

had said they'd spend that night and their next day of rest.
The trail was well marked and, even if rough, it was easy to
follow. It inscribed, in the map Jones had drawn for them, a
sweeping arc that stretched from Gain's Ferry on the Sabine
in far east Texas to San Antonio in south central Texas. The
arc skirted the northern edge of a vast impenetrable wilderness that the Indians called the Big Woods and the white men
called the Big Thicket.

It was an Indian summer day, hot and muggy. Men and
mules alike were tired and cranky after a long week of travel.
The women sat dazed and listless, waiting for another day of
jolting, rocking motion to come to an end. The children were
so bored they had stopped making mischief. Tommy Matlan
lay on the rear gate of his parents' wagon and stared at the
ground and then, wistfully—oh, what he would have given
for a horse of his own—stared at True as he rode by.

The trail skirted natural barriers of marshland, angled around
fallen trees, forded innumerable creeks too small to name.
Held to a walk for the past week, Firetail tossed his mane and
fought the bit. To let the stallion run would be suicidal, and
yet True understood the great beast's desire to stretch his
legs. In a minor concession, he eased Firetail into a trot as he
passed the Matlans' wagon. Next in line were the Michaelsons.
He glanced to his right. As usual, Elizabeth was driving, with
Lottie at her side. Lottie smiled invitingly at him, in the
process eliciting a scowl from Joseph, on horseback on her
side of the wagon.

"Any problems?" True asked. "Be glad to drive for
awhile."

Elizabeth shook her head no, but did not answer or look at
him.

True shrugged. She'd refused to have anything to do with
him since that night on the bluff when he'd kissed her and
told her he was going to marry her. She would set his plate in
front of him, hand him a cup of coffee, and that was that.
True grinned and tipped his hat. He could wait. She'd come
around. He had every confidence in the world. "See you at
supper," he said cheerfully, and rode off.

Buckland and Mila Kania were in the lead again. True
exchanged pleasantries with them, then let Firetail break into
a canter in order to catch up to Jones and the Campbell boys,
who led the way. Three quarters of the way asleep, Jones
nodded in the saddle as his gray gelding plodded forward

diligently. The big horse knew the trail well, and needed no direction. Still not believing Jones's assurances that they needn't fear an Indian attack for a good many miles yet, Mackenzie and Dennis Campbell rode with guns ready, just behind the wagon train master. True waved to them and rode past, letting Firetail break into a slow gallop as the ground rose and the trail through the virgin pines widened. Firetail snorted in delight. Behind him, great clods of the pine needle carpet flew from his feet to reveal a deep reddish brown sandy loam. A mile ahead of the wagon train, True rounded a bend into a clearing and found Hogjaw, Andrew, and an Indian.

They had run into Indians several times on the journey from Solitary to Natchez. Each time, to True's continuing amazement, Hogjaw had known either the Indians or someone else from their tribe. Choctaw, Natchez, or Alabama, they were all friends of the mountain man—even the Comanches, strangely enough given his past run-ins with them. Comanches, like the rest of the horse Indians—Apache, Sioux, Cheyenne, and so on—had a different way of thinking, Hogjaw had told him more than once. Just because they scalped you one day didn't mean they weren't going to be your friend the next. A man had to take them as they came and keep an eye peeled. Fiercer, prouder men never set face on earth, and if a man stood up to them, they respected him for it, especially if he had something they wanted to trade for. And even more especially if he'd been scalped, lived to tell about it, and went back to walk bravely among the People.

It was a hell of a price to pay for respect, True thought, holding up his hand, palm out, in a sign of friendship as he rode toward the trio. The brave wore a breechclout and buckskin leggings. Beadwork of porcupine quills and glass baubles obtained from some passing trader decorated his chest. He carried a bow and a quiver of feathered arrows slung across his back.

"Coushatta," Hogjaw said by way of identification. "One of the Caddo tribes. Good people."

True extended his hand as Hogjaw went on to introduce him to the brave in Spanish.

"His name is Runs the Deer," Andrew said excitedly. "His people are camped about two days ride to the south."

"Brings us welcome news," Hogjaw added. "Seems the Comanche are raiding further to the west this year. Be a disappointment to the Campbell boys, but mighty comforting to the rest of the folks, includin' me. Looks like we got us a long, clear ride to San Antonio, True boy.''

"Fine with me," True said. "What's that all about?"

The brave had taken off a wide, multicolored beaded belt and was holding it up in one hand while he gestured at Firetail with the other.

"He wants to trade his wampum belt for that hammerhead roan of yours." Hogjaw grinned. "Injuns don't worry much about looks neither."

"No trade," True replied, shaking his head.

Though it was apparent that Runs the Deer understood, Hogjaw conveyed the message, then translated a second offer. "He says the belt is worth many horses, but to show you that he is serious and respects you, he'll throw in the nag he's ridin' and the pick of his wives."

"Nope," True said. "No deal."

Runs the Deer scowled, and grunted what sounded like a question that True didn't need translated.

"Tell him," he added quickly, "that it's no reflection on him, his horse, or his wives. This horse is special, and I'll trade him to no man. And what are you up to?" he went on to Andrew while Hogjaw translated. "You look like the cat that ate the bird."

"Yeah. Well . . ." Andrew seemed to have trouble meeting True's eyes. "What I decided is, ah . . . Well, since there isn't that much chance of trouble, I figured I'd be leaving."

"What?" True asked, his eyebrows rising in surprise. "Where to?"

"Runs the Deer has invited me to visit with his people," Andrew blurted. "Seems like a good chance to—"

"I know his father," Hogjaw interrupted, obviously on Andrew's side. "Ol' Blade is the chief now and Runs the Deer is next in line for the job. Be a right nice experience for Andrew here."

"What about the land grant?"

"Hell, True, we don't even know if we're gonna take them up on that. Besides, I'm too young to settle down. I want to see the elephant."

"A man owes it to himself," Hogjaw said approvingly.

"See the elephant?" True exclaimed, upset with Leakey

and not bothering to hide it. "This was your notion, wasn't it? Even gave him the reasons why he ought to go."

"It's my life," Andrew retorted angrily.

Hogjaw feigned innocence. "Argue with that and you're arguing with yourself, True boy."

True searched for some way to dispute Hogjaw's logic, then grudgingly conceded that the mountain man was right. "Well . . ."

"C'mon, brother. You know Pa would think it was a good idea."

"I don't know," True said, stalling for time. "There's just the three of us. Joseph'll have something to say—"

"Joseph won't have anything to say," Andrew interrupted. "This is between Runs the Deer and myself." He leaned forward in his saddle to grip True's wrist. "I'm going, True. I'll join up with you in San Antonio later on. It's settled."

And so it was. The look in Andrew's eyes told him so. "When are you leaving?" True finally asked, resigned.

Andrew gave a whoop of joy. "This afternoon, soon as I shake Joseph's hand and gather my gear from the wagon." He reached over and clasped True's shoulder. "I don't have to go alone. You could come with us."

"He can't," Hogjaw said. Both True and Andrew looked at the mountain man. "True's got a different path to walk."

"Oh?" Andrew said.

"He's right," True said, the image of Elizabeth strong in his mind. He nodded in the direction of the coming wagons. "You better think up some good words. Big brother may take some convincing."

Andrew grinned. "I have a few minutes before they get here. I guess Runs the Deer and I will just wait for them. Least I can do is gather some firewood as a last gesture."

"This where we're camping, then?" True asked.

Hogjaw nodded. "Yup." He pointed with his nose. "Plenty of fresh water. A chance for everybody to look at the sky for once. Couldn't do much better. Want to scout around a little first, though. Comin' with me, True? Little place up ahead where you can let that ugly thing run his legs off for a minute."

"Sounds good to me."

The mountain man rattled off a string of Spanish to Runs the Deer, then turned back to Andrew as he started to ride away. "Mind you holler out first thing you hear horses.

Them Campbell boys is primed an' ready to open up on the first redskin they see. Don't want 'em startin' a war with the Coushatta.''

Old man and young rode in silence for the first few hundred yards. Finally, True pulled up. "I thought you said there was an open place where Firetail could run.''

Mama, Hogjaw's mule, kept to her steady plodding pace. "There is," Hogjaw said. "Bout a hundred miles down the road.''

"What the hell?" True spurred Firetail, and caught up.

"Take it easy, True boy," the mountain man said laconically. "Sometimes two talkin' is better'n three.''

"Oh, really?" True fumed. "Well, all I got to say is you sure know a lot for being such an ugly old bastard. Or think you do, anyway.''

Hogjaw mulled that over for a moment. "Comanches took my scalp, True boy," he allowed at last. "They left the brains right where they were." He winked, and his left fist shot out and caught True in the biceps, almost knocking him off Firetail. "C'mon, younker. You too, Mama," he added, kicking the jenny in the ribs. "Let's find us a deer or two for supper.''

In the quiet of a glade, in the stillness of an autumn afternoon, in the wilderness that was Texas, three brothers sat in silence, searching for something more to say. Something more than goodbye. But words wouldn't come, as they seldom do for family. There are words of farewell for enemies and for friends, but for family only a silent special tightness in the throat. Joseph, the eldest, was the first to break the silence. "Guess I don't have to tell you to take care of yourself, little brother.''

Andrew shook his hand, turned to True, and grasped his.

"Be thinking—" A frog was in True's throat. He coughed to clear it. "See you.''

"Yeah," Andrew said, confused at finding his former excitement suddenly tinged with regret. Tom Gunn Paxton always said that everything had its price. There was never joy without sorrow appearing somewhere down the line. Andrew understood his father's words more keenly now than ever before. On the brink of adventure, he was about to be separated completely from his family. He was exhilarated, he was frightened. Quite suddenly, he felt very grown up. "In San Antone," he said, and turned his mare away from them.

"In San Antone," True called to Andrew's back. "We'll be there."

Runs the Deer waited patiently at the edge of the clearing. Reaching him, Andrew did as he had been taught, and did not look back.

Another week had passed. Tired, yet perked up by the open sky above them and the prospect of a day of rest, everyone set to work with a will. Jack Kemper, Buckland Kania, Scott, Dennis, and Mackenzie Campbell built a temporary corral for the stock, rubbed them down, and saw to their water. Nels Matlan cleared a place a little way downcreek for the women to bathe the next morning. True butchered the pair of small, tender doe he and Hogjaw had killed earlier. Joan Campbell made a bread pudding. The children, Tommy, Ruthie, and Dianne, collected enough firewood to last the morrow. Joseph and Lottie, with Hogjaw to guide them, collected a huge bowl full of edible greens and roots. Kevin and Mildred Thatche went hunting for nuts and returned with a whole peck of chinquapins, from whose burred shells they extracted two quarts of delicate nut meats which they set aside to roast. Mila, Helen, Eustacia, and Elizabeth, after she had seen to Hester, set up for dinner around a common fire. Best of all, Thaddeus Jones backtracked along their trail to a bee tree he had noticed and, daring the angry insects, robbed them of their dark winter's store. The dark man's cheeks were lumpy and swollen, but he did not complain. Later, their stomachs already full, the settlers poured the thick molasses-like honey over Joan's bread pudding. Even the Kempers were in the best of humor.

The night was balmy. The sight of stars worked a miracle on their spirits. Nels and Eustacia Matlan entertained with a series of dramatic readings from Shakespeare, the rhyme and meter of which lulled the children to early sleep but thrilled the amusement-starved adults. Buckland and Mila Kania followed with jew's harp and accordian and, while the children were carried to bed in their wagons, struck up a tune. Nels and Eustacia were the first to dance, but only because Mildred protested when Kevin took her hand and led her into the firelight. By the first chorus, Scott and Joan Campbell, Jack and Helen Kemper, and Dennis Campbell and Lottie had joined them.

Elizabeth left the group and walked to the wagon to check on Hester. There she found the plate she had left on the seat, untouched except by ants and moths who had claimed squatters' rights to the bread pudding and honey. Discouraged, Elizabeth dumped the food under a nearby bush before returning to the wagon and looking in on the huddled form beneath a blanket. "Mother? You haven't eaten in two days."

Hester stirred, rolled onto her side, and stared at the quilt folded next to her on the bedding.

"Mother, please. You can't just lie there day after . . ." Elizabeth gave up, leaned against the backboard, and let the canvas fall into place. The journey since crossing the Mississippi could be measured in the ever descending stages of her mother's depression, against which Elizabeth felt totally helpless. Whatever was happening in Hester's mind was privy only to herself, and Elizabeth, the outsider, was incapable of reaching in and touching and helping. Only Hester could cure Hester. To recover, she had to will her own recovery.

"There's dancing going on," a voice said from behind her.

Elizabeth spun about to see True standing in the shadows. "I know," she said. "Everyone sounds so merry."

"Except you."

"Yes," Elizabeth snapped, immediately wishing she could take it back. "I'm sorry," she apologized. "You're right. Except me."

True wanted to hold her, almost did but then, unsure how she would react, he gestured toward the main campfire. "Will you dance with me? I'd like you to."

Elizabeth felt herself blushing. "I'm . . . I'm not dressed for dancing."

"Clothes don't matter," True said softly. "Never did, never will." Suddenly she was in his arms and weeping silently against his chest. True held her, let his cheek touch the top of her head. "On the other hand," he said, "we could just sit."

The trunk was large enough for both of them. Side by side, his arm around her, they listened to the music and the laughter, and together watched the stars. Elizabeth could hear his heart beat, feel him breathing evenly and slowly. She had wanted this, yet had fought it with every ounce of her strength. Somehow it was dangerous to let a man touch her. It was wrong to follow in Lottie's coquettish footsteps. Her father had laid his hands on her and in so doing made frightening and revolting that which should have been joyful, yet she had known all along that not all windows opened onto bleak vistas, not all doors led to degradation. It was wrong to let the memory of his touch sully her whole life.

The stars wheeled. His voice soft and deep, True told her of Solitary, of his mother and father, of his youth. He told her of his dreams, his hopes, those fantasies he had shared with no one else. As he talked, the roiling maelstrom in Elizabeth's mind slowed, and the pain and anxiety that had plagued her for the past weeks faded. She wasn't yet sure if she wanted anything of True Paxton, only that for the first time in months she felt needed, and warm, and safe.

"Well, you should have seen his face," True said. "Looked just like . . . Well, you ever see a squirrel misjudge a leap and fall from a tree?"

No answer.

He craned his neck, tried to see her face without disturbing her. "Elizabeth?" he asked, oh so softly. "Elizabeth?"

No answer. Only her breath, soft as a feather on his hand.

"Well, I'll be durned." He smiled, leaned back against the wagon, and fit her head more snugly against his shoulder and chin. "She's asleep."

Chapter XIV

They were well into November. On Monday, the tenth, a day and a half after Andrew's departure with Runs the Deer and refreshed from their Sunday rest, the wagon train set out early in the morning. The only rest for the next two weeks would be a half day the following Sunday. The nights turned chilly, the days remained warm. Each morning the valleys were filled with fog. They ate well. The woods, unlike those of Pennsylvania which had been hunted off years ago, were full of squirrel and deer and turkey and bear. Human beings were few and far between. An occasional settlement or isolated cabin lay across their path, but there was little time to stop. A half hour at the most might be spared for trading news of the trail ahead and the civilized world behind. Their lives inextricably intertwined for the duration of the journey, the settlers had become a small but compact community that handled the daily routines with increasing efficiency.

Still, under pressure, tempers flared and personalities grated. Jack and Helen Kemper, the former storekeepers, became even more withdrawn. Kevin Thatche became obsessively protective of his pregnant wife, and took great pains to protect her from Hogjaw. Hogjaw, though he proclaimed their fears to be a lot of hooey, cooperated and stayed out of Mildred's sight. Buckland Kania learned to shorten the blessing he spoke over the evening meal. Tommy Matlan hid his primer and refused to do his lessons. Nels took his belt to his son and then made him walk for two days before relenting and letting him ride one of the extra horses on the third day.

Only one wheel broke. They made up the lost time Thursday evening, not camping until deep into dusk. When a harness broke, it was replaced and put aside to be patched later. Mama took lame on Tuesday. Hogjaw tried to ride the jenny he and the Paxtons had brought with them, but soon gave up and walked for the next three days. Jones was everywhere up and down the line, pushing and prodding, cursing recalcitrant mules, dishing out encouragement by the eyedropper or ladleful as need be. Everyone looked forward to Saturday night. With luck, they had been told, they would camp at the Trinity River, the more or less halfway point between Gain's Ferry and San Antonio. Their spirits rose when they arrived early, around noon on Friday, crossed without incident, and found their campground would be a large meadow. There, hung head down from a cottonwood, was a yearling black bear Hogjaw and True had shot that morning on their forward scout.

Jones proclaimed a holiday. Everyone was tired and needed the rest. They would camp in that same spot through Saturday and Sunday, and not move until Monday morning. The announcement was greeted with cheers, and everyone turned to with a will. The wagons were drawn up, stock watered and put to the first real grass it had seen in over a week, and supper was well on its way, before dusk. Three hours later, a full meal under everyone's belts, the camp lay in slumber. Only True, Hogjaw, and Jones were awake. True on watch and slowly riding circles around the camp, and the two older hands quietly smoking and talking in front of a miniscule fire.

Many hours later, one other awoke and lay with open eyes that stared blankly at the canvas over her head. Hester had dreamed of the box, and couldn't put it out of her mind. Her mother had given it to her when, as a child, she had been ill. The box was made of gum wood and its lid was held closed with a little brass latch her father had fashioned. Her mother had carved tulips in the wood, and painted them crimson and butter yellow and indigo. Hester's favorite color was indigo. Tulips in a row and coiling one about the other on the lid. More tulips laboriously etched into the brass by her father.

Oh, how she had loved that box! Filled it with the collected treasures of childhood, mementos of happy, sunlit days, of laughter, of beauty. Now, in the prairie night and in her mind, she reopened the box and peeked beneath the lid. Everything was there just as she had remembered it. Beads. A shell from some distant sea. Bits of colored glass, red, blue, and the amber of autumn leaves. A tiny chair her father had carved for her doll house. A horse chestnut—how sad that its rich chocolate brown had faded. And best of all, three miniature dolls she had found beneath her pillow one birthday morning. They had names, Hester remembered. They were . . .

What? What? She couldn't remember the names, she thought, panicking. If she could hold the box again, touch the dolls, she'd remember, though. She was sure. All she had to do was take it in her hands and open it and touch them. The names would come back.

But where was it? Her head moved, her eyes swiveled about in their sockets, but all she could see was a blank sky of canvas. She wanted it. Wanted it. Where was it? Where? Lost in the fire? No, not in the fire. Surely not in the fire and turned to ashes along with Mommy and Daddy the night the house burned. At her Auntie's Em's house, where she went to live next? No, not there, either. Auntie Em didn't believe in dolls.

Poor Hester. Couldn't find her keep-pretty. Mommy and Daddy gone. That wasn't nice of them, even if they couldn't help it. Shouldn't have gone and left her all alone. So frightened. Was that why she had married so young? No. Better not think about that. Alone again was bad enough without thinking. Poor Hester. Foolish Hester. Sad Hester. If only she could find the box, though. One day soon she'd had to look more thoroughly. Look everywhere. One day soon.

Saturday was one of those glorious Texas fall days when the sun was warm and the air just cool enough to feel good on the skin. They had all slept well, and woke really rested for the first time in days. There was work to be done, but no one minded. Laughter and chatter filled the meadow. The women sewed and cooked and aired bedding and washed clothes in the river. The men greased all the wagon wheels. Harness was mended, horses actually curried. Off to one side, Jones, Leakey, True, and Joseph rigged a makeshift farriery. Two trimming and two shoeing—Tommy Matlan was kept proudly busy helping—they worked their way through every animal there by the middle of the afternoon. By five, the vast majority of the work was done and all the men hiked a hundred yards downriver to bathe and swim and generally act as though they were Tommy Matlan's age again.

Dinner was a feast. Great sizzling steaks of juicy dark black bear meat were laid out on a plank. Onions and carrots, traded two settlements back for a half tub of axle grease, had been roasted in a pit. The ever present beans were seasoned with bear fat and tiny green peppers so hot that even Thaddeus Jones had to blink and blow and wipe the perspiration from the back of his neck. Last but not least, Mila Kania and Eustacia Matlan brought out the monumental surprise of the journey, four apple pies. The men groaned and rolled their eyes and said they couldn't eat another bite. But the pies were gone before the coffee had cooled enough to drink. Hogjaw, after an appreciative belch, proclaimed Mila and Eustacia the heroes of the feast and, bowing gallantly, kissed their hands. Jack Kemper was taken with a fit of generosity and, ignoring his wife's scowl, broke out one of the jugs of whiskey he'd been saving to trade in San Antonio.

The party—Jones called it a fiesta—announced by a blast from Hogjaw's bugle, started at sundown with a square dance. Thaddeus Jones did the honors for the first, calling the old standard, "Turkey in the Straw." Hogjaw followed with one he'd made up, "Go See the Varmint, and Step on the Elephant's Trunk." By the time they finished, everyone was laughing so hard they had to take a break and pass around Jack Kemper's jug again. When they resumed, it was to dance to some of Mila's favorites, polkas that her father and mother had remembered from the old country and taught her as a child.

"May I have this dance, mam'selle?" True asked, with a sweeping, comical bow to Elizabeth.

Elizabeth smiled skeptically. "I'd probably step on your feet."

"Never you mind that. I step on them myself."

They'd talked a good deal during the last two weeks. Elizabeth still wasn't sure exactly what she felt about True, especially in the face of his obvious desire for her. At one moment, recognizing that she needed him, she feared becoming too dependent on him and rejected his company. At another, attracted to him in spite of the constant warnings she gave herself, she welcomed his proximity. "I . . . I'd better check on Mother first," she finally said.

True reached out and untied the leather throng holding her hair away from her face. Golden curls spilled around her shoulders and neck. "I'll wait right here," he said. "Don't take too long."

"I won't."

The lantern inside the wagon was turned down. Hester lay

'on her pallet, as she had for the past three weeks. "Mother?" Elizabeth said, entering. "Are you awake?"

There was no answer. Quickly, Elizabeth opened the trunk, pulled out her yellow dress and good shoes. "There's dancing," she said, stripping off her work shirt and trousers. "You'd enjoy watching. Everyone is having so much fun and the fresh air would do you good." Chattering more gaily then she felt in light of her mother's despondency, Elizabeth dressed. "It'll be so much better next week. Open ground, Mr. Jones says. We'll be able to see the sky again. Every day! Won't that be nice? And in another three weeks we'll be in San Antonio." She laughed, falsely but brightly. "You'll see then how silly you're being, Mama. And you'll feel better, too. Why, you'll simply have to! Especially when you see our land. Won't that be a marvelous Christmas present? I know you'll love it. We all will!" Ready, she knelt and smoothed Hester's brow. "I'll be nearby if you need anything. I'm going to dance with True. He's very nice, Mama. I think I like him a great deal, did you know that? I wish you could watch us dance."

Still, Hester didn't move. Elizabeth adjusted her mother's blanket and quietly crawled out of the wagon. True was waiting for her as he'd promised. "Well!" he said, obviously approving the change. "You're beautiful." He glanced toward the wagon. "She doing any better?"

"I wish I knew what to say to her," Elizabeth said, worried. "She just lies there. And doesn't eat enough to keep a bird alive."

"We'll be in San Antonio soon. She'll snap out of it then."

"I hope so. I keep telling myself that—"

"In the meantime, you, my lady, need to snap out of it yourself." He took her hand, led her toward the firelight. "C'mon. A smile will do you good. Best medicine for melancholy I know."

And so it was. Mila's accordian squealed a sprightly tune, accompanied by Buckland on the jew's harp and Hogjaw Leakey beating the rhythm with a pair of horseshoes on a wheel rim. Arm in arm, feet flying, they spun round and round, two-stepping to a polka. "Step to it, yonkers, step to it!" Hogjaw yelled.

Little Tommy Matlan danced by with Ruthie Campbell in tow. The Thatches cut their pace in half in deference to

Mildred's condition. Nels and Eustacia found themselves in a contest with Scott and Joan. In the midst of it all, Thaddeus let out a Comanche war whoop and jumped in with an ungainly hop and side kick. Leaping high in the air, he slapped his beaver hat against his thigh, came down, and twirled about madly before leaping again. The gaiety was infectious. Elizabeth felt her heart pumping wildly. Faces skidded past in a blur. Laughter rose in her throat. For the moment, there was neither fear nor loneliness, only the firm, joyful pressure of True's hands holding hers, the strength that flowed from him to her, and an overwhelming sense of well-being.

And then, suddenly, the music stopped. His face furrowed with worry as he looked past her, True froze. Elizabeth turned around, saw the trouble, and knew exactly what had happened because she had seen it happen before. Never content in a relationship until she had become the object of a quarrel, Lottie had been lavishing attention on Dennis Campbell throughout the evening. Her intent, of course, had been to make Joseph jealous, and she had succeeded. Tired of being ignored, Joseph had cut in between her and Dennis and claimed his turn to dance. Hurriedly trying to stop them before they came to blows, Elizabeth started forward, only to find herself spun about by True and propelled toward the periphery of the group.

"I'll take my turn with her now," Joseph said, reaching for Lottie.

"The hell you say, Paxton," Dennis said, pushing Lottie behind him. "You've let us know you're the lord of the manor back in Carolina, but here you're no better than anyone else. Lottie's begun this dance with me, and by God she'll end it with me. *And* have another," he finished belligerently.

"Lads! . . ." Scott called, hurrying toward his son and Joseph.

"Boys, boys!" Reverend Kania waved his arms helplessly. "Please, this is a festive gathering."

"I said I'll have my turn!" Joseph roared, his anger fueled by Jack Kemper's whiskey. "And by God yourself, this farce is over!" Without warning, he grabbed Dennis by the shirt and threw him aside. "Get away from her!"

Taken by surprise, Dennis flew backward, tripped over a log, and fell heavily, his head slapping the dirt with a dull thud. At the same time, his brother Mackenzie charged through the circle of onlookers and buried his shoulder in Joseph's midsection. Joseph grunted and went down. "Sonofabitch!" Mackenzie swore. "C'mon. Get up so I can knock you down again!"

The women screamed and ran for the wagons. Kevin Thatche led his pregnant wife to safety. Nels Matlan stood in front of Eustacia to keep her from harm. Scott Campbell moved to stop the fight, but Hogjaw restrained him. "It's a fair fight so far," he said. "Best let 'em get it out of their system."

Pale and gasping for breath, Joseph pushed himself to his feet. Mackenzie feinted with a left and threw a looping right that sailed over Joseph's head, then dropped unconscious as Joseph caught him on the side of the head with a forearm.

"Okay. Fight's over, boys," Hogjaw announced. "Why don't you all—"

"No it ain't," Dennis said, stepping over his brother and brandishing a length of firewood.

His eyes narrowing, Joseph slipped his knife from its scabbard and, crouching, stepped back and waited for an opening.

It was no longer a fair fight, no longer a question of a mere lump or two. Realizing the situation had to be defused before it was too late, True grabbed Hogjaw's rifle from where it stood propped next to the fire and fired into the ground between Joseph and Dennis. Dirt flew into the air, and the startled antagonists turned in the direction of the shot. "Man said the fight was over," True said, his voice uncommonly loud in the ringing silence. "Scott. Reverend. Step in front of them."

Scott hurried to his son's side and took the club. Buckland Kania moved as quickly to Joseph and held out his hand for the knife. Joseph stared sullenly at True, glanced around the circle of faces and focused on Lottie, who stood to one side, her hand to her mouth. "I keep my knife," he said quietly, ignoring the minister's outstretched hand and sheathing the broad blade.

Thaddeus Jones walked forward and hooked his thumbs in his belt. "Long day today and plenty to do tomorrow," he announced. "Best pack it in for the night, I suspect."

No one had any better idea under the circumstances. Joan Campbell led Ruthie and Dianne off to their wagon. Eyes wide, Tommy Matlan circled Joseph at a safe distance and ran to his mother. True tossed the rifle to Hogjaw. The mountain man caught it in a massive fist and, with an approving nod in True's direction, began immediately to reload. "We need to talk," True said, catching up with Elizabeth before she'd gone too far.

"About what?" Elizabeth snapped, turning on him. "Your brother or my sister?"

"Don't blame me, damn it," True answered, grabbing her arm. "I'm not the one who started that fight. I'm the one who ended it, remember?"

Elizabeth glared at him, almost spat a rejoinder, but at last lowered her eyes. "I'm sorry, True. It's catching, I guess."

"Yeah." He touched her arm and smiled ruefully. "Shouldn't've grabbed you like that. Look, we both need to calm down. Walk with me?"

"No," she whispered. "Not tonight. I need to get back. Mother will be worried." She searched his face for signs of anger, and when she saw none, smiled at him. "Tomorrow?"

"If you say so."

"Goodnight, True."

"Goodnight, Elizabeth." He touched her cheek. "I love you."

"I . . . I know." The faint smell of gunpowder lingered on his hand. "Goodnight."

Why couldn't she say it, she wondered, hurrying toward the wagon. Because she mistrusted all men so much that she couldn't love any man? Because she was afraid to admit her feelings yet? Because she wasn't totally sure of herself, and couldn't stand the thought of playing Lottie's game? Because her father still looked over her shoulder, because she could still feel his touch? That was a distinct possibility, she admitted bitterly, arriving at her wagon and looking around for her sister.

"Walking with True again?" Lottie asked with a smirk, emerging from the bushes where she had gone to relieve herself.

An answer wasn't required. Lottie was merely trying to sidestep the real issue. "I trust you're happy now," Elizabeth said, seething with anger.

"I don't know what you're talking about and neither do you," Lottie minced, miffed that her younger sister should take such a tone.

"Of course not." Elizabeth stationed herself between Lottie and the rear of the wagon. "Well, congratulations anyway.

You have them at each other's throats. I hope you're proud of yourself.''

"What I am is tired, Elizabeth. So if you don't mind, I'm going to bed."

"Not until you hear what I have to say."

"Will you please move so I can climb into the wagon?"

"No. You wanted them to fight. Just like back home. The Lottie Michaelson trial to test the mettle of her suitors and cull out the inferior ones. It makes you feel important, doesn't it? And tomorrow you'll be mooning once again over Joseph."

"Move," Lottie ordered, trying to shove past. But Elizabeth, though younger, was as tall as her sister and more than a match for her. She pushed Lottie back and stood her ground. "It has to stop, Lottie. Someone might have been hurt, even killed. And all because of your vanity."

"Why don't you just mind your own business?"

"This *is* my business," Elizabeth hissed. "I'm tired of being Loose Lottie Michaelson's sister and putting up with the stares and snide comments and innuendoes. Once we reach San Antonio and divide our land, you can prance about like a cow in heat all you want, but for right now, spare me, please! You might even help out some, or is that too much to ask of the spoiled hussy you've become?"

Her face a furious mask, Lottie started toward her sister, but then squealed and jumped back when a far more macabre visage appeared out of the shadows.

"Sound carries," Hogjaw said laconically. "Especially whispers at this time of night. Everything all right?"

"How dare you sneak up on us like that!" Lottie exclaimed.

"Well, bein' as I'm supposed to be responsible for you, an' since I thought maybe I heard a cat fight, I figured I ought to just make sure nothin' was amiss." Hogjaw smiled amiably. "Of course, if I'm buttin' in where I'm not wanted . . ."

"You aren't, Hogjaw," Elizabeth said, secretly grateful for the interruption. "Thank you for your concern."

"Think nothin' of it, ma'am," he said, doffing his hat and melting into the shadows. His voice drifted back to them from the trees. "Nothin' of it at all. You gals sleep tight, now. 'Night.''

"Well?" Elizabeth asked, once his footsteps faded and they were left alone.

"I'll check on Mother," Lottie said.

"Throw me out my shirt and pants and a blanket." Elizabeth yawned. "I'll sleep under the wagon."

"If you want."

The sounds of night. Crickets and other, unnamed insects, strange to those from so far away. A creaking wagon spring, the flap of convas falling closed. A muffled goodnight, a child asking for a blanket. A loud yawn and the first tentative snore. Down among the willows, True walked the rope corral, tightened a knot here, adjusted the height there, then ducked inside to check the animals. The dark shadows moved about like ghosts, now and again nudging him or moving away to go about the business of cropping the thick, sweet grass that tasted so good after the miles of forest. He stopped last at Firetail, stood by his side, and gazed up at the stars. "You're one hell of a horse," he finally said, scratching the stallion's ears when Firetail lowered his head and pushed against True's chest. "A lousy substitute, but a hell of a horse."

"That you, True?"

It was Joseph's voice—sober now, from the sound of it. "Yo," True answered softly.

Joseph threaded his way through the animals to stand next to him. "Problems?"

"Naw. Better safe than sorry, is all. Thought I'd look them over before I turned in." He nodded toward the opposite side of the corral. "Jones is sleeping over there. I told him I'd take this side."

"Good idea." Joseph paused awkwardly. "True?"

True knew his brother well, knew what was coming next. "Yeah."

"We're brothers, right?"

"Of course."

"And blood runs thick between kin."

"So they say."

"You should've sided with me, True. Not gone against me like that in front of the others."

"I didn't go against you. I went against someone getting killed over a tease. She egged you on, Joseph."

"You have no call to talk about her like that."

"Look, Joseph—"

"Don't say it." Joseph's voice bore a warning that brooked no argument. "Just don't. The point is, the Paxtons are supposed to stick together, like Andrew and I did for you in Natchez Under the Hill.''

"I didn't start that fight. And you had no call starting the one tonight.''

"Doesn't matter, damn it!'' Joseph said, more hurt than angry. "Trouble with one of us is trouble with us all.''

"Not when you're wrong, Joseph.'' True took a deep breath, waiting for the explosion that never came. "I'm sorry.''

"So am I, True,'' Joseph finally said. "So am I.''

Firetail nickered softly as Joseph stalked off toward the wagons and the orange glow of the campfire. True stroked the stallion's muzzle, reached under his neck and kneaded the great bunched jaw muscles. Telling Joseph the truth hadn't been easy. But then, not much was, these days. "A lousy substitute,'' he said again, leaving the stallion and walking back to the edge of the trees to stand and stare at the Michaelson wagon.

Her hands had been calloused from work, but had seemed soft to him nevertheless. She had danced lightly, as gracefully as a bird in flight. Her laughter had been as full and rich as her body. Her hair had shone bright gold in the firelight, and her eyes had glittered with liquid warmth. "Sure were pretty tonight, Elizabeth,'' he whispered, wanting her as he savored the taste of her name. "You sure were pretty.''

And as he walked back into the shadows toward a lonely bedroll, he had no way of knowing that Elizabeth was watching him. Watching and remembering, too. And wanting just as badly.

Chapter XV

The pall that hung over Sunday morning's camp didn't fade until the end of services when the Reverend Buckland Kania, after the last hymn and before the benediction, raised his arms and gestured for silence. "There's one thing more," he said in the hush, "and though it shouldn't have to be said, it does." He paused, looked into each set of eyes and read the concern there.

"We've been thrown together by a loving God. Together, we've traveled a long way through trying circumstances, and together we'll reach the goal we've set. But only if we pull together, united.

"Now, we all known what happened here last night. We can all feel it as a weight on our hearts. The Lord has given us good weather. He has kept the heathen from our throats. He has seen that we have food in abundance. He has, above all else, blessed us with fine companions and given us the strength to endure."

He stopped again. This time his eyes sought Joseph, then Dennis, then Mackenzie, and finally Lottie. "We seek a new land and a new life," he went on at last. "What does it avail us to carry with us animosity and dissension and rancor?"

Only a cardinal dared break the silence.

"I beg that you look to your hearts for the answer, and that from this hour forth we travel in peace as trusting friends and as good neighbors. Let us pray."

Even Hogjaw bowed his head.

"And now, the Lord bless thee and keep thee, the Lord make His face to shine upon thee and be gracious unto thee, the Lord lift up His countenance upon thee and give thee peace. Amen."

A moment later, a stern-faced Joseph stood in front of

Dennis and Mackenzie and offered them his hand. Ten minutes after that they were drinking coffee together. The rift was not healed, as True could tell from the tension in their voices, but at least it was patched. With any luck at all, the patch would hold until they reached San Antonio.

The remainder of the day was given over to resting, to swimming, to desultory talk. Jones had planned it that way, had known they would reach the Trinity a day earlier than the settlers expected. Not that he was particularly devious, but he understood how much an unexpected extra day of rest boosted morale. The good Lord knew they'd need every minute he could give them if they were to see their way through the next week.

Angling away from the campsite, the wagon train master struck out downriver for an hour or two of solitude, the last he'd get for three weeks. It was high noon, the lazy time of day. Hogjaw was alseep in the sun, resting like an old, tough coyote who knew enough to catch a few winks whenever he had the chance. A subdued Joseph was off walking alone. The Campbell men and Nels Matlan were off at the edge of camp where they'd driven a couple of stakes and were playing horseshoes. True had wandered off to the river and found himself a cottonwood to sit in. The women were gathered in a circle next to the Campbells' wagon, where they chattered and gossiped and sewed.

> "Oh, the green hills of Kaintuck
> Are as pretty as can be
> But my black haired señorita
> Is the only gal for me. . . ."

Jones cocked an ear and listened, decided he was far enough away to be left alone, and lay back to watch the sky go by and listen to the slow clock of the seasons turning as the world spun in its course. There'd been too little time for that of late. Too little time to laze about and let his mind go blank and wander. That was the problem with bringing in too many new people from the East. Oh, being a wagon master wasn't bad work as work went, but it spoiled the wilderness, cluttered it up with talk and busy bodies charging around, intent on civilizing things.

Which was why he had never been to Kentucky, he thought, even though he didn't mind singing about it. Kentucky or any of the rest of that part of the world where his people, as some folks called them, lived and toiled and died as slaves. Well, he mused, that was their problem, not his. Thaddeus Jones was a Mexican citizen and planned to remain one. He had a wife and four kids in Santa Catarina, a mother and father long buried, and a brother and sister somewhere around Mexico City, the last he'd heard. That was enough people for any one man to have, just as Mexico was enough country without wandering all over the continent the way Hogjaw did.

Mexico City. Jones yawned, blinked his eyes to keep them open, and then decided the hell with it and let them close. Mexico City. It had been a long time. Ten years? Nine? Whatever. Might be a good idea to look up his sister and brother once he'd left off this batch in San Antonio. Head on south, pick up his wife and kids, and just keep on riding. Be a long trip, of course. Mexico City was a far piece from Santa Catarina, not to mention San Antonio, he thought, drifting off. Nothing new there, though. He'd been a long way from a lot of places in his time. One more wouldn't hurt.

Everything had been ready the previous night, before they went to bed, even to ground-tethering the stock next to their respective wagons. The group had wakened long before dawn, had eaten hastily, put out their fires, harnessed, and left. Now, two hours after the sun had risen, they were passing through the last dense stand of pine. Prairie land, deep in grass and dotted with motts of post oak, lay ahead of them.

The Kempers were fourth in line. They had just started down a long, gentle slope when Jones galloped past them to meet a quarter mile ahead with True and Hogjaw. Minutes later, as the forward scouts split and rode off to either side, Jones galloped back to meet the rest of the train.

"This is it!" he shouted, stopping them with an upraised hand. "The prairies. The way we're goin', it's about a hundred and twenty miles. I want to make that by Saturday evening, so like I said before, we'll be stretchin' it. Remember, now, this here's a sea of dry grass, so be careful with fire. Believe me, I've seen what it can do when it gets started out here. Anything go wrong, holler out fast. Otherwise—" He took off his hat and waved it over his head. "—let's go!"

The dust kicked up by the lead wagons and the mules hung in a cloud around them and stuck to their skin. "Hell of a hot day," Jack said. "Why don't you soak a couple of cloths for us. Never should've left Pennsylvania."

Uncharacteristically dutiful, Helen crawled over the back of the seat and emerged from the interior of the wagon a moment later with two wet rags. "What's done is done," she said, handing her husband one of them. "Best quit thinking of what's behind us."

Kemper wiped his forehead and face. "Too damn hot for November," he said, his voice garbled by the cloth. "I said, it's too damn hot for November."

"I heard you, for heaven's sake," Helen snapped. She pressed the cloth over her throat and inside her blouse, dabbing her bony shoulders.

"Well then, answer."

"You didn't ask a question. You were just carrying on."

"I wasn't just carrying on. I was—"

"Hush."

Dennis and Mackenzie Campbell rode past, trotting their horses into the lead to check out a creek ahead and locate an easy crossing place before the wagons got there. "I wasn't carrying on," Jack said once the youths were safely out of earshot. "It's just that it would be nice to have some snow. I miss snow."

"Snow," Helen snorted.

"We could have gone north and east as easy as south and west. New York, Connecticut, Massachusetts. Hell, anything'd be better than this."

"I think," Helen said coldly, "that we've discussed this all before, and complaining only makes things worse. Texas was the best choice. We are out of the reach of any sort of authority. Believe me, I know best."

"*Believe* you. *Listen* to you." Jack removed his hat and wiped the freckled scalp that rose domelike above a fringe of hair. "Maybe I should never have listened to you in the first place."

Helen's face was red with heat and prickly with dust. The cloth helped only so long as she held it against her skin. "Then you still would have been a common teller with no future but to count other people's money, deposit and withdraw other people's money, figure other people's interest. You would be a clerk and nothing more," she snapped contemptuously."

"But not a criminal," Jack replied evenly. "You forgot to mention that."

"No, you would not be a criminal. Nor would you have deed to over a thousand acres of land, and the prospect of being wealthy and respected."

"All right. All right," Jack said, capitulating.

Helen looked out over the flowing prairie. "It's precious little thanks I get. Everything I've done has been in your own interest, and to help us rise above an intolerable situation. The bank will reinvest and recoup its losses. No one will be hurt. How has anyone been hurt? And you have something to look forward to. A chance to be somebody."

Jack rubbed his eyes, held the cloth over his nose. It was only the first hour out from under the trees and already he was sick and tired of eating dust, of grit in his eyelids. He wasn't due to be lead wagon for another three days, and then the order would repeat itself. Take comfort, he counseled himself. Save your sanity and take comfort. Another few weeks couldn't be all that bad. Before long, he'd have his own land and a store. And like Helen kept saying, he'd be somebody.

There was frost on the ground Tuesday morning, but by noon it had evaporated under a hot sun. Monday night's camp had been interrupted by the constant howl of coyotes, and tired though they had been, almost everyone had slept fitfully. Breakfast had been a hasty affair, lunch only a little longer, and that because of the animals, not the people. Now, as the afternoon waned, the wagons crawled out of a creekbed and struck out across the rolling land again.

Elizabeth had no idea of how many miles they had made that day, nor did she really care. For weeks before, she had wished for the end of the trees, and now that they no longer shaded her, she wished they were back. Her hair was tied up and covered with a hat but still felt full of dust. Her clothes itched, her eyes burned, and the steady jolting of the wagon tried to lure her to sleep at the same time it bounced her awake. The only thing that kept her sane was the sound of Thaddeus Jones's melancholy ballad. She didn't understand the exact meaning of the words, but the rhythmic phrasing and plaintive tune conveyed a poignancy of their own.

Boring boring boring, with more of the same to look forward to for the next four days. Elizabeth glanced sideways at Lottie and tried to think of something to say. They'd talked about Hester. They'd talked about the weather, about the journey, about the food, about everything except their own deteriorating relationship. "It's nice to have the lead," she finally said.

Evidently deep in her own thoughts, Lottie looked at Elizabeth as if she had spoken utter gibberish. "Uh, yes," she replied, uncertain what she was agreeing with. Joseph hadn't spoken to her since Saturday night. Neither had Dennis or Mackenzie. Not that the latter two particularly mattered. Her ploy had been designed to arouse Joseph's ardor.

All it had brought her was embarrassment and a stern lecture from Hogjaw, the likes of which her father never would have dared deliver to her. At least he had delivered it to her in private. Strangely enough, she had taken it to heart. She couldn't explain why. Perhaps it was the trip. Perhaps she was just ready to listen. Perhaps she was too tired to fight anymore. The reasons weren't even very important, she finally decided. What was important was Joseph, and that she loved him.

What a damned fool I've been. All I had to do was tell him. Now I have to convince him.

The way things were going, she wasn't sure she could.

Wednesday felt more like Friday. They had traveled until near dark on Tuesday night and everyone was tired. The prairie had lost its fascination. Light beige grass stretched to the horizon on all sides. The few oaks scattered about on the face of the land did nothing to break the monotony. The only relief to tired, sore eyes was an occasional patch of still bright red and yellow sumac.

Nels Matlan kept a firm hand on the reins. If he never saw the back side of a mule again he'd die happy. Behind him in the wagon, he listened to Eustacia explaining a math problem to Tommy and the Campbell girls. That was one thing that wouldn't change. Education. The children would need it even more than he had, where they were going. They didn't understand that now, of course. Education never made sense, at first.

Nels grinned as he recalled the far different childhood he had spent. His father was a minister and his mother a teacher at a small private preparatory school. They had ingrained in him an appreciation of learning. Perfectly at home with his books and letters, preferring the relative safety and security of the city, he had never dreamed of becoming a pioneer. And yet, on the very day he had read the notice of the Mexican land grants for sale, he had contacted Señor Medina and committed his savings to the venture. To his surprise and joy, Eustacia had accepted the decision quietly and without complaint. Her only response had been, "When do we leave?" To his dying day, he would never be able to repay her faith and loyalty.

Mules, dust, heat, cold, fatigue, books, land, miles, strangers, friends, ever new vistas, horizons beyond expectation. He hadn't been able to add them all up yet, but he had come to one absolute conviction.

He was glad he had come.

Thursday was taking forever. Or felt as if it was. The horses were tiring, the mules balking when led to the traces. They were fed oats to keep up their strength, but already they looked gaunt. The constant travel was hard on the humans, but harder by far on the animals that pulled the loaded wagons.

It rained Thursday afternoon. Surprisingly enough, unlike the forest trails that turned to mud, the prairie remained firm. It had to do with the thick mattress of grass, Scott Campbell supposed as he pulled his slouch hat lower over his face. That and the soil, which seemed to drink the water. A good day for rain, he mused. It seemed to perk up the animals and certainly laid low the dust, which was important since he was last in line that day. Behind him, if he leaned far out and looked around the wagon, he could see their tracks. Already, the water-swollen grass had started to stand straight again.

The boys, along with the Paxton brothers and Leakey, Jack Kemper and Nels Matlan, had ridden ahead to the next river, whatever the hell Jones had called it. They had carried axes and picks and shovels and pulleys to prepare the way for the wagons when they got there. Scott and Reverend Kania and Kevin Thatche had been left behind to make sure nothing happened to the women.

"Here," he said to Joan as she emerged from the wagon. "You take it for a while. I'm going to ride out to the side."

He leaped down from the seat, untied the mare from the rear of the wagon, tightened the cinch on her saddle, and rode off on an arc that would take him in a wide circle around the wagons. You never could tell, Jones had said. Just because they hadn't seen any Indians didn't mean there weren't any around. Scott Campbell wasn't a man to take chances when it came to his wife and children. For if they were taken, what else was there?

Friday was almost too much to bear. They had slept little the night before. One horse had had to be shot. Just as they camped, they had discovered bad wheels on two wagons, and had labored long past dark to repair them. The ground was wet and cold. Buckland Kania had come down with a fever. Dennis Campbell had sprained an ankle so badly he could not walk on it. The effective loss of two men put just that much more strain on those who were left. No one wanted to move on Friday morning, but Thaddeus Jones rousted them out anyway, driving them from their blankets with curses and a well-placed kick or two. Damn and by damn, he had said, but they were going to make the Colorado River by Saturday night. When they finally got moving, they hit the first of the limestone outcroppings.

"Damn rocks," Kevin Thatche cursed. "And if it isn't rocks it's dust and if it isn't dust it's rain. Damn!"

"How much farther to San Antonio?" Mildred asked from his side, trying to defuse his anger with their private joke.

Kevin's frown melted, at least momentarily. "Just around the bend," he said. "You sure you wouldn't be more comfortable in back?"

Mildred winced and held her swollen abdomen. "I don't know. Maybe."

"Go on, then," Kevin said tenderly. "Jones says we'll be past this in a little while."

They had borrowed blankets and quilts and arranged a thick pallet to cushion Mildred's ride. She climbed awkwardly over the seat and, ducking her head, stepped inside and lay down heavily. If he would only come, she thought, uncomfortable on her back and trying her side. Behind her, she could see Joan Campbell through the open rear of the wagon, and waved to her before closing her eyes in an attempt to dull her mind against the jolting. For a moment, she dozed, but then awoke abruptly, inexplicably thinking about her parents and wondering if they had ceased looking for her.

Mildred's father was a doctor, Kevin's an attorney. Both men had envisioned far grander futures for their children than to be unmarried and pregnant on a wagon train in the middle of a foreign country. But she and Kevin had had their own ideas about the future. Desperately in love and despite the obstacles placed before them by their well-meaning parents, they had succeeded in escaping. The savings account instituted by his father at Kevin's birth had been enough to purchase their share of the Medina land grant and buy them a place on the wagon train. They had mailed their parents letters from St. Louis and told them not to worry.

A heavy shadow passed over the wagon. Mildred craned her neck, saw the same shadow pass over the Campbells' wagon and, a moment later, a stand of three tall oaks by the side of the trail.

"Not to worry," she repeated to herself for the umpteenth time. Inside her, the baby kicked again.

Saturday was more a waking dream than anything else. Only the promised arrival at the Colorado River kept them going, and then as sleepwalkers. The mules smelled the water first, pricked their ears forward, and picked up the pace. Within minutes, the word had spread back to the settlers from Jones. However faintly at first, their spirits stirred, and rose. The hellish week had come to an end! Soon they would rest.

And rest they did. The stock was put out in record time as bodies revived just long enough for the necessary chores. Uncooped at last, Tommy Matlan and Ruthie and Dianne Campbell raced around wildly. No one complained. They were all too stupified, too glad just to have stopped.

Later, as night approached, each family made its own campfire and sat about in relative privacy, the general thinking being that there was such a thing as too much community, and a time to temper social protocol with a degree of healthy solitude. Elizabeth dropped the last of the firewood she had gathered next to the cookfire, and added a few pieces around the edge to warm them up. Lottie was busily frying bacon, while Hester sat off a little to one side, stared at the fire, and sipped a cup of broth. "Did she ask for that?" Elizabeth asked, surprised to see her mother taking nourishment again.

Lottie wiped her forehead with the back of her wrist. "Yes. I didn't believe it myself. She smiled, too."

They were under trees again, which was a comfort after the open spaces of the prairie. The Michaelson wagon was close to the Paxtons', as usual. Elizabeth nudged the coffee pot nearer to the fire and caught herself looking for True, who had gone out hunting with Hogjaw. "They haven't come back yet?" she asked Lottie.

"I didn't hear—"

"Oh, the bear stuck his paw in the honey tree, and the bee said buzz, buzz, buzz. Oh, the bear took a taste, and licked with glee, the sweetest honey that was, was, was. . . ."

The deep bellowing voice singing off key indicated Hogjaw was returning to camp. He always sang as a way of identifying himself to the guard. As he was prone to say, it wasn't the melody that kept a man alive, but whether he could caterwaller loud enough to wake the Devil, scare a crazed grizzly, and keep some blood and thunder storekeeper from scratching an itchy finger on the trouble side of a Hawken rifle trigger.

True was with him, and smiled at Elizabeth. "Sorry we're late," he said, leaning his rifle against a log.

"And empty-handed," Joseph noted, coming over from his wagon.

"Not exactly," Hogjaw said. He hung three skinned and cleaned squirrels on the end of a spit away from the fire. "Didn't know we was having bacon. I wouldn't have shot these."

"You hadn't come back, so I thought I'd better start something before it got too late." Lottie pulled the frypan off the fire, and set it aside. "No matter. We can eat them tomorrow."

Hogjaw had noticed Hester eating, and sidled up to Lottie. "She take anything more than broth?" he asked, jabbing a thumb in Hester's direction.

"Some bread. That's all."

"Might oughta cut up one of them squirrels and make some stew for her," Hogjaw suggested. "Maybe she's comin' around. Meat'd do her good." He winked at Elizabeth, sniffed the air comically. "Do me good, too. We about ready to eat?"

Their meal was bread, bacon, beans, and onions. Joseph and Lottie, having made their peace a few days earlier, sat together and talked quietly. His mind on other matters, True dabbed at his food, and then, excusing himself, disappeared into the night. When Hester finished eating, Elizabeth took her to the river and helped her wash her face and arms before leading her back to the wagon where she changed her mother's clothes and put her to bed. By the time she was finished,

Hogjaw had left the camp and bedded down in the woods to get some sleep before Jones woke him at midnight for the watch.

Lottie was starting off with Joseph when Elizabeth called to her. "What?" she asked, turning and frowning.

"Could you stay and watch to see that Mother's all right?"

"Where are you going?" Lottie asked.

"I'd like to bathe. I haven't had time yet."

Lottie was obviously displeased, but couldn't complain because she had gone off to the river while Elizabeth was setting up camp. She glanced at Joseph and then at the wagon where Hester slept. "Well . . ." She threw up her hands in disgust. "Well, hurry," she whispered to her departing sister, and grudgingly accompanied Joseph back to camp.

A half moon was low, but gave enough light to see by. Elizabeth took her time, feeling her way through the trees to the river. The night was quiet. After the long, difficult week, almost everyone was asleep, early though it was. The river was shallow with small, tublike holes where the water had worn depressions in the rocky bottom. Elizabeth stripped quickly and, gasping, entered the cold water. Five minutes later, chilly but refreshed, she slipped into the clean dress she had brought with her.

The dress, blotting the water from her skin, clung to her. She stood on a rock at the edge of the water, rinsed one foot and slipped it into her shoe, then rinsed the other and raising it, lost her balance and started to topple.

"It's me. Don't yell," True said, catching her from behind and pulling her to him.

Her heart thudding wildly, Elizabeth spun to face him. "My God, you scared me! What do you think you're—"

"This," True said, and kissed her.

His arms were around her, his body pressed against hers. His lips were warm, his tongue a darting, enticing instrument of passion. She could feel his thighs and the growing hardness touched her where not even her father had dared. The thought flashed through Elizabeth's mind that she should struggle, should fight him, but her body disagreed and she found herself surrendering to the rising emotions within her. Thoroughly confused by this inability to resist, she returned his kiss with abandon, pressed her breasts against him, crushed her flesh to his.

It was he who broke off the kiss and took a step back. "I

love you, Elizabeth Michaelson,'' he said, and gently cupped her breasts in his hands.

His sun-bleached, tousled, hair shone in the moonlight. His eyes were slits of gleaming brilliance. Elizabeth shuddered and closed her eyes. His hands warmed her through the cool dampness of her dress. Her breasts ached and her loins burned where his hardness had touched her. Hardly aware she was doing so, she placed her palms against his chest, then ran them along his forearms to briefly press his hands tighter to her breasts before gently removing them. ''Well,'' she managed to say, ''you have all the nerve.''

''I suppose I do,'' True admitted, a little embarrassed himself and unsure of what to do with his hands. ''If I only had the guile, this courtship might be easier.''

''Courtship?'' Elizabeth exclaimed, much louder than she had intended. ''Courtship!'' she repeated, whispering this time.

''I warned you before, Elizabeth, though I admit it wasn't with the golden tongue Joseph possesses. He can bring a quail to ground with his charm. Me, I have to make the best of a situation any way I can.''

She reached to touch his cheek. ''You're doing very well, I think, Mr. Paxton. Very well indeed.''

''Elizabeth? I . . .'' He paused, tongue-tied. ''I . . .'' His voice was husky, almost choked. ''I want you, Elizabeth. I haven't ever . . . that is, I haven't ever wanted somebody like I do you.''

Softly, Elizabeth came to him, resting her head against his chest. ''I know,'' she said, almost too quietly to be heard. A frown creased her forehead. Her father's touch. Her mother, ill and wasting. The land that was to be hers, and all it meant. She wanted True, but was afraid. Wanted to depend on him, but was afraid of that, too. She needed time. Time to prove herself, to know herself. ''I know.''

She was intensely aware of his arms around her, of the warmth they generated in the closeness of the moment. She could feel his heart beat, his breath on her hair. With a sudden flash, she realized he must have seen her naked while she bathed. She stiffened momentarily but then relaxed, for the thought secretly pleased her in some strange, forbidden way. She forced herself to push away from him. ''I can't, though. *We* can't.'' Her eyes caught his, told him that she loved him even if she couldn't say so in words. "It's not you, True. It's me. Someday . . . But not yet. Please understand?"

True started to speak, halted, tried again, and at last smiled wanly and shook his head. "Elizabeth Michaelson," he finally said, "you are the most impossible woman I have ever met."

"And you are the most . . . the most . . ." A lump was in her throat and she felt her eyes tearing. Blindly, too shaken to say more, Elizabeth stood on tiptoe and kissed him, then as quickly stooped to pick up her dirty clothes and ran off through the trees.

The path seemed different, the trees out of place. Elizabeth did not remember the stumbling, awkward return to camp, only that she arrived from a different direction than that from which she had departed. Making no more noise than a cloud passing the moon, she stole quietly past the Kanias' wagon, ducked under a low limb, and found herself next to the Paxton wagon where the sound of labored breathing and a shuddering moan stopped her in her tracks. The canvas had been torn by a tree limb jutting onto the trail, and through the tear, illuminated by the dull glow of a lantern and the moonlight filtering through the canvas, she saw . . . flesh on flesh. Beads of perspiration like jewels scattered on flesh. Legs wrapped about a waist. Large, white, muscular buttocks driving down, rising and falling.

Lottie's voice, and Joseph's, blending. Lottie's whispered cry, Joseph's gutteral answer.

"Now."

"Now."

"Now!"

Lottie turning. Her mouth an open, silent "O," her glazed eyes focusing on her sister.

Joseph groaning, his back arched, his eyes closed as his seed exploded from him.

Lottie's eyes, accusing and delighting and alive with satiation, as full as after a feast when hunger has been met.

The smell of heated flesh, salt smell of sweat and fluid animal scent. Backing, reeling, fighting for control, Elizabeth panicked as though her father's arms were reaching out for her in the darkness. Carl Michaelson had wanted that. That!

Damn him, damn him, damn him!

Sobbing, Elizabeth fled and fell, lay panting at the base of a huge old sweet-smelling cedar. There, her mind whirling in confusion, she tried to sort out and separate the beauty of love from the awful secret of her father's sordid lust. It was impossible. Lust and love mingled inextricably until only the grunting, sweating release of beasts, blind in their orgiastic fury, remained.

At long last, exhausted, she pushed herself to her knees. It was no use. Thinking was too painful. She would sleep instead, and then go about her work. There was comfort in the necessity of daily tasks.

On leaden feet, ordering one leg before the other, Elizabeth walked to the wagon. Sleep, she thought, climbing onto the lazy board and ducking under the canvas. Sleep . . .

Her breath caught in her throat and her pulse hammered in her temples. Her hands, bloodless talons, gripped the wood siding. It took a long, horrifying moment for her to fully comprehend.

Hester Michaelson was gone.

Chapter XVI

True found her late the next afternoon, almost a half mile from camp. It was plain to everyone what had happened. Hester had walked off into the night searching for Lord knew what. Somehow finding the river, she had walked north through the shallows, emerging only when the water became too deep, and struck out for higher ground. A hundred yards farther, she had tripped and tumbled into a ravine where her head caught in a crook formed by two branches. Her neck had snapped cleanly and quickly: there could have been no more than a flash of pain, and then instant death.

Death.

Elizabeth stared coldly at the dark rich earth cresting over the lip of the grave and at the simple wooden cross with her mother's name carved on it. Morning light slid through the trees. In the distance, crows cawed and warned the wild world that humans were present. Reverend Kania's reading from the New Testament was so much gibberish to her. Lottie, cradled in Joseph's embrace, wept and wept and wept.

When the service ended, Thaddeus Jones searched for the easiest way to announce that the wagon train must continue. It was Monday morning and they had to be on their way. San Antonio was still many agonizing miles down a long trail. "You know we got to leave her," he finally said. "Hard as it is to say or do, it might as well be now." He cleared his throat. "True or Hogjaw can drive for you, if you want. I'll put someone else on to scout."

"That won't be necessary," Elizabeth said coldly, brushing past him and walking determinedly through the other families, whose bereaved faces showed their sorrow over this latest misfortune. As if on signal, the rest of the settlers started for their wagons. Only Hogjaw lingered at the gravesite,

and only Buckland Kania saw him give a sad shake of his
disfigured head and heard him mutter, ". . . the howling
wilderness.''

Wagons wheeled, axles creaked. The settlers took their
places in line. Joseph led Lottie to her wagon, but when she
started to climb up beside her sister, Elizabeth shoved her
back and grabbed a whip to drive home the point. "You
couldn't wait, could you?'' she hissed. "You couldn't watch
her for half an hour, you had to race off to Joseph. A pair of
rutting animals, that's what you are. Rutting animals while
your own mother died!''

Stricken, Lottie's hand flew to her mouth and she began to
wail again.

"Now look here," Joseph said, color coming to his face.
"Just who the hell do you think you are?"

"You stay away from me, Joseph Paxton. You have your
own wagon. Put her in it and let her ride with you. You can
ride to San Antonio or ride to Hell. I don't care which, but
you stay away from me. Both of you."

Her face buried in her hands, Lottie stifled a cry, and ran.
Joseph's mouth opened as if he would answer, but then
closed in a grim line. Quivering with rage, he stalked off after
Lottie and helped her into his wagon.

A whip cracked. Scott Campbell shouted at his mules and
took the lead. True walked Firetail abreast of the Michaelson
wagon. "Elizabeth?"

*I will not cry. I will drive this wagon, and I will do what
has to be done.*

"Elizabeth?"

She turned, and though her expression was one of lashing
anger, he saw the wounded desperation behind the mask. She
looked at and through him, then leaned down to untie the
reins and take them in her hands. "Leave me alone," she
said, her voice raw with anguish. "Please, for right now,
leave me alone."

True nodded in silent acquiescence. He wanted to go to her
yet knew how impossible that was, for she was not yet ready
to share her sorrow. One day she would, though. Of that he
was certain. Mounting, he rode ahead, ignoring the heart that
implored him to return.

They forded the river, climbed the opposite bank, and left
the mount of earth, the crudely fashioned marker beneath
which Hester Michaelson slept her final sleep. The right

wheels struck a root, but Elizabeth did not notice. The mules strained against the rising hills, eased down the lengthening slopes. She did not notice that either.

Lottie's fault.

Lottie. Always Lottie. I left too. I left her alone. I never loved her enough. My fault. Mine.

"No!" she said aloud, surprised by her own voice and looking around to make sure no one had heard.

My mother and father. Both gone. Not enough love for either. When does it stop? Where does the blame lie?

She had told Lottie to stay. Lottie had agreed. And then left. Left.

All gone. All.

Elizabeth wiped her swollen eyes. She was the last. Her family was dead. All dead. Lottie too, as far as she was concerned. She was alone.

PART THREE

Chapter XVII

A man reined in his horse, waved his hat in a great circle, and let out a whoop of recognition. Behind him, the drivers of a half dozen wagons broke column and drew up in a ragged line along the crest of a ridge. They were all strangely silent as they gazed down at the city below them, for they had traveled many weeks and many miles and found it difficult to believe they now looked upon their destination. They had placed their lives and their life savings on the line, had left homes and families and friends to strike out for the unknown. Now, their fears were allayed and joy blossomed in their hearts. The moment was too precious to be marred by cheers or shouts, at least at first.

And then, the spell was broken.

"San Antonio?" True asked, hardly daring to believe.

"You got it, True boy." Hogjaw raised his voice so all could hear. "There she is, folks. Old San Antone. Feast your eyes and stretch your grins! You done by God made it!"

One and all, they poured from the wagons, shouted and cheered. Hats flew into the air. Nels and Eustacia Matlan danced, were joined by Scott and Joan Campbell. Wagonmaster Thaddeus Jones broke out his bottle. Dennis and Mackenzie Campbell and Joseph wasted powder firing at the sky. "Wait!" Buckland Kania shouted, holding up his hands for silence. "Please."

Slowly, the settlers sobered. They gathered about the man of God in a loose semicircle, and bowed their heads.

"God . . ." He paused, blinked back tears. "We're here, You brought us here, and . . . Well, God, for once in my life I don't know what to say, except . . . Thank You. We all just plain . . . thank You."

A horse stamped its hoof, nickered softly. A passing breeze

ruffled and popped one of the canvas wagon covers and went on to whisper softly through a cedar. A mule shook its head and set harness jangling. Half a century before "the shot heard 'round the world" began the American Revolution, San Antonio had been a center of commerce, an established hub of trade and civilization in Spanish America. On that deceptively warm December afternoon more than a century later, it seemed little changed. Gray and brown and whitewashed adobe houses sat alone tree-lined dirt streets. A river undulated through the heart of town, and the thin lines of meandering aqueducts and irrigation ditches glimmered in the sunlight. Everything looked very peaceful from a mile away. San Antonio appeared to be a city without pretense, and yet as inviting as the mysterious veiled smile of a señorita.

A road intersected the ridge, sprang from the trail of wagon ruts to become a full-fledged highway called *El Camino Viejo de las Carretas* or, as Jones translated roughly, the Old Cart Road. True looked back at the weatherbeaten, patched wagons. "Fitting," he muttered to himself, including the settlers in his assessment. They were not the same people who had set out from Natchez, Mississippi two months earlier. Their clothes were worn and patched. Their skin had become tough and leathery, tanned by sun and wind alike. Their faces had hardened, as had their eyes. Laughter came less readily. The wilderness had changed them. Texas had transformed them. True was vaguely aware that the metamorphosis would continue. The vastness of the land would continue to work its way on them: a journey's end was also the next journey's beginning.

"I hope our land looks like that," Mila Kania said.

"More rolling in places, flatter in others. How you divvy it up is for you to figure out. My job's about done." Jones straightened in the saddle and rubbed his leg where it hurt when a weather change was coming. "Right now—" He pointed to where a blue gray line of clouds dulled the northern sky. "That there's one of them northers I was tellin' you about. It's gonna get cold as hell around here before nightfall, so I reckon we'd best get down there."

"To our land?" Nels Matlan asked.

Jones shook his head and pointed further south. "Medina's *hacienda* is to the south of town over that rise. Your land's a little farther out. We'll check in with the local authorities before we head out that way, probably tomorrow morning."

"Why can't some of us start for Medina's right now?" Jack Kemper asked, anxious to see the raw substance of his Texas empire.

" 'Cause things just ain't done that way, in the first place, and because of what those fellas travelin' east told us the other day in the second. Bein' in Mexico and subject to Mex law ain't exactly the same as in the U.S. Out here, when there's a new regime, it's best to find out which way the wind's blowin' before you run off tryin' to do too much. I don't personally know this Santa Anna who's the new president, but I do know General Cos, and he's a damned popinjay. If we go through town without payin' our respects, his feelin's'll be hurt and he'll likely send us some grief out of pure cussedness. In any case, we're gonna want a warm place for the night. Ain't gonna make that much . . ."

"Oh, my God!"

Everyone turned toward the cry. Mildred Thatche was doubled over and clutching her abdomen. A stunned Kevin, his eyes wide with panic, had his arms around her. Eustacia hurriedly recruited three of the men to help carry Mildred to her wagon and then climbed in with her. A moment later, she stuck her head out the back. "You'd better come help, Joan," she called. "And Mr. Jones, there's a higher law than that of Mexico. The baby is coming. If there's a hotel and a real bed in that town, we'd better get her there. Now!"

"Damn and holy damn!" Jones swore, riding to the wagon. He dismounted, climbed onto the driver's seat and took the reins. "Climb up, Kevin boy, and hold on tight. Hogjaw, get my horse. Let's go!"

They all moved as one, hurrying to horse and wagon. Seconds later, with the Thatches' wagon in the lead, the re-formed column rumbled off the ridge and down the hill toward town.

General Perfecto Cos smoothed his moustache across the pencil-thin line of his lips. His expression one of pensive appraisal, he listened to Thaddeus Jones explain the reason for the hurried flight of this new group of settlers from the north into his city. "I see," he muttered at last. "The birth of an infant. I see." One eyebrow raised. "But you must understand my soldiers' alarm. I will have your belongings released to you."

Jones translated roughly to True and Scott and motioned

for them to go tell the other settlers while the general issued orders to his adjutant. Scott left, True remained. "That storm's almost here," True pointed out. "Is there some place the rest of us can go?"

"There is an inn on *Calle de la Acequia* just off the *Plaza de las Islas*," Cos answered, understanding True's English but responding in Spanish. "*La Casa del Rio*. It should serve your needs." He turned back to Jones. "And the mother, you say, is being taken care of? You are sure?"

"Padre Salva has given her a bed in the infirmary behind the cathedral," Jones said. "I have faith in him."

"But of course, Señor Jones. I forget you are no stranger to San Antonio," Cos purred. "Unfortunately, those you lead are strangers. It becomes my duty to press further. You have enlightened me as to the stages of your journey, but I remain woefully ignorant of where it is destined to end."

"Here, General. These folks bear deeds to the land Señor Cirilio Medina, my employer, offered as grants and sold while he was up north. He hired me to bring them here, which I have done. As soon as I lead them to Señor Medina's *hacienda*, I will have earned the money he paid me."

"Ahhhhh. Señor Cirilio Medina." Cos sighed knowingly, rose, and walked away from his desk. The afternoon sunlight, streaming through the windows, glinted from the gold buttons and braid adorning his uniform. "Yes. A good man. And honest."

"I have always found him so, General," Jones said.

"Who? What?" True whispered.

"Shut up," Jones snapped under his breath. Something was wrong and he didn't need distractions. "We've got problems."

"What?"

"I don't know what yet. Shhh . . ."

His adjutant had anticipated the general's desire and opened the French doors. Cos strode through them onto the balcony overlooking the military plaza. Below him, to the obvious relief of the settlers—among whom he particularly noted a striking blond young woman standing next to what was probably the ugliest man he had ever seen—the wagons were being pulled out of a guarded compound. The first hint of the coming norther made Cos suck in his breath and feel profound gratitude for his woolen uniform. "Medina," he said, reentering the room. "Good, honest, and fool enough to prefer the deposed Bustamente over our new and glorious leader, Major General Antonio Lopez de Santa Anna, President of Mexico.''

"Oh, shit!" Jones muttered in English.

True felt the flesh crawl on the back of his neck.

Cos sat in the thronelike chair. The wood creaked despite his slender build. "Times change," he said matter of factly. "Titles change. Life is a river of unending progression, is it not?''

Jones's expression was one of humble perplexity. "The general will forgive me if I do not understand what this matter has to do with these innocent settlers who have entered Mexico in all good faith, and with no knowledge of either Bustamente or President Santa Anna.''

"Then I must make myself understood," Cos said with a deceptively pleasant smile. "The unfortunate Medina is no longer with us. His place and his lands have been given by General Santa Anna to Major Luther O'Shannon in recognition of his most important services during the unpleasant demise of our late president.''

"What in the *hell* is he talking about?" True asked, beside himself.

The general suffered the upstart young *norteamericano* a withering glance. "As a result," he went on coldly to Jones, "the matter must be discussed with Major O'Shannon. I will add, however, that the manner in which your party conducts itself during your visit to San Antonio de Bexar is and will be of extreme interest to me. You do understand that the preservation of peace and order in this province is my responsibility.''

"I can assure you, General Cos, that the folks I accompany are law-abiding people," Jones said, his tone a little too pleasant for True's liking. "With respect for your person and your title, they are grateful for your assistance, and will indeed present themselves to Señor O'Shannon at their, and his, earliest convenience. And now, with your kind permission? . . .''

"Of course, Señor Jones. Good day.''

They were dismissed. Jones grabbed True by the arm and propelled the volatile younger man out the door before giving him a quick, rough translation of what had happened.

"They can't do this to us!" True exploded as they made their way downstairs.

"They haven't done anything yet," the wagon train master

replied. "First thing to learn here, boy, is to leave while the military is still neutral. All Cos was saying is that we need to ride out to see this O'Shannon fella. If there's anybody to get riled at it's ol' Cirilio. I know he hated Santy Anna's guts, but to cut his own throat in the process was a damn fool thing to do. Hell, I credited him with more sense than that.''

A blast of arctic wind struck them as they emerged from the ornate front doors of the Military Governor's Palace. The norther was hitting, sending dust flying. Local merchants whose stalls lined the plaza scurried to put away their goods and head home. Women of dusky beauty carrying armloads of homespun goods cried out to their children to help them. Men clad in the blousy garments of *péons* staggered under loads of winter vegetables. Children, all agog at the black man and the strangely light-complected *norteamericanos*, laughed and ran about underfoot. Usually listless soldiers hurriedly led mules and horses to shelter or ran for their barracks to get heavy winter cloaks.

"Well, it's here,'' Jones yelled above the shrieking wind to the settlers who waited for him to guide them to a place where they could spend the night. "I'll tell you what's happening as soon as we get inside. Meanwhile, it's gonna get a lot colder, and fast. Follow me.''

The temperature plummeted sharply. Shortly after five, with the stock stabled and the exhausted settlers assigned rooms, everyone except the Thatches and Eustacia Matlan, who were still at the infirmary, gathered in the large main room of *La Casa del Rio* to hear Thaddeus Jones explain the changes that had taken place since his departure from San Antonio some four months earlier.

"It's gone,'' a stunned Nels said.

"We don't know that for sure,'' Jones pointed out, trying to ease the shock.

"We paid good money. All we had, mostly. And now you're saying the bastards stole it from us!'' Scott Campbell's voice shook and his face was bloodless. At his side, Joan wept silently.

Jack Kemper rose and his fist slammed down on the table. No one looked at him, but they all shared his anger. "I'm not going to let it happen,'' he said, his voice choked. "I say we ride out to this O'Shannon's place right now and find out what the hell's going on.''

"You're damned right!'' Scott chimed in, warming to

Kemper for the first time since they'd met. "Dennis, Mackenzie, you've been itching to use those guns. Well, now you can go get them."

"Now wait just a minute—" Jones began.

"Wait, hell!" Scott roared.

"Sit down and let the man talk," Hogjaw growled from the far end of the table.

"Who the hell's side are you on, anyway?" Kemper asked. "You're supposed to be looking out for those girls. Well, they're losing too, same as the rest of us. I say Campbell and I are right. We get our guns and *take* our land, if need be."

Dennis and Mackenzie pushed back from the table. "Anyone else joining us?" Dennis asked, looking pointedly from Joseph to True.

Elizabeth clutched True's hand so hard her knuckles were white. Lottie clung to Joseph's arm. True didn't move. "I'm for listening to Jones," he finally said. "He knows more about this than any of the rest of us. Joseph?"

Every head in the room swiveled to Joseph, who deferred to Hogjaw with a sullen nod. "I don't know who this O'Shannon is," Hogjaw said, his voice a low rumble, "but I do know this much. If he's here with Santy Anna's blessin', you can bet he ain't here alone. He'll have men. Fightin' men and plenty of 'em. Goin' after him would be like goin' after an old grizz with nothin' but a butter knife, which only a damn fool would do." No one dared interrupt him. "I fer one just spent fifty some years workin' hard at not bein' a damn fool. I ain't about to start now. And as fer land, I never yet met a dead man who gave a hoot about it one way or t'other."

" 'Nuff said?" Jones asked in the silence that followed. "Campbell? Kemper?"

Scott glared around the table, at last sighed in resignation, and waved his boys back to their seats. Jack Kemper, suddenly alone, followed reluctantly.

"Good," the wagon train master went on. "Now, tomorrow mornin' is soon enough for anything. Ain't nothin' gonna change before then, so there's no sense in goin' off halfcocked, which means we'll want to keep calm and do some plannin'."

There wasn't anything to plan, really. They did talk, though, and as Jones had hoped, they calmed down. Outside, night descended, the dark matching the settlers' moods. The howling wind stalked the streets and searched for crevices in the adobe. Numbing cold waited those who stepped outdoors. Slowly, the talk died. What should have been a joyous occasion for the newcomers had turned into one fraught with doubt and uncertainty. About the only thing good any of them could say about their arrival was that they were under a solid roof instead of camping out. Not even the Thatches found relief, for word had been sent from the infirmary that Mildred had not yet delivered. Isolated, nursing their fears, the original band sat around the main room of *La Casa* and stared at the walls and each other.

True, Joseph, and Hogjaw had fled the glum atmosphere. After all, they hadn't come to Texas to settle on land already bought. They had lost nothing but their option money, one hundred dollars. Their dreams had not been shattered. And yet, as they stood at the bar in a tiny *cantina* adjoining the lobby where a wizened, sour old man attended, a pall hung over them.

The *cantina* was well lit with coal oil lanterns. A half dozen Mexes, as Hogjaw called the native San Antonians, sat around a large round table and talked in low tones. A cracked mirror behind the bar doubled the shelves of cups, glasses, and variously labeled bottles of Scotch, rum, and whiskey. Hogjaw pointed to a clear bottle filled with a milky liquid and ordered for the three of them.

"If you don't mind," Joseph snapped, "I'll order for myself. Rum."

"The only thing that makes that stuff rum," Hogjaw countered, "is the tobacco juice added to it. Pepper and wood ashes turn the same thing into Scotch. And that one labeled 'Kantuky Sippin Whiskey' is more of the first with a little rattlesnake venom and black powder poured in."

The bartender poured their drinks. Joseph drank his first and pointed for another immediately, followed by a third. "Kind of bitter," he said. "What is it?"

"Mescal. The drink of the people. They make it from a cactus called *maguey*. Best take it easy, Joseph," Hogjaw warned. "It'll lay you out flat afore you know it."

A while later Joseph sipped his fourth and leaned forward on his elbows to stare at his reflection in the mirror while he tried to remember just exactly what had happened, what had brought him to bay, cornered him into marrying Lottie

Michaelson. There was nothing wrong with her physical attributes, of course. In fact, he couldn't remember when he had experienced such an insatiable and voracious creature. But marriage? That wasn't what he'd set out to do. Not by a long shot.

Entrapped, that's what he'd been. He carried a vivid memory of Lottie sobbing all that first day after her mother died, and then into the night as he held her. Somehow, he had felt sorry for her, he guessed, and he had asked her to marry him and she had accepted. Within seconds, she had changed from a weeping, lost girl to a vixen who covered him with heated kisses and, with her full, ripe thighs pulling him deep inside her, drove him wild with fierce, impassioned lovemaking. The Reverend Kania had married them the next night when they camped. It wasn't until two nights later, in the still hours of the morning as he stood watch over the sleeping wagons, that the full realization of what he had done hit him.

He was married, and marriage was not what he had set out to find. Lottie Michaelson was a peculiar sort of profit, one he could in no way honorably leave. At least there was the land, he had thought, and work enough to keep him occupied. And if the marriage became unbearable, he could always slip away with the knowledge that he hadn't left her destitute. A woman with over a full section of land and a working farm would always be able to attract someone to care for and protect her. His conscience would be clear.

And then came the unpleasant news of that afternoon, and with it the feeling that he was trapped for good with no escape possible. Joseph glared defiantly at Hogjaw, finished his fourth drink, and shakily poured himself a fifth.

The letdown of a journey ended, the cold, the disappointment, had all conspired to make him vulnerable, and the mescal was hitting him hard. Joseph didn't particularly care, though. Drunk was as good as anything else under the circumstances. A little giddy, he raised his cup to toast himself and then froze as the image of Elizabeth Michaelson glided past the door that led to the lobby. "Bitch!" he cursed, downing the drink and shoving away from the bar.

True and Hogjaw watched him weave through the tables on his way to the lobby. Worried, they exchanged glances, paid for the drinks, and left in time to see him catch up with Elizabeth at the front door of the inn.

"Where do you think you're going?" he asked her, catching her by one arm and spinning her around to face him.

Elizabeth grimaced with pain. "Let go of my arm," she hissed.

Joseph staggered backward, pulling her with him. "I asked you a question," he said, bracing himself against a chair.

"None of your business."

"That's right. None. Never anybody's business unless you make it so. You made it my business when you kicked Lottie out of her own wagon and made her ride with me. 'S'your fault. 'S'all your fault."

"I imagine you kept her happier than my drudgery ever could," Elizabeth said, trying to pry his hand loose.

Joseph shook her. "She's your sister, goddamnit. Yours."

"Her name is Lottie Paxton."

"Her name is Lottie Paxton," Joseph mimicked in a drunken falsetto. "Well, who made you queen? Who gave you the right to judge anybody? You hated her from the moment we took up together, and I know why."

"You're hurting me," Elizabeth said between her teeth.

"Because she was getting something you've never had, that's why!"

"Let her go, Joseph," True said, coming up behind him.

Elizabeth looked past Joseph to True. "I'll be all right," she said quickly, seeing the murderous look in True's eyes.

True's hand snaked out and caught Joseph's wrist. "I said, let her go!"

Joseph released Elizabeth's arm and, whirling, slapped True's hand away. "Are you taking her side again?"

"Against a man twice her size?" True asked, keeping Joseph's attention diverted while Elizabeth slipped out the door. "You're damned right."

"Oh, yeah?" Joseph mumbled. "Well . . ." His face suddenly turned pale. "I don't . . . I don't . . . feel so . . . good," he stammered, and crumpled to the floor before True could catch him.

"I'll carry him up to his lady fair," Hogjaw said to True. "You follow Elizabeth. With soldiers thicker than maggots on ripe meat, she might just find more trouble she can't handle."

Elizabeth had been wearing a shawl, but that would offer precious little protection against the cold. True nodded gratefully to Hogjaw, stepped over Joseph, and hurriedly grabbed a pair of coats from the rack by the door. Outside the front had passed, leaving the sky clear. The wind was even fiercer, and cut through True's shirt like a knife. Few of the adobe buildings had windows and there were no streetlights, but a half-moon and all God's stars, bright in the snapping cold, lit the streets. True caught a glimpse of movement ahead of him and ran across the plaza to the *Calle de Calabozo*, whose ominous translation was Street of Dungeons, which in a sense was true if one headed west to the army barracks and the prison beneath the Military Governor's Palace. At the corner, he turned and headed east, relieved to see her ahead of him. Quickening his steps, he soon drew abreast of her. "You'll catch pneumonia if you stay out too long, you know. I'm sorry about Joseph."

"I have my shawl," Elizabeth said curtly, hiding the relief she felt in learning that the steps she had heard pursuing her had been his.

A strong gust of wind whipped around a corner and pushed her against him. True draped the extra coat around her and led her into the shadowed doorway of a *hacienda* where the wind couldn't reach them. "You're being silly, you know."

"He was terrible," Elizabeth sobbed. "And after . . . everything that's happened today . . ."

"Shhh. It's over with," True crooned, stroking her hair. "He won't try that again, I promise. You'll see. . . ."

The taste of her on his lips was almost more than he could bear. Elizabeth tried at first to resist his kiss but then, her knees as weak as her resolve, she wrapped her arms around him and hungrily pressed her body to his. She had been so alone. So many lonely weeks. And he had always been near. To help at the crossings, at camp. Never demanding, always giving. "True, True," she whispered. "I'm glad you followed me. I wanted you to follow me."

"And catch you?"

"And catch me." Her hands reached up to take his face. "The land doesn't matter," she whispered huskily. "It does, but not really. Not if you catch me."

"You mean that?" True asked, incredulous. "You really mean that?"

Elizabeth cocked her head to one side and looked up at him. "Of course. Isn't that what you wanted?"

"Lady, lady!" True yelled, vying with the wind. He caught

her in a bear hug and, lifting her off her feet, whirled her around. "You just try me again and see!"

Laughing, dizzy, Elizabeth ducked out of his embrace and darted out into the street.

"Watch out!"

"*Cuídase!*"

Both warnings came at once. Startled, Elizabeth stopped dead as a powerful ivory white stallion all but reared out of the ground in front of her. The stallion pawed the air and rolled its eyes, almost fell over backward, but finally got all four feet safely back to earth. Its rider, a young man dressed all in black and silver, quickly regained control and, unable to hide his surprise, stared down at Elizabeth.

Elizabeth regained her balance and tried to walk around him, but the rider backed his stallion to cut her off. She tried to go forward and again, his eyes glinting with intrigue, he blocked her path. "*Buenos noches, señorita. Lo siento mucho, pero . . .*" He stopped as True emerged from the shadows and took Elizabeth's arm. "Ah! *Gringos!*" His eyes bore into True's. "You will wait one little moment until I finish my business, no?"

"No," True started to say, but then froze as four more mounted *vaqueros* appeared out of the shadows across the street. One of the men led an attractive, middle-aged Mexican woman, the other three pointedly blocked the path back to the inn. Alert and poised, True stepped between them and Elizabeth. "Just what the hell is going on here?" he asked.

The young man on the horse ignored him. "*Vente,*" he said brusquely. The woman obediently ran to him. "You see," he said to True as the woman held up bound wrists, "I left her some semblance of honor." In the same instant, a stiletto flashed in the moonlight and the ropes holding the woman's wrists fell to the ground. No sooner was she free than he wheeled his horse and rode across the street to face a storekeeper's house.

"Miguel. Miguel Hernandez!"

A man of about fifty years with a lined and weary face appeared at the window.

"You have bragged that if you ever caught me with your señora you would thrash me and send me crying to my father," he said, reverting to Spanish. "Well, here I am, and here is your señora. She has spent the day with me." He grabbed the woman as she stumbled past him and lifted her so that he might kiss her. When he dropped her, one hand clung to her blouse and ripped it open. "Look. The wind is cold, but sweat still clings to her breasts!" So saying, he reached into a pouch at his side and removed a gold coin that he threw against the door of the shop. The giggling woman staggered to the door, picked up the coin, and turned toward the young man and his companions. Pleased with herself, she bit the coin and then, with a look of sly pleasure, reached underneath her dress. The *vaqueros* cheered when she brought her hand out empty, waved triumphantly to them, and disappeared inside the house.

The little drama was finished. With good-natured shouts, the four *vaqueros* rode off, leaving the young man on the white stallion alone. Slowly, he walked his horse across the street, stopped a few short paces in front of Elizabeth and True. His belt buckle flashed silver in the moonlight. The buttons on his waist-length jacket were silver, as were the wide shiny spurs on his high boots. He doffed a flat-brimmed black hat and made a sweeping bow. "This is a land where golded-haired women are rare indeed. You are beautiful, señorita. My compliments." His smile faded, to be replaced with a frown. "You," he said, pointing at True, "will leave now."

True smiled, stepped away from Elizabeth. "Why don't you try shoving one of those shiny gold coins up your ass?" he asked matter-of-factly.

The young man's face contorted in fury. He raked his spurs against the stallion's flanks, streaking the white flesh with crimson. The animal lunged at True. Elizabeth screamed. True dove to one side, barely averted being trampled, hit the ground rolling and sprang to his feet, his Arkansas Toothpick flashing in the cold air. The young man wheeled his stallion and once again charged. True feinted to his left and ducked to his right, at the same time slashing upward to sever the reins where they joined the bit. Following through, he slapped the flat of the blade across the animal's rump as horse and rider shot past.

"Hey!" the rider shouted, almost falling as the reins hung uselessly in his hands, and then grabbing madly for the stallion's mane when the animal swerved and galloped out of control. Within seconds, horse and rider had disappeared down the wide street. The young man's curses lingered, and then faded in the relentless wind.

True watched for a moment before he turned. Elizabeth

was staring at him. He shrugged as if nothing important had happened and, with a smug smile, returned the knife to its sheath. "About ready to head back?" he asked.

"Yes." She took his arm and clung to him. "I wonder who he was?"

"Dunno."

There had been emergencies on the trail, but she had never seem him move with such fluid grace and a precision that was almost frightening. Dodging, side-stepping, rising, pivoting, he had looked more like a dancer than a man in a fight for his life. And he loved her. Loved her. Had said so himself. Suddenly, Elizabeth realized that she loved him too, and had for some time even if she had been too stubborn to admit it. Just as suddenly, she realized that the young man on the white stallion would not let matters rest as they were, and that True had made a dangerous enemy. "He will hate you," she said, frightened. "He is dangerous."

True inhaled deeply, felt the cold, clear air clean in his lungs. His mind raced a million miles ahead of his body. He could feel the blood coursing through him, was so intensely aware of the moment that he was sure he had never truly been alive before. Danger and hate were little more than feeble jokes. He could do anything because the grandest prize of all walked at his side, and loved him. And feared for him, too, which wouldn't do. Not for anything did he want her to be frightened. The characteristic Paxton grin, impish and irrepressible, lit his face as he looked down at her. "Oh?" he asked. "Do you think it was something I said?"

Chapter XVIII

Monday morning dawned bright and clear as a dazzling sun rose to set afire the frost that whitened the land. The wind had died during the night and the smoke that rose from each house ascended in straight lines like slender trunks that expanded into short-lived, puffy crowns before dissipating. Those San Antonians who lived in adobe buildings were still warm, for the thick walls of their homes had resisted the wind and still retained some heat. The poorer, *peónes* of mixed race for the most part, suffered in drafty *jacalitos*, poorly constructed thatched hovels of vertical sticks crudely chinked with mud.

Inside *La Casa del Rio*, the large common room was warm and cozy. One by one, the would-be settlers, still bleary-eyed from their first night's sleep in real beds but unable to resist the mouth-watering aroma of puffed and golden biscuits, staggered downstairs to be greeted by the sight of plates heaped with crisp bacon and fresh-fried eggs. True had passed an uneasy night. At first, returning to his room, he had been unable to sleep through sheer jubilation. Joy had given way to worry, though, and when he did finally drop off, he was plagued with dreams of lost land and a newfound enemy. "Cold up there," he grumbled, planting himself in front of the fire.

Mama Flores, proprietor of *La Casa*, all skirts and busy hands and smiles, bustled by. "You'll see. It is the way here. Winter one day, summer the next. Summer never leaves San Antonio de Bexar for very long. We say the sun sleeps here. Carlotta! *Café para el señor, por favor. Inmediatamente!*"

"Me too," Hogjaw growled from a chair next to the hearth. True had thought that the mountain man was asleep, but he had been awake the better part of an hour, and simply too comfortable to move.

171

"La cara, también," Mama Flores added, hurrying off to the other side of the room.

"What's *la cara?"* True asked.

Hogjaw glanced up at him from heavy eyebrows. "The face," he finally said. "She thinks it's funny. I don't."

True knew when to take a hint, yawned widely in order not to laugh, and accepted a mug of steaming black coffee from a doe-eyed girl who twisted away from him with a flourish of her long skirt and a none too subtle wiggle of her hips. "Carlotta!" Mama Flores scolded from all the way across the room. The girl giggled and, flashing a backward smile at True, hurried into the kitchen.

"She likes you," Hogjaw drawled, blowing on his coffee.

"She likes all handsome young *caballeros,"* Mama Flores said, stopping in front of True and planting her fists on her hips. "Her husband does not so much, *comprende?"*

"Good coffee," True said, rapidly changing the subject.

The room was coming alive. The girls returned carrying plates of bacon and eggs. A half dozen single men had entered from the street, and three or four other guests had made their way downstairs. Hogjaw unfolded from the depths of the chair and sauntered over to the table with the largest platter of biscuits. Without waiting for anyone else, he dragged the platter, a plate of butter, and a bowl of honey in front of him and began to eat, shoving half a biscuit in his mouth at a time.

The Campbells came down next and took a small table for themselves. The Kempers followed right on their heels and, unwilling to sit with any of the locals, took a place at the main table but as far from Hogjaw as possible. Joseph and the Matlans came down together. The Matlans joined Hogjaw, but Joseph filled two plates and started upstairs again, only to meet Elizabeth halfway up. True watched, waiting for a confrontation, but the two only glanced at each other and passed without words. Relieved, True crossed the room to meet Elizabeth at the bottom of the stairs. "Sleep well?" he asked, escorting her to a place on the bench next to Hogjaw.

"I think so. My back is sore, though."

"From sleeping in a bed," Hogjaw said, filling his plate with bacon and eggs. "Ground's better for you."

"For you, maybe," Elizabeth said. She sniffed the air and looked around the table. "I'm famished. Would someone please pass something. Anything? And is that coffee?"

She and True served themselves and dug in. As if by mutual consent, no one spoke about the events of the day before and the impending loss of their land. They would have to speak about it soon enough in any event, and there seemed little point in broaching the subject any earlier than necessary. The first platters of food had been emptied and replaced with full ones when the front door opened to let Thaddeus Jones in. *"Cierra la puerta!"* Mama Flores shouted immediately above the clank of silver and plates.

"Yes, ma'am," Jones called jovially, hurriedly closing the door as ordered and cutting off the cold draft. The wagon train master shed coat and hat and, wiping his hands on his smooth, worn buckskin shirt, called for a plate and cup. "Smells good," he said, sitting across from Hogjaw. Carlotta placed utensils in front of him and he set to with a will, filling coffee cup first and then transferring most of the contents of the platter of eggs and bacon onto his plate.

Leakey glowered at him, then quickly snared the last two eggs and pieces of bacon while he had the chance. "How's the little gal?" he asked.

Jones swallowed, took another bite, and spoke around it. "I've just come from the Padre's. Seems like last night was nothing but a warning. Anytime, now, it appears, from the way Miz Kania talked. Them nuns is takin' good care of Miz Thatche."

"How's Kevin?" Elizabeth asked.

"Don't worry about him. Padre Salva's the Lord's man, right enough, but he's a practical one as well. He put the lad to sleep last night with a half bottle of Holy wine, and has him started on the other half already this morning. Kevin ain't worried at all."

"Powerful stuff, the Lord's brew," Hogjaw said, snagging the last biscuit from under Jones's outstretched hand.

The atmosphere had changed with Jones's entrance. What joviality and light remarks that followed were forced and carried with them an impatience to get on with business. No one wanted to talk in front of strangers, however, so it wasn't until a half hour later, when the last of the locals left, that Jones rose and cleared his throat. An immediate hush fell over the room.

"Well, I guess it's time. We can't sit around and pretend forever. Some of us are gonna have to ride out to O'Shannon's and hear what the major has to say."

Scott Campbell rose and walked over to Jones's table. "I'll go," he said. "So will my sons."

"You are fine, but—no offense, Mr. Campbell—your lads have a touch of the temper about them. I think this will be an exercise in gathering your cards and playing them one by one rather than grabbing the whole deck and tossin' it high."

"I'll go too," Nels Matlan said. "What about Thatche and Kania?"

"I already talked to them," Jones said. "Neither will be going. They've left it in your hands."

"I'll ride with you," Jack Kemper chimed in. "And the sooner we leave, the better. I'd prefer to see my land before another sun sets."

"Not many anxious men in Texas," Hogjaw muttered, sopping his plate dry with a fragment of biscuit. All eyes turned to him as he dropped the morsel into his mouth and licked his fingers. "They don't last. Sooner or later they stick a leg in a rattler's mouth or walk into a Comanche lance or drop their trousers and wind up shittin' in their long johns."

Kemper slammed his fist on the table. "See here! You have the manners of your namesake. A hog! There are ladies at this table!"

Hogjaw dutifully removed his coonskin cap. "Pardon," he said, taking in each of the women with a glance before turning back to Kemper. His eyes shone with murderous intent. "Then too, sometimes an anxious man is liable to let his mouth write a draught his fists can't collect."

Kemper paled and quickly sat down.

"I'll go too," True said, hastily breaking the awkward silence that followed.

"You don't own land," Campbell snapped.

"My brothers and I own an option on one half of two thousand hectares," True countered. "Right?" he asked Elizabeth.

"Yes. Which my sister and I intend to honor. Furthermore, I intend to represent my own claim."

"A woman?" Jones asked, scratching his head. "No offense, miss, but I'm not sure how that'll sit."

Elizabeth's eyes flashed as she stood. "I have a voice, Mr. Jones. I exercise command of the English language. My father bought that land. The deed is in the Michaelson name. I am a Michaelson and I intend to petition for what is rightfully mine."

"Why can't I ever talk you out of anything?" Jones said ruefully. "Very well. No need to add to the group, unless someone else wants to get frostbit. Any questions?" He paused, looked around the room. "We leave in an hour, then. Gentlemen, you'd better see to your horses. Mama Flores has a carriage you can use, miss. I reckon one of us can drive for you."

"And I reckon," Elizabeth said with heavy sarcasm, "that I've just driven a mule team from Natchez to San Antonio. I think I'm quite capable of driving myself, thank you."

"Yes, ma'am, I suppose you are," Jones said, capitulating. "You go on and get ready. I'll have it out front for you. Well? What's holdin' everybody up?"

Everyone scrambled for the door at once, leaving Jones and Hogjaw alone. "Well?" Hogjaw asked. "What's eatin' you?"

"What'd you think?" Jones snapped. "Go out there cartin' a woman along on men's business. Goddamn, but that woman's hardheaded. Don't she ever let up?"

"Nope," Hogjaw chuckled. "She's a filly that ain't gonna let herself be broke without a fight. That's one thing I'll say for True."

"Oh? What?"

"She's the only kind worth havin'." Hogjaw uncoiled from the bench, jammed on his hat, and turned in the open front door. "You wait and see, Blackie. They're gonna make one hell of a pair. One *hell* of a pair."

For Luther O'Shannon, a day beginning the same as the day before and the day before that was cause for pleasure. Monotony, especially the monotony of place, was a condition to be relished. He had served Santa Anna well. This northern province of Mexico was just unsettled enough that he could find good reasons to justify his remaining there. He had land, title, position, wealth, and power. He had peace, with the promise of action.

"Luther O'Shannon," he said aloud, staring at the whitewashed adobe and the dark, heavy beams that crisscrossed the ceiling overhead, "you've finally backed the right man. Took the right job at the right time, you did, and it's rosy days ahead."

The dark-haired figure next to him in the great bed yawned and snuggled up against him. "What are you talking about?" she asked in Spanish.

"About things that don't concern you."

"You promised to speak Spanish."

"Only when you please me."

"Oh? Like this?" She reached beneath the sheet and stroked his hard belly and then, giggling, let her hand slide down to tug gently at him.

O'Shannon laughed deep in his throat and, gripping the woman's hair, yanked her head back against the pillow and parted her lips with a bruising kiss. He kissed her ear, ran his tongue down the side of her neck and nuzzled her throat until she purred happily. When her back arched with desire, he cupped one of her breasts, blew softly on the nipple until it swelled and hardened, and then suddenly bit into the dusky flesh. Lucita howled in pain. O'Shannon flipped her over, gave her naked buttocks a resounding smack, and rolled out of bed.

The mirror was kind to him, and he stared at himself with the practiced eye of a man given to self-love. Recognizing the vice, he reveled in it and faulted himself not one iota. At fifty, he had the hard supple body of a man twenty years younger. His pectorals were firm, and when he pressed his upper arms against his sides and tensed, they bulged satisfyingly. His forearms were still hard and strong, his biceps like rocks, and the skin under his triceps taut and firm. He placed a hand on the flat of his belly and rubbed in a small circle, adding pressure and then pinching to see if any fat had accumulated. The belly was always the first to go. Fat there was a harbinger of worse to come. He noted a little give, but not enough to worry about. Not bad at all, he thought, for one who lived so well. Only the deep lines around his eyes, the flecks of brilliant white in his deep black hair and sideburns, gave away his age. O'Shannon did not complain. Women liked a mature man. He was more than happy to make himself available, especially if they were young and fiery.

Which reminded him. O'Shannon stepped sideways and glanced at his wife's reflection in the mirror. She was rubbing her wounded breast and glaring at him. When she noticed him watching her, she quickly replaced her frown with a manufactured winsome smile, climbed out of the bed, and followed him as he walked to the window. "You hurt me," she said petulantly. "Why do you have to be so hateful?"

"Don't be a fool," O'Shannon said, opening the window onto the courtyard. "You know you love it."

The house was a hollowed-out two-story square with bedrooms, study, library, sitting rooms, and dining room all facing the courtyard. O'Shannon stared down through the wrought-iron grillwork. The courtyard, awash in the summer with brightly hued flowers, was bleak and bristling now with dusty green gray cacti. Birds nested there, though, finding protection among the thorny branches. Their songs taunted winter when other parts of the countryside loomed gloomy, cold, and silent.

A musky warmth emanated from Lucita. His bite forgotten, she ran her hand along his flank, felt the muscles quiver beneath her touch. At sixteen, Lucita was as adept at arousing a man as was her mother, an exotic courtesan who had long been a favorite among the politicos in Mexico City. O'Shannon had taken a fancy to Lucita during a drunken orgy after Santa Anna's takeover and had married her as a favor to the new president, who owed her mother a favor in return for certain crucial information regarding Bustamente before his fall. O'Shannon hadn't really minded. Lucita represented a pleasant interlude. By the time he tired of her and took a fifth wife, Santa Anna would have forgotten all about her. So would O'Shannon, for that matter. The only wife he wanted to remember was his first, a Spanish *contessa* who had borne him a son. She alone burned in his memory, and could never be replaced.

Lucita's fondling had had the desired effect. "I do not love being hurt," she said, seizing his erection. She cupped his testicles and began to apply pressure. "Maybe I should hurt you now, no?"

"Don't bother me. It is morning and I wish to be alone," O'Shannon snapped, more concerned with the weather than with his wife. It was cold out, probably below freezing, and he would have to exercise indoors unless he wished to risk pneumonia. "See to my breakfast, and tell Emiliano we will be using the ballroom this morning. He will need to move the mats from the roof soon so they can warm up."

He was ignoring the pain she was causing, as he always did. There were limits, though, and Lucita knew that when she reached them he would strike without warning. Apprehensive, she let her husband go and peevishly turned her back on him. "That is maid's work. Always you tell me to see to breakfast. I am the mistress of this house. Let the—"

"You are boring me, Lucita," O'Shannon said, cutting her off with a peremptory wave of his hand.

"And you are treating me like a servant. I will not be ordered about like a common kitchen maid." Lucita tossed her head. Her long black hair whipped about her naked shoulders. "Be careful, husband. Do not forget. My mother has the ear of Santa Anna."

O'Shannon laughed derisively. "More than his ear, unless I miss my guess."

"Such talk!" Lucita said, feigning shock. "The president has given you much, and you ridicule him."

O'Shannon slammed the window shut. "He has given me nothing I did not earn. Don't forget, love, it was I who fashioned his army into a fighting unit to rival Napoleon's best. It was I who was responsible for ousting Bustamente and placing Santa Anna in the president's palace."

Her attack thwarted, Lucita pouted, sidled up to him and rubbed her breast against his chest. "You do not love me."

"I never said I did." O'Shannon felt himself rising in her hand. "But what do you care, little one? I have given you title and nobility, money, and a fine *hacienda*. I have given you pleasure, and when that wasn't enough, a virile stepson to rut with as you choose."

Lucita's fingers clawed and she struck at his face. "Bastard!"

O'Shannon caught her wrist and twisted until she gasped with pain, then scooped her up and threw her onto the bed.

"I never—" she spat, trying to free her imprisoned wrists.

"Of course it's true. I do not mind, little one. You are a most desirable piece of flesh. I would have done the same thing were I in his place."

"He took me by force. He violated me."

"Nobody violates a whore."

"You would excuse him even if he were the Devil!"

Taunts, complaints, demands, even insolence, were permissible. As a matter of principal, though, O'Shannon did not allow anyone to cast aspersions on Ramez, his son. Viciously, he grabbed a handful of Lucita's long, black hair and jerked her head sideways. "He is my son," he whispered venomously. "My only son. A man loves his only son. If you are so unlucky as to bear a child by me, I will forget him as I have all my other bastard children who roam the world. Do you understand me?"

"Let me go!" Lucita hissed. "I hate you. Let me go!"

O'Shannon rolled her onto her stomach and lifted her hips. Lucita tried to fight him, then screeched with pain as his fingers dug into her and he entered her from behind, driving with deep savage thrusts that left her clawing at the bedsheets and cursing him through clenched teeth. When he finished, his seed spent and his phallus limp, he eased back on his haunches and shoved her away from him.

"I was wrong," Lucita whimpered into a pillow. "Ramez is not the Devil. You are."

Chapter XIX

Impatient, True had decided to ride ahead, and now waited on the bluffs south of town where the road forked, the right hand disappearing to the southwest as it stretched toward Laredo, the left to a narrower, less worn trail leading directly south toward O'Shannon's. There was little wind and the air was crackling cold in the bright sunlight that rapidly melted the frost from the boulders strewn about him. True breathed deeply and drank in the land. It would take over six weeks to travel from the Sabine River crossing to San Antonio; as much, Jones had said, to El Paso. From verdant, almost tropical forest to arid, empty desert. Rolling hills, plains as flat as the palm of his hand, and even, out of sight to the west, untamed mountains. Breathtakingly vast, it was a land that inspired superlatives and wild flights of imagination that transcended hardship and danger. As ominous as yesterday's news had been, True refused to believe the men and women he had come to know so well over the past weeks would be denied their stake in that land. There was so much of it available, and all that space was so empty, compared to the East, that they could surely work out a compromise. What the settlers ended up with might not be the paradise they had expected, but it would be a start.

The cold bored through his coat. True dug his hands deeper into his pockets and glanced back toward town where he could distinguish three horsemen and a carriage proceeding along the *Camino Real a Laredo*, the Royal Road to Laredo. Plumes of coffee-colored dust drifted away from the horses' hooves and the churning wheels of the carriage. Firetail whinnied and pawed the ground. "Easy," True said, his voice soft and calming. "Easy, boy. They'll be here soon enough."

He could feel the tension already. The settlers had ridden

too far and had gone through too much to have their dream destroyed. Campbell with his wife and sons and daughters, all ready to build. Kemper driven by his unspoken desires. Elizabeth, fighting every inch of the way, burying her father and mother, and still indomitable. Elizabeth with the golden hair and soft lips, whose sweet spirit filled the hours of his days and nights with fantasies both desirable and frightening. If anything happened to her . . .

Was that what being in love was like? It was certainly not what he had expected. But then, he had not foreseen heading West either, hadn't pictured himself as one apt to act precipitately. He rocked forward slightly, and leaned back to feel the gold amulet touch his chest. More than he knew, perhaps, he was his mother's son and acted, like her, according to dictates that defied rational thought. Adriana was a creature of the elements. She listened when they whispered to her of what must be. She had tried to teach her sons to listen, too. Listen to the murmur of the earth. Listen to the secrets of the wind. Listen to the merry music of streams and the solemn, ponderous musings of frozen rivers and ice-hung branches. Adriana was a God-fearing woman but did not seek the divine beneath lofty spires or in the shadows of hand-wrought artifacts that man, throughout history, had pummeled and shaped and fired in the vain hope of achieving perfection. She found God in the unhindered progress of the seasons, in the whispered poetry of the stars. She found God in the act of growing older and sensing the grace of wisdom, and in their opposites, eternal youth and unabashed passion. All his knowing days True had wanted to be like her, for to be like her was to be free, truly free and blessed with life. Now, watching Elizabeth approach, he was suddenly aware that the years had not been wasted, that the lessons taught him by his mother and complemented by his father and Hogjaw, were not in vain. Everything he needed was inside him. All he had lacked was love, and that he had found. Elizabeth Michaelson completed him. With her at his side, nothing was impossible.

True had dismounted and was stomping his feet to start the circulation in them when he heard the horses. Moments later, they appeared around a bend and drew up beside him. "It's a lonely land," Jones said, looking around at the wilderness that made San Antonio appear to be an island set down in an uncharted sea.

"Makes a man want to run to his mother," Scott added, agreeing with the black man.

"That it does, bucko. In this land, an extry powder horn and sack of balls is worth all the mothers in creation, though. The Comanch' has little respect for motherhood."

"I still don't see what the fuss is about," Kemper said scornfully. "You've gone on and on about Comanches, and I've yet to see a single one of them."

A yellow-toothed smile spread across Jones's face, as if he knew something Jack Kemper didn't know, or that he might find out too late. "You'd best keep an eye peeled nonetheless. Most folks around here count heavy on seein' 'em—seein' 'em *first*, that is. Man has a tendency to live a little longer that way."

"Mr. Jones," Elizabeth broke in, "are you leading us to O'Shannon's, or do you intend for us to split up and whoever finds it first signal the others?"

"Gettin' a mite touchy, Miss Michaelson?"

"It's a woman's prerogative, Mr. Jones."

"Seems like I've heard of them." Jones chuckled. "Prerogatives, that is. Well, there's our trail," he added, pointing south. "You can lead the way if you want."

"Mind if I ride with you?" True asked.

Elizabeth's smile was both honey-sweet and tinged with daring. "If you can catch me," she said, tapping the mare with the tip of her whip.

The animal bounded forward. "Hey!" True yelped, leaping away barely in time to save his toes.

"She's got the temperament of a MacGregor I once knew," Scott said.

"Women," Jones concurred, the tone of his voice summing up his opinion of the fairer sex.

True swung aboard Firetail and started off after the carriage. "Catch Firetail for me in a minute, will you?" he asked Jones as the hammerhead stallion raced past the wagon train master's gray.

Outrunning a carriage was an easy task for the roan. Elizabeth looked back, saw him closing the gap, and vigorously applied the whip to the mare, who tried her best but was quickly overtaken. "What are you doing?" Elizabeth screamed as True guided Firetail alongside her.

Instead of answering, True swung his right leg over the

horse as if dismounting, held his weight with his hands on the
saddle, and placed his right foot in the left stirrup.

"You're crazy!" Elizabeth yelled. Her knuckles were
bloodless as she clutched the reins, and her head jerked back
and forth as she looked from True to the trail ahead and back.
"Don't do it! I'll stop!"

The carriage rocked as it hit a stone. Firetail's pace didn't
vary. As calmly as if he were stepping off a porch, True
pulled his right foot out of the stirrup, pushed away from
Firetail, and landed beside Elizabeth, jolting her to one side.

The carriage rocked precariously. Elizabeth's face was as
white as a sheet. True clasped his hands behind his head and
propped his legs on the edge of the footrest. "You're crazy!"
Elizabeth shouted angrily.

"A man's prerogative," True replied. "Besides, there's
something I wanted to tell you."

"You're totally mad!"

"Nope. Not that. Slow down and I'll tell you."

Elizabeth pulled gently on the reins and gradually slowed
the mare to a trot. "What then?" she asked, still angry.

True leaned toward her to speak directly into her ear. "You
sure are pretty this morning."

"What?" Elizabeth asked, astounded. "You . . . you risked
. . . You mean you . . . Oh!"

"It seemed important at the time. Here." He reached over
and put his hands over hers on the reins. "Let me drive."

Meekly, Elizabeth let go and took his arm in hers. "True?"
she said.

"Mmm?"

"Don't do things like that again. Please?"

True smiled, braced his thigh against hers, and clucked to
the mare. "Wouldn't want you to think I didn't care."

"I don't think that, True." Her voice was low and rich and
she held tightly onto his arm. "I haven't thought that for a
long, long time."

Sometime around noon, nine men came riding up the gentle slope overlooking what formerly had been the Medina
ranch. Stables, outbuildings for storage and cooking, and
housing for the *vaqueros* formed orderly extensions radiating
from the central *hacienda*, the two-story brick and adobe
edifice that looked more like a fortress than a home. The
closer the riders came, the more they looked like soldiers.

Disconcerted, True noted their leader wore a flowing black cape over a black suit trimmed with silver, and rode a white stallion. The column of eight men who followed him were dressed identically in blue greatcoats trimmed with scarlet stitchery and carried twelve-foot-long lances with slim, lethal-looking iron points. True glanced down at his own homemade linsey woolsey shirt and pants, his bulky coat sewn from a green plaid wool blanket. He had given little thought to fine clothes while westering, and though he had brought a suit with him, it was tightly rolled and packed in a saddlebag back at the inn.

The settlers reined in their horses and waited a few yards down the slope while the riders from the *hacienda* approached and, at a command from their leader, fanned out in a semicircle. "I am Ramez O'Shannon," the leader announced, walking his horse closer. "General Cos informed us of your impending arrival and your wish to speak to my father, who awaits you at . . ."

Recognizing True and Elizabeth, he stopped in midsentence and stared at them. When he resumed, his voice was tight with anger, reflecting the hatred in his eyes. "You are on O'Shannon land. Our holdings are not generally open to strangers. However—" He flashed a smile at Elizabeth, who remained impassive. "—exceptions can always be made in the case of a beautiful señorita." He glanced briefly at Campbell, Kemper, and Jones, returned to Elizabeth bowed with a flourish of his hat. "You are welcome, gentlemen. For a short while. And now, if you would be so kind as to . . ."

Firetail interrupted him with a scream of fury as he plunged and yanked at the rope tethering him to the carriage. The white stallion whinnied a return challenge and fought against his master's firm control. "What is that?" Ramez asked archly, pointing at Firetail.

"What?" True asked, feigning innocence and looking around. "Oh, that. A horse," he said, as if explaining the obvious to a child. "His name is Firetail."

Ramez laughed. "A horse, eh? Maybe, *gringo*, his mother was frightened by a burro and this is why he is so ugly."

Jones edged his gray closer to the carriage and tried to signal True to shut up, but to no avail. "Where I come from," True drawled, "looks aren't the first thing we value in an animal."

"And what is, *Señor Gringo?*"

"Speed, to begin with, and then control." He smiled grimly. "We train them to obey so we can still handle them in case something happens to the reins."

The merriment left Ramez's face. His mouth turned down in a scowl. "What is your name, *gringo?*"

"Paxton. True Paxton."

"Paxton," Ramez repeated, as if skewering the name on the point of a lance. "There is that which we must settle one day, Señor Paxton. Perhaps soon." He bowed once again to Elizabeth. "My padon, lady, for this unseemly behavior in your presence. Such matters are better considered in private. And now—" He raised his hand, turned, and spoke rapidly in Spanish to his men, who broke into two groups of four to let the settlers pass. "—if you will all follow me, please."

The small procession, followed by the newly-formed semicircle of *vaqueros,* rode down the hill toward the *hacienda.* "What the hell was that all about?" a worried Jones asked.

True related the story of the confrontation the night before, finishing with, "If I'd known who he was, I wouldn't have come along today."

"You didn't have to antagonize him all over again," Elizabeth hissed, flashing a conciliatory smile at Ramez when he turned to see what they were talking about.

"I didn't try to," True said glumly. "It just came out that way."

Jones told Campbell and Kemper what had happened, and turned back to True. "Nobody's blamin' you, True boy. You done what you had to, but see if you can try to keep your mouth shut from now on. You're in a tight spot as it is, without makin' things worse."

Seen up close, the *hacienda* was even more impressive. Newly whitewashed adobe walls reflected the sunlight. Fired tile in bright colors had been inlaid over the doors and windows. The roof was covered with alternating red and green tiles, a splash of color that dominated the countryside. A great iron gate set in the surrounding wall swung open magically at their approach, then closed behind them as they entered the enclosed compound.

"Place hasn't changed much," Jones observed, rubbing the back of his neck. "That's what I like about Mexico. Nothing changes much. Not the land, not the people."

"Would you mind telling me, then," Kemper sniffed,

"why we are going to see a man named O'Shannon instead of Medina?"

"Well," Jones amended lamely, "it *looks* the same. You can come back to a place a year later or twenty years later and nothin's very different."

"Sounds awful," Kemper said.

"Comforting in a way," Scott Campbell suggested.

"If I'd wanted permanence, I would have spent the rest of my life in Philadelphia."

The younger O'Shannon had halted outside an intricately fashioned iron grill that protected the recessed main entry to the *hacienda*. "Your horses will be cared for," he announced, dismounting and moving to Elizabeth's side of the carriage to offer her his hand.

Servants appeared to lead the horses away. Another, an old lady, emerged from the *hacienda* and opened the grill. Afoot, Ramez proved to be several inches shorter than True, a difference for which he compensated by strutting like a boy prince as he took Elizabeth's arm and led the way up the steps. "At the risk of being brash, may I inquire your name, señorita?" he asked.

"Elizabeth Michaelson," Elizabeth answered, sensing True move closer to her.

"A beautiful name for a beautiful lady. You must be my guest here sometime soon. We are relatively new to these parts, and my father loves to entertain. Your presence would brighten our house, and help us forget our isolation." He tossed his cloak to a servant and beamed at Elizabeth. "May I assist you with your wrap?"

True snorted in disgust. Jones nudged him with an elbow. Elizabeth wondered if True really thought she was so stupid that she didn't see through Ramez, especially after his exhibition in the street the night before, and smiled reassuringly at him when Ramez was behind her and couldn't see her face. Somewhere off to their left, what sounded like a sword fight was in progress, and the clash of steel against steel rang through the sparsely appointed foyer. "My father at exercise," Ramez explained as he waited for the men to take off their coats and hang them on the rack. "If you'll come with me, then. I'm sure he won't mind being interrupted."

The rooms were spacious and appointed with dark furniture that contrasted sharply with the thick wool rugs that had been spread for the winter across the cold tile flooring. Sunlight poured through windows with real glass, more glass than the settlers had seen in one place since they had embarked on the riverboat that took them down the Mississippi. Servants, mostly young girls, could be seen peeking around doorways and bustling from one room to another. Greasewood candelabras bristling with candles that filled the air with the sweet smell of beeswax hung from the ceilings. Elizabeth caught a glimpse of the central courtyard and thought to herself that it must be beautiful in the summer.

The sound of swordplay increased. Ramez stopped in what was apparently a gaming room, the walls of which were hung with paintings of battle scenes. "My father is the artist," he said, gesturing with a sweep of his arm. "He's proficient at everything he does."

Elizabeth noticed a hint of bitterness in Ramez's voice, and in that brief moment discovered a degree of kinship with him, for she too had lived in a strong father's shadow, and failed. "O'Shannon is hardly a name I expected to find in Mexico," she said, trying to lighten the atmosphere.

"My father is Irish," Ramez said. "My mother was Castillian Spanish, not at all like the *mestizo* and *negrito* mixed blood we see around here. Father is a soldier. He has plied his trade in France with Napoleon and in Greece killing Turks. He fought with Bolivar in Venezuela and against the English in Ireland. Now he is here in Mexico, and I—" He could not hide his dislike for the situation in which he found himself, "—am with him." A particularly loud clatter of swords, followed by a string of badly pronounced Spanish, interrupted him. "He is in there if you are ready."

The ballroom they entered was by far the most impressive room they had seen so far. It ran the full length of one side of the *hacienda*. Windows bordered with tiny stained-glass designs and covered with intricate wrought ironwork looked out into the courtyard. Three crystal teardrop chandeliers hung from the ceiling. Massive oak tables and chairs had been shoved back against the walls, leaving the brown, tan, and cream mosaic tile floor clear. Of the three men in the room, two were dusky, short, and obviously Mexican. The third, Luther O'Shannon, was trim and light-complected with a shock of salt and pepper hair that was brushed straight back from his forehead and hung down to his shoulders. A sheen of sweat gleamed on his tight, bunched muscles as he danced away from one blade and parried another slash that, if not halfheartedly delivered, might have done him injury. "Come, Emiliano!" he roared in Spanish. "You aren't trying. And you, Sancho! I'm counting on you. What man learns unless he is pressed to the limit? Come, the first man to draw my blood may have my saddle. The silver one."

The smaller man, Emiliano, danced to one side as O'Shannon beat back a laborious attack by Sancho, and then closed from the side. At the last second, O'Shannon, catching him out of the corner of his eye, twisted and kicked the legs out from under the Mexican. Emiliano tumbled to the floor and rolled quickly out of the way of his employer's saber. At the same time, O'Shannon stepped into Sancho's renewed attack and, swinging backhanded from the side, slashed across and upward and sent Sancho's weapon flying across the room. So ferocious was the attack that Sancho was thrown off balance and tripped over his own feet. With a roar of laughter, O'Shannon leaped toward him and stabbed with the saber. Sancho yelped with fear and, the blade barely pricking his chest, fell backward and sat heavily, legs splayed and dignity shattered.

O'Shannon turned in disdain from his fallen opponents and, fully aware of his visitors and the effect his swordplay had had on them, accepted a wet towel and a tankard of wine from a girl who appeared through an archway. "The saber is a slashing weapon," he said, toasting himself. "It is difficult to master, but in capable hands there is no more lethal weapon for hand-to-hand fighting."

His gaze swept across the men, lingered on Elizabeth as he drank from the tankard. "I am Luther O'Shannon. You have met my son, I see. And across the room—" He gestured to Lucita, who was half hidden in a large, soft armchair. "—is my wife, Lucita. She is angry with me and pouts to demonstrate her disapproval."

He did not motion for them to sit, so the five visitors remained standing, awkwardly bunched together. "We don't know what General Cos has told you," Jones began, breaking the silence, "but I might as well go on and explain my part in this. My name is Jones. Señor Medina hired me to bring these here settlers to him, so here I am."

"And no Medina," O'Shannon said, with a little cluck of dismay. "Are any of you adept with a saber? I am a willing student. You there." He pointed his tankard at True. "Your name."

"True Paxton," True answered, stepping forward.

"True. An interesting name at that. Well, now, True Paxton, you have the look of a capable man. I can read good breeding in your eyes. Can you handle a saber with any skill?"

"I doubt it. The blade's too long to suit me."

"An interesting observation," O'Shannon remarked. "You'll permit me?" He raised his saber and lifted the flap of True's coat. "Then what do you prefer? A pistol? Ah! The knife." His eyebrows rose. "Although it is a little long for a knife. A bayonet perhaps?"

True brushed the tip of the sword away. "We call it an Arkansas Toothpick, where I come from. Heavier than the average knife, shorter than your saber." His eyes bore into O'Shannon's. "It's difficult to master, but in capable hands there is no more lethal weapon for hand-to-hand fighting."

O'Shannon studied True for any trace of derision, then finally nodded. Behind him, set on winning a silver saddle, Emiliano had risen from the floor and was creeping up behind his employer. O'Shannon was no fool, though. He had spent too much time at sabers and knew his fellow man too well. Reading precisely what was happening in True's eyes and Elizabeth's gasp, he whirled at the last second. The blades met in a singing of steel and a raw metallic rasp, and the basket hilts collided as the two men closed. Before Emiliano knew what had happened, O'Shannon had pushed him backward and sliced open his thigh. The Mexican groaned and dropped his saber to clasp his leg as blood began to well from the cut.

"Greed, Emiliano," O'Shannon said in Spanish. "Greed is your undoing." He tossed his saber to Sancho and clapped his hands twice. Immediately, Sancho rushed to help his companion from the room.

"Well, then," the Irishman said, reverting to English and ignoring the servant girl who hurried to wipe away the blossoms of blood staining the floor. "I suppose that is the end of my exercise for the day. Unfortunate, but it can't be helped." He strolled across the floor to the table by his wife's chair and refilled his tankard from a pitcher. "So. Why have you come to me? Why have you come to my land?"

"Because we own part of it," Elizabeth said before any of the men could speak.

O'Shannon looked over his shoulder in mock surprise. "What? The woman speaks? You are beautiful, my dear, but is this not men's business?"

Elizabeth's face reddened but she held her ground. "My father bought the land, but he is now dead, as is my mother. My sister and I are their heirs, so it is my business. No man need speak for me concerning land that I own."

"Land that you own, eh?" O'Shannon chuckled. Lucita smiled up at him. "Did you hear that, my dear? Land that they own." A puzzled look crossed his face. He set down the tankard and leaned back against the table. "You must pardon me, my dear. All of you, of course. But I know nothing of land that you own."

"We purchased grants of land," Scott Campbell said, his voice hollow with anticipation. "We paid for them with hard money. Eight thousand hectares between us."

"And we have deeds to the property and a map of the ranch showing which sections are ours," Kemper added.

"Really?" O'Shannon asked. He ambled across the open floor toward the settlers. "I trust you have them with you. May I see them?"

Jones pulled a large package out from under his coat. "These are all of 'em," he said, handing them to O'Shannon. "I checked 'em myself."

"Mmm-hmmm." O'Shannon took the packet, broke it open, and walked back to the fireplace and perused them one by one.

The settlers waited. Ramez perched on one of the table tops. Lucita rose and brought him a glass of wine. Her eyes never left Elizabeth, whom she studied as if inspecting a rival.

"As you can see," Kemper said, filling the awkward silence, "everything is perfectly legal. All notarized by the local authorities as well as those in Mexico City."

"I see. Yes, I see," O'Shannon answered at last. "There is, however, a problem." His smile was diabolical. "The authorities whose signatures I read here are, how shall I put it, no longer authorities. And this transaction was between you and Medina, who no longer owns this ranch. I do. These grants—" He tossed them into the fireplace. "—are useless."

"No!" Elizabeth exclaimed, rushing across the room toward the fireplace.

True was a step ahead of her and restrained her from reaching into the flames. Already, the papers had caught fire and were burning fiercely.

"You had no right!" Kemper shouted, his face pale as a sheet.

"It isn't a question of right," O'Shannon sneered. "They were valueless. Mere scratchings on paper. Nowhere was the name O'Shannon mentioned."

Campbell stepped forward, his hands balled into white-knuckled fists. "We assumed you were a gentleman," he said, his voice hoarse with emotion.

"Assume what you will as long as you do not take me for a fool."

Kemper was trembling with rage, and tried to pull the pistol he carried. Jones quickly stepped behind him and grabbed him by the elbows. "We paid!" Kemper screamed, straining against Jones. "We paid, damn you to hell!"

O'Shannon appeared unperturbed. "You paid Medina," he said with a shrug. "Find Medina. Your quarrel is with him, not with me."

"Our quarrel *is* with you," Campbell insisted. "The land was bought and paid for almost five months ago. It was ours before you took it over. You are, in effect, taking—stealing—something you didn't own in the first place."

Not many men had called O'Shannon a thief and gotten away with it. The Irishman's features grew taut with controlled fury. "What is your name?" he asked, his voice an icy chill.

"Campbell. Scott Campbell."

"And you are a lawyer, Mr. Campbell? One versed in Mexican law?"

Campbell's mouth opened, then closed. "No," he finally admitted.

"Then I suggest," O'Shannon went on, "that you are ignorant of the facts, and haven't a leg to stand on. The land is mine. I say so, and can prove it in any Mexican court if you should have the temerity to challenge me. The only way you will get so much as one square yard of my land—" His smiled was a thin, white line. "—is to pay me for it."

"But we can't," Elizabeth whispered, staring at the ashes of a dream. "We have so little left. Medina took it all."

O'Shannon's outburst had ended and he had regained his composure. "Then, my dear, you and your friends have my sympathy. But not my land. There is nothing I can do for you."

"They could appeal to Santa Anna's court," Jones broke in from across the room. "He might help."

"An idle threat, Mr. Jones. One that you of all people should know better than to make." O'Shannon shrugged eloquently. "But by all means, feel free to try. I will be in Mexico City in a couple of months myself. If they wish, I will be most pleased to arrange an audience for them. A piece of advice, though. Our president has no love for those who supported Bustamente. I would not mention Medina's name if I were you." He turned to the table and refilled his tankard. "This isn't a bad wine. Will you join me?"

They stared at him, struck speechless by the casual way this man had devastated them, had made their hardships and suffering meaningless.

"No? Then I must bid you good day. I have a great deal to accomplish today, and am already late." His brows furrowed. "Ah, I can see you blame me. But I must insist you consider your request from my point of view. Surely you do not expect me simply to present you with a significant portion of my land just because Cirilio Medina robbed you." O'Shannon looked into each of their faces, read the emptiness there. "I will tell you what I will do, though. Pay me what you paid Medina, and the land is yours. It's good land, too. Many springs, good grass . . ."

"You know we have no money," Campbell muttered dully.

"There's nothing more we can do here," True said. He took Elizabeth by the arm and led her away from the fireplace. "Let's go before someone does something stupid. There'll be another day."

They didn't as much as say goodbye. Confused, heartbroken, angry, they left, following a servant who preceded them to the main entrance where their horses were waiting. "He can't do this," Campbell said, slumping dejectedly in his saddle.

No one replied. It was too obvious that Luther O'Shannon had justice on his side. At least his form of justice.

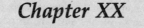

Chapter XX

"Jones is leaving! The bastard is pulling out! Down at the stable."

"Sonofabitch! I'll be right along," Joseph said, grabbing for his boots. "You stay here," he told Lottie, who still lay in bed. "I'm going with Kemper."

They met the three Campbell men at the side door and hurried with them to the stables to find a small knot of people gathered at the front door. "What's going on?" Scott snapped, brushing past Nels Matlan.

Jones stood by his gray, behind which was tethered another riding horse and a pack horse. "It's true, then," Joseph growled. He pushed between True and Elizabeth to confront the black man. "Where the hell do you think you're going?"

Jones's expression narrowed. He stared long and hard at Joseph. "I done what I was paid to do. Or at least half paid, seeing as Medina ain't around to hand me the rest. I'm going home."

"But . . . but how can you leave? I mean, just . . . leave . . . like that?" Nels Matlan's voice trailed off.

"Eight days to Christmas," Jones explained. "I got a family, and I want to see 'em. Might not make it by Christmas day, but I'll come close."

"You brought us here," Joseph said, defiant and angry. "You got us in this trouble. And now, damn your hide, you aren't going to run out on us."

"Joseph, no!" True warned, reaching out and catching his brother's arm as Joseph took a menacing step toward Jones.

Jospeh swung around and shoved True back, spun back toward Jones, who suddenly had his rifle cocked and pointed at Joseph's belly. "End of discussion," the black man said flatly. "You understand," he added to Leakey.

The mountain man's gnarled face was free of accusation or blame. He nodded. "It ain't none of his business."

"Well, it's mine," Kemper snorted. "Hell, leaving us stranded like this . . ."

"Is your back broke?" Jones asked, a little angry now himself. "Your hands curled up with the arthuritis? What the hell? You're a man, aren't you? The good Lord give you a brain, didn't he? There ain't a one of you here don't have at least a couple hundred dollars in his poke. There's plenty of others who've had a hell of a lot less to start with."

"That ain't the point—"

"The hell it ain't." Jones looked scathingly at Kemper, then glared at each of them in turn. "So you lost your land. Well, so what? There's worse things, and if you can't get past that then you wouldn't've made it *with* the land. Now, it's true I brought you here; but I didn't have to haul you draggin' and kickin', 'cause you wanted to come. And if the goin' turns out to be rough, it ain't my fault."

"Ah, let him go," Mackenzie sneered. "We don't need no chicken-livered nigger to help us."

Scott Campbell whirled and slapped his son hard enough to fatten his lip and draw blood. "I'll not have that talk from one of mine," he snapped. "Mr. Jones—" Scott extended his hand to Jones. "—I apologize for my son. He spoke too hastily, and without thought. I for one thank you for everything you've done for us, and wish you a safe journey home."

His face as red as his hair, Mackenzie stalked off. Jones watched him go. "I don't hold a younker's temper against him," he said, shaking Scott's hand. "He'll get over it."

"He might, but I won't," Joseph snarled. "and if I learn you had a hand in misleading my wife and these other people, you'd better keep a sharp eye to the horizon, Jones. Or by heaven, you'll not see me coming for you. And I'll not give a warning."

Hogjaw watched Joseph follow Mackenzie. "Them boys've got more grit than sense," he said, shaking Jones's hand.

"You'll need men with grit in the days ahead. Nels?" Jones shook Matlan's hand. "Land ain't everything. There's plenty of settlements begging for teachers and schools. True, you take care. Mark my word. I seen that look in your eye. If I find where Medina took off to, I'll send word, but in the meantime, leave O'Shannon be. He has the law on his side in the first place, and in the second he's tough as a cedar stump. I'd say he could take the measure of any man here. Or—'' He fixed his gaze on Elizabeth. ''—woman.''

''We'll see,'' True said, pumping the black man's hand.

''Well, I'm off, then.'' Jones swung into his saddle. ''I wish you folks all the luck. Sorry I couldn't do more to help.'' He winced, and hitched his weather-plagued leg into a more comfortable position. ''Keep an eye on 'em, Hogjaw. Dependin', I'll drift up this way come summer or fall. See if any of you are still here.''

''We will be,'' Elizabeth replied.

''Miss Elizabeth, I have learned better than to take turns with you.'' Thaddeus Jones tipped his hat to her. ''If you say so, it won't by God surprise me if you are.'' He waved one last time, kicked his gray in the ribs. ''Old horse,'' he said, ''let's be goin'!''

Hogjaw never let goodbyes bother him. The rest, both those who felt betrayed and those who understood, found it harder to adjust. Thaddeus Jones, wagon train master, guide, protector, had been an integral part of their lives for more than ten weeks. He had led them through the wilderness. He had ordered their days and nights. He had laughed with them, eaten with them, worked with them, counseled them. More than anything else, he was at home in this strange land in which they found themselves. When he was with them they were not alone: in his absence, they were cast adrift, unsure of themselves and how to proceed.

The feeling wore off only gradually. The Christmas season was on them, and San Antonio was bustling with visitors. Scott Campbell was the first to find work when he was hired on as a farrier, shoeing horses at the stable. Nels Matlan was the next. Through his conversations with Padre Salva, he met a visitor from a settlement called Washington-on-the Brazos, where a man by the name of Travis was parceling out sections of a large grant for a tidy profit. Washington-on-the-Brazos had recently lost its sole teacher in a riding accident, and though the job paid little, Nels, Eustacia, and Tommy would be able to take over the dead teacher's house. The settler promised to discuss the matter with the rest of the parents, and to send word back to Nels sometime after the first of the year.

The others could find nothing so concrete. Reverend Kania

proposed to begin riding circuit and serving the scattered
Protestant settlements that were gradually growing up in the
area. Kevin Thatche was busy worrying about Mildred, who
still hadn't delivered after her initial scare. Jack Kemper
made the rounds of San Antonio's merchants looking for one
to help stake him in a trading post. Joseph and True, along
with Lottie and Elizabeth, decided to wait for Andrew to
return before making any further decisions.

Sunday, the twentieth, only five days before Christmas,
was the first day that each and every one of them smiled.
They were gathered at Mama Flores's *Casa del Rio* for the
evening meal when the front door flew open and Kevin
Thatche stumbled in. "My God!" Joan Campbell gasped, the
first to see him.

"He's white as a sheet."

Nels Matlan was at his side in two steps. "What is it,
Kevin?" he demanded.

Kevin stared blankly at Nels, then at the faces turned
toward him. "A boy," he finally managed. "It's . . . a . . .
boy!"

Joan Campbell cried in relief as the questions battered
Kevin.

"How is he?"

"How's Mildred?"

"How big is he?"

"What you gonna call him, Kevin?"

"Here, now!" Hogjaw roared, cutting them all off and
taking over. Swiftly, he walked to Kevin's side and took his
arm. "First things first. The boy's gonna do fine and so'll his
mama. You'll all see how big he is in a day or so, and what
he's gonna go by don't matter. What does matter, what this
younker needs," he proclaimed, "is a belt of the best!"

Grinning like an idiot, Kevin accepted their cheers, their
handshakes, the good-natured pummeling.

"Kemper?" Hogjaw went on. "We've had our words, but
you've got the only decent whiskey I've seen this side of the
Mississippi. Name your price and break out one of them jugs.
We got us a brand new Texian and I'm by God the one
buyin' to celebrate the fact!"

Here, at last, was something to celebrate, a reason for good
cheer in the face of bleak prospects. Mama Flores and her
multitudinous family joined in the party, as did some of her

regular customers. Someone appeared with a violin, someone else with a trumpet. Chairs and tables were pushed back to make room for dancing. It was as if a canopy of gloom had burst and let the sun shine through, not solely because of the child, but also because the settlers were starved for laughter. By midnight, Mexican-American relations had been cemented, in spite of the language barrier, by two jugs of fine Pennsylvania corn whiskey. And when everyone tottered off to bed, all slept well for the first time in nights.

Monday morning dawned springlike. Remarkably, no one felt the worst for the carousing. The party had been a tonic of the best sort. Scott Campbell whistled on his way to the stables. Kemper actually greeted Hogjaw with a smile. Lottie and Elizabeth exchanged more than half a dozen words for the first time since the morning after Hester's death. Best of all, even though the weather was most un-Christmaslike for northerners used to snow and the sound of sleigh bells, everyone began to enter, however faintly at first, the spirit of the season.

The birth of Kevin Michael Thatche, Jr., as he had been named, proved to be a catalyst in more ways than one. Their obsession with O'Shannon broken for the time being, the settlers emerged from the dark mood into which they had fallen and began to look to the future. The men rented an empty lot to the north of town and took the wagons there to set up a semipermanent camp where everyone with the exception of the Thatches, who wanted to keep the baby inside for awhile, could live more cheaply than at Mama Flores's. All hands turned to the preparation for the christening. The women sewed, the men busied themselves making a crib, a cradle, and, though a year or two premature, a high chair. Mildred was beside herself with joy and spent those hours when she wasn't with her new son under the tutelage of Joan and Eustacia.

True, Nels, and the Campbell boys spent the last two days before Christmas roaming the city and inviting every American colonist they could find to a Christmas Eve service and, on Christmas day, Kevin, Jr.'s christening and christening party. Hogjaw waited until the day before Christmas to take Tommy Matlan into the hills and bring home a ten-foot-tall cedar. By the time Christmas Eve itself rolled around, the city was awash with celebration. Gunfire and the pop and whoosh of homemade fireworks filled the clear night air. At eleven, upwards of a hundred colonists watched respectfully as the procession carrying the baby Jesus to his creche in front of the cathedral wended its way through the streets. An hour later, at the same time Padre Salva was offering midnight mass for the predominately Catholic Mexican inhabitants of San Antonio, the settlers gathered in the circle of wagons for their own simple service of prayer and thanksgiving. Stars twinkled overhead. Somewhere in the distance, a coyote sang a forlorn accompaniment to their spirited *Adeste Fidelis,* and then, as if hushed by the solemnity of the occasion, remained silent through Buckland Kania's reading of the traditional first nineteen verses of Luke.

"And it came to pass in those days, that there went out a decree from Caesar Augustus, that all the world should be taxed. . . ."

Elizabeth stood next to True, her hand in his. She had heard for more years than she could remember the moving story of the birth of the baby Jesus, but this year it had taken on added significance. Not three paces in front of her, lying in his own cradle and cushioned by a straw-filled mattress, lay young Kevin. And as he suggested the Christ Child to her, he also awakened her own maternal instincts.

Suddenly, she knew she did not want to wait any longer. Her parents were dead. She had traveled some fifteen hundred miles, far from all that was familiar. She had neither quailed at the struggle nor begged for help. She had remained resolute in the face of calamity and loss, and had not allowed herself the luxury of collapse and dependency. She had been strong enough, had proved her own strength to herself. The promised land had turned out to be a chimera, but the man she had found was very real, and she loved him.

"But Mary kept all these things, and pondered them in her heart," Reverend Kania said, finishing the text that Elizabeth had barely heard. "Let us pray. Oh, God, tonight we celebrate the birth of Thy Son, who Thou in Thy infinite wisdom and mercy and love sent to us that night so long ago. . . ."

Elizabeth bowed her head and folded her hands, but could not, try though she might, concentrate on Reverend Kania's prayer. True was too much on her mind. His presence, the barely discernible movement of his chest as he breathed, the feel of his hand linked with hers. Here was the miracle that had borne the human race down all its years of passion, turmoil, and strife.

The miracle was love.

Cash money was a scarce commodity, but a truly joyous Christmas had never depended on money. The children had decorated the tree during the hours before the service, with Hogjaw as their overseer. The women had cooked venison roasts and vegetables and baked pies and cakes. And before slipping away for the night, parents surreptitiously placed wrapped packages around the base of the tree, which stood in the center of the circled wagons.

Christmas came the next morning with the sound of pounding feet and whoops of happiness as everyone gathered again at the tree. Great pots of coffee brewed over half a dozen open fires. Almost two dozen children milled around the tree, waiting. The smell of fresh biscuits set mouths to watering. The second the sun peeked over the horizon, Hogjaw took his place under the tree and began handing out presents. A doll here, a shirt or pair of gloves there. A sack of hard candy, whittled horses, soldiers, tops, and wagons. A first gun for a twelve year old, whose eyes glowed with pride. A necklace for a sweetheart, a kerchief for a new bride. No gift was of great value, except as measured by the love with which it had been given, and received. Breakfast was catch as catch can, hot biscuits and butter and honey snatched on the run. Before anyone realized how quickly the time had flown, Buckland Kania was beating on a huge iron pot and calling them all to a mercifully short worship service.

And then Christmas dinner! The biscuits were long forgotten, and everyone dug in with a will. Whole roasts disappeared, along with mountains of mashed potatoes with gravy, and loaves of steaming, fresh bread. There was hot buttered rum for the adults, milk laced with molasses for the children, and best of all, a whole table full of pies and cakes to fill every last empty cranny in every last groaning stomach. Afterward, while the women cleaned up and the children played, the men gathered in groups, loosened their belts, and talked desultorily of weather and politics and land and horses.

The temperature was climbing into the high seventies when everyone trooped down to the river at the western edge of town for the baptism. There, under a canopy of leafless cottonwoods, the Reverend Kania baptized two adults and three older children before he called Kevin and Mildred forward. A hush fell over the crowd, for this christening was special. The Thatche child, unlike the others, was born a Texian, as the colonists had taken to calling themselves. He was one of the very first of what they hoped would soon become a swelling tide.

Kevin, Jr. didn't exactly agree, but that was because he didn't like the cold river water sprinkled on his head. Mildred quickly wiped it away so he wouldn't take a chill. When she turned around to walk back up the bank, Hogjaw was standing in front of her. "He's a fine looker, Mrs. Thatche," the old man said, his face plastered with what passed for a grin.

Mildred's face reddened.

"I could 'a told you before, but it wouldn't've done no good, I reckon. Contrary to what all them old wives say, my kind of looks ain't catchin'."

Kevin's face was as red as Mildred's. "I guess we owe you an apology, Mr. Leakey," he said. "We just weren't thinking too straight. He's our first, though, and we were scared. You never can tell. . . ."

"I didn't mind," Hogjaw said, sparing the lad any further explanation. "You was takin' care as you saw fit, which is all a man can ask for. I ain't never had one of my own that I know of, but I understand. Lookee—" The old man's face jellied around, finally settled into a frown of concentration. "I know Presbyterians don't hold much with Godfatherin', but would you mind if I held the tad for jest a minute?"

Mildred looked alarmed, but Kevin rose to the occasion, gingerly took Kevin, Jr. from her arms and handed him to Hogjaw.

"Kind of fragile lookin', ain't he," the mountain man said, his eyes rapt as he cupped the tiny infant in his great hands. "Tiny. Don't weigh more'n a medium size grasshopper." Abruptly, he ducked his head until his nose was just above the baby's. Little Kevin opened his eyes, squawled, and flailed his arms. One little fist connected with a jaw flap and set it swaying before Hogjaw raised his head again. "You're a mite young fer sharin' blood, little tad, so I done it that way. We shared each other's breath now, which means we're kin of a sort. I got me a grandson and you got you a brand new granddaddy. If ever you need anything, little tad, or if ever you find yourself in trouble, you come runnin'. So long as ol' Hogjaw's alive, he'll be there to help.''

"Mr. Leakey—"

"You call me Hogjaw now, son-o. You too, little missus. And the pleasure's mine," Hogjaw said as he looked up from the child. "You two younkers remember, now. You got kin, and kin are fer help when help is needed." Moving slowly and carefully, as if the child would break in his hands, he handed Kevin, Jr. back to his mother and then, awed, pointed out to the gathered crowd where the baby had struck him. "You see that?" he crowed, his eyes glistening with pride. "That was a right he got me with. A real haymaker. Little cuss slugged me, he did."

"The mellowing of Hogjaw," True told Elizabeth a little while later on the way to Mama Flores's, where the christening party was going to be held. He shook his head in wonder. "Who would have guessed that that crusty old man could be so sentimental."

"I think it's . . . nice," Elizabeth said, giving his arm a squeeze.

"Oh, I'm not saying it isn't," True explained. "It's just a surprise, is all."

Everyone, including many of the other colonists, had chipped in to help pay for the party at *La Casa del Rio*. Mama Flores had sent her children and in-laws to the settlers' camp to pick up the leftovers from Christmas dinner, and added platters of *tamales, enchiladas,* chicken *mole,* and barbecued goat, enough to feed an army. The rafters were festooned with ribbons and *piñatas*. As the afternoon wore on, as many new guests arrived as old ones left. Spanish and American mingled as friends, shouted at each other in the mistaken hope that volume would increase understanding.

Evening came, lanterns and candles were lit, the furniture was moved to the wall, and the dancing started. Off in one corner, an ebullient Padre Salva, a roly-poly man with the face of a cherub and the hands of a stone mason, shared a cup with the lean and ascetic-looking Buckland Kania. Staunch Roman Catholic and ardent Presbyterian appeared to be getting along famously as they engaged in a heated debate over papal authority.

True and a half dozen other men had been in the adjoining bar talking about a horse farm one of them proposed to start.

When the discussion veered to politics, True eased away from the table and headed for the main room to find Elizabeth and ask her if she wanted to dance. "Lose something?" Hogjaw's voice asked from just behind him.

"Not sure," True drawled. "You find something?"

Someone had stuffed paper flowers all around the brim of Hogjaw's hat and tied a bright green ribbon around his neck. The mountain man's sagging face was beet red from a combination of too much drinking and dancing. "Just happiness, is all. I swear, these little Mex gals is the prettiest things!" Hogjaw hiccuped, and swayed alarmingly. He gestured with his head in the direction of the door, and almost fell over that way, catching himself at the last second. "Out there," he said. "Wouldn't let that girl walk alone if I was you."

True grabbed Hogjaw's arm. "Elizabeth?"

"None other, boy-o. None other." He winked suggestively. "Nice night for walkin', wouldn't you say?"

"Excuse me." True snatched his hat from the rack, elbowed his way across the dance floor, and escaped into the street. The sky was clear, the night quiet except for the muted noise of the party he had left behind.

Halfway down the block, Elizabeth heard the noise swell and then stop. "True?" she asked, sure she recognized the approaching figure from the way he walked.

"Me," True answered, hurrying to catch up with her. "Where you going?"

"Back. Someone said you were talking about horses. I thought . . ." Her voice trailed off. "It's been a long day. I was tired."

A high cloud still in the sunlight far to the west glowed with a purple sheen that faded as they watched. Aware of each other, yet not speaking, True and Elizabeth ambled down the street toward the lot where the wagons were parked. Somewhere off to their right, a guitar strummed a mournful melody to accompany a sweet, tired voice. Elizabeth didn't understand the words, but could imagine lovers standing close together in front of the amber glow of a fire, silhouettes of faces captured in a moment long dreamed of, when pretense is forgotten and all that is left is the honesty of two souls touching.

Honesty. It was easier, somehow, when the blush lay hidden and obscure. Easier, yet difficult too, as if she were balancing on a pinnacle and reaching for a star. She might fail and fall, but she might succeed, too, and in capturing one of night's far diamonds, burn her hand and find pain in beauty and fulfillment.

They held hands. Simply, as children do. When they reached the circle of wagons, they stopped by the dying fire and stood for a long moment looking at each other. "We're alone," Elizabeth said, whispering.

"Everyone else is at the party. No one is here."

"Except us."

"Except us."

True moved first, lit a lantern and, taking her by the hand, led her toward her wagon, secluded in the shadows. A dove whistled eerily from the darkness, startling them both and making them smile shyly. At last, Elizabeth turned and climbed into the wagon. True followed, hanging the lantern on a hook before closing the rear flaps against the growing chill.

Elizabeth waited, her back to him. True stepped close, parted her long, golden curls and kissed the back of her neck. He reached around and unfastened the buttons running down the front of her dress. The dress dropped to the floor, a gray, lifeless mass in comparision with the chaste white chemise and the tawny limbs beneath the filmy fabric. Slipping the straps over her shoulders, he knelt and pulled the undergarment down to her ankles, kissing the length of her spine as he did, kissing the twin perfect mounds above her thighs, kissing the backs of her knees.

Elizabeth rocked backward and almost lost her balance as a liquid warm weakness spread through her. True caught her, helped her down to the pallet, and then disrobed and stood before her, aroused and primal.

"I love you, True," Elizabeth said, reaching for him.

"And I love you," True said, kneeling in front of her.

Elizabeth blushed. "I don't know . . . That is, I haven't ever—"

"Shhh." True touched her lips with one finger, then bowed to kiss her breasts.

Elizabeth shuddered with pleasure and fear, and with trembling fingers, dared to touch his shoulder.

"Neither have I," True whispered. "Dearest, dearest, dearest . . ."

When they met and joined, Elizabeth cried out once in pain

that was soon forgotten in the whispered, hasty stirrings of their embrace. As they moved together to become one, all that they had been before was forgotten and left behind in the fire of their love. And all that they would be thereafter was born in those same flames that, consuming them, left them weak with awe and trembling with wonder.

Chapter XXI

Carl Michaelson took her by the arm and pulled her to him. He was smiling, joking, laughing even as his free arm swept in an arc that took in the full, verdant fields brimming with life. Elizabeth cringed at his side. She couldn't remember exactly why she was frightened, only that she was. It was silly, wasn't it? This was her father. His arm around her waist was strong and protective, the all-encompassing symbol of his love for her. Shyly, feeling very much the little girl, Elizabeth relaxed and smiled up at him just as him arm tightened around her waist and his free hand fondled her breasts. Still she smiled, even as his face changed, twisted with hate and lust, leered down at her. His right arm had slipped down so that his hand cupped her buttock and pulled her to him, her groin to his, grinding into her through the thick, coarse denim. His left hand squeezed one breast and then the other, pinched viciously. His breath was hot on her face, his eyes bloodshot and gleaming wildly.

"Please don't, Father," Elizabeth pleaded, amazed at how calm she sounded. "Please don't do that."

She slipped from his grasp just before he disappeared. The light had changed and she was wandering alone and in a strange place. Laughter followed her. She was terrified, yet again strangely calm, as if being terrified were quite natural. The ground around her was bare and littered with rocks and dank weeds. A dancing couple whirled past her, stopped and pointed at her, and continued on their way. She was holding a lantern that was lit but cast no light until—why she did not know—she leaned over and peered into her father's face.

He looked so different! Elizabeth stared down at him with clinical detachment. He was dead, she thought. He didn't move, only stared back at her with sightless eyes through a mask of caked blood. As she watched, she realized she was wet and that the ground was a soup of mud. Rainwater washed the blood from her father's face, collected in his open mouth, a miniature pond fringed with bristling stubble. He looked surprised, she thought, surprised and not amused to learn that death should have taken him by its pale hand and led him into the dreamless sleep. . . .

Elizabeth's eyes opened and her mind struggled through the mired depths of the dream. Overhead, the ribbed canvas was pale gray with early morning light. At her side—she stiffened suddenly, then relaxed as the memory flooded back—True lay asleep, his lips slightly parted, his hair tousled. Elizabeth shifted carefully, rolled onto her side with her back to him. She had had the same dream twice before, once deep in the pine woods of east Texas, again the night they buried Hester. She wasn't sure what it meant, but each of those other times when she woke she had been filled with a sense of brutal misfortune, of babes snatched from cradles, of the hungry dragged from feasts, of poor souls dispatched at the moment of their glory. Of death taking the strong and driving the weak mad. And each time, too, she felt anger and a cloaking guilt that stifled her and left her breathless. This morning she felt different, as if the dream had perhaps visited her for the last time, had come calling in the night to test her and, finding a new Elizabeth grown immune to its horrors, crept away.

"You have freckles here," a morning-deep voice said. True's hand touched her shoulder blade outside the covers, slid under the covers and cupped her breast.

Elizabeth rolled onto her back. "Is that so terrible?"

"Of course not." He pulled down the cover, kissed the valley between her breasts. "And there, too. I never suspected."

"I never suspected a lot of things," Elizabeth said. She twisted a lock of his hair around her finger, closed her eyes and arched her back as his head moved and he kissed her under her breasts. The moment was as sweet as his touch, as warm as their bodies under the covers. "True?"

"Mmm?"

"What are you thinking?"

He sat up abruptly and the covers fell away from him. "Well . . ." He scratched his head, yawned and stretched mightily. "That I'm hungry." He looked down at her with an impish grin. "What about you?"

"Oh, I don't know." Elizabeth turned toward him and kissed his side. She walked her fingers over his thigh, took him in her hand. "Maybe a little," she purred lazily. She smiled to herself as he hardened and, groaning, lay back beside her. "I guess I could fix us . . . some breakfast . . ."

"Ah. . ."

"If you want . . ." Her hair cascaded over her breasts and onto his chest as she hitched up on one elbow to look down at him. "You knew all along it would come to this, didn't you."

True wrapped a lock of her hair around her breast and kissed the nipple where it peeked through. "I didn't exactly keep it a secret." His other hand slid down her stomach, spread her thighs. "You knew it, too," he said, slipping his leg under hers and slowly entering her.

"I never . . . True!"

"Confess," he whispered, rolling to lie on top of her.

Her eyes widened, became misty. "True . . ."

"Confess." His hips rose and fell, each thrust more demanding than the last. "From the first moment we met, you knew. Confess."

No past, no future. Only the excruciating present, almost unbearable in its intensity. Rising to meet him, she wrapped her arms and legs around him. "Yes," she gasped. "Yes." And crying out, "Yes!"

The world hadn't gone away, only receded for a few moments. True fought into his boots, pulled his pants' legs down over them. "Well?" he asked.

Elizabeth moved away from the front flap, let it close slowly. "Helen Kemper is out there," she said, a little apprehensively.

"I'll just sneak out the side, then, and circle around the Thatches' wagon."

"She'll still see you. She's facing this way. Unless she swallowed her tongue during the night, everyone will know by noon."

True held her face between his palms. "Do you care that much what the others think?"

"Do you need to ask?" Elizabeth retorted, her eyes flashing. "Of course . . ." She stopped and, suddenly subdued, sank back on her haunches. "Yes," she whispered. "I do care. We're not married, and I don't want people to think that

I . . . that we . . . Darn it, True!'' Her eyes swam with tears. ''I don't want anybody to say that I'm a loose woman, or that you . . . you hung around me just because I . . . we . . .''

True took her hands. The firm set of her mouth, the determination she exuded, the strength of character that had kept her going through the long miles, the beauty of their lovemaking . . . ''You are a very special lady, Elizabeth,'' he said. ''I love you.''

Elizabeth laughed self-consciously and brushed a tear from her cheek. ''I've never been called a lady by anyone else. Mother always thought of me as a little girl, and Father just . . . Lottie's baby sister, I guess . . .'' She trailed off, hoping she had concealed the strain in her voice.

''I'll check on Mrs. Kemper,'' True said, sensing her discomfort but not pressing the matter. If Elizabeth confided in him one day, so be it. Everyone had wounds of all colors and configurations that needed healing. Love was the one sure balm, and love needed time. ''She's facing the other way,'' he whispered, quickly unlacing the canvas and making a hole large enough to crawl out of. He gave her a quick kiss and disappeared out the side. ''See you in a few minutes.''

The morning air was chilly. True ducked into the Thatches' wagon, where he'd been staying, made a few morning sounds, yawned hugely as he stepped out again, this time in plain view, and stumbled sleepily off to the latrine they'd set up at the periphery of the camp. ''Morning, Mrs. Kemper,'' he said a few minutes later, standing over the fire to warm his hands. ''Pretty day. That coffee sure smells good.''

Helen Kemper had a nose for subterfuge. Glancing at True out of the corner of one eye, she tried to figure out what he was up to. ''Left early last night,'' she said, pouring him a cup of coffee. ''Not sick, I hope.''

''No, ma'am. Thanks. Just had about all I could take of cigar smoke, is all.'' He grinned apologetically. ''That and tequila, of course. You have some extra bacon I could borrow? Pay you back this afternoon.''

''There on the sideboard,'' Helen said, nodding, then swiveling her head to watch Elizabeth emerge from her wagon.

They wanted to laugh and shout, to dance about with joy. Never had the air felt so crisp, the sky seemed so blue. True felt ten feet tall, Elizabeth as if she'd been reborn. But Helen Kemper's eyes were narrow with suspicion, so they played at bored nonchalance while they wolfed down their breakfast.

"Going into town," True announced a while later after he'd scraped and washed his plate. "Anyone want to come along?"

"Who? Me?" Elizabeth asked innocently, biting her tongue to keep from laughing.

Almost everyone else was up by that time, stirring about making and eating breakfast, doing their morning chores. "Or anyone else?" True said, hoping there would be no takers.

"Maybe I'll check in on Mildred," Elizabeth said. "Wait a second. I'll walk with you."

"Scott left before daybreak," Joan Campbell said. "Would you carry his breakfast to him?"

"Happy to." True took the tin of beans and bacon Joan handed him, crossed to join Elizabeth at the edge of the road. "See you all later. Ready?"

The sun was just over the horizon by the time the first building blocked the camp's view of them. No sooner than they knew Helen Kemper couldn't see them, they dropped all pretence of propriety. "I thought I'd die!" Elizabeth said, dissolving in laughter.

"You're a born conspirator," True said, laughing. "Good morning, Mrs. Kemper," he mimicked Elizabeth. "Your biscuits smell heavenly." He wrapped one arm around her and hugged her to him. "Lovely. Sugar would melt in your mouth."

"Well, I *had* to say *some*thing." She giggled. "You looked so painfully innocent."

They chatted easily, at home with each other as they walked. The adobe buildings to either side brightened as the sun climbed above the horizon. A small black dog snuffled out from an alley and, spying intruders, immediately set in motion a progressive chorus of howls. True threw a stone at the pooch, who leaped in the air and scampered off yelping as if he'd been dealt a mortal wound. They delivered Scott's breakfast and, since they were at the stable, decided to spend the morning exploring the countryside. Elizabeth went to say hello to Mildred and ask Mama Flores to pack them a lunch while True saddled Firetail and another horse.

"Younker," a voice called from above.

True glanced up to see Hogjaw peering out of the loft door. He held a rifle with a powder horn tied to the barrel. When he dropped it, True whipped out a hand and caught it just above the flint. "What's this for?"

"Keep it primed and close to hand. Graveyard's full of folks sent to perdition within sight of town. I won't be needin' it, seein' as I still got some of the happiness I was tellin' you about last night up here with me." He cackled with delight. "By God, but there's a flash in the old pan yet!"

Leakey had a habit of popping up in the most uncanny ways, True thought, shaking his head. He slung the rifle over his shoulder and led the horses around to the front of Mama Flores's just in time to meet Elizabeth. True helped her onto her horse, tied the lunch behind Firetail's saddle, and mounted. "Pick a way," he said. "Any way."

With their horses fresh and trotting easily, they headed east. San Antonio was returning to normal after the Christmas holiday. Roosters were crowing, each trying to outdo the other. Women yelled at each other and at their children, who screeched back and raced along the street, trailing little dust devils. The smell of *tortillas* heating over hearths or outdoor cookfires permeated the air. They passed a woman in a black shawl making her way across the plaza toward the church. Unheeding of the grief in the woman's shuffling steps and bowed back, two children played tag around her as if she were little more than a tree trunk.

A goat bleated a greeting to them. A basketmaker waved to them from beneath a load of vines and reeds piled high on his back. A potter outside a nearby *jacalito* was busily firing his wares in a pit filled with wood shavings. Inside the eddying, swirling cloud of smoke, his bright *serape* glowed with a veritable rainbow of colors. True stiffened as a soldier, his face puffy from a night's carousing with one of the whores from a nearby brothel, scowled at them as they rode by. Unshaven, his uniform in disarray, the soldier reeked of stale *pulque* and the dank odor of sex. True did not relax until they were well past the man, out of his sight around a corner.

A few hundred yards past the last house on the edge of the city proper, they came to one of the aqueducts. The stone waterway had been built years earlier with priestly engineering and Pueblo Indian labor. Missionaries and Indians alike were long departed but their handiwork continued to carry water to the fields and the rapidly growing city. The temperature climbed as the sun rose and spilled bright light across the land and through the cottonwood trees that clustered at intervals along the aqueduct. The water overhead whispered as it flowed smoothly through the closely fit stonework. Both True and Elizabeth unbuttoned their coats and relaxed, content to let the horses lead them where they willed.

The aqueduct ended and still they rode until, her back stiff and her legs beginning to get sore, Elizabeth called a halt on the bank of a rocky, tree-lined stream. Puffy white clouds, mirrored in the smooth water sailed across the blue sky overhead. When the wind stirred, the barren branches clicked and rasped lightly, like a multitude of small, scurrying animals. After an initial moment of suspicion, True and Elizabeth caught each other listening, their faces knotted with concern. Laughing, they stepped close and kissed, kissed again, and yet again.

"It's getting hot," True finally said, breaking the embrace and shedding his coat. "I'm hungry. How about you?"

"Ummm, not yet." Elizabeth took off her coat and draped it over a shrub. Downstream a few yards, the water trickled musically over a tiny natural dam of round, moss green stones, polishing and smoothing, wearing them to perfection before eroding them away entirely as the final step in one of nature's age-old chores. Elizabeth hopped from stone to stone, found one path across the stream, another back, and then, lazy in the gentle winter sun, found a place to sit on a tree trunk jutting out from the bank.

"What'cha thinking?" True said around a mouthful of *tortilla* as he joined her.

"Oh, I don't know." Elizabeth rested her head against his shoulder. "You. Me. The day. This place. Everything is so beautiful."

True grunted and took another bite. "Wouldn't want to be here during a heavy rain," he said, pointing to the piled remains of trees and boulders that had been carried by a current far more powerful than that which bubbled merrily underfoot. He reached to one side and plucked a tangle of grass from a bush. "The water was at least head deep right here during the last flood. Pretty dangerous."

"We had floods in Pennsylvania too, Mister Paxton," Elizabeth said.

"Sorry," True apologized. "Didn't mean to—"

"No, no." Elizabeth sighed, regretting her reply. "I guess I'm too accustomed to defending myself."

"You don't have to defend yourself with me."

"I know." Elizabeth reached up and nipped him on the

ear, at the same time tickling him. "You have to from me, though."

"Hey!" True pinned her wrists and pulled her to him. "See what you did?" he asked, mock seriously.

"No. What?"

"You made me drop my *tortilla,* that's what." His voice was deep and gently provoking. Softly, he kissed her lips, each eye, and her neck. "Now, aren't you ashamed."

"Not in the least," Elizabeth purred, her head back and her eyes closed.

"Oh, yeah? Well, then . . ." Suddenly, he grabbed her hat and sent it spinning across the creek.

"True!" Her hat arced up, caught the wind and curved back to the same side of the creek but further downstream. Elizabeth jumped up and ran to catch it, heard True giving chase, squealed and ran past the hat. True growled and almost caught her, but tripped on a loose rock. Elizabeth bolted into the lead and ducked beneath a low branch. She heard True grunt with surprise and looked back to see him wrestling with the branch. Finally he shoved it over his head, then returned to the chase.

A startled rabbit bounded away from a clump of greenbriar, zigzagged across open ground, and disappeared. Laughing, Elizabeth followed the rabbit across the tiny meadow and into the shaded coolness of a thick cedar grove. "I know you're in there," True sang from somewhere behind her. Elizabeth heard him crashing through the dense growth, ducked around a matted wall of grapevines, and cried out in surprise as she almost collided with Ramez O'Shannon's stallion.

True burst from the thicket behind her. "Now I . . ." His voice faltered and died as he came to a halt. They were standing in one of the many concealed clearings that broke up the heavy brushland along the creek. Less than twenty feet in front of them, the white stallion and its companion, a brown gelding wearing a side saddle, yanked at their tethers and, unable to pull free, rolled their eyes in alarm.

"What are you doing on my land?" a voice called to them.

True stepped in front of Elizabeth, checked his knife to make sure it was loose enough to draw easily, and watched Ramez emerge from the tangled brush on the far side of the clearing. His black and silver jacket was unbuttoned, his thick black hair tousled. His ruffled shirt was open and loosely

tucked in at the waist. "Your father's land, don't you mean?"
True taunted, regaining his composure quickly.

Ramez sneered. "My land," he insisted. "One thousand
hectares deeded to me to do with as I please." Cocky, he
posed with hands on hips. "And I please to be alone on it.
You are intruding. It is fortunate for you I do not have a gun
close at hand."

"It is fortunate for *you*," True responded, his eyes narrowing.

Ramez had the gall to laugh. "You frighten me terribly,
señor." He held out his hands and shook them violently.
"See how I tremble?" The shaking stopped and one long,
slender finger pointed arrogantly at True. "From now on,
gringo, guard where you ride. Do not trespass again."

"I'll ride where—"

"True!" Elizabeth placed a hand on True's arm. "There is
trouble enough without adding more."

The tension was palpable. Ramez stood smugly confident,
sure that his own demeanor and his father's well-known
reputation would protect him from harm. True's breath was
shallow, his face white with anger. He was poised, ready to
spring, restrained only by Elizabeth's touch and the sound of
her voice. Slowly he relaxed, glanced sideways at Elizabeth
to show her he was under control and that she needn't worry.
"You're a lucky boy, O'Shannon," he finally said, and
turning on his heel, led Elizabeth back the way they had
come.

Ramez waited until they were gone, then brushed a strand
of hair from his face and stepped back into a hidden bare spot
under the concealing cedars. There, crouching on a pallet
made of *serapes,* Lucita awaited him. "They're gone," Ramez
said, switching to Spanish. "You needn't worry."

"I thought it was Luther," Lucita said, wide-eyed and
almost sick with fear.

"Father gave me this land to do with as I please. He never
rides on it. It's a point of honor. And you know he is an
honorable man."

"Still, I was afraid," Lucita said, lying back seductively
and drawing up her skirts.

Ramez knelt between her legs and touched her with his
riding crop. "Do not be afraid of him, woman," he said
hoarsely. "Be afraid of me."

*   *   *

A quarter mile away, True guided Firetail to the right, up the first long, low ridge of hills to the east of the creek. From his vantage point, the land spread out in a rolling, fertile-looking plain. Woodlands followed the stream back to the south. The undergrowth thinned rapidly on the western side and gave way to peach-colored grasslands broken by occasional groves of trees. "His land!" True exclaimed, the idea springing full blown. "By God! That's it!"

"What's it!" Elizabeth asked.

"Beautiful here, isn't it?" True said, not really paying attention. He pointed. "Good place for a house there. There, too, where that shadow of the cloud touches the hill. What do you think? Like to live there?"

"I think," Elizabeth said dryly, "that it belongs to Ramez O'Shannon."

"Yes!" True shouted to the hills, and threw back his head and laughed. Roared! "His to do with as he pleases!"

"Whatever? . . ."

The laughter stopped as abruptly as it had begun. True stood in his stirrups and looked across Ramez O'Shannon's land. "It's going to be ours, Elizabeth," he said, his voice soft and strong. "All ours. Yours, Lottie's, Scott's, Kevin's . . . all of ours. It and more like it." He reached across the short space between them and took her hand. "You'll see, Elizabeth. You'll see." He kissed her fingertips. "But right now, let's get back to town. Like Hogjaw says, time's a wastin'!"

He whirled Firetail in a circle and slapped Elizabeth's gelding across the rump. A second later, galloping side by side down the slope, they were flying like the wind, a wind blowing fresh and clear and out of the west. A wind with the promise of hope after all. True Paxton had a plan.

Chapter XXII

Luther O'Shannon stood on Señor Cirilio Medina. It wasn't very difficult. Cerilio Medina was at rest six feet beneath the dry Texas sod, sleeping dreamlessly in the company of worms and slowly returning to the inevitable dust of the original Creator. Luther often came to this spot to think, to enjoy the private conversation of the wind, and to dream of County Kilgarry with its hills of emerald clover sweeping down in ripples to the white-flecked, cloud gray bay.

The geography and climate of the two locales contrasted vividly, but O'Shannon had somehow connected the two places in his mind on that evening he led Medina to his death. The mesquite grove had been picked almost by random. It was far enough away from the *hacienda* for privacy, yet close enough to reach without an undue waste of time. Time had, after all, been of the essence. Only three hours earlier, he had confiscated Medina's ranch with the help of a handful of soldiers borrowed from General Cos, and since these things, if done at all, were best done quickly, he had begun that final trek shortly thereafter. Medina had talked of his home during the walk. He had been born and brought up in a palm-swept village on the east coast, and remembered it vividly. As O'Shannon listened, he had realized that Medina hoped that his death might mean a sort of homecoming, and that his spirit would find that tranquil innocence again. The Irishman was not insensitive to these nostalgic wanderings and wonderings: he too had childhood memories. He too had known poverty and ached to climb out of it. He too had understood that the only avenue open to him was to learn to fight better than most men could. He too had left a small village and clawed his way to prominence, and yet wistfully desired that which had been left behind. Out of mercy—he called it respect for a fellow soldier—Luther O'Shannon had fired in midsentence, in mid-dream. Perhaps, if there were any justice or luck at all, Medina's soul would fly from his body and soar over that shimmering white coast lined with dusty green palms, and see himself below, still young and tan and lithe and unencumbered. The lead ball knocked him to the earth, sprawled in the lifeless frozen spasm of a collapsed marionette.

A man's birthplace sticks in his craw. Three months later, Luther O'Shannon stared down at the slight mound beneath his feet. "Did you find it?" he asked. "Was it as you remembered, señor?"

The dead man kept his answer to himself. The enemies O'Shannon buried stayed silent, stayed dead, except in his dreams, where the fallen marionettes often rose to dance again. Contemplative, O'Shannon pursued the metaphor, expanded it from the moldering Medina to the world at large as he walked back toward the *hacienda*. It was a simple metaphor, but it worked well enough. To regain control, a man had to manipulate many strings, keep in mind where each led, and what the consequences were of twitching it. Even his son Ramez was one string. What other children O'Shannon might have had were conveniently forgotten. One son was enough to keep in line. Lucita, headstrong and sensual nearly to a fault, was another. Santa Anna was far away but an important and difficult string: distance was necessary because the land he had bestowed was far away from Mexico City, and dangerous because one never knew who *el Presidente* was listening to at any given moment. Closer to home, yet another string attached to the settlers, whose numbers were increasing almost daily. Land-hungry, industrious, and imbued with a sense of individuality and self-esteem, they were an irritating thorn in his side—which was an apt description for General Cos, too, the final string.

Cos was one of those officers O'Shannon considered inevitable in every soldier's life. The general had no appreciation of the finer aspects of the art of warfare. He had been assigned the farflung outpost of San Antonio by Bustamente because his family was very wealthy and had to be placated, and because the former president believed he would do the least amount of harm there. Santa Anna had allowed him to remain for the same reasons. Unfortunately, the general appeared to be little more than a frightened martinet, one who gave too much weight to the *peónes'* love of Medina and their anger over his fall, and not enough weight to the disruptive influence of the settlers. The day would come when O'Shannon would have to advise Santa Anna that Cos needed to be removed. There was plenty of time, however, to mull over the potential dangers of that particular problem. Ah, well, O'Shannon sighed inwardly, letting himself in at the front door and starting down the hall to his study.

"There you are." Dressed in a riding outfit, an angry Lucita stood in the doorway. "I've been looking all over for you."

"Oh?" It still took the Irishman a moment to make the mental switch from English to Spanish. "I've been out, as you can see," he answered waspishly. "What do you want?"

"Your son," Lucita fumed. "Can you teach him no manners? Pah! He is as bad as his father!"

O'Shannon brushed her aside and entered the study, which he also used as an office. "Really?" he asked dryly. "What has he insulted this time, your honor or your intelligence? If either is possible."

"He promised to escort me to San Antonio today to pick up my gown for the New Year's Fiesta, but he is nowhere to be found," she explained indignantly. "Now I don't know how I shall ever—"

"Be quiet, Lucita. In God's name just be quiet." O'Shannon poured himself a cup of coffee from the urn on his desk. "If you'd get up in time, these things wouldn't happen and I wouldn't have to listen to you chatter like a molting hen. Ramez left two hours ago."

"Two hours?" Lucita sputtered.

O'Shannon sipped his coffee. "In order to be there by noon. Something about a horse race. Now, will you get out of here and leave me in peace?"

"Oh!" Lucita angrily stamped her foot and spun around, her face childlike with an ugly pout. "A horse race? He prefers a horse race?" she shouted to the house at large. Her voice rang through the hall, followed by a curse and the sound of breaking pottery as she knocked over a plant. "I spit on a horse race, do you hear me? What is so special about a stupid horse race?"

It was in a manner of speaking, practice.

Firetail had begun to pull abreast of the bay mare as they rounded the corner and entered *Calle de la Soledad*, then headed at a dead run toward the *Plaza de las Islas* and *La Casa del Rio*. The citizens of San Antonio, *mestizos,* Indians, colonists, and soldiers shouted bets at each other and cheered on the two horses. All knew that the *norteamericano* named True Paxton had wagered a substantial sum in this race against Don Raphael Sanchez's fleetest mare. Most of the onlookers waited in the plaza itself to watch the finish. Two poles with a banner stretched between them had been erected just for the occasion.

Joseph Paxton had positioned himself in the front rank of the spectators, about a hundred feet from the finish line. The second the horses thundered past him, he grinned with relief and, having seen enough, began to work his way through the crowd toward a wagon set a few yards from and in a direct line with the poles. His goal was Ramez O'Shannon, who was watching the race with two friends, young officers under Cos's command.

A cheer erupted from the crowd. A good head taller than anyone around him, Joseph could see Ramez leaning forward intently as Firetail stretched his lead to a full head and neck, and won the race. He could also see as Don Raphael, stationed on the balcony of the hotel, gave a disappointed wag of his round, good-natured face and, with surprising haste, vanished inside. All around, the crowd milled about, arguing about the race while they paid and collected on the bets they had made.

"What do you think of that, Ramez O'Shannon?" Joseph asked, stopping by the wagon and talking loud enough for the young man and his friends and anyone nearby to hear.

Ramez looked down at Joseph and scoffed. "A race between nags. And the *gringo*'s nightmare of a horse barely won."

"Poor sentiments from one of your station, sir." An expert in his angler's role, Joseph knew exactly how much line to let go before he set the hook. "I would have thought you'd be as excited as everyone else to see such a magnificent contest between the best that San Antonio has to offer and a truly remarkable, if unknown, animal."

"Best?" Ramez laughed aloud, and his companions joined in. "Why, only two months ago my Torbellino bested Sanchez's nag by better than two lengths."

"Two months ago?" Joseph asked skeptically. The crowd was beginning to take notice. He gave a twitch to the line. "And where did this miracle occur? Was anyone present?"

He smiled and shrugged. "I wasn't. Perhaps this happened in a dream. Your dream, for instance."

Muffled laughter rippled through the crowd. Ramez colored. "Outside of town," he was compelled to explain. "The ridge road that circles the city. A challenging course. One for horses of breeding."

Joseph took off his hat and scratched his head. "Well," he said with a wink to a bystander, "the roan *was* bred, I can assure you of that."

Ramez's lips were a thin line. "Do you bait me, *gringo?* Have you taken leave of your senses?"

"Neither. I state a fact." Suddenly, Joseph sounded very businesslike. "It is a fact too that the roan can run anywhere, providing the wager is of interest."

"Torbellino," Ramez sneered, "would wait for that ugliest of animals at the finish post."

"And turn to find that fastest of animals already there ahead of him."

"Not one day in ten, *gringo*. But the question is meaningless. I would never disgrace Torbellino by matching him against that poor creature you so generously call a stallion."

Joseph nodded. The fish was solidly on the line, and he could start hauling it in. "Not only a stallion, but a winner, as you just saw."

"By a fluke," Ramez said, with a laconic wave of dismissal. "Sanchez's mare lost a step and was thrown off stride."

"A man can always find an argument when he is afraid."

Ramez had turned to jump down from the wagon, and spun around at the accusation. "You dare!" he sputtered.

"That's the problem. I dare and you don't." Joseph shrugged and smiled wryly. "But then you have your reasons, and must bed your fears in your own time."

Ramez's friends tried to restrain him, but the youth tore free of their grasp and stalked across the wagon bed to tower over Joseph. "Fool!" he spat. "You impugn the honor of the O'Shannons."

"Not at all," Joseph said mildly. "I am not the one afraid. You are. I only point out the obvious."

A crowd had gathered to listen. Someone sniggered, but shut up the second he felt Ramez's eyes meet his. It was not wise to offend an O'Shannon. No matter how little one had, one could always have less.

Ramez was trapped. "Name your wager!" he blustered, trying to save face. "Name it!"

Joseph and True had been over the figures a dozen times. They had six thousand dollars between them, including Andrew's share of the money they had carried all the way from South Carolina. That and five hundred pooled from the others, plus the five hundred won from Sanchez, made a fair-sized purse. Joseph paused, waiting for silence, and then spoke out for all to hear. "Seven thousand dollars American money. In gold. A man's wager."

A collective sigh hummed through the crowd. Ramez's friends quite suddenly looked uncomfortable and Ramez himself blanched. Having always received what he needed from his father, he had no money to speak of. And Luther would never agree to such a sum.

"Never mind," Joseph went on blandly, as if he had known all along what the answer would be. "I recognize your problem. You are thinking of another excuse. Very well. I will save you the trouble and call off the race." He started to walk away. His parting shot was icy with contempt. "You need fear no longer."

A hundred eyes stared at him. Ramez felt sick to his stomach. "The land!" he blurted out before he could think.

"Land?" Joseph asked skeptically, stopping in his tracks. His heart thudded. Hook, line and sinker!

"A thousand *hectares* of fine land. The best there is. More than enough to match your sum."

Joseph looked dubious. "That's seven dollars a *hectare*," he said. "That's more than twice what some people I know paid for land some fifteen miles south of here," he pointed out, in obvious reference to the land O'Shannon had taken from Medina. "Sounds a little steep to me."

"Fifteen hundred, then," Ramez said. "All I have." A light sweat beaded his brow. "This land is better. It's closer to town. There's better water. My top offer."

"Well . . ." Joseph didn't want to give in too easily, nor did he want to let this biggest fish of all get away. "How do I know you own this land?" he asked.

"I will bring the deed to Padre Salva. And you, *gringo*, will leave your money with him." Ramez was regaining his confidence. The money was as good as his. He smiled to show what a silly matter it all was. "What better place to find my reward than the church? That is, unless *you* are the one now thinking of an argument."

"Not on your life, sonny." Joseph held out his hand. "We have a bet."

Ramez ignored the proffered handshake. "You say when and I'll say where. Fair enough?"

"New Year's Day," Joseph said without hesitation. "At ten in the morning."

"The Ridge Road circle," Ramez decreed. "With the start and finish at the end of the plaza at *Calle de la Quinta*. See that Salva receives the money, *gringo*."

"And you be sure the priest receives the deed. Until then?"

"I will be there, as will Torbellino. First to start and first to return."

Those who had been listening scampered off to spread the news. Another race, this one between Ramez O'Shannon and the *norteamericano* with the ugly horse. And such a wager! So much money and so much land! This would be a New Year's Day no one would be likely to forget.

Joseph ambled toward the hotel and cut through the alley to the stables where True was busy rubbing down Firetail. "How's he doing?" he asked, his keen eye already noting that the stallion looked to be in perfect shape.

"Happy as a lark," True said. He shook out the tow sack, refolded it, and waited. "Well?" he finally asked, trying not to appear too anxious.

"All fifteen hundred hectares," Joseph said with great slow relish. "How close was it?"

"Could have had her by four lengths easy," True said, getting back to work on Firetail. "When and where?"

There had been tension between the two for the past few weeks, but it had faded quickly once there was work to be done. Joseph recounted the conversation and enumerated the details.

"Better than two lengths," True said, comparing the four lengths he thought he could count on to the two by which the white stallion had beaten Sanchez's mare. It might be a close race. He threw a blanket over Firetail and left him for Scott Campbell, who would rub him down again in a half hour. "I hope so, big brother," he said, "I'll tell you what, though."

"What?" Joseph asked, leading the way out of the stable.

"I think we have a race on our hands. A *real* race, this

time. And just in case, I think we ought to take turns sleeping with our animal. Any argument?''

"Not a one," Joseph said, his head wagging slowly up and down. "I saw that boy's eyes. He's a crafty little sonofabitch. If not before, then during the race. Watch him." They stepped into the shade of Mama Flores's balcony.

A crowd of well-wishers, winners all, waited for True. Across the large open room, Don Raphael Sanchez sat in one of the large chairs by the fireplace, sipped a glass of wine, and waited to pay his debt. True made his way through the crowd, shook hands, exchanged pleasantries, and invited everyone to the bar, where he said he'd join them in a few moments. "Ah, the thrill of victory," Don Raphael told Elizabeth, who waited for True at his side. "Were it not for your beauty, señorita, I would deeply regret that Mama Flores introduced me to this *vaquero* of yours."

"And I'm sorry someone as nice as you had to lose," Elizabeth replied simply, smiling up at True as he joined them.

"My compliments on a race well run," True said, stretching his lanky body into a third chair.

Don Raphael regarded True quizzically, at last smiled and produced a small sack containing the five hundred dollars he had lost. "Interestingly run might be a more appropriate term, don't you think?" he asked.

"Sir?"

"Come, come, my young friend." Don Raphael jiggled the sack up and down and listened to the clinking of the coins. "I am an old man, one who delights in observation. I have spent a good many years studying horses and riders. Among other things," he added, smiling in Elizabeth's direction. "You were holding back your remarkable animal. You took a chance on losing rather than claim the victory cleanly and without question."

He chuckled and sipped at his wine again. "This puzzled me a little until a friend bore me the news of another challenge accepted. Another race. With Ramez O'Shannon." His head bobbed up and down. "The white stallion, Torbellino, eh? Ah, clever, clever. I understand completely."

True managed to look bewildered. "Mr. O'Shannon was watching just like everyone else. I don't see—"

Don Raphael made a little clucking noise and wagged his finger at True. "You have used me, señor."

"I won the race fairly," True protested.

"But of course. Please do not misunderstand me. I placed the wager, and I lost. You had no idea of how quick my animal was, and could have lost. Still—" His voice dropped and he leaned forward. "—you used me—how do you say? —adroitly. And though it has cost me, I am appreciative. Let me tell you something."

Intrigued, True leaned closer, as did Joseph, who pulled up a bench and straddled it.

"I am a landowner of modest means, a man who survives by remaining neutral in great and small affairs alike. There is, however, a wind blowing through Mexico, and I am unsure of just how long I will be able to maintain this neutrality. I like you. You are smart and, I think, honest. I like Americans. They work hard and dare to dream." His quick eyes checked the room. No one was paying undue attention. "This, now, is confidential, and I trust you will not repeat it. I was Cirilio Medina's good friend, and they killed him in cold blood. I was a friend to Bustamente, and he is deposed and dead. Though I must appear to be so, I am no friend of Santa Anna's, much less this Luther O'Shannon and the whelp he calls a son." Don Raphael's eyes glowed with unmasked hatred, then quickly converted to his usual bland appearance as he remembered he was in public. "Anything that discomforts these people pleases me," he went on in a normal tone, "so I am glad you won and hope you win again. And that my five hundred dollars—I see now why you insisted on dollars—will be of use in what you are trying to do. Fifteen hundred *hectares* will serve you quite well."

Don Raphael's eyes narrowed and his voice grew hoarse. "It is little enough I can do for you now, but perhaps worth something. Torbellino is a far better horse than my mare, and when they raced he did not have to try very hard to win. He is very fast, and his rider is full of tricks, so you must be wary. I think you will beat him, though. If you do, there are those who will sell you cows for a very fair price, and teach you about this land which is different from that so far to the north. We are not bold, but that much we will dare. If you win."

The smile returned and the old man stood and dropped the bag of gold coins into True's outstretched hand. "I will be here to watch, my friends." He bowed deeply to Elizabeth, nodded his head to True and Joseph. "Señorita. Señores. Until we meet again, eh?"

In silence True, Elizabeth, and Joseph watched him leave. "Well, shit!" Joseph said, immediately adding a contrite, "Sorry," to Elizabeth.

"Didn't have to try very hard," True said, the words ringing in his ears. "There goes our two lengths." He looked at Joseph. "Well? What do you think?"

"I think Andrew's gonna be mad enough to whip us both single-handed if we lose his two thousand. And I don't know as I'd blame him," Joseph admitted ruefully.

"You *did* win today," Elizabeth pointed out, trying to inject a ray of hope into the gloom.

"Yeah," True said. "Today. What about Thursday?"

Joseph stood, swung one leg over the bench, and hitched up his pants. "I'll tell you what about Thursday," he said with a grim smile. "Lottie may have a fit, but I'm gonna get out there, pretend that animal is the emperor of all North America, and rub him down myself."

The crystal goblet exploded into streaming slivers of glass that sprayed outward from the stone fireplace and sprinkled the floor in front of the hearth. Luther O'Shannon tromped through the twinkling shards, pacing from one side of the room to the other. His boots clicked authoritatively on the tile, thudded on the rugs. Pride and a meticulous devotion to self-discipline were the two characteristics a man needed if he wished to be the cream that rose to the top of what O'Shannon metaphorically referred to as the scummy milk pail of humanity. These, with an accompanying sense of self-esteem, he had given his son—or so he had thought. And hoped. Only to find out that the silly ass . . . "Leave us!" he thundered to Lucita, who lounged in one of the great chairs next to the fireplace.

Lucita began to protest, but wisdom asserted itself. She shrugged, rose, and stalked petulantly from the room.

"Fifteen hundred *hectares!*" Luther roared, reverting to English as the door clicked shut behind Lucita. "Fifteen hundred of the very best *hectares* north of the Rio Grande. I gave you that land so you could make something of yourself."

"I will," Ramez retorted confidently. "Seven thousand dollars."

"If you win."

"I'll win. Torbellino will run circles around the roan." He chuckled. "You should have seen him, Father, trying so hard to beat Sanchez's bay and just barely winning.'' Ramez walked over to the table and poured a glass of *pulque* for himself. The milky white liquor gave off a sour aroma. He wrinkled his nose. A *peón*'s drink. But good to sleep on.

O'Shannon sank tiredly into the chair Lucita had vacated. ''You have had enough. Leave it!''

Ramez glared at his father, but obeyed.

''Did it ever occur to you,'' O'Shannon asked patiently, ''that this True Paxton might have heard of Torbellino's race with the mare?''

''Impossible!'' Ramez snorted. ''Why on earth would he and his damn brother make such a foolish wager then, when they know I can beat them?''

The elder O'Shannon tried not to sound too painfully aware of his son's shortsightedness. ''Because perhaps they know more than you give them credit for knowing.''

''I think,'' Ramez said, drawing himself up to his full height, ''that you are being specious, Father. This argument is designed to keep me from doing as I wish. You gave me the land to do with as I pleased. I please to wager it on Torbellino's speed. When the race is finished, I will have land *and* money.''

''A wise man does not wager his land. The land he owns is the basis of his fortune. If he loses it, he loses all. I don't like it.''

''Because at last I will be independent of you?'' Ramez asked softly. ''Father, please. Stand aside in this matter.''

Stand aside. The cream rose to the top of the milk on its own, after all was said and done. A man could give his son only so much, and no more. Slowly, Luther O'Shannon uncoiled from the chair, walked over to Ramez, and placed his hands on his shoulders. ''Aside, is it? I am old and in the way, is that it?'' He sighed, cupped his hand around the back of his son's head, and gave him a playful, affectionate shake. ''Very well, Ramez. The land is yours to do with as you wish. But one thing.'' His voice dropped and he stared directly into Ramez's eyes. ''Do anything but lose.''

Ramez exuded confidence. ''I will not lose, Father.''

''The Ridge Road can be dangerous—''

''I have ridden it many times. The southern height is the key, but Torbellino is sure-footed and I have handled worse.''

''Under no circumstances will you allow True Paxton to

win," O'Shannon insisted, as if he had not heard what his son had said. "Do you understand me?"

Ramez returned his father's stare without blinking. "Of course, Father."

"Good." O'Shannon turned away wearily. "Then off to bed with you. You'll have a long day tomorrow."

Ramez sighed. He detested being treated like a child, but he was tired and would have to start for San Antonio early in the morning so Torbellino would be well rested by Thursday. "Very well," he said stiffly. "Good night, Father."

The door clicked closed again, and O'Shannon was alone. Tired himself, he picked up the glass of *pulque* Ramez had poured and sank into the chair by the fire. He tasted the liquor and scowled. *Pulque* was meant to be drunk from clay, not fine crystal. Everything had its place. Liquor as well as people. Trouble began when they left their place.

He stared into the flames. A servant moved in front of him and swept up the powdery fragments, then silently left. O'Shannon tried to recall Ramez's mother, the way she had looked before the cholera had sapped her strength and wrung the flesh from her young bones, but all he could remember was a skin-tight mask of death, so he moved his thoughts elsewhere. To the race, to the wager. To True Paxton, a stranger from the North who had entered Luther O'Shannon's private, contented world. He stirred. Misgivings nibbled at his mind. But Ramez deserved to have his day and his chance. No argument about that.

Outside, the south wind had stilled. Luther O'Shannon listened, but could hear nothing except the sound of the fire. He wouldn't sleep this night, nor the next, nor the next. Soon he would have company, though. Before the night was over, the north wind would be baying at the door.

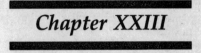

Chapter XXIII

Emperor, as they had taken to calling Firetail after Joseph's comment two days earlier, was resting. True dozed in a pile of hay just outside the stallion's stall. It had been a rough two days, and there were another twenty-two hours to go before the race. Their preparations had been exhaustive. The same afternoon that Joseph made the bet with Ramez, True had found a man who knew the course O'Shannon had picked, and rode around it on one of the stable horses. Three hours later, right around five o'clock, he had ridden Firetail slowly around it again, after which Firetail received his third rubdown of the day. Afterward, Joseph himself picked a bag of oats and another of corn at random and set them aside. With equal care, he and he alone carried the emperor's water from the well.

No less than three people had warned them to beware of the O'Shannons, so just to be sure, True and Joseph had taken turns staying awake at the stable. Firetail wasn't used to such constant attention and responded with increased nervousness, as if he knew something was up, but that was the price they paid. A norther had blown in Monday night. By Tuesday morning it was cold enough to leave a skim of ice on standing water. The sun came out Tuesday around one, and True took the occasion to half walk, half run Firetail around the course. They kept the same vigil Tuesday night as they had Monday.

No one suspicious had come to the stables or been seen lurking around when Firetail was let outdoors. By Wednesday at noon, while the rest of the town geared up for the New Year's Eve festivities, True had begun to think they had imagined threats where there were none, and were acting like a couple of little old ladies. He was about ready to leave the stable when the door opened and Joseph came ambling in with lunch. "If it doesn't snow and we don't all freeze to death before morning, I guess we'll have a race," he said, handing True a plate wrapped in a towel. "Old timers say tomorrow's gonna be the same as today. We never ran him in weather like this before."

True opened the towel and sniffed at his food.

"He likes the cold," he said, spooning beans laced with hot chili onto a *tortilla*. "These smell good. Just what the doctor ordered."

"Yeah. Feed your horse some of them beans and he'll by God live up to his name," Joseph growled, his lips turning up at the corners.

"Can't be that bad. Just a bunch of beans." True took a bite. "Jeee-sussss!" he gasped.

Joseph tried not to grin. "Told you," he drawled. "But go on and eat up. Wouldn't want Firetail to feel all alone in the world."

True drank some water and bit a hunk out of a plain *tortilla*. "You sure have a funny way of cheering someone up," he said.

"You did look a little glum. Just thought I'd take your mind off the race for a minute."

"With a brother like you . . . ." True's grin faded. "I keep telling myself that O'Shannon's horse will be running in the same weather as ours. And that ought to even everything out."

"Sounds reasonable." Pensive, Joseph walked into the stall and ran a practiced hand over Firetail's flank. "Feels good. One more time around and he'll be as ready as he ever will. When are you leaving?"

"Few minutes. Elizabeth's coming by. We're going to ride it together.

"Oh? You two been riding a lot lately." Joseph emerged from the stall, stood over True. "And not just on horseback."

True's face hardened. "None of your business, big brother."

"Or so I hear," Joseph amended with a shrug.

"Well, maybe you've been listening too hard."

"Have it your way," Joseph said. "I've listened too hard."

True searched his brother's face for a hint of sarcasm. Finding none, he softened, rolled another *tortilla* full of beans, and handed it to him. "Here. Put some fire in *your* tail."

Joseph clapped True on the shoulder, took a seat next to him, and began to eat. In seconds, his face was reddening. "I want you to win that race," he said, trying to talk and gasp at the same time. He took a swallow of coffee, which only made it worse, and switched to water. "It's never *really* mattered before, but this time we have to win."

"That was the general idea," True agreed, recalling his initial inspiration after his encounter with Ramez O'Shannon by the creek.

"You know why I came to Texas?"

It was a surprising question, seemingly out of context with the subject at hand. True looked sharply at his brother, but could find no signs of rancor or of the anger that usually drove him. Inside the stall, as if impatient for an answer, Firetail drummed on the plank floor. "No," True said. "Why?"

"I came along for the ride." Joseph swallowed his beans and took another sip of water. "At twenty-seven years, that's a hell of a reason to do anything. I've been thinking, though—surprise, eh?—and time was when this would have been just another bet. If luck went against us, so what? Find a warm whore for a cold night, get drunk, and the hell with it. Why not?"

"Joseph . . ."

"No. I'm not through." Joseph stared at the tiny, iridescent drops of oil floating on top of his coffee as if they carried a message that, if he were clever enough, he could decipher. "I couldn't sleep last night. Just lay there next to Lottie and stared at the ceiling. Jason was cut out for running Paxton Shipping. I knew it but I resented him anyway. As for you and Andrew, I figured because you came from a mother different from mine, that it always had to be me against you."

"I never felt that way," True said softly. "I can't imagine Andrew did, either."

"Doesn't matter. As far as I was concerned, you did. Mainly because Father favored you. No—" He held up a hand to stop True. "That's a fact, and I don't blame him. I did for a long time, but not now. I was the eldest in age only. You were the one we all followed. Look, we even followed you to Texas."

"Hogjaw—"

"Brought us. He took you. Andrew and I tagged along. What I'm getting at . . ." He trailed off, looked for the right words. "Lottie . . . I don't know if I love her, True. I've never loved any woman I've bedded. But we're married and so be it. And I love what's inside of her." He looked at True for the first time since he'd started talking. "She's carrying my child, True. Son or daughter, I don't care. It's my child. And I want a house to raise it in. A house of my own on land that I own. So this race matters. I don't want to go grubbing and scratching about, True."

Horse sounds. Wind through cracks in the walls. The door creaked open. "True?" It was Elizabeth.

"In here," True called, with an apologetic glance at Joseph.

"Doesn't matter," Joseph said. "I'm finished anyways. All talked out. There's work to be done. You two go on."

"Joseph . . ."

"I said go on," Joseph repeated gruffly. "I have to get some sleep if I'm gonna stay up all night with the emperor here."

"All right." True rose, reached out to touch Joseph but pulled his hand away at the last moment. "We won't lose," he promised quietly so Elizabeth wouldn't hear.

"It's almost one," Elizabeth said, appearing out of the gloomy front part of the stable. "You ready?"

"Just finishing eating," True said, taking her hand and giving it a squeeze. "Joseph and I've been talking tactics and strategy. Sleep well?"

"Mmm-hmmm. Morning, Joseph."

"Morning?" Joseph sounded like his old self again. "Don't let Hogjaw ever catch you calling afternoon morning. He'll try to trade faces with you." He set down his plate and started into Firetail's stall. "You saddle hers. I'll take care of Firetail."

Easier said than done, True thought, genuinely worried about the race. Working quickly, he saddled the same little chestnut mare Elizabeth had ridden for the past two days, then walked both horses to the front door and, after helping Elizabeth mount and waving goodbye to Joseph, headed Firetail toward the *Calle de la Quinta*. "Quiet today," he finally said, when Elizabeth hadn't spoken for the first few minutes.

"Oh?" Elizabeth said, a little coolly. "Nothing to say, I guess."

They rode in silence, following the path the race would take. The trail was actually an assortment of paths that, as seen from a map, continually bore to the left and traced an uneven but closed loop that hung from the southern edge of town. Someone had erected flags along the course since the day before, and True had time to think for the first half mile or so. Elizabeth was withdrawn to the point of truculence. He had to admit he hadn't paid much—any, really—attention to her for the past two days. But that wasn't his fault. A great deal was at stake and he had been hard on the grind. The least she could do was understand.

The course began to rise into the hills, and True concentrated on the job at hand. His eyes sweeping every inch of the trail, he took note of slopes and angles, of dips or obstructions that might cause a mishap. Twice he rode a section, turned Firetail about and retraced his steps, and then rode it at a gallop. The worst, most dangerous part of the course lay at the extreme southern end. There, the horses were forced to run up a gradually sloping hill, climb a truly brutal twenty yards amid a jumble of boulders, and zigzag another hundred yards or so along the rim of a limestone cliff before beginning a long, slow, angling descent that would take them back to town. True rode Firetail up the steepest part of the climb, walked him back down, and let him walk up it again to make sure both of them knew the exact route they would take through the boulders. "This is the hard part," he told Elizabeth, holding her chestnut's bridle as he led the way along the rim.

"You realize this is insane, don't you?" Elizabeth asked in return, trying not to look over the edge.

"You want that land or not?"

The little mare shied. Elizabeth gasped and held onto the saddle horn. "Of course," she snapped, more in fear than anger.

The path widened and True led them all into a sheltered spot out of the wind. "Then don't make it any harder than it already is," he said, handing back the reins to Elizabeth. He let one hand rest on her thigh. "Please?" he asked gently. "I need all the help I can get, Elizabeth."

Elizabeth swung down off her horse, leaned against a wagon-sized boulder. Men were such an intolerable mixture of shrewdness and density, she thought. All True had to do was tell her he still loved her, that he wanted to marry her. All he had to do was set aside the race for a few moments, take her in his arms, and kiss her. That wasn't asking too much, was it? She too had been busy. She had carried water. She had brought him his meals, listened to his and Joseph's endless speculation about each and every aspect of the race. She wasn't being selfish. She had a right to be indignant. Of course the race was important. But not as important as the two of them. Nothing was that important. When a man and a woman were in love . . .

"Stay here," True said shortly, unwilling to wait any longer for a response. "We're going over this a few more times, and then head back to town."

When a man and a woman were in love . . . Elizabeth sighed, wished she were warm again. He was so damned intense! It wasn't as if he'd never raced before. He had. Often. The stakes were higher this time, of course, but the race itself couldn't be *that* different. A little smile creased the corners of her mouth as she sank further out of the cutting wind. All the help he could get? Very well. Very well, indeed. A hint of mystery to distract him would do for starters. And then? Joseph was due to watch Firetail that night while True relaxed and got some rest. The smile deepened, then faded and became secretive. He would rest, surely enough. And relax, too. Of *that*, if nothing else, Elizabeth was certain.

The trail flirted dangerously with the rim and a steep, boulder-strewn apron of rubble created by countless years of rain and ice and wind. True looked over the serrated edge and chipped loose a large chunk of timeworn limestone with his bootheel. A man on horseback might make it down the apron if he could keep his horse's head up and not panic. Not that he wanted to try it, he thought, leading Firetail back to the beginning of the treacherous section. The course's incline was rugged enough without riding off a cliff. Slowly, checking each foot of the way, he walked the route again before mounting and riding back. Ramez O'Shannon and Torbellino had raced that stretch before, had run it again that very morning according to rumor. True's only chance was to become as well acquainted with it as possible in the short time allotted to him.

Three times they walked the ridge. On the fourth, True gave Firetail his head and let him run. Neck stretched, hooves sending a shower of pebbles and rocks down the slope, the hammerhead stallion thundered along the hundred crooked yards without a misstep.

"Well?" True asked, reining to a halt and dropping to the ground by Elizabeth's side. "What do you think?"

"I think you worry too much," Elizabeth said.

"Oh, really?" True patted Firetail's neck. "Looked easy, did it?"

"Not terribly difficult."

"That's because we're alone. If we both get here at the same time, though, this little exercise will pay off, believe me. You about ready?"

"I'm about frozen," Elizabeth said, leading the chestnut out of the rocks and preparing to mount.

"Beautiful from here," True said, restraining her.

"San Antonio is very pretty."

"I mean you."

"Oh," Elizabeth said with calculated coolness, the first part of her plan.

True tried to put his arms around her. "For heaven's sake, Elizabeth," he said, exasperated when she stepped away.

"Don't blaspheme."

"Blaspheme? Who the hell is blaspheming, goddamn it?"

Their breath clouded on the air, was swept away rapidly. "Shall we go back?" Elizabeth asked. "I'm cold."

"I'll say," True snapped, instantly regretting his tone.

Elizabeth put her foot in the stirrup and, angry despite herself, mounted the chestnut.

"Oh, boy!" True said, throwing up his hands. "Look. I surrender. Aren't you even going to tell me what I've done?"

"Maybe it's what you haven't done," Elizabeth answered dryly and, clucking to the mare, rode off.

Eager to be back in a warm stall with a bait of oats, the little mare trotted off smartly. Behind her, True tilted his hat back on his head and scratched his forehead. Now what was eating Elizabeth, he wondered? He had bayed at her heels all the way to Texas. He was trying to win her land back. He certainly hadn't forced her into bed. He had repeatedly vowed his love, and already had begun plans for a cabin for them. What more could a woman want?

Realization struck like a battering ram. "True Paxton," he said, springing onto Firetail's back and riding after her, "you're a dimwitted, loose-brained, cross-eyed, sod-poor excuse for a future husband!''

With all his plans and expectations for the two of them, one thing had cleanly slipped his mind. One very important thing that—as soon as the race was over and won—involved a preacher.

Chapter XXIV

New Year's Day morning dawned crackling cold but without the wind that had kept most of San Antonio indoors for the last two days. Elizabeth woke to a half-emtpy pallet. The covers were cold as ice where True had slept. He had been up and gone long ago, probably before light. A slow smile crept over her face as she remembered the night before. They had slipped away early from the usual gathering of friends in town, as much to be together as for True to get a good night's sleep. His mind on the race, True had been tense and jittery as they began to make love, but then, avid and all-consuming. And he certainly had relaxed, she thought, remembering how he had dropped off and slept like a log. But then, so had she. Warm and satiated and feeling very much in love, she had slept soundly.

A little frown replaced her smile. He still hadn't proposed, darn him. Once the race was over and before the sun set, he most certainly would though—if she had to drag it out of him. The first day of the new year was a good time for beginnings. The whole rest of their life together would begin that day. Of that she was determined.

Quickly, shivering against the cold, Elizabeth rolled out of the blankets, dug in her trunk, and pulled on a pair of corduroy trousers for warmth. Her chemise and yellow dress, True's favorite, followed, topped off with her father's old coat, which she and Joan had altered while still on the trail. The sleeves needed rolling up, but the shoulders fit well, and the whole garment hung well below her hips.

The camp was deserted. Hurrying, Elizabeth moved the coffee closer to the fire before visiting the latrine and taking a quick wash-up. She had just poured her coffee when the church bells began to ring. One, two. She counted unconsciously, pulled the coffee off the fire. Three, four. Nine o'clock, probably. The crowd would have begun to gather. Lots of hangovers and bleary eyes, she imagined. Five, six. She smiled warmly, remembering the children who gathered at the church and the animated light in the eyes of the one chosen to ring the bells. Something about children and bells. She would have a dinner bell next to the door of her house, just like they'd had in Pennsylvania. When she had been good, her mother had let her ring it to call her father from the fields. Seven, eight. She felt in her pocket, touched the ribbon she'd bought three days ago for True to wear. He'd probably think it was silly, but wouldn't say so. And if his face got the slightest bit red, she'd . . . Nine, ten.

Ten!

She froze. Impossible! She had miscounted. Surely she hadn't slept that long. Not ten! It couldn't be that late. Frantic, she dropped her coffee cup and ran out of the camp toward town.

True!

I'm here! Right here! Don't start without me. Her heart was throbbing, her breath rasping in her throat. There must be time. Please, God, slow the time, stretch the seconds.

True!

She had to hurry, had to catch him before the race started. What would he think? He's miss her, think she was angry, or worse, that something had happened to her. If he lost the race, then she would be to blame. Late? Too late. Unless . . .

True ignored the crowd as he looked for Elizabeth. Damn it, where was she? Joseph hadn't seen her. Neither had Nels or Hogjaw. She couldn't be angry again, not after the night they'd spent together. Unless she was miffed because he'd left without waking her. Surely she'd understand that, though. She could be sick, he supposed. But that didn't make sense. Someone else would have known, and told him. The only alternative left was that someone had . . . The O'Shannons! He and Joseph had been watching Firetail. What if the threat lay elsewhere? What if they'd done something to . . .

No. He wasn't going to let himself think that way. It didn't make sense. There was no point in holding or hurting Elizabeth unless they told him they were doing so. For that matter, what did they even know about Elizabeth? True hadn't exactly hidden his affection for her, but for an outsider to know how important she was to him would be difficult.

The race. Think about the race. First things first. Some logical explanation. Probably something silly and unimportant. Concentrate on the immediate problem. Winning.

The bells had rung ten o'clock. General Cos had arrived and was talking to Luther O'Shannon. True kept an eye on them. Less ostentatiously dressed than his son, O'Shannon rode a massive steel gray stallion and radiated an aura of capability and confidence. Perhaps that, True reflected, was the reason for Ramez's exaggerated cockiness. Weak and ineffectual by comparison to the one man in the world he wanted so badly to emulate, Ramez's only recourse was a desperate combination of fancy clothes and a brash demeanor. It was a sad imitation at best. True preferred the elder O'Shannon's ruthlessness to his son's empty arrogance.

General Cos held out his hand and took a pistol from his aide. Ramez quieted Torbellino and patted him on the neck, keeping him well away from Firetail. His master affected an appearance of contemptuous calm, but Torbellino, knowing the race was about to begin, pranced about nervously. Neither True nor Ramez had spoken to each other, only exchanged cold nods of acknowledgment. Fine with me, True thought, edging Firetail toward the starting pole. The next few minutes would tell everything that needed to be said. If only Elizabeth were . . .

"True Paxton."

True's heart leaped into his throat as Luther O'Shannon approached him. Was this it? The veiled, nor not-so-veiled, threat? He tried to think of how he would answer, but his mind was a whirling blank.

"I suspect what you have done," O'Shannon said, icily calm. "My son is young and quick-tempered and you baited him well. I, however, am not so easily tricked, and have cautioned him to take you and your mount seriously."

No threat, then! True's heart slowed and his mind returned to the race. So Ramez knew. Did that make any difference? "So?" he asked, wondering what O'Shannon was getting at.

"So the race might be closer than anyone expects. And this. I have, with your permission, thrust a saber into the wood pillar at the corner of the plaza at the *Calle de la Quinta*. Rather than trust judges to call the finish, the winner will be the man who draws the saber from the wood. I trust that is satisfactory?''

''No complaints here,'' True called flatly. ''That way there won't be any question when I beat the pants off your son.''

True thought the remark would anger O'Shannon, but the Irishman merely smiled faintly and nodded. ''You too are young,'' he said matter-of-factly. ''And brash. I hope—'' He touched the gray's flank and the animal backed smartly away from True. ''—you are not too disillusioned.'' Not waiting for an answer, he wheeled his horse, stopped briefly to whisper something to his son, and withdrew to the edge of the plaza.

General Cos raised his arms and the crowd quieted while he announced the conditions of the race and the wager. True patted Firetail's neck. The roan stallion pawed at the earth and shook his mane. Ramez took off his hat and threw it to one of his father's men. ''Get 'im, True,'' Joseph shouted from somewhere to the left.

Cos lifted his pistol, pointed it to the sky.

''I wish,'' True began silently, ''Elizabeth was—''

The shot startled him. Ramez on Torbellino leaped into an instant lead. Right behind him, Firetail exploded into motion. A roar of approval sounded from the plaza. True rose in the stirrups and crouched low over Firetail's withers. The race was on, and the first trick was to stay close enough to Torbellino on the flats so he could overtake on the hills and pass before they reached the climb that led to the rim. Nothing else mattered.

Elizabeth could see True's head over the crowd. Sobbing, she beat her way through the rear ranks and into the press of excited humanity. She heard the shot and saw True's head disappear as he crouched over the saddle, but didn't associate either of those with the start of the race until, a fraction of a second later, the roar of the crowd blotted out everything else. ''No!'' she screamed, unheard. ''Wait! You can't—'' A hand caught her wrist and held her in a relentless grip. ''Let me go! Let me go! Help!''

''Calm down, durn ya!''

She looked up, saw Hogjaw at her side. ''I didn't know it was so late,'' she yelled above the noise. ''Did True—''

''No time for talk now,'' Hogjaw interrupted. ''This way.

Just grab aholt of my coat and follow. A start never meant a tick's worth. The finish is where the game is played.''

She took a second too long to agree, almost lost him, then grabbed the back of his coat and let herself be dragged along. Without him, she never would have made it through the crowd that was already moving toward the shiny saber thrust into the post. She was almost sorry she did, because when they reached the rope that separated the throng from the space left open for the racing horses, there was nothing left to do but wait. And that was the hardest part of all.

Torbellino was well ahead and running alone by the time they passed the last *jacalito* and entered open country. The flat road was hard-packed and easy to run on, just the sort of conditions that the white stallion liked. Ahead, the foothills rose into the morning sun. The flag that marked the turnoff into the moutains barely wiggled in the light breeze. Ramez took the turn and glanced over his shoulder. The roan was a good fifteen lengths behind him, running well but not, it appeared, gaining. If he could hold the lead through the climb and along the rim, there was no question but that he would walk away with the colonists' money. And oh, but victory would be sweet.

A flag was a blur as they passed it. Torbellino leaned into the curve, and powered up the slope. Ramez checked behind him again and saw, to his astonishment, that the roan, evidently stronger than Torbellino, was beginning to narrow the distance between them. There were still a thousand or more yards to go before the hard climb. If he could just hold him off that long . . .

Another flag. A sharp climbing turn to the left and then again to the right. Torbellino missed a step and Firetail picked up another two lengths. Only five hundred yards, and already the gap had shrunk to no more than three lengths. The three times Ramez had raced this route he had allowed Torbellino to slack off a little on this rise so that he would be rested for the run into town. In none of the three previous races, though, had a horse challenged him so strongly, much less threatened to overtake him. Worried, Ramez put the quirt to Torbellino's flank, slashed down again and again as he bent around the final flag on the ascent.

At that moment, bent low over Torbellino, he first heard the whistle of Firetail's breath. He dared a glance to his right.

The great roan's head was even with his own, then inched ahead, even with Torbellino's. Horrified, Ramez watched the great legs driving up and down, the hooves drumming the packed earth, the heaving chest gulping in huge draughts of the frigid air. And in that same instant, he thought he heard his father's voice in his ear. "Don't let him win," he had said. "Do anything but lose."

Less than a hundred yards away, the labyrinth of boulders loomed above them. A vague hollowness ate at Ramez's stomach. His throat burned. Panic tore though him, made him slash at Torbellino until the blood welled from the steaming white flanks. Even so the roan pulled ahead and swerved in front of him, blotting out the world. Never before in a race had Torbellino seen another horse's tail or eaten another horse's dust. *Do anything but lose.* But he'd never lost. Never in his life. An O'Shannon didn't lose, didn't know the meaning of the word. Not Luther O'Shannon. Not Luther O'Shannon's son.

Both men slowed their mounts as the first boulders flashed by and the incline steepened. Firetail picked his way through the route True had chosen the day before. Behind him and to his right, Torbellino followed a slightly longer but smoother path as he heaved his way upward. Ramez took chances, drove the white stallion on, and suddenly, as the horse faltered, saw the pink flecks in the saliva that flowed from his mouth. Torbellino was coming abreast of Firetail, but only because he was being driven beyond his limits. True Paxton knew it, too, Ramez could tell. The *gringo*'s horse had strength to spare, was taking the climb with ease. Torbellino had spirit, but was broken, finished. There was a chance he would gain the height first, but he was so tired his chances of winning had diminished to near zero.

Do anything but lose. Ramez could see the look of disgust on his father's face. *Do anything but lose.* The son had failed the father once again. *Do anything but lose.* Torbellino stumbled. Ramez jerked viciously on the reins, pulled him upright, slashed him with the quirt. *I will have land and money.* Had he said that? *Now you have neither money nor land.* His father would say that. *Do anything but lose!*

The roan gained the height first and Torbellino broke out of the boulders right behind him. The wind rushed past Ramez's ears. Pounding hooves. The labored scream of Torbellino's breathing. His father's voice thundering in his brain. His own boasts, come back to haunt him. The muted laughter of the *peónes*. Crazed, Ramez forced Torbellino into one final surge that took him abreast of Firetail on the narrow trail and then, as the blood-streaked white stallion, so magnificent only five short minutes earlier, broke, just as he started to fall back, winded, Ramez jerked him to the left, deliberately into the roan.

True braced himself. In that lengthening time given to men in a crisis, he realized what Ramez had done, saw with terrible clarity that which he had considered the day before, and then was too busy to think past each dizzying second.

They were off the trail and over the side. The valley floor tilted crazily below. Firetail was bracing, relaxing, leaning back, throwing his weight to one side or the other to keep his balance. Close at his side, showering him with rocks and dirt, Torbellino followed, with Ramez caught in the devastating consequences of his folly. True leaned back, set Firetail almost on his haunches, helped him around the first boulder. The same stone caught Torbellino's front legs and broke them. With a shrill whinny of pain, Torbellino collapsed and rolled over with Ramez caught in his saddle. Ramez screamed and tried to jump free, but couldn't. The ornate pommel stabbed him in the belly, bursting his abdomen as the full weight of more than half a ton of horse rolled over him once, and then again and again and again, tumbling like a great broken doll that spilled, instead of sawdust, real blood and entrails.

True saw none of this. His world encompassed a space no larger than himself, his horse, and the next boulder racing uphill to meet him. The ground in front of him slanted sickeningly. He pulled his right foot out of the stirrup and shoved hard against the side of the hill. Firetail skewed to his left, and pointed into the slide again. Chips of flying limestone cut True's cheeks and slashed his hands. A boulder inflated to fill the horizon and reach out with what seemed like a life of its own to smash into his arm. He could feel the bone give, was sure he heart it snap, though he felt nothing.

Lean back in the saddle. Keep his head up. Good boy. Good boy.

Death was in the winter dust. Death in the noise, in the preternatural quiet, lurking to either side and ahead. Death waiting for one slip, one miniscule misjudgment. Just one.

Gradually, the world straightened and Firetail's wild, sliding ride slowed as the slope bottomed out. Legs stiff, head up, eyes wild, the stallion stopped and stood trembling on flat ground. A rock sang by, bounced and rolled to a stop. Another half dozen, then another three, and one final stone. And then silence. Slowly, still dazed, True slid from Firetail's back, staggered to one side, and leaned against a boulder. At first he thought he was going to throw up, but the sudden pain in his arm and the dim, faraway memory of snapping bone brought him back to his senses. As if in a drunken stupor, he unbuttoned his coat and slung the broken arm inside it. Only then did he have the presence to check Firetail.

The roan's sides were heaving. His coat was dark with sweat and caked mud where the dust had clung to him. His head bobbed up and down as he breathed. Though a gash had been ripped in his left rear leg, all four hooves were planted squarely on the ground. Not yet able to talk, True stumbled toward him and walked around him, checking each leg carefully. It was a miracle, but there were no broken bones. Then he went to look for Ramez O'Shannon and Torbellino.

Vision blurred, the world swam away and came back. Half hidden behind a great boulder, Torbellino's battered hind quarters lay twisted in a loose pile of small stones that had slid over him. True limped in that direction. What was left of Ramez lay behind the boulder. His fine clothes were torn and soaked with blood. One leg bent upward beneath his torso. His back was twisted in a grotesque angle. Only his face, so finely chiseled, so brittlely handsome, was untouched. He looked terribly small and frail, like a child.

As if in a dream, True whistled Firetail to him and bade him stand still during the dizzying, numbing chore of lifting the corpse one-handed over the roan's withers. Firetail shied at the extra weight, but calmed down quickly when True mounted and headed him back toward town. The ride was a nightmare that unfolded as he watched, awake and vaguely curious as to its outcome. Soon, from what direction he wasn't sure, he was joined by a half score of riders come to see what had caused the delay. At their head, he led the shocked, silent procession through the streets of San Antonio and across the plaza to the finish line and the waiting crowd.

No one cheered. No one rushed to greet him when they saw the broken body draped across his horse, the blood running down the roan's leg, the blank, white look on True's face.

The drama played itself out slowly, as if it had been rehearsed and each participant knew his role to perfection. His face a mask of emotionless calm, Luther O'Shannon stepped from the crowd and stood alone. The staring onlookers, unconsciously stepped backward. Elizabeth gasped and tried to run to True but was restrained by Hogjaw. "You have to let him do it himself," the mountain man whispered in her ear.

True walked Firetail to the post, reached out his good right arm and, with a bloody hand, jerked the saber free.

The crowd sighed as one. Luther O'Shannon's face, drained of color, revealed nothing.

True turned Firetail, stopped him in front of O'Shannon. O'Shannon gestured curtly with one hand. Two of his men hurried forward and gingerly lifted the broken corpse from Firetail's withers and laid him on the ground. Luther O'Shannon remained perfectly still.

A whisper rippled through the crowd. True's eyes raked over it. The whisper faded quickly. The crowd was silent again.

True threw the saber down in front of O'Shannon. It hit the packed earth with a dull, mournful clang.

"Our land," he said, spraying a red mist from his swollen cut lips, and then waited.

The silence grew. At last, Luther O'Shannon, his eyes hooded and feverish with hatred, nodded. When he spoke, his voice was a harsh, anguished whisper that held no tint of the terrible lust for vengeance that already consumed his being. "Your land," he said. "But not yet paid for, Paxton. Not yet in full."

True nodded his understanding and turned away from O'Shannon to see Elizabeth and the tears of love on her face. He nudged Firetail, who walked toward her as she broke from Hogjaw's grip and ran to him.

The roan stopped.

True looked down as she touched his leg. A look stilled her before she could speak.

"Eliz . . . abeth . . ." he said, focusing with great effort on her. "Will . . . you . . . marry . . . me?"

She caught him as he fell.

PART FOUR

1835

Chapter XXV

They built with cedar, and stone, and mortar crushed and mixed with their own hands. Working together, they raised four walls and a roof for each family—not much as houses went, but winter was almost over and it was time to plow and sow. No one complained. They were home at last.

The two months since the race on New Year's Day had flown quickly. A splinted and patched-up True and taken title to what had been Ramez O'Shannon's land the day after the race. Less than a week later, feeling the need for more land and with the advice of Raphael Sanchez and the consent of the other settlers, True and Joseph had traded the fifteen hundred *hectares* plus three thousand dollars for a six thousand-*hectare* tract twenty miles south of San Antonio and just east of Luther O'Shannon. True and Joseph owned the land, of course, but as they had promised, they offered to parcel it out equally among all seven families and Andrew, share and share alike with an eye to water and grass and wood, and on more than favorable terms. At a little under three square miles per family—not a great ranch to be sure, but a decent start— the urge to remain together was overpowering. Nels Matlan sent word to Washington-on-the-Brazos declining the teaching job they had offered him. Scott Campbell quit his job at the stable. Buckland Kania decided to sell most of his share back to True and Joseph and, debt free, build his church on what was left and make it the center of his circuit. Even the Kempers, who had dreamed of easy empires, chose to establish their trading post near their fellow travelers.

By the end of January, the land had been divided and a small collection of cabins, sufficiently distant from one another for privacy yet close enough to afford a modicum of protection and mutual benefit, had sprung up. They called their settlement Agradecido, the Spanish word for grateful. And if anyone worried about the threat their neighbor to the west might pose, they put it out of mind when the griefstricken O'Shannon vacated his *hacienda* and moved to Mexico City during the first week of February. In any case, Ramez had spilled his own blood and the settlers were guiltless. Not a one of them, though, no matter how lofty his ideals or how deep his friendship for True, would have changed his name to Paxton. Not for a moment.

And not for a moment did True wish to be anything other than a Paxton. He reveled in his new life with Elizabeth on land he could call his own. He loved the smell of the freshly turned earth and watched avidly for the first shoots of spring wheat to appear. At night, he learned the coyotes' songs, by day, the whistle of the cardinals and the soft hoot of the doves. He noted where the sun rose and set, how the wind bent the grass, when the clouds carried rain. Each day he carefully exercised his arm and felt the muscles grow around the knitting bone. And at last, when the first week of March had passed, he decided it was time to do a full day's work.

Determined, he tilted a barrel of seed corn, caught the lower rim with his right hand, and reached around the middle with his left arm. A bushel, he told himself. Sixty-six pounds plus the weight of the barrel. Just enough for a decent test. He exhaled, inhaled, exhaled . . . and lifted. Pain stabbed through his arm and turned his stomach, but the bone didn't give. As he stood and held on, the pain receded and left no more than a vague, deep ache.

"My God, I knew it! You couldn't wait, could you?" Elizabeth said from the doorway. "I married the stubbornest man in all creation."

True gritted his teeth and forced a grin. "It's been nine weeks since Hogjaw set it, and I've been working up to this. Nine weeks is time enough for anyone to go about dangling his hand. I either have two good arms or I don't."

"I'm more worried about your head and what's obviously rattling loose inside," Elizabeth replied archly, spinning in the doorway and reentering the cabin.

The imperious performance set True in motion. He let loose a wild whoop, dropped the barrel, and charged the doorway, leaping through and catching Elizabeth midway across the room. Smothering her scream against his chest, he picked her up and tossed her onto the down mattress.

"What are you doing?" she yelled, discovering the answer as he fought aside her kicking legs and bunched her skirt around her waist. "True! No!" She pummeled his chest, trued to get a knee between his legs, and failed. "It's the middle of the day, True!"

"Sorry ma'am. I can't hear. Something loose in my head."

"I take it back," Elizabeth shouted. "I take it back."

"Eh?" True said, holding her down with his weight until he undid his trousers. "What's that? What's that?"

Her fists beat a tattoo on his back. "I said I take it back!" she screamed, laughing and then suddenly gasping as he entered her. "I said . . . Oh, True . . ." She wrapped her arms around his neck and returned his kiss. Half-dressed, wishing she could feel her breasts against his naked chest, she kissed him again and moved with him, against him, around him, to and away from him, but never far away. "True True True," she whispered against his cheek, into his ear. "Dearest dearest dear . . ." Her wide eyes stared into his as they fused and stiffened and shared the sweet agony.

Slowly, slowly her eyes closed as his head sank to rest by hers. She could feel the tug on her hair, his weight pleasant on her, pressing her into the mattress. Her arms around him, she held him as she held the memories. The night he had first kissed her. The terrifying leap into her carriage. His face, bleeding, in the plaza when he fell into her arms. The almost childlike solemnity of his "I do," to Reverend Kania's posed question.

It had been the second of January. What better time to begin a new life? The ceremony had been quiet, with only five people present, True and herself, Reverend Kania, Joseph, and Hogjaw to give the bride away. Lottie was not there, but Elizabeth did not let the coolness between them spoil the happiness of her day. Afterward, with evening closing around them like a blanket, they had walked openly to her—to their, she reminded herself—wagon. And found that someone had brought them flowers and turned down the pallet. They had needed nothing else. Not that night.

And not now, she thought dreamily. Now with his hard strength melting in her. Not now, with their house and their furniture and their land . . .

Dearest dearest dearest. My own True love . . .

The wood was a warm color in the spring afternoon. "I

was making a pie," she said, her voice sleepy as she studied a patch of sunlight on the wall by the bed.

"Is that what you call it?" True asked, his voice muffled by the pillow. "Never heard of it referred to as making a pie. Lots of other things."

"Silly," Elizabeth said. She took his hand and diverted it from further explorations along the inside of her thigh. "The day is half over and there's so much to do."

"Like baking pies?"

"And more. It's a special day," she added, her eyes drifting to the dresser. Cursing his nearly useless left arm, True had built the dresser by lantern light over the past two weeks. And if the drawers weren't completely finished, the top was, and held a single clay pot from which jutted a half dozen budding rose stems. Yellow roses, flower of memory. The weather was cool but mild, the sun bright, the soil moist. Elizabeth didn't know much about planting roses in the Texas climate, but she felt in her bones that the time was right. She sat up, her golden hair draping across her shoulders. "I want to plant Grandfather Michaelson's roses."

True reached up and entangled his fingers in the thick curling strands of gold. "Yellow rose," he whispered, and pulled her down to him. He stroked her face and her hair, soft as the breezes that bent the prairie grass. "You are my yellow rose, Elizabeth. I love you."

Elizabeth nestled against him. "I love you, True."

Pies and roses could wait.

She set the roses on the east side of the house so the sun could kiss the budding leaves and coax to life the yellow petals that would soon unfold. Her fingers kneaded and turned the sandy soil, spread the roots just so in the earth, and patted the ground around the stems with as much care as a woman with her child.

A child. Her time had come a week earlier, and when she had started right on schedule she felt a vague bitterness spread through her. Now she stared at her flat stomach and wondered when. Joan and Eustacia had their children. Mildred positively glowed with the joy of motherhood. Even Lottie was pregnant.

But not Elizabeth. Maybe it was just something else she didn't do well. As she couldn't be her father's son, now she couldn't be a mother to a babe of her own.

She stared at the roses, the yellow roses waiting patiently to burst forth with hew life—as she must wait. And self-pity certainly didn't help, she thought, patting the earth once again. There would be time. She smiled a little naughtily to herself. "Pies," she whispered. "we'll just have to bake lots of—"

A shadow crept over her. Curious, because she hadn't heard True come out of the house, she turned and looked up and, her heart leaping to her throat, she screamed.

Inside the cabin, True heard the scream, heard it cut short even as his hands closed around the rifle over the mantle. Three leaping steps brought him barreling through the door, rifle ready and finding its target, a short, wiry-looking half-robed savage on horseback. The Indian carried a rifle across his lap, but held his hands in the air to show he meant no harm.

"You no shoot-um little brother," the savage said, as if reading his lines from a Thespian's prompter.

Blond hair! The Indian had blond hair! "Andrew!" True whispered, setting the rifle down. "Andrew!" he whooped joyously. "By heaven, it's Andrew!"

Andrew Paxton slipped from the back of his horse and wrapped his arms around True. "Who else? How many blond Indians do you know, anyway?"

True laughed, held Andrew at arms' length, and gazed fondly at him. "Just you, little brother."

"Well, goddamn!"

"If you're just going to stand around and cuss . . ." Andrew turned to Elizabeth and bowed comically. "Didn't mean to give you a start, Elizabeth. These are everyday clothes among the Coushattas." He grinned down in the direction of his beaded vest, buckskin breeches, and moccasins.

The two brothers stared at each other, studying the changes. It was obvious Andrew still had his wild streak, equally obvious that True fit easily into the mold of husband and builder.

"Joseph told me you were married," Andrew said. "I found it difficult to believe him. Now that I see you two, though, I can hardly recall a time when you weren't married. You spent a long time looking for the right one, brother. Glad to see you didn't wait around when you found her. Last time I saw you, the two of you were at loggerheads. You still got a temper, Elizabeth?"

Elizabeth put her fists on her hips and stood her ground. "You'll find out soon enough, Andrew Paxton, if you keep dredging up the past."

"Yes, ma'am!" Andrew laughed, holding his hands in front of him as if to protect himself.

"And if you don't take dinner with us," Elizabeth added with mock ferocity.

"Whatever you say, ma'am. I will be forever in your debt." He looked at True, raised his eyebrows and jerked his head toward Elizabeth. "You think it's safe for me to take care of my horse first?"

Elizabeth went inside to put on coffee. True and Andrew led the horse to the corral True had finished only two days earlier. It was like old times, in a way. Neither of them spoke while Andrew unsaddled his mount and True filled the water trough. Firetail eyed Andrew suspiciously, but finally let his nose be rubbed for a moment before retreating skittishly to the far set of rails. "So this is it," Andrew finally said, leaning on the corral and looking out over the land.

"Well . . ." True began, a little hesitantly.

"I heard all about it," Andrew interrupted.

True glanced sideways at him.

"Ran into Hogjaw in San Antonio. He made it sound pretty exciting. Sorry I missed the race."

"Don't be," True said. "We came *that* close to losing everything." He cleared his throat. "Your money, too."

"Hogjaw left that part out." Andrew grinned and clapped True on the shoulder. "Joseph didn't, though. Hell, True, it was just money. And besides, you won."

True's face was red. "We did set aside a share of land for you. I didn't want you to think—"

"I won't if you quit talking about it." An exaggerated scowl replaced Andrew's grin. "Us Injuns don't go much for the white man's money, anyway. Beads are more our style. You think she's got that coffee hot?"

The matter was closed for good. Easy in each other's company, happy to be reunited, the two brothers ambled across the wide yard. "I trust you haven't turned Indian so completely you've lost your taste for beef stew and apple pie," True said, ushering Andrew into the house.

Andrew took a deep, appreciative sniff, and shook his head. "Hope you eat early, and made plenty."

"Will and did," Elizabeth said. "We never know when Hogjaw might stop by."

"He won't today. He and the Campbell boys were on their way to a buffalo hunt when I saw him. Mmm. Coffee's good. I always end up burning mine." Andrew sipped his coffee and took his time. "Joseph and Scott will be along about suppertime, though.. Them and a friend I've been traveling with."

"Not another Indian I hope," Elizabeth said.

"Nope," Andrew chuckled. "A white man I met when I was living with the Indians. But just about as dangerous as any redskin you'll ever meet. A fellow by the name of Travis. Colonel William Barrett Travis."

Travis was everything True and Elizabeth had heard. He was a handsome, courteous southerner with the blood of South Carolina aristocracy pounding in his veins. Buck Travis, as some called him, was a man driven by pride, well-educated, a good speaker, and an excellent conversationalist. He was a rebel who had found a cause in which he could believe. Mexico's hold on this far-off position of the state of Coahuila was tenuous, and the whites outnumbered the Mexicans by more than three to one. Stephen Austin had petitioned the central government of Mexico for separate statehood, but Travis had a far grander dream: nothing less than the birth of a new nation. For True, who wanted only to live and build in peace, a more dangerous guest could not have sat at his table.

"A most excellent repast, Mrs. Paxton," Travis said as the last of the plates were cleared. "Yours is the type of hospitality of which legends are made."

Joseph grunted his assent. Scott Campbell slapped the table in frustration. "There it goes again," he said. "Always somebody beating me to praising the food."

Elizabeth laughed. "Though I thank him, I'm afraid Mr. Travis overstates his case."

"Quick-witted and witty, too," Travis said, enjoying the banter. "A quality rarely seen in women of these parts."

"Not really," Elizabeth protested. "It is just that men seldom take the opportunity to listen, so busy are they with the clamor of their own conversation."

"You'd better stop while you're even," True broke in, with a wink to Elizabeth. He slid a bottle of whiskey across the table. "Let her get ahead and you'll never catch up."

Don Raphael Sanchez, an unexpected companion of Travis, helped himself to a drink. "Ah, Señora Paxton. When my friend Buck Travis asked me to accompany him to your home, I all but harnessed the carriage myself, so anxious was I to see you. Know that if Señor True ever fails to appreciate you to the fullest, you have but to send word and I shall whisk you away to my *hacienda*, where you shall be installed as no less than a queen."

True opened his mouth to say something, but clamped it shut again as he recalled Don Raphael's words and attitude that afternoon when his horse had lost the race with Firetail. Then he had spoken of political neutrality: now he was in the company of Travis. Had he broken completely with Santa Anna and Mexico? Was he consorting openly with Travis, or merely protecting himself in case the revolutionaries carried the day?

Elizabeth's face had reddened and her mind was racing. All this to-do over a beef stew was disconcerting. Something significant was happening tonight, and she didn't think she liked it, whatever it was. "A gallant proposal, Señor Sanchez," she replied, wondering what came next.

"I fear the next will not be so gallant," Andrew said.

The tone of his voice changed the whole atmosphere in the room. Joseph put down his drink untouched. Travis slouched back in his chair and took in everyone with hooded eyes. Sanchez stared at Andrew, wondering how far the young man had been taken into Travis's confidence.

"I did not think this was a completely innocent visit," True remarked neutrally. "Not with our most noteworthy firebrand here for company."

Andrew stiffened.

"True . . ." Elizabeth warned.

"Sorry, Mr. Travis," True said. "You are welcome here. But you will forgive me if I don't extend the same cordiality to your sympathies."

Travis appeared unperturbed. "Perhaps I may change your mind," he suggested.

"I doubt it. I first heard your name a week after we crossed the Sabine into Mexico. That was—" He paused. "—around four months ago. Since then I've heard it often, and always linked with talk of insurrection, rebellion, and revolution. And I don't like that kind of talk."

"Not just talk," Travis said. "Action, which is sure to

come. Our cause is worthy and someone has to lead. Since that task seems to have fallen to me, I'm duty bound to perform it as well as I can."

"I appreciate that. But you must appreciate, too, that I have no wish to become a pawn in your game."

Pawn and game were not words that Travis took lightly. His face hardened. "Not mine," he said, leaning forward. "Santa Anna's."

True shrugged. "The Mexican government has been quiet lately, and will probably remain so if we don't provoke them further."

"Quiet?" Travis asked indignantly. "They've closed the borders, tried to stop immigration from the States, which means our families and friends can't join us. They've occupied our towns and imposed import tariffs on the goods and tools we need. They threaten to take our land and harass us in a thousand ways. When King George did that, the whole country rose—"

"I don't want what's mine taken from me," True interrupted, "but at the same time, I can't fault Mexico for wanting to keep something it's had for a long time."

Travis glanced at Don Raphael Sanchez. The Mexican sighed and folded his hands over his ample belly. "Word has come, Señor True—a letter from my brother—that there is a movement afoot in the capital to revoke all foreign ownership of land within a fifty-mile radius of San Antonio." He noted True's shocked reaction and nodded his head. "Yes, I have reason to believe it is the truth. If it is, and if they are successful here, we can be sure they will try the same thing in Washington-on-the-Brazos, Anahuac, Brazoria, and other areas with dense colonist populations."

Scott Campbell, who had risen to help himself to a second serving of pie, sank slowly onto the bench seat. "They wouldn't dare," he said, flushing angrily.

"The Mexican government would dare anything, no matter how unlawful," Travis said. "That's why we must be rid of it once and for all. We're Texans, damn it. Not Americans, not Mexicans. This land is *our* land. Unless we're such a bunch of yellow-bellies that we *want* to give it back."

Joseph drummed his fingers on the table. True poured himself a shot of whiskey. Andrew watched his brothers, and said nothing.

"I endorse, with one important reservation, Señor Travis's

view," Don Raphael said, breaking the silence. "I think there is a good chance that it is not too late for words. There are voices in Mexico City speaking against us. If those voices can be neutralized—"

"Whose voices?" Scott Campbell asked, interrupting.

"Luther O'Shannon is one of them," True replied before Don Raphael could speak. "Any bets?"

The Mexican nodded. "Santa Anna is not a man totally devoid of reason, though. He has been known to listen."

"To one with the strength of his convictions," Don Raphael said. "And shrewd enough to win a horse race by a nose."

A cup crashed. Splinters of porcelain littered the floor at Elizabeth's feet. As the men's heads turned toward her, she stared at her trembling hands. "Excuse me," she said, barely in control of her voice, and escaped behind the blanket that partitioned the bedroom from the rest of the cabin.

Footsteps approached the blanket and stopped. Elizabeth sat heavily on the bed, then lay back and held her hands tightly over her stomach. Her father was dead, her mother too. She and her sister were estranged. If True left she would be alone. "No!" she screamed in her head. Completely alone. "No no no no no no . . ."

But the men continued to talk. And despite all her efforts, she could not drown out their voices.

Elizabeth woke up when the door slammed. The light on the ceiling was dim and the night was quiet. A moment later, the blanket curtain was pulled back and True entered. "Are you asleep?" he whispered, sitting on the edge of the bed.

"When are you leaving?"

"Do you know me so well?"

"When are you leaving?"

"I won't be alone. Don Raphael is going with me. Joseph volunteered to come too, but with Lottie pregnant—"

"When?"

True stared into the darkness. "Early next week," he finally said, his voice low. "Monday, I think."

"Six days. That's all we have."

"Well . . ." He cleared his throat. "Less. I'm leaving for San Antonio tomorrow. Don Raphael helped us write a petition. I need to get as many signatures as possible before I leave."

Her voice was bitter. "One day, then. One night."

"I'm sorry, Beth. God, I'm sorry. But I'm sort of responsible, at least for O'Shannon's animosity. Someone has to do it. I . . . Ah, hell, Elizabeth. I don't know. I just feel it has to be me. The least I can do is try."

Silence in a night shrouded with misgivings.

"Elizabeth?"

The still passing of the minutes.

"You will be here when I come back, won't you? You'll still be here?"

Silence.

And then from the covers, movement, her hand finding its way . . . into his.

Chapter XXVI

The journey took three weeks, to which were added two days when the rains forced Don Raphael and True to huddle in damp discomfort in a farmer's shack at the base of Xochimilco, around whose peak they had to travel to reach Mexico City. At last, after contending with raging streams, mudslides, fallen trees, and their own fatigue, the two men reached the city. The hour was late, the night dark. Estimo Sanchez, Don Raphael's brother, was not in when their carriage discharged them in front of a great white house that lay like a jewel at the edge of a park. Neither True nor Don Raphael complained; they left word with the staff and tumbled into the first real beds they had slept in for over three weeks.

True woke early and with little sense of where he was. Sleepily, he pulled back the curtains and saw that his room looked onto a balcony that ran the length of the house. Beyond the wrought-iron railing, a high carpet of trees obscured the city, beyond which, outlined against the predawn light, rose the majestic mountains that had, in ancient times, protected the abode of the gods. It was too damn early to be overwhelmed. Still blurry-eyed, he stumbled back to his bed and, luxury of luxuries, fell immediately to sleep again.

The sun was streaming through the windows when he woke the second time. Rested and alert, he reveled in the scent of clean sheets and the cool spring breeze that wafted through the open window. A man was standing on the balcony, his back to True's room. He puffed languidly on a cigar and rocked on his heels, rocked and watched the clouds clip the mountaintops and the new day freshen. Soon he was joined by Don Raphael. From their greeting, True assumed the man was Estimo, a belief confirmed when the two men embraced warmly.

They had laid out a robe for him. True rose, then explored until he found a small room where he could relieve himself. A wash basin full of water scented with lemon sat on the stand next to his bed. When he had washed, he donned the robe and, ready to face the day, walked onto the balcony.

"Ah! Our *norteamericano* friend joins us. You are Señor Paxton, my brother tells me. Welcome to Mexico City—and my house."

Estimo was a leaner, younger version of his brother, to whom he bore a distinct facial resemblance. Raphael completed the introductions and the three sat down to coffee, fresh rolls, sweet butter, and preserves in the European style to which True had become accustomed at the Alabaster House in Charleston. The coffee was flavored with hints of chocolate and cinnamon and tasted altogether refreshing. The croissants and sweet rolls were exquisitely baked, soft and flaky and still hot.

"My eldest daughter tells me you met last night," Estimo said in heavily accented English. "And that she regrets very much that you are married. Do you like the coffee? It is blended especially for me."

"Very much," True answered, deciding to treat the comment on Estimo's daughter as a social nicety and let it go at that. He spread butter on a roll, sipped appreciatively at his coffee. "A far, far cry from what I've grown used to. I think I could very easily become spoiled."

Pleased, Estimo laughed and refilled True's cup. "Tell me," he asked, leaning back and lighting a fresh cigar. "What do you think of our city?"

"I'm afraid I've seen practically nothing of it," True responded. "We arrived late, it was dark, and I was very tired. I certainly got an impression of life, though—people bustling all over the place."

"Yes. Many people and many more to come. All seeking peace and prosperity, of course. The pot at the end of the rainbow, I think you say, which they seldom find." He shrugged and puffed on his cigar. "Ah, well. Men strive to survive and endure, and must be content with that which is given them."

Estimo didn't look as if he had too many worries in that regard, True thought. If anything, he was probably much better off than Don Raphael. Lord only knew how much it cost to maintain the style of life to which he was obviously well-accustomed. "Unfortunately," True said, "that which has been given is too often taken away in the next breath."

"Clever!" Estimo said, at the same time sharply clapping his hands. A maid appeared immediately, took away the coffee pot, and left another in its place. Steam rose from the spout and drifted lazily upward for a foot before the breeze whisked it away. "You turn a philosophical observation into harsh reality. Clever. You were right, Raphael. Your *norte-americano* friend is not a patient man."

"There's no time for patience," True pointed out. He gestured back to his room. "I carry a petition signed by a lot of people who are afraid they're going to lose most of what they've paid and fought for. They're good people who want nothing more than to prosper and to live in peace, as you have pointed out. At the same time, I have a home and a wife that I miss, and the sooner I return, the better. I'm sure you understand I mean no disrespect."

"Of course not. You speak words I too have said in my time."

"Then down to business," True said with a sideways glance at Don Raphael.

"Very well." Estimo sat back, twirled the silvered tips of his extravagant moustache, and pondered. "Today is Thursday. A week from next Tuesday, I shall announce your arrival to the proper authorities."

"A week from . . ." True blanched. "But that's almost two weeks from now! Isn't there any way—"

"This week is nearly over and the people I need to talk to will be unavailable, I'm sure," Estimo explained, as if talking to a child. "Next week is Holy Week, so of course nothing will be done then. I'm afraid the Monday after Easter Sunday is never a very good day—so much to catch up on." He nodded. "Yes, the Tuesday after next is the earliest."

Easter week, True thought, his spirits sagging. What a time for him to arrive! And what would he do for twelve days? See the sights? Twiddle his thumbs? Doleful, he stared at his croissant and wished it were one of Elizabeth's biscuits. Croissant be damned, there had to be some quicker way. Had to!

But there wasn't. The days dragged on in idle luxury. No matter how much he wanted to be done with his business and away, it was remarkably easy to sleep late, eat well, and spend hours just ambling through the park. Dinner was usually at nine, and always attended by a score or more friends of Estimo and Eulalia, his wife. Holy Week was a whirl of parties and balls and parades, during which True twice caught glimpses of, but thankfully never encountered, Luther O'Shannon. The weather was beautiful, the city exciting. Voices in a multitude of languages argued, appealed, insulted, laughed, chattered, gossiped, tying and untying the timeless human bonds of existence. Dogs barked, goats bleated, roosters crowed no matter the time of day, chickens squawked and flapped furious feathered retreats from the turmoil of the street. Wagons lumbered and streaked past, creaky and clattery; stately carriages rolled by in stern displays of opulence. Vendors, beggars, the common man and the prince all rubbed elbows in kaleidoscopic whirls of color. The bells of the cathedral worried flights of pigeons into the air with their pealed messages of forgiveness and hope, of resurrection promised and life hereafter. And then Good Friday. Accompanied by Don Raphael, True watched the altar of the cathedral as the priests stripped it bare, and walked the silent gray streets devoid of life, in mourning for the crucified Christ. Saturday, a deluge inundated the city, and Sunday morning, as if on cue, the day of Resurrection dawned clear as bells that pealed forth the good news.

The next two days were the worst. Monday, because it seemed as if something should be happening, Tuesday because Estimo simply disappeared. True paced his room and the balcony, prowled the halls, tried to concentrate on the one book in English he'd found in Estimo's library. Nothing worked. Estimo didn't reappear in the house until nearly dinner time. "Well?" True asked nervously.

"Next Tuesday," Estimo said, beaming. "You have been granted an audience at two in the afternoon with *el Presidente* Santa Anna himself."

"Excellent!" Raphael exclaimed, in contrast to True's disappointment. "The sooner the better for us, I say."

"The first appointment is for True Paxton alone. We have been granted an audience three days later. The president wishes to discuss the matter of the *norteamericano* colonists separately from that which concerns the Sanchez family and ranch."

"But we came together," Raphael protested. "Our causes are allied. The same man speaks against us both."

Estimo shrugged. "Of course, my brother, but I was in no

position to argue. "The wheels grind slowly. These matters take time and patience. In any case, it is of no importance. I have given much to Santa Anna's cause, and he will listen closely to us—unless, of course, he has discovered I also supported Senor Bustamente."

"My Spanish," True said. "It hardly exists. Will there be someone there to translate for me? Could you do it?"

"The president has his own translators, I'm afraid." Estimo laughed and clapped True on the shoulder. "But don't worry, my friend. All these things will be taken care of in due time. Remember, you have another week to suffer. In the meantime, I have spent a busy day, it is almost nine o'clock, and I believe dinner is waiting." He gestured for True to lead the way into the dining room where the rest of the family and that night's guests waited. "Gentlemen?"

The week crawled. True didn't know whether he was more bored or more worried. Elizabeth would be alone for another month at the rate things were going. Joseph and Scott were watching out for her, to be sure, but only from a distance. It was that distance—those two miles—that bothered him. A gun couldn't be heard from two miles away. Or a scream. If she got sick, or if Indians chanced by . . . No, he commanded himself over and over again, you can't keep thinking that way. Think about something else. Food, drink, walks. The sights of the city: the ragged children; the beautiful señoritas in their brightly colored skirts and dazzling white blouses; the old crone who begged at the corner of the park; the three legged dog that trotted past the house every afternoon at four o'clock precisely. Anything . . .

And at last Tuesday. Excited, True rose, and dressed in the finery Estimo had arranged for him. When he finished, he looked at himself in the mirror and decided that except for his hair and skin color, he might have passed for a *vaquero* in his burgundy waistcoat, crimson sash, tight burgundy trousers worked with silver filigree, shiny black boots, and flat-brimmed hat. He was too nervous to eat. So much depended on this one interview. So much land, so many lives, so many dreams. He doubted if he could heal completely the rift that had grown between the colonists and the government, but if he could start the process by assuring Santa Anna of his sincerity, the moderates might be given a little more time to cool the passions fanned by the hotheads on either side. A little more time. *Any* time. Blood need not be spilled, was his message. There are many, many of us who do not want to see the earth run red.

One o'clock. He took leave of the Sanchez family, climbed into the coach, and, with the well wishes of his host ringing in his ears, rode away toward the *Plaza Central* and the president's palace. The ride through the city left him unmoved, for he was deep in reflection, still uncertain, after his long wait, of how to counter the lies Luther O'Shannon had spewed about the colonists around San Antonio. He must prove that rebellion against the Mexican government was in no way the intent of the settlers who had signed the petition he carried.

The coach jolted to a stop. True looked out to see a massive walled structure, at whose base lay a motley arrangement of makeshift shelters teeming with ragged, unwashed children playing in refuse. "Hey!" True called to the driver. "This isn't the palace." His Spanish was broken, but he was sure he could be understood, and equally sure he wasn't mistaken. He'd seen the palace the week before on a drive with Don Raphael. This was someplace else. Somewhere he instinctively knew he didn't want to be. He climbed out of the coach and shouted up at his impassive driver. "I'm supposed to go to the president's palace. The palace!"

The children shouted. A half dozen women emerged from the shacks and ran toward the gates as they groaned open, only to be battered aside by five soldiers and an officer who marched toward the coach.

"What the hell?" True asked, confused and reverting to English.

"A close approximation, Mr. Paxton," a voice said from behind him. Recognizing the voice, True whirled about in time to see Luther O'Shannon, bristling in the gold and silver braid of a Mexican officer, step around the coach and salute. He was not smiling. "My compliments, Mr. Paxton. And welcome to Ciudadela Prison."

True lunged. A musket stock cracked against his skull. He hit the ground face first, tasted dirt, heard the racket of the coach as it drove off. Only dimly aware of what was happening, he saw his blood upon the earth, and then the clear blue sky as a booted foot dug into his side and rolled him over. A roaring sound filled his ears and the sky began to spin. High over him, bending lower, Luther O'Shannon's face loomed, and he was vaguely conscious of the critically important petition being plucked from his breast pocket. He tried to speak, but his voice faded as the face receded and he slipped into the abyss of unconsciousness.

"What did he say?" the officer asked.

"Elizabeth," O'Shannon replied, remembering in time to revert to Spanish. "I believe he said, 'Elizabeth.' His wife."

"Ah . . ." the officer replied knowingly. "A wife. Another wife to join the others. Always they come to wait and beg for news. They give themselves to the guards for carrying messages and food to their husbands inside. His wife will come also, to offer herself, no?"

"Perhaps," O'Shannon said, his eyes narrowing with anticipation. "Perhaps, Captain. But not to the guards."

Chapter XXVII

On the sixty-sixth day after True left, toward the end of May and with the late spring sunshine warm around her shoulders, Elizabeth carved another notch in the corner gate post of the corral. Sixty-six, she repeated to herself. Two months and six days. There was some hope in the number. He had been gone one week longer than Don Raphael had estimated; with luck he would return before too many more notches had been carved. A muffled curse and a jingle of harness from the stable told her that Firetail was saddled and, in retaliation, had probably tried to take a bite out of Hogjaw's leg or rear. Elizabeth smiled and ran back to the cabin to put away the knife and close up.

"Mule marrow! If this horse were mine, he wouldn't be for long!" the mountain man shouted, emerging from the stable.

"Now, Hogjaw, you just need patience," Elizabeth called back. She adjusted her bonnet, closed the door after her, and checked once again to make sure the coins she carried wrapped in a kerchief were safely pinned in her pocket. "Firetail will grow to like you."

"No, ma'am. No, he won't. And I won't grow to like him, neither. That way we understand each other right from the start."

Hogjaw had been furious when he returned from his buffalo hunt with the Mackenzie boys and learned True had undertaken such a fool venture as going to Mexico City without him. That night he had prowled the streets of San Antonio and looked for someone to fight, but finding a scarcity of volunteers, had decided to hie himself out to the farm where he could build a shelter and camp out until True returned. After all, it might be a Comanche spring. One never knew. That no such trouble had come along didn't matter. There had been work enough to keep him occupied. He'd finished the stable True had started and built a smokehouse from scratch. Now, faced with the prospect of totally rebuilding the outhouse if he didn't want to go crazy with boredom—a one-armed man and a woman should have gotten help in the first place—he was damned well ready for True to get back. Ever optimistic, he shaded his eyes and inspected the semicircle of trees where the San Antonio River looped back on itself.

Hoping for a second that Hogjaw had spied True emerging from the shaded distance, Elizabeth looked also and saw nothing but the willows and a hawk carving lazy circles in the still sky. "Well," she said with a sigh, "I guess I'm about ready."

Hogjaw spat to one side, handed Firetail's reins to her. "Reckon I'll ride with you, if you don't mind," he said.

"Of course not. Is something the matter?"

"Should there be?" he snapped in return.

"No," Elizabeth answered, taken aback by his anger. "I just—"

"Ah, hell, Elizabeth. I'm sorry. Edgy, I reckon." He sniffed the air like an old buck antelope searching for trouble. "Too damned quiet! Seems likely we ought to have some unfriendly visitors or somethin'. Makes me nervous when things go right for too long." The mountain man disappeared into the stable and came out a few moments later with the pack horse and the long-eared, narrow-faced Mama, the mule he had ridden farther in the past five years than most men rode in a lifetime. "Damn good thing I'm along," he grumped, slinging his rifle over his shoulder before mounting. "Little girl like you ridin' unarmed—it's plumb loco. Well, you comin' or not?"

The day was beautiful. High cumulus clouds bloomed across a sky that was blue beyond imagination. The land was dappled with vibrant colors: red Indian paintbrush, dusky bluebonnets, bright yellow prickly pear blossoms alive with bumble bees, and everywhere the green of spring-lush grass. As always, Elizabeth experienced initial delight, and then a steadily increasing tension as she neared Lottie's place. The conflict and tension between them had never been resolved, rather lay festering like an old wound that refused to heal. The two sisters were careful to be polite to each other, but if Elizabeth had ever hoped their relationship would reach beyond the obligatory support required by the frontier setting in which they lived, she was soon disabused of the notion. The most recent example involved Joseph's daily ride to check on Elizabeth. Lottie had accompanied him on the fourth day, and her resentment was obvious. Elizabeth almost pointed out that True hadn't left simply to inconvenience Lottie, but held her tongue. There was no sense in arguing. True was a natural leader, and she was quickly learning to put up with the occasional jealousy and bad feelings that leadership naturally engendered.

Joseph and Lottie had built their place some two miles north and east of True and Elizabeth. Slightly hillier there, their homestead lay off the trail in a shallow valley through which ran a small but ever-running spring-fed creek. As the trail dropped into the valley, Elizabeth found herself reigning Firetail to a stop. Joseph and Lottie's cabin had been built at the base of a bluff that protected them from the north wind. A stable and corral lay fifty yards to the west, the smokehouse and another small outbuilding to the east along the bluff. Hogjaw's help notwithstanding, each of them looked more complete and finished than Elizabeth's buildings, the result, no doubt, of True's broken arm and then his absence.

"We goin' to San Antone or not?" Hogjaw asked.

"Wait." Elizabeth glimpsed movement in the open doorway of the cabin and shaded her eyes against the morning sun. A moment later Lottie, her belly distended with child, stepped into the yard and moved toward the garden she had planted between the house and the smokehouse.

Suddenly, the antagonism between the two of them seemed to Elizabeth more like the dull ache of a deep bruise that one wished, more than anything else, would go away and leave one in peace. She was tired of the uncomfortable chance encounters, the awkward unexpected meetings. She was sickened by their childish, petty bickering. She was ashamed of her own apparent inability to understand and forgive and love. And she remembered how frightened Mildred Thatch had been of having her baby in the wilderness. Lottie probably felt the same way, but was too proud to take the first step or ask for help. And Elizabeth had been too proud to offer.

"Well?" Hogjaw asked, startling her.

Elizabeth spurred Firetail, caught up with the mountain man, and reined in. "Here's the money and the list of things I want," she said, handing him the knotted kerchief. "You'll get them for me, won't you? I was just looking for an excuse to see if there was any word from True or Don Raphael."

Puzzled, Hogjaw scratched beneath his cap. "I don't understand. Where are you gonna be?"

"Where I should have been a long time ago." She smiled, and briefly rested her hand on his arm. "You know how it is between Lottie and me, Hogjaw. Maybe it isn't too late, though. I'll be with her, and I'll watch for you on your way back this afternoon. Just give a yell." She wheeled Firetail. "Or come sit," she called over her shoulder. "We'll have fresh coffee for you."

Hogjaw watched her go, at last gave Mama a nudge and started her down the trail. "Come on, old lady," he said. "People are comin' to their senses back there. Be nice to see for a change, but we'd best leave 'em to their privacy."

Far behind him, Lottie heard the horse approach and looked up as Elizabeth brought Firetail to a halt at the edge of the garden. "Good morning," Lottie said guardedly. Smudged dirt tracks, the paths of tears, streaked her cheeks. "You need something?"

Elizabeth didn't answer immediately, rather dismounted and looked around. The wagon was gone, which meant Joseph was either out hauling wood or had gone to town. A faint column of smoke rose from the cabin chimney. A cow and her calf stood silently in the corral. Slowly, Elizabeth climbed through the fence and stepped across the rows of onions and carrots and turnips, then stood staring down at her sister where she bent over the soil. Lottie started to speak, caught her breath as the child in her womb kicked. She gasped, clutched at the earth, and turned her face to hide the new tears that welled in her eyes. Suddenly, Elizabeth knelt at her side and put her arms around her.

And then they were both crying.

Lottie had cleaned house, bathed, and fixed lunch by the time Elizabeth finished in the garden. "You never could bring in a garden," Elizabeth chided, dumping a double handful of baby carrots and onions she'd thinned from the thickly planted rows onto the drainboard. "Vegetables have to be coaxed from the ground. It's like getting a young'un to take his castor oil, it takes patience and coddling," she added, recalling one of her grandfather's axioms.

"That may be true," Lottie said, laughing. She pulled an

apple pie out of the oven and held it under Elizabeth's nose. Juice bubbled up through the slits in the golden crust. "But you never could bake."

Elizabeth sniffed. "Mmm! Touché." She watched as Lottie placed the pie on the windowsill to cool. "I'll forgive you your garden if you'll forgive me my pies. Even Stephen?"

Eyes bright with happiness, the two sisters embraced. "Even Stephen," Lottie said. "Darn!" She stepped back, wiping the tears from her face. "You've got me started again."

"Nothing that a little food won't help," Elizabeth said, walking to the sink and tipping some water into the wash basin. Working the lather under her nails, she began to scrub her hands. Lottie had added lilac to her soap. The scent reminded Elizabeth of the Pennsylvania farm and the sachet their grandmother had kept in her linen closet. "However did you get lilac?" she asked over her shoulder.

"Joseph found a bush growing next to the foundation of a house he ran across up in the hills. Earlier settlers, we think." Lottie dished out stew for both of them, reheated some cornbread left over from the night before, and poured two glasses of buttermilk. "It was either razed or else it just burned down by itself. We're going to try to plant some here. It'll look pretty out front, don't you think? Or maybe," she said laughing, "I'll put it all around the outhouse."

They both ate ravenously. The buttermilk was tart and refreshing, the cornbread delicious, and no stew ever tasted better. Best of all, between eating and washing dishes and making coffee, there was time to talk. Talk of memories of childhood, talk of the new world they'd found, of their husbands in particular and the foibles of men in general. Talk to fill in the six-month gap of their lives as sisters, and to forge, at last, a closeness they had never felt before.

"And now look what we've done," Lottie exclaimed as the sun crept onto the tabletop between them. "Joseph should be home almost any minute." A sly look crossed her face. "I wanted the pie to be a surprise for him, but I don't think he'll mind if we sample it. Just to make sure, of course."

Elizabeth nodded seriously. "A good idea. Besides, Hogjaw is due back from San Antonio. And if he gets here before we eat our share, there won't be a crumb left."

"Hogjaw!" Lottie shuddered. She got up, retrieved the pie from the window and began to cut it. "Sometimes you amaze me. I know he means well and all, but I just can't see how you stand to have him around. Every time he visits here I have to add some of Joseph's whiskey to my coffee to keep from getting the willies.''

"I'm used to him, I suppose," Elizabeth said, ashamed for not defending Hogjaw more strenuously and yet afraid to test her newfound friendship with her sister.

"Maybe so. Still . . . You want more coffee?''

"Good Lord, no," Elizabeth groaned. "I've had enough to last me a year.''

"Let's go out on the porch. It's cooler there in the afternoons. And—'' Lottie rubbed her back. "—I think I've had about all I can take of those kitchen chairs for one day.'' She handed Elizabeth her pie, walked out onto the porch, and sank into one of the rockers Joseph had built. "Ahhhh!" she sighed, glad to be off her feet again. She looked down at herself and lightly patted her abdomen. "Lord, I must look a sight.''

Elizabeth pulled her chair closer to the rail. "Nonsense. You look happy.''

"I am, I suppose," Lottie said. She smiled wryly. "When I'm not weeping and wailing like I was this morning when you found me. I don't know what to think. One day I'm as brave as Daniel in the lions' den, and then my little wonder here gives a kick and I realize how alone we really are, and how far from any kind of help.''

"Now you're feeling sorry for yourself," Elizabeth laughed. "Joan and Eustacia are no more than twenty minutes away and you know it.''

"Maybe so. It's still scary, though.''

"Don't complain," Elizabeth said lightly to hide her disappointment. "I just wish I had cause to be scared that way. It would be worth it.''

"And then it'll be *my* turn to come by your place and tell *you* not to worry. I promise not to be too condescending.'' Lottie grinned widely. "Would you look at us? We came out here to eat pie, and instead we sit and talk sad talk.'' She waited for Elizabeth to take a bite, then tasted her piece. "Well," she said, making a little face. "It isn't one of my better efforts. Too much honey in the crust, I think. That and the dried apples . . .''

"That's right. Rub it in," Elizabeth laughed. "The crust on the cobbler I baked last night made excellent shingles for the smokehouse.''

"You probably didn't add salt. You never add salt."

"Salt's for curing."

"You always say things like that. Always."

Elizabeth talked around a mouthful of pie. "Salt is for beans, then."

"It is also for pie crust, as Grandmother and Mother tried to tell you for years. I don't know why they kept trying. Convincing you of anything is a task I gave up long ago."

The sisters glared at one another for a moment. Then the frowns melted and both of them laughed. "Well, I'm glad to see some things remain the same," Lottie said.

"A touch of constancy in a land of ever changing moods and seasons," Elizabeth said, paraphrasing one of Reverend Kania's trail sermons.

"Amen!" Lottie sighed. "Nothing like a touch—" Suddenly, she tensed and touched her abdomen as the baby within her kicked hard.

"Lottie? . . ." Elizabeth said, concerned.

"He kicked, is all," Lottie whispered. "It always startles me."

"Lottie, go inside!" Elizabeth's voice had changed dramatically, grown urgent, insistent.

Lottie glanced at Elizabeth, then quickly toward the mouth of the valley and the intersecting trail. At first she saw nothing remarkable. The edge of a cloud had cut the sun and left the blackjack oaks and towering cedars in shadow. A meadowlark whistled, bobbed, and flitted across the pasture. The afternoon was pure and still, bright with wild flowers. A crow called. Nearer, squirrels chattered and scolded among themselves. The world was filled with the harmony of a spring day.

And one thing more. With fear.

Lottie sucked in air between her teeth and held herself perfectly still. She too had seen the Indians at the edge of the trees. And their grotesque adornments were the dab and slash of warpaint.

"Oh, my God!" Lottie whispered in a choked voice.

Three Indians walked their horses out of the grove and stopped, watching the cabin and the women.

"Lottie! Is there a gun?"

"Oh, my God! What are they?"

"Comanches, I think. Is there a gun?"

Lottie stared at the Indians.

"Damn it, Lottie!" Elizabeth did not take her eyes off the braves.

"Yes. Over the fireplace."

"Bring it to me."

"What are you going to do?"

"Stand up slowly. Walk inside and bring me the gun." Elizabeth dabbed at her lip with the hem of her apron. "Now!" she commanded hoarsely.

It seemed to take forever, but Lottie finally rose and walked slowly inside. Once out of sight, Elizabeth could hear her run to the fireplace. *Of course. A rifle over the mantle.* She remembered seeing it earlier, remembered thinking about it. Her father had taught her how to shoot, but never how to kill a man. She would have to get mad, as mad as she'd been that day in Natchez Under the Hill. Or afraid. *That won't be a problem. I am afraid.* The world began to spin. Her knees trembled. *Breathe, you foolish girl.* She forced herself to exhale, heard the air whistle past her teeth as she inhaled. *Christ! Maybe they're friendly.* She clasped her hands together to keep them from trembling too. *Sure. Like the ones Hogjaw met were friendly. The ones who left him with a nightmare face. How will I look? No. They will have to kill me!*

"It's by the door, right behind you. Oh, Jesus!" Lottie sounded panic-stricken. "They're coming, Bethie. They're attacking!"

"Stay inside, Lottie. No. Climb out the back window and hide in the root cellar. Make sure you keep the cabin between you and them. Do it now!"

Elizabeth reached into the cabin and grabbed the rifle. She had no time to see if Lottie had obeyed, only to advance to the edge of the porch as the Comanches raced toward the cabin, their bloodcurdling screeches tearing the pristine silence.

True!

She raised the rifle, sighted on the closest warrior, then gasped in horror. The flint . . . there was no flint! The rifle would not fire unless the flint struck the frizzen and set off the gunpowder with its sparks. Frantic, she looked up to see if the nearest savage was upon her, and to her surprise found he had veered from his course and was retreating. Swiftly, she shifted her aim to the second brave and then, when he turned aside, the third. The rifle was useless, but they didn't know that.

The third Indian waved his lance and crouched low on his horse as he rode parallel to the porch, wheeled, and rode back in an attempt to lure the white-skinned woman into wasting a shot. The muzzle never wavered, nor did she shoot. Like a true warrior, he realized, she was going to wait for a killing shot, and he did not want to be the one sent to the Great Spirit by a woman's hand. Let one of the others, and he would swoop down like the mighty hawk and lift her scalp and hang the magic golden hair from his beaded belt. Keeping flat against his mount, he swerved away and rode until he was out of range. When he joined his companions, he realized they had entertained similar thoughts. The golden-haired woman was disconcerting. She was powerful medicine. The matter required thought and discussion.

Elizabeth lowered the rifle and waited.

Seated on their ponies just beyond the garden, the warriors argued among themselves. Now and then they pointed at her, stabbed their lances in her direction. At last, with a chorus of yips and howls, they wheeled their horses and charged the house again.

"Your average Injun, now, is brave but cautious. But he likes things in their place. He don't cotton to the strange." Elizabeth remembered Hogjaw's words. Something, maybe her actions, was definitely bothering them. She held the rifle in front of her, and as the Indians closed in, threw it to her shoulder.

Once again, the Indians swerved aside. This time they stopped in the south meadow, beyond rifle range.

Impasse.

"Disdain in the face of danger. Raw courage. That's what the heathens respect. That and nothin' else." Hogjaw had said that, too. Elizabeth didn't know if it were true, but decided, for lack of a better plan, to take a chance. Willing herself to move in spite of the numbing paralysis that stiffened her limbs, she sat in the rocking chair, balanced the rifle across the railing, and began to finish her pie.

The Comanche braves had intended to make a simple raid. Thoroughly confused, they watched Elizabeth and tried to figure out what was happening. There were no men present. White women were easily frightened and killed or abducted, depending on the whim of the attackers, but here was one who did not scream or wail or run. She appeared not to pay them any mind. It was obvious she could handle the rifle, for she waited for the shot that killed. The braves argued.

Elizabeth finished her pie, wiped her mouth with her apron, and stood. She didn't see how she could endure the tension much longer. She had bought time for Lottie, done her best. It was time to do something positive. Her heart in her throat, she picked up the rifle, stepped off the porch, and began walking toward the Indians. They watched her come on, her stride unwavering, her skirt trailing in the dust, her shining gold hair streaming out behind her in the breeze.

A creature of beauty, a creature of vengeance. A creature obviously commanded by the Great Spirit, or worse by the Owl, which everyone knew was the Messenger of Death.

It wasn't worth learning the truth. The warriors yanked viciously on the rope bridles and spun their ponies. The horses reared and plunged. The Comanches yipped and howled to show they were not afraid, but shrewd men who had seen through the trap laid for them. Before the white woman had come a dozen paces closer, they had galloped up the valley and disappeared, leaving behind no more than a filmy cloud of brown dust to waft across the garden and Elizabeth.

It was over. Dazed, Elizabeth stopped, held the rifle close to her to keep her hands from shaking, and ordered a semblance of strength to her knees, which seemed to have turned to water. She could feel a cold sweat beading her forehead and knew she had to sit down, fast. Turning around as if frightening away a Comanche raiding party were an everyday occurrence, she walked back to the house.

Lottie was in the doorway. "I found this in the kitchen," she said, holding up a short-handled axe. She looked frightened and utterly ineffectual, but her determination added a whole new dimension to her beauty. "I thought I could help."

"They're gone," Elizabeth said. "I think I'll sit down now," she added, and fainted dead away.

Hogjaw's lumpy, floppy face wasn't the easiest thing to set eyes on when regaining consciousness, but Elizabeth found it beautiful.

"We come riding up hell-bent on rescue and found Lottie tryin' to drag you into the house. Sure as hell gave me a start. I figured you'd done took a Comanche lance and was a goner."

Elizabeth's vision improved. She saw Lottie sitting in a chair, Joseph standing by her side.

"We ran into three Comanche bucks," Joseph explained, "riding like Lucifer himself was after them. Hogjaw winged one of the rascals before they cleared the west hill."

"Only one place they could have been comin' from was this farm," Hogjaw went on. "So when we seen you stretched out and Lottie strugglin' with you . . ." His face warped into a semblance of a smile and his eyes looked more tender than Elizabeth ever remembered seeing them. "Well, I'm just thankin' God you're still alive, missy. Just thankin' God."

"I'm sorry I gave you a start," Elizabeth said, sitting up.

"Start? Hellfire, girl! That was the whole P-plumb race. Start and finish." He rose suddenly. "Gol-D! The pack horse! I forgot all about her." He patted Elizabeth's arm, moved toward the door. "You rest up now, missy. I'll go catch her an' be back in two shakes."

"You go help, Joseph," Lottie said. She got out of her chair and shooed Joseph after Hogjaw. "Leave a bucket of fresh water on the back stoop before you get too far. Elizabeth could use a wash."

Joseph walked obediently to the back door, then stopped and turned. "Lottie told me what . . . how you . . . that is, what happened," he said, searching for the right words. "I . . . well . . . Blast it! I mean . . ." The frown lines on his forehead softened and a slow smile lit his face. "Thank you, Elizabeth. All three of us . . . thank you," he blurted, and quickly closed the door before Elizabeth could answer.

"And now," Lottie said, obviously taking over, "I am going to help you clean up, little sister. And when we're ready to let them back in, we'll keep Joseph and Mr. Hogjaw Leakey away from the pie and let the women have seconds for a change. Like Mother always used to say, 'All's well that ends well.' "

And all was well. For three days—three notches in the gate post. For three days of planting and sewing and humming lonely ballads at sunset, and waking to begin a day anew. On the fourth day, a *vaquero* rode into the yard and came to her door. He carried a letter from Mexico City. The scarlet wax bore the deal of Don Raphael Sanchez. With a sudden dread stabbing at her heart, Elizabeth tore it open and read:

Most Excellent Lady:

I send news of the most unfortunate circumstances. Your husband, True Paxton, is imprisoned. . . .

Elizabeth continued to read, but the world had come crashing down long before she finished.

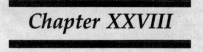

Chapter XXVIII

Ciudadela. A waking nightmare of endless hours, empty hearts, and broken bodies. Fragments of survival.

The cells were more like pig sties buried within the bowels of the massive yellow stone building. The prisoners were fed like swine, watered like swine, herded like swine. Their language was a series of grunts, barely enough to communicate. Some, during the depth of night when the worst dreams came, squealed like swine. And like swine, they had reverted to a feral existence in which survival was everything.

Deprived of sunrise and sunset, True measured the passing of time by the severity of the headaches that plagued him. Only as he recovered from the concussion caused by the blow to his head did he learn to discern the difference between day and night. Day was when he could see the filth he lived in. Night was when he could not. Day was when he was let outside the inner building to walk with his scurvy-ridden fellow prisoners under the blazing sun. Night was when the iron gates clanged shut, and the darkness was so complete he could barely see his hand before his face. For a while, his fellow prisoners studied him. Gradually, he blended in and they took little notice. Only one prisoner, the one they called Tarantula, continued to keep him under surveillance. Tarantula was stockier and more powerful than the others, the type of man for whom Ciudadela had been created. True instinctively knew to be wary of him; he kept his distance, and waited.

Where there was space, a man slept in it. Where there was food—worm-eaten *tortillas* or greasy beans or half-rotten lettuce—men fought for the lion's share. And when the women came, men died for the choicest ones.

Trying not to, True listened. The darkness was alive with

groaning men and women, the carnal noise of madness. The
darkness seethed with the salt smell of sweat and semen. The
darkness was a rutting beast that knew neither tenderness nor
love nor temperance. Some of the women were wives become
harlots. Others had never been anything but the cheapest
whores, the destitute of the streets gathering the last sordid
pesos of their waning, worried lives.

A hand touched his leg. True opened his eyes, saw a
spectral shape at his side, and held up his hands to ward it
off. A woman's voice crooned an obscenity at him. "No,"
he croaked.

Clawlike fingers wrapped around his wrist, pulled his hand
to a sweaty, oily-feeling, pendulous breast. *"Como que no?"*
the voice asked. The woman moved closer and True could
feel damp, coarse pubic hair against his arm. *"Gringo,"* she
said. *"Mucho dinero, no?"*

"Déjame!" True hissed, as always having mentally to
translate from English to Spanish before he spoke. Leave me
alone. *"Déjame."*

The woman grabbed his testicles with her free hand. "They
are very full, no?" she said in Spanish simple enough for him
to understand. "I can make them empty." She cackled. Her
breast swayed against his hand. "No money. It is good.
Another white man already paid me. For you."

She started to crawl on top of him. True pulled up one leg
and kicked, felt his foot sink deep into the fat, slippery flesh
of her stomach. The prostitute gasped and, the wind knocked
out of her, rolled onto her back. No sooner had she hit the
floor than other shapes moved out of the darkness. Like
vultures to carrion, the poorest prisoners, those with neither
wives nor money, gathered around and one by one mounted
her. Horror-stricken and yet fascinated, True watched the
macabre, ghostly dance. When one finished, another took his
place. After the third, he closed his eyes and pretended to
sleep.

Pretended he wasn't losing his mind.

He willed his thoughts to Texas, to a simple cabin and a
woman of warmth and tenderness. *Eighteen now, dearest
Elizabeth, Elizabeth mine, Elizabeth of my heart. You are
eighteen and I have been gone how many days and weeks and
eternities from your life?*

He tried to count, but the days and nights were all the
same. A man soon learned not to tabulate the time, for such

additions served no purpose save to feed the madness. Why know how much of one's life was being wasted and robbed? Thoughts were better placed elsewhere. Escape, for example. But how? It took strength to climb the high walls, purpose to overwhelm the many guards. Bad food and worse water soon robbed a man of both. Swine did not climb, nor did they plot.

There was only one escape.

He must picture hair the color of ripening wheat rippling in the summer sun. Picture skin like rich cream, sweet to the taste. Picture eyes wide and limpid, misting at the moment of consummation. Picture moist lips, the flick of a tongue. Relive the touch of soft fingers, now playful, now earnest and searching.

The mind soared when flesh could not, and triumphed over stone walls and armed guards and the cries of the forgotten damned.

The amulet looked valuable. But then, everything has value to a man who has nothing. He had been watching a long time and had glimpsed, twice now, the shining metal through a tear in the *gringo*'s shirt. The medal consumed him, filled his dreams. He found himself lusting after it the way he sometimes lusted after a piece of meat or a woman. He knew he would think of little else until it was his, until he could see and feel it in his hand.

Juan Torres missed very little. His eyes were long accustomed to the dark, squalid inner cells of the Ciudadela. His nose was keen, capable of sorting subtleties from the general stench. His fingers were deft and well-trained, even if it was they which had failed him on the day he tried to remove the golden ring from the Archbishop's finger. Juan preferred the inside, went out into the main courtyard only when forced to, perhaps to bathe in the rain or when an official count of the prisoners was taken at the whimsy of some petty official. These occurences were minor inconveniences, but Juan took them in stride. He thought it was a fine idea for the Commandant to learn how many had died: such discoveries always led to an infusion of new prisoners, most of whom brought something that Juan found useful once he got it in his hands.

The time had come. Juan leaned forward slowly, peeled the ragged shirt he wore from the chalky moist wall. Moving smoothly, he straightened and stepped over a huddled, sleeping form, over a second and a third and—oh, so cautiously—a fourth. Soft as a feather, his right knee touched the ground at the *gringo*'s side. His breathing was shallow, as silent as the flight of an owl.

Juan was the prince of thieves, a *don* among the *peónes* of Ciudadela. None were as silent as he. None were as quick, for he was like the lightning flash that is gone before its path is seen. None were as light of touch, for he was like a ghost that drifts along the lonely vastness of the Sierra Blanco, touches everything but is not felt.

See? The gringo sleeps.

See? Your fingers touch the thong around his neck. The prize is . . .

True's hand snared the wrist.

. . . yours. . . .

True's fingers bit deep into the flesh, pinched muscle, tendon, and nerve. He heard the intake of breath between broken teeth. He twisted, levered down. Soon the arm bent and the shadow at his side leaned forward until its forehead touched the stone floor. "I will gladly break it," True whispered in his clumsy Spanish.

Silence. A drip of water. The rustling of a rat, one of the lucky ones that had not been caught and eaten.

"Permit me to introduce myself," Juan said. He was afraid his arm would be torn loose from the socket, but had known pain before and hid it well. "I am your humble servant, Juan Torres."

The accent was strange to True's ears, but he could understand well enough. "Pleased to meet you, Juan Torres. My name is True Paxton."

"Yes. I have heard the name. A *gringo*."

"And a light sleeper."

"A man of many talents," Juan agreed obsequiously, at the same time trying to ease the pressure on his arm. A twinge of fresh pain showed him his folly. He grunted in agony in the hope he could placate the *gringo*. "You are hurting me," he said.

"Really?"

"I think you will break my arm."

"Really?"

"If you do, my little Conchita, who visits me every Sunday, will mourn I can no longer put both my arms around her sweet flesh."

True eased his hold on the wiry little man. "My heart is touched. I would not be the source of Conchita's grief."

Juan sighed with relief, sat up, and squatted with his back against the wall. "It is rare to find compassion in Ciudadela," he said gratefully, rubbing the circulation back into his numb arm. "I think you are a great man."

True didn't know whether or not Juan was being facetious, but his nerves had been so keyed up that talking was a release. He slipped the thong from around his neck and dangled the amulet in front of the would-be thief. "This was a gift from my mother."

The metal glittered dully in the dim light. It would never be his now, Juan knew. The moment had passed. "What isn't?" he asked with a resigned shrug.

"Would you steal such a gift? The last she gave me?"

"Of course," Juan answered.

True sighed, replaced the thong around his neck and tucked the amulet under his shirt.

"But I would regret it," Juan added.

"Small comfort."

"All the comfort there is, in Ciudadela." Curious, Juan lowered his voice and leaned close to True. "Tell me, *gringo*. You must have many enemies. The other *gringos* are kept apart, but you . . . you are here with us."

True stiffened. "Others? North Americans?"

"Yes. I have heard names."

"A man called Austin?"

"Yes. That was one."

Silence. The drip of water. A muffled snore. So that was the fate of at least one of Texas's other emissaries.

"You know him?" Juan asked.

"No. Only of him. Where are they?"

"Another building? Who knows." Juan waited, hoping the *gringo* would ask him to find out so he could ingratiate himself. A *gringo*, even one with enemies, could be a powerful ally. "And your enemies?" he asked at last, when True didn't speak.

There was a long wait. "I have only one," True finally said. "But one is enough, no?"

"One is always enough when he is the right one."

"Yes." The water dripped. The walls seemed to lean inward. "Leave me now," True said. "We will talk another time. Now I want to sleep."

The Mexican was gone as swiftly as a thought. True waited a moment before he decided he really could sleep again, then lay back down. He grunted, rubbed the small of his back, rearranged the scanty pile of straw he had gleaned over the past week. Juan Torres, he thought. A slight man, darker complected than many of the others, a loner. True folded his arms over his chest, wiggled around to work a lump of straw out from under his right kidney. Torres lived well enough, from all appearances. His clothes were better than most in Ciudadela. He looked well fed. A good friend to have, perhaps, if one wanted friends. Fifty other prisoners in the cell snored, shuffled, jostled for space. The ones with bad dreams tossed and turned, called out in their sleep. The others, those with access to *pulque* brought in by the prostitutes, slept as dead men. True closed his eyes and, willing one corner of his mind to stay alert, dropped off into a shallow slumber.

Four men away, Juan Torres crept to his own meager bedding, a ragged ticking, filled with corn husks, bartered from a guard in return for the favors of Conchita. As he stretched out, a hand bit into his biceps and a fetid breath touched his face. "Little fly had best watch the company he keeps," a voice said in his ear.

Tarantula! Juan forced himself to relax. Tarantula was a permanent resident of Ciudadela because he had murdered his parents in cold blood. It was not wise to appear too confident when Tarantula talked to one, but neither was it wise to appear frightened, for then it could be reasoned that one had cause to be frightened. "Company, friend?" Juan whispered, somehow managing to keep his voice calm. "I spoke to him but briefly. We are not companions."

"I hope not," Tarantula hissed. "Flies sometimes overhear that which is not meant for their ears, and then buzz about where they should not be heard. I would hate to think that you were telling the North American things he is not supposed to know. If you did, I would have to wring your worthless neck, little man, and I hate to do things like that without being paid."

Juan knew it was dangerous to ask, but he had to know the answer. "Then someone has paid you for him, yes?"

"Does a fly walk on the web of the spider? He had better grow fangs, first."

"Juan Torres walks only where it is safe," Juan said.

"Good. But just to be sure—for if he learns of this I will

know who whispered in his ear—I will tell you." Tarantula's hand groped for Juan's. "Soon, I will break this *gringo* as I break . . . this."

He bent Juan's little finger back against his wrist. There was a tiny pop followed by a barely louder crack of bone, and Juan fainted. Tarantula rolled over, pulled his blanket around him and drifted easily off to sleep. His point had been made. The only thing left to do was wait for the money. Maybe it would arrive in the morning, maybe the day after that. It didn't really matter. Tarantula could wait. He had all the time in the world.

They had moved him. Why, he did not know. It was difficult to think. Two nights before, a fever and explosive diarrhea had come on him. His head spun, his gut rumbled with gas and ached continually. The cell he was in was as small as a closet. Stone walls on three sides. Bars on the fourth. Past the iron bars, the hallway was bleak and feature-less in sallow lamplight.

Someone screamed. The sound echoed dully through the corridors, seeped into the soul, and left it trembling. Crouch-ing, True shivered and wrapped his arms around his knees for warmth. *Bastards! Bastards! Swine! Got to get . . .*

A door creaked open, slammed shut. Another scream, this one truncated at its height, and then footsteps, the abrupt click of boots smartly striking the stone floor. When they stopped, True looked up and saw Luther O'Shannon standing outside his cell. "What do you want?" he asked dully, his words slurred and thick.

O'Shannon stared at him as one would stare at an animal caught in a trap. Stared and said nothing.

"Damn you!" True coughed, heaving himself to his feet and standing propped against the back wall. He stank of his own ordure. His temper was brittle. Vermin crawled beneath his clothes. His gut rumbled painfully. "Answer me," he demanded. "What do you want?"

O'Shannon watched.

True wiped the perspiration from his forehead. The Irishman was toying with him, but he did not have the strength to remain calm. A scream tearing his throat, he lunged across the cubicle and stretched his arms through the bars. His face slammed into iron, his hands clawed the air inches from O'Shannon's face.

O'Shannon watched. A glimmer of amusement flickered over his face.

"Someday," True gasped, his arms dropping to dangle limply between the bars. "Someday, you sonofabitch!"

Luther O'Shannon watched.

True's knees collapsed, and he slid down the bars to the stone floor.

He was taken back to the large cell, thrown in with everyone else. The fever persisted. So did the diarrhea. Secretly, always in the night when everyone else was asleep, someone he thought he knew brought him warm gruel thickened with little chunks of unspoiled meat. Once he tried to ask who, but was answered with a finger touching his lips to demand silence. He did not ask again. Gradually, the fever subsided and his stool cleared and his gut stopped rumbling so fearfully. Why, he did not know, for he had been closer to death than ever before.

His father had the answer. True saw him once, just after they came at him, the one called Tarantula and three friends.

The prisoners had been allowed into the courtyard for a wash in the rain followed by their daily ration of *tortillas* and beans. After half an hour, they had been herded back into the stygian confines of the inner walls. True's eyes had not yet adjusted to the darkness when he heard the first whisper.

Tarantula and his three cronies had remained inside and could see quite well. Swiftly, before anyone knew what was happening, they closed in on him from four sides. True sensed them coming and swung blindly just before a fist slammed into his jaw. Even while he fell, others hammered his stomach, ribs, and groin. The punishment did not last long. Just long enough. They left him curled in a corner, his breathing ragged, blood streaming from his nose and mouth.

It was then that True saw his father. Thomas Gunn Paxton was sitting on a log. Behind him, patchy through the vine-covered trees, Solitary showed bright and gleaming in a blood red sun. Thomas was sharpening the blade of his cutlass. He looked much younger than True remembered, and quite fierce, too. "I'm dying, Father," True whispered.

Thomas Gunn Paxton glanced up. "No you're not."

"I'm not?"

"Not unless you want to. Why else do you think you

survived this long? You didn't want to die. We Paxtons are a stubborn lot.''

True was staring at a wall, a stone wall smeared with his own blood. He moved his hands. He placed them under his shoulders and pushed himself to his knees. Pain ripped through his chest and he choked back a scream.

"If you think that hurts," Thomas Gunn Paxton said, "wait until you stand."

"I can't!" True said, his voice an almost meaningless croak.

"You want me to tell your mother that?"

His father faded before his eyes. Only the blood on the wall was left. Slowly, True got one knee off the ground and, using his hands on the wall, clawed his way up until he was standing.

Now that is pain! He braced himself, leaned back against the wall. *Oh, Christ!*

The world finally ceased its spinning. Objects and people solidified, held still long enough to be seen. True shuffled through the prisoners, all of whom made way for him as if physical contact with him might bring retaliation down upon their heads. He ran into one man, angled off as if the contact had bruised him. He peered into blank, carefully neutral faces, went from one to another like a sleepwalker. He tripped over a loose brick and, sucking in his breath and gritting his teeth, willed himself to reach down and pick it up.

Tarantula was facing his cohorts, allowing them each a sip from the bottle of *pulque* he had purchased from one of the guards for double what it should have cost even on the inside. His back was to True, and he was so busy bragging about his new source of wealth that he did not hear True coming. True did not ask him to turn around, only lurched out of the crowd and swung with all his might. Brick met bone and bone gave. Tarantula stumbled forward. True hit him again and he fell to his knees. When he tried to stand, True hit him a third time.

The dull crunch of tissue and bone. A sickening, hollow sound. Tarantula hit the floor face first, his left leg kicking out once. The bully's companions melted into the gathering men. Incredulous that the dreaded Tarantula had been crushed, they stared at True and the nearly dead man at his feet.

"We Paxtons are a stubborn lot," True said in English, and aimed his body toward the corner he always occupied.

The corner wouldn't stay in one place. Vision dimmed,

cleared, exploded into pinpricks of light. The walls melted, coalesced again, shifted crazily. Suddenly, a supporting arm encircled his waist. Blinking, he could see it belonged to Juan Torres, and for some reason he remembered the gruel and knew who had brought it to him. "You . . . you . . ." He tried, but his tongue wouldn't work.

"There is no need of thanks, friend," Juan said, snapping at the other prisoners to clear a path. He helped True to his corner, eased him into a sitting position."You see—" His teeth flashed as he smiled. "—Juan is a man to be trusted despite what others may say. And the one called Tarantula, I do not think he will bother any of us again."

One eye in the wily brown face winked. True thought it took a long, long time. *"Sopa,"* he mumbled, remembering the Spanish word for soup. *"Sopa."*

"Yes. It was me. Any other man in here would have killed me if he had caught me the way you did. You did not. Now, lie quietly. I will bring you more soup later." The teeth, all True could distinguish of his face in the gloom, flashed again as Juan held up a crudely fashioned dagger, a length of hammered, jagged iron set in a wooden handle. "And when it is dark," he hissed in a hate-filled voice, "the spider will learn, if he is still alive, that the fly does have fangs."

Juan had disappeared. True stared uncomprehendingly around the room, at the shadowed shapes, the ghostly images of the nightmare world. The pain in his side was almost intolerable, but the victory he had scored, however minor, tasted good. Only then did it dawn on him that there would be other cutthroats willing to take O'Shannon's money. As many others as there were prisoners. And just before he passed out, he wondered how many more victories he had left in him.

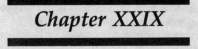

Chapter XXIX

Veracruz. Elizabeth liked the sound of the name, but she would have liked it more under different circumstances. The last ten days had been packed with tension, worry, and fatigue, all stemming from the note from Don Raphael. Her first step had been to ride to Joseph and Lottie's house, where she had spent the night. All three of them had agreed that her only course was to go to Mexico City with Hogjaw and try to get True released. Joseph had dug the money out from under the hearth and given it to her the next morning. Five thousand American dollars in gold was a frightening sum, but there was no way to tell how much would be needed. Some of it she packed in her valises, some in Hogjaw's warkit, and some in his thick, leather money belt. At least it wouldn't all be stolen or lost at once.

They left for Corpus Christi on horseback Saturday morning. By the time they got there Monday, Elizabeth was so sore she could hardly walk. A day was spent locating passage to Veracruz, a difficult job because no one wanted to sail south. Luck was with them, though. By Monday evening they had found a captain, and on Wednesday morning they embarked for the run down the Mexican coast. Their luggage was lighter by one hundred twenty-dollar gold pieces and Elizabeth was so tired they had to rig a sling to lift her into the schooner, but at least they were on their way. Hogjaw helped her into a bunk in the captain's cabin, assured her that they were moving at a remarkable pace, all things considered, and fussed around until she had dropped off to sleep.

The next four days were frustrating beyond compare because it was difficult to see that they were making any progress whatsoever while all the time True was languishing in prison. They were also a blessing in disguise. The weather was

balmy and the breezes, except for a brief squall, moderate.
Elizabeth, forced to fill the time somehow, alternated between
sleeping and working the stiffness out of her legs and back.
On Monday, the eighth of June, they sighted Veracruz. Elizabeth was on deck with the first hail of the lookout. Already
the swirling, screeching gulls had come out to meet them.
Before too many minutes had passed, a dark blue ridge of
land that rose out of the water resolved itself into a shoreline
of gently rising tree-covered hills. And by the time Elizabeth
had come back on deck after going below to pack, she could
hear the surf white as new snow and, beyond, white sand,
whitewashed buildings, and red-tiled roofs. They were still
more than two hundred miles from Mexico City, but at least
the distance had become reasonable. Before too many more
days passed, she would be reunited with True.

" 'Lizabeth?" Hogjaw joined her at the rail. His deerskin
garments looked out of place on board ship, but he didn't
care. Neither did anyone else. In fact, the Mexican sailors
went out of their way to neither complain nor deride. Except
for wondering, very privately, how one so ugly came to be
traveling with one so beautiful, they made a point of ignoring
the hulking mountain man. "You got all your stuff together?
Captain Hernandez has a boat ready to take us to shore as
soon as we drop anchor."

"The sooner the better," Elizabeth said, pointing to the
pair of valises by the door leading to the captain's cabin.

Sooner turned out to be another excruciating half hour. At
last, though, the anchor chair rumbled through the hawse
hole, and the schooner snubbed against the line and came to a
dead stop. Aloft, men crawled through the rigging making
everything secure. Below, a crew of six swung the captain's
gig over the side and lowered it into the water. Within
another minute, the gig with Hernandez himself at the tiller
was dancing across the water.

The ride was an unsettling fifteen minutes of climbing
swells and digging into troughs that the sailors considered
inconsequential. Elizabeth's knuckles were white as she clutched
the board seat on either side of her. Hogjaw put on a good
show, but kept a tight hold on the gunwale and was heard to
sigh with relief as they slid onto the sand and came to a
jarring halt. He would rather have ridden an old bull buffalo
across Texas, he announced later, than take that short ride
again. And if it hadn't been for Elizabeth and True . . .

Hernandez accompanied them to town where the haggling and spending began again. In the end, a messenger was dispatched to Sanchez in Mexico City with the news that Elizabeth was on her way, and a request to be met by someone in Puebla, a little over halfway there. The messenger was gone before they had been in town for an hour, but it took the better part of the day to arrange transportation for themselves. Not until two mornings later did they climb into a dilapidated ruin of a coach drawn by a mismatched pair of ancient geldings that looked more fit to be rendered for glue than to take them on a trip through the mountains further inland. "I know this man," Hernandez assured them. "He will stop at decent inns, and you will be in Puebla in four days' time."

"Four days?" Hogjaw asked. "Hell, I could do it in less than two."

"Alone and with two or three good horses, yes. But with the lady?" Hernandez shrugged, a gesture that suggested the impossibility of such a preposterous idea. "The roads twist much, Señor Leakey, and climb far higher than you think. Be happy with four days. If it rains, it could take many more."

"You will be waiting when we return?" Elizabeth broke in, anxious to leave.

"I will wait for the agreed-upon time," Hernandez said. "Meanwhile—" He slammed shut the door and signaled for the driver to start. "—you are wasting time. Adiós!"

The coach started with a jerk that threw Elizabeth against the back of the seat. "A month," she said. "What day is it?"

"The third," Hogjaw growled. "Gives us until the third of July."

"Do you think he'll wait?"

"We paid him enough." An evil smile played among the creases and folds of Hogjaw's face. "If he doesn't, he'd better find him another ocean to sail in. And hope to hell I never heard of it."

Puebla was cool, at least, so the dust that rose around them in choking clouds didn't stick and cling and itch as it had in the more humid Veracruz. It wasn't hard to find the center of town, or the single decent hotel where they were to meet Sanchez's man. By that time Elizabeth had come to expect delays. A broken wheel that took a half day to fix, and another half day spent waiting for a bridge to be repaired, had taught her better than she cared to know. She was not at all surprised to learn that no one was waiting for them at the hotel. Nor was she surprised when she came down, the next morning, with an embarrassing case of diarrhea, and was forced to spend the better part of the next two days in a most indelicate position on a chamber pot in her room. By that time, exhausted, disillusioned, dehydrated, and bloated with the home remedy given her by the hotel owner's wife, she was not even surprised when the most magnificent coach and four she had ever seen drove up to the hotel and let out a rather fierce-looking young man who strode through the door as if he owned the place and asked for her by name.

His name—the part Elizabeth could decipher from a long, run-togther string of syllables—was Pedro Sanchez, and he was the second-born son of Estimo Sanchez. That he and his horses were fatigued and would need to rest a day or so before beginning the trip back was a bit of news Elizabeth was prepared to take in stride. Later, beaming with approval, Hogjaw found the time to praise her. She was learning to roll with the punches, he said, and not to kick and scream when faced with adversity. In this particular case, such a course was especially wise. Mex prisons were notorious, he explained, and though True had been tough as a nail when they'd last seen him, he'd probably be more than a little wore down. The faster they could get him out, the better. Saving her strength and wits for when she got to Mexico City and could actually *do* something was smart.

Thursday morning, about ready to leave Puebla at last, Hogjaw forgot his own advice. Their bags were packed and they were waiting out front, when the coach pulled up at the front door and Pedro stepped out. "You are ready?" he asked in broken, schoolboy English.

"Absolutely," Elizabeth replied, accepting his helping hand and climbing into the coach.

Hogjaw started to follow, but Pedro placed a hand on the mountain man's brawny arm. "You will ride up top with the servants, señor," he said in his most imperious tone.

"What?" Hogjaw asked, shaking off the offending hand.

"You will ride up top with the other servants."

Hogjaw's cheeks flapped alarmingly as he scratched his chin. "Hmmm. Well, younker, I'll tell you what."

"Señor?"

"I'll either ride inside with the lady or you can pick your left ear up off'n the ground. Take your pick."

"Ear?" Pedro asked, not sure he was understanding correctly. A bit flustered, he glanced down at the ground. "But my ear is not on the ground, señor."

Hogjaw smiled and his face did a little dance all its own. The stitch scars on his skull gleamed like a pale wreath.

Pedro, the second-born son of Estimo Sanchez, paled. "You may," he said quickly, "ride inside with us, señor."

Two more nights of restless sleep. Two and a half more days of bone-wearying travel. Dry stream beds. Lonely passes. High, arid plains. And towns whose names were music as the coach swung north to avoid washed-out roads and to enter the city from the northeast. Tlaxcala, Apizaco, Calpulalpan, Texcoco. Names Pedro helped her learn how to pronounce while Hogjaw sat glowering in the corner he had staked out for himself. Village after village after village, some more prosperous than others, but all with nearly identical adobe houses arranged in squares surrounded by the shacks and huts of *los povres,* the poor ones. Some few of these shacks were blessed with laughing children, but most were occupied only by wracked and bent old men and women who stared sullenly at the passing carriage, the symbol of everything they dared not dream of in their poverty-stricken world.

The closer they came, the more crowded was the road that snaked through the marshes and around Lago de Texcoco, the lake that lay on the northeastern edge of Mexico City. Pure-bred Spaniards rode in coaches much like the one in which Elizabeth rode, and scattered travelers on foot or riding burros; *mestizos* and other half-breeds of all colors, along with purebred Indians clad in dirty white cotton trousers, whose lot it was to eke out a living at the bottom rung of the creaky ladder of existence, moved aside as they knew they must. The Sanchez coach stopped for no one, and much abuse was hurled at its passing by men fighting to keep their burros under control or by vendors with their merchandise strapped to their backs in great, precariously balanced piles.

Pedro appeared to care not one whit. How unlike Don Raphael this man was, Elizabeth thought, wondering if his father Estimo was at all like Don Raphael, or if the differences between the two brothers were as great as those between

True and Joseph. There was little time to think, though. The sights were too fascinating. People, buildings, animals, all jumbled in one teeming, seething mass, as different from her quiet homestead south of San Antonio as it was from Philadelphia. The coach had slowed, at least, in deference to the crowds, and then slowed further as it entered a broad, tree-lined street. The whole character of their surroundings changed. Loud became quiet. The bustling crowds diminished, replaced by an occasional servant with well-dressed children in tow. The rank odor of humanity was dispelled by the sweet aroma of flowers. Before Elizabeth could quite catch her breath, the coach was driving through gates of wrought iron woven into figurative designs. Inside, the grounds were like a park. Fountains jetted water into the air, released it to bubble over marbled tiers alive with carvings that looked as if they might have come from Paris itself. Banks of flowers rose at precise angles to sculpted hedges. And by the time they reached the end of the drive, servants were approaching the coach to help the passengers out and up the blue tile steps leading to a pair of massive mahogany and brass doors.

"Mighty fancy place your daddy has," Hogjaw commented.

"This is not my father's house, señor," the young man replied stiffly.

The door to the coach opened and the young man stepped out and offered his hand to Elizabeth, who already felt shabby in her gingham dress and cotton bonnet. She thought of True then, and embarrassment, not for her dress but that she should have worried about such nonsense, reddened her cheeks. "If not your father's, then whose?" she asked, stepping down.

"Mine, dear lady."

Elizabeth turned, brightened at seeing Don Raphael, saw next a slightly built man beside him who looked as if he might be his brother, and then cringed as if slapped, when she recognized the man at their side.

Pistol drawn and swinging upward, Hogjaw leaped from the carriage.

"Come come, my uncouth friend," Luther O'Shannon said. "You really ought to put that down before you hurt someone. Unless you wish to start a war with Mrs. Paxton in the middle. It would be a shame for such a beauty to be marred by fire and shot."

Hogjaw looked around and counted a dozen Mexican soldiers with their muskets aimed at him and Elizabeth. "Damn!" he said, the pistol steady on O'Shannon. "You'll by God go first, then."

"First, last, whatever," O'Shannon said coolly. "I've faced death as many times as you have, old man. You don't care, I don't care. But the lady? . . ."

The argument was compelling. Slowly, Hogjaw took the pistol off cock and lowered it, then handed it to the soldier who stepped forward to disarm him. "Don't fret, 'Lizabeth," he mumbled. "Always been a way out before. There'll be one this time too."

"That is better, my shaggy friend. Napoleon always used to say that the best war was won without firing a shot. I heartily agree. And now, if you will be my guest?" O'Shannon nodded to the soldiers who moved in to lead Hogjaw toward the carriage house at the base of the side wall. "You see? A victorious commander can be generous. And as for you, my lady . . ."

Elizabeth stared at Don Raphael who, unable to meet her eyes, kept his head lowered.

". . . you must be tired after such a long and tedious journey. The girls will take you to your room. Do not hesitate to ask for anything you want." He let a thin smile cross his face. "Within reason, of course."

Elizabeth hesitated, watched Hogjaw disappear around the corner of the house, and then, scorning O'Shannon with a single glance of contempt, followed the servants up the blue tile stairs.

"You promised she would not be harmed," Don Raphael said when the doors shut behind Elizabeth. "And that True Paxton would be set free."

His son was dead and Paxton had not yet paid in full for the life he had taken. Under the circumstances, promises were meaningless. Still, O'Shannon was not a man to be trifled with. "Do you doubt my word?" he asked in a tone as sharp as a shard of broken glass.

"I don't know," Don Raphael answered with a directness that frightened his brother. "Should I?"

O'Shannon had baited his trap as adroitly as True Paxton had his, and the results would be equally devastating. Nothing would bring back Ramez, but the vengeance he had in mind would ease the pain. And whether or not

Sanchez liked it was totally beyond his concern. "That's up to you, my fat friend," he said, a death's-head grin parting his lips. "Quite frankly, I don't give a damn one way or the other."

Chapter XXX

Three interminable days passed. Three days during which she was allowed to eat and sleep and pace and worry, but not to leave her room or speak with anyone who knew anything. Her food arrived on trays, was well-cooked and nourishing, but tasted like sawdust. The servants made her bed, saw to her clothes, carried bath water for her. For some inexplicable reason, a seamstress appeared and took her measurements. Each night a fire was lighted in the fireplace. She was incarcerated in opulence, every bit as much a prisoner as True, and there wasn't a thing she could do about it. The balcony was guarded at all times by two soldiers; another soldier was stationed outside her door. Only once was there a brief glimmer of hope. On the second day, one of the two maids allowed in her room slipped her a tiny piece of paper with her lunch. Later, alone, she unfolded it and read: "I am trying. Don't give up. R." Something about the note bothered her, though she could not say what. The first night she had cried herself to sleep. That second night, she lay dry-eyed for a long, long time before finally dropping off. Sometime in the early morning she woke, having dreamed of True, and a strange note she was sure hadn't come from Don Raphael. In the morning, she was too tired to solve the mystery, and at last gave up out of frustration.

Wednesday, she woke up crying and couldn't stop. Just to hear English, a sentence she recognized, would have helped, but every word spoken to her was in Spanish. She felt so alone, so isolated, with no one to turn to for help. O'Shannon had her completely at his mercy, was playing with her as a cat played with a mouse before killing it. That had been clear from the beginning. What wasn't clear, especially after more than three days of absolutely nothing happening, was what

295

course his vengeance would take. If only Hogjaw . . . But Lord only knew where they were keeping him or what they had done to him. She doubted that O'Shannon had had him killed. On the other hand, the mountain man's death would serve . . .

Stop! You've got to stop!

Elizabeth clapped her hands to the side of her head as if to keep it from exploding. She *had* to remain calm. Wild suppositions, confusion, fear—these were what O'Shannon wanted from her. Confidence, calm, and cool thinking were the only weapons in her arsenal. Steeling herself, she forced the tears to stop and—hunger served O'Shannon's purpose—made herself eat the lunch the maid had brought.

The bath water was perfumed that afternoon. Elizabeth bathed and saw no sign of surrender in the act, if for no other reason than that she knew she would function better if she cared for herself. She continued being wary, though, for the pace of the servants had quickened. Something was in the air. She had to think, to anticipate, to plan ahead. Needing silence, she rested her head against the back of the tub and slid down until her ears were under water. What did O'Shannon want? Why was she here? She distrusted the obvious answer, that she wanted to take her, because he could have done that—or tried to, she corrected herself—within an hour after her arrival.

Oh, True! Where are you? If only I could let you know I am near. . . . No. I won't let myself do that. Think. Think, girl!

Don Raphael's treachery was totally unexpected. Why would he do such a thing to her? Did O'Shannon have something on him, too? Even so, it was galling. She had expected a friend waiting for her, and had counted on his support and help. Betrayal was a bitter wound. O'Shannon's animosity was expected—she had considered that from the first moment—but to have Don Raphael turn against her as well . . .

Furious, she stood and stepped from the bath and snatched a towel from one of the maids who stood waiting to dry her. "I'll dry myself, damn you," she snapped. "I'm not a child."

Something *was* up! Her heart thudding in her chest, Elizabeth let herself be helped into a chemise and then sat docilely while one woman with a severe and dominating air dried, brushed, and coiffed her hair and another, a shy young girl, trimmed and buffed her fingernails. That finished, she was led to the next room and stood in front of a mirror while a magnificent gown was lowered over her head. In all her young life she had never seen such a shimmering, jewel-encrusted creation—pink rose silk stitched with pearls and gleaming silver teardrops, wound with fragile chains of gold. The bodice of lace and glittering gold fabric cinched her waist and held her breasts indecently high. As a crowning touch, an exquisite abalone-shell comb set with diamonds and hung with a shoulder-length black mantilla was thrust into her hair.

"But why?" she asked the hairdresser, unable to believe her eyes. "Why? Where is he taking me?"

"You wait," the hairdresser said, the first words she had spoken. *"No hablo ingles."*

I don't speak English. Elizabeth knew that much Spanish. She'd heard it enough times. Understanding didn't help, though. She wanted an answer. Any answer. Something concrete, to which she could respond. She was tired of being treated like a dumb animal, groomed like a sacrificial lamb to be led to the altar of O'Shannon's revenge.

The door to her room opened and Don Raphael entered. Elizabeth whirled to face first him, then the maids. "Leave me," she snapped. "Now. Get out!"

This was one command that needed no translation. Hairdresser, manicurist, and the other two maids hurriedly curtsied and, eager to escape, scampered past Don Raphael and closed the door after them.

"Well?" Elizabeth asked in the dead silence that followed. At last she had someone on whom she could focus her anger. "How *nice* of you to come," she said, acid dripping from each word. "Where is he? What is happening? What are they *doing* to me?"

Don Raphael walked to the fireplace and stationed himself in front of the blaze that had been started an hour earlier to dispel the chill of the mountain night. The hearth was fashioned of shiny turquoise tile worked with slivers of white clay. The mantel was a single huge, intricately carved piece of oak. Arranged along its length, golden plates taken from Aztec temples gleamed dully in the early evening light. Don Raphael wiped a finger across his reflection in the polished oak, and stared into the flames. "A fire," he said, not answering her. "Now there is a world one can understand. The progression is simple. A log has no choice but to burn and become ash. In life, though? Ah, much more difficult. We do what we must, I suppose.''

"True always said we do what we choose to do. Anything else is just an excuse," Elizabeth said, by no means ready to forgive. "You remember True? My husband? He was your friend.''

"And still is," Don Raphael said, finally looking at her. "No. Let me speak, please. I thought our trip here would be fruitful. If I hadn't thought so, I wouldn't have come myself or let Señor True come. I would have joined Señor Travis outright and have done with it. Only after Señor True drove off to meet with Santa Anna that morning did I realize things were not entirely what they seemed to be.''

Don Raphael sat heavily, and stared at his steepled fingers. "My brother, Estimo, sold Señor True to Luther O'Shannon in return for the favortism and protection of President Antonio Lopez de Santa Anna. You must understand. These are precarious days, days of the Devil. It is unwise to be considered an enemy of Santa Anna. Estimo was convinced that our homes and families were in great danger, that every *centavo* we possess was at stake. So he promised O'Shannon he would deliver Señor True to him, and he did. By the time I dragged the full story out of him, Señor True was in prison. In Mexico, that which is done is not easily undone.''

"There was nothing you could do," Elizabeth said, mocking sympathy.

"There was nothing for me to do. I was powerless.''

"Really?" Elizabeth sat near the window, arranged herself in a high-backed chair of polished maple cushioned with padded satin. She could see herself reflected in the mirror, but the image belonged to someone else, she thought, someone she wasn't at all sure she knew. "Not so powerless you couldn't write a letter that you knew would bring me running.''

"I didn't write that letter," Don Raphael said quietly.

"Liar! Of course you wrote it. For every precious *centavo* you didn't want to lose.''

Don Raphael looked more sad than angry. "How many times have you seen my hand?" he asked. "Think carefully, now.''

"I . . . I don't know. Never, I guess." But he wouldn't trick her this way. "Except for that letter.''

"And the note I sent you yesterday. Do you have either of them?''

Elizabeth was more confused than ever. "There was something . . . something wrong about that note," she stammered. "I dreamed you hadn't sent it. That it . . . that you . . ."

"The note was mine," Don Raphael said, striding to the desk. He dipped a pen in the inkwell, scratched something on a piece of paper, and handed it to Elizabeth. "Does this look familiar?" he asked.

It read, "I am trying. Don't give up. R." And the handwriting was identical to that of the note she had received the day before.

"Estimo wrote the letter sent to you in San Antonio. I sent one too, but some days after his left. Mine is probably waiting for you there now. I learned of Estimo's the day the messenger from Veracruz arrived here." He took the paper from her hands and threw it into the fire. "I'm sorry, Elizabeth. I knew it was dangerous for you to be here."

Elizabeth stared at her hands, twisted the simple gold band on her ring finger. "What does he want with me?" she whispered. "Do you know?"

"Revenge. Exactly what or how I don't know. All he has told me is that he will free True, and that you will not be harmed. I believe he will keep his word."

"Something else, then," Elizabeth said, a cold chill running up her back. "Something worse."

"I'm afraid so. An eye for an eye is not enough for Luther O'Shannon. I will try to help any way I can, but be warned. I am weak and he is very, very strong. Strong enough that I . . . that I . . ." Don Raphael's face turned beet red and he lowered his eyes. "I have not dared to fight him openly. And I would have written the letter myself if he had ordered me to. It is a terrible thing to say, but I would have. I thought you should know that."

She was beyond anger. His admission left her cold, empty, and even more helpless. "It's all right," she said dully. "I understand." She could taste the bitterness. "You'd have had no choice, I suppose. It's all right."

"No, it isn't." Don Raphael shook his head sadly. "You see, I am his lackey." Slowly, he walked to the door, and spoke without looking at her. "For whatever the reason—Who knows? Spite?—I was sent with this message. Señor O'Shannon will dine with you at eight. One of the maid's will show you the way."

The sound of the fire ameliorated the deathlike quality of

the silence. "I suppose I have no choice?" Elizabeth asked, then blushed as she realized that that had been precisely Don Raphael's justification.

"Perhaps you see how it is after all," Don Raphael said, mercifully refraining from looking at her. "I am an old man, Elizabeth. I have seen much. The loss of a loved one is a terrible thing, but to live without honor . . . without . . ."

"Don Raphael? Stop. Please." Elizabeth rose and went to him, placed her hands on his arms and rested her cheek against his back. "Perhaps you are right," she admitted, haltingly. "These are days of the Devil."

Don Raphael patted her hand. The muscles in his back remained tense. "I am sorry, Elizabeth. So very sorry," he said, and, taking her hand from his arm, escaped.

Elizabeth watched him go, his shoulders sagging, saw the shadows envelop him, a sad gentleman in rumpled brown finery adrift in the chaos of a changing world. "Days of the Devil," she whispered to herself as the door closed behind Don Raphael. "And his name is Luther O'Shannon."

The Devil had refrained from luncheon in order to appreciate dinner fully. He was very hungry. According to his orders, the menu began with a Chablis followed by consommé served with Sherry Isabella. A Sauterne would accompany the boiled and chilled sliced bass with rémoulade sauce. The main course would be roast ribs of beef *a jus,* fresh steamed green beans and glazed tiny new carrots. Pâté de fois gras and a Château d'Yquem would follow, after which would come braised lamb over steamed asparagus points, and sherbet made from ice carried from the mountains. A simple cinnamon-flavored flan would serve as dessert, after which, if they so desired, cheeses, fresh fruits, and Château Margeaux. Coffee and liqueur, of course, finished the list, after which . . . Quite pleased with himself, O'Shannon chuckled in glee. His years in France had served him well. These things were best done in style.

For the moment, the table was bare save for a low centerpiece of fresh flowers and, for Elizabeth as she halted in the doorway, a confusing array of silverware and goblets. Dressed in a red and gold uniform, O'Shannon stood off to one side in front of the fireplace. His salt and pepper hair was brushed back from his forehead and his beard was close cropped to follow the unforgiving line of his jaw. "Enchanting," he said, coming to take her hand and lead her to her place at the table. "Absolutely enchanting. You grace this humble house with beauty that exceeds the divine. Surely Homer had you in mind when he told of Hera, Queen of Olympus." He seated her, took his own place at the other end of the table, and clapped his hands. Immediately a servant appeared to pour the Chablis. "A toast then, to you."

Elizabeth willed her hand not to shake as she picked up her glass and held it out. "And to you," she said, her voice surprisingly firm. "And your appalling combination of courtesy and barbarism."

O'Shannon drank slowly in contrast to Elizabeth, who finished her wine quickly, placed the goblet to one side, and would not allow the servant to refill it. "Your heart may soften to me before the night is over," he said at last, gesturing lazily with one finger to the servant at his side. "But come, you must be famished."

The consommé and sherry appeared as if by magic. "I am hungry," Elizabeth said, "for answers. What do you want with us? By what right did you imprison True?"

"Right?" O'Shannon asked, amused. He sipped his consommé delicately, to prove that one so accomplished in warfare and intrigue could also be civilized. "Santa Anna has need of capable commanders. I am a capable commander and he sets quite a store by me. In addition to which, I have always made it a policy to curry the favor of those in power. As a result, I become powerful. So you see it is not a question of right at all, but of might."

"That doesn't answer my question."

"The consommé is cold," O'Shannon snapped, and barked something in Spanish to the servant. Immediately, the bowls and wineglasses were whisked from the table and quickly replaced with the bass and Sauterne. "Very well," the Irishman said, his composure regained. "Your husband killed my son. That is all the right I need."

The combination of wine and tension were making Elizabeth dizzy. She pushed the Sauterne away. "He tried to kill True and almost did, breaking his neck in the process," she said. "You know that's what happened, and you know True had nothing to do with it."

"I know he took my son from me." Each word flat and equally emphasized, as terrifying as the dry, brittle sound of a rattlesnake. O'Shannon stabbed a piece of bass, followed it with a swallow of Sauterne. "In any case," he said, forgetting how civilized he was and talking around a full mouth, "the question of his imprisonment is moot. He'll be let out tonight and brought here tomorrow morning."

Elizabeth's fork caught on the edge of her plate. Fighting for control, she laid it down carefully and hid her hands in her lap. "Here?" she asked. The color drained from her face and she was forced to wet her lips before she could speak. "Why?"

"You're not eating your bass. It's really very good."

"*Why?* Is that all? You'll simply bring him here?"

O'Shannon's lips pulled tight against his teeth as he smiled. "Not exactly."

"What, then?"

"I intend to put the two of you, with your very ugly friend, of course, in a coach bound for Veracruz. Or to have him shot. The decision is in your hands."

That *was* it, after all! Her body for her husband's life! A plain and simple proposition, and yet . . . Why all the extravagant ceremony? Why the ritualistic dinner? Why the jewels and fine clothes and expensive wines? There had to be more. *Had* to be. "I . . . I don't understand," Elizabeth stammered.

"Come, come, Mrs. Paxton. You aren't unintelligent. You don't lack imagination. Of course you understand. You have from the beginning. What I do with your husband tomorrow morning depends on what you do with me tonight."

There it was in so many words. Somehow, the bass disappeared. In its place was set down a great chunk of pink meat surrounded by dark juice and shot through with fingers of blood. A fly buzzed over the table, circled the centerpiece, and landed on a piece of bread. A fitting sign of decay, Elizabeth thought, searching desperately for something, anything to break the numbing spell she was under. A sour note in a picture of elegance. A log in the fireplace fell with a crunch and a whoosh of sparks. O'Shannon's knife scraped his plate as he cut his meat. The fly crawled across the bread, stopped to clean itself, and went on. "Your beautiful wife . . .'" Elizabeth began, faltering.

"Is now a beautiful ex-wife." O'Shannon lifted an exquisite linen napkin to his mouth. "And happier, I assume. Free to bed whomever she wishes and not worry about it."

There had to be something to say. Some correct response.

If she could mollify him, show some sympathy . . . "I'm sorry," Elizabeth said lamely.

O'Shannon shrugged. "No need to be. It is in the nature of the young to be unfaithful. I expected no less." He beamed, as if speaking of such things at dinner was absolutely natural. "Ah, young girls. They have spirit, but the brains of cactuses. And scratch even worse. You are a very rare commodity, Mrs. Pax . . . May I call you Elizabeth?"

"Can I stop you?"

"Of course not. Rare indeed. A woman of youth, intelligence, beauty . . . and all wasted, as far as I can see. Please. Try the ribs. They're delicious. So tender you don't even need a knife, really. You have no idea how hard it is to teach these people to cook meat correctly."

Elizabeth pushed at her meat, forced herself to take a tiny bite.

"To think you're wasting your life on a barren frontier. On a *farm!* Paris . . . Greece. Have you ever tasted *ouzo*? Have you strolled beneath the elms along the Rue de Chantal? Danced and dined with true aristocracy, the pulse of civilization? Laughed, lived, tempted yourself with affairs in the French manner? Do you know that the gulls sound different over Montmartre Sound? It's true. Their lilting cries are distinguishable from those over Venice or Tripoli."

"I have no desire to know those things," Elizabeth said plainly. "I'd rather, as you call it, waste my life on a frontier farm."

"I know," O'Shannon said with exaggerated sadness. "I knew that when I spoke. It is a shame, though. Beauty like yours is born for the world to enjoy." Abruptly, he rose and walked to Elizabeth's end of the table, stood behind her and placed his hands on her shoulders.

Elizabeth shuddered, made herself sit still.

"Young and beautiful. And frightened. It is as it should be, as I knew it would be." O'Shannon's voice was understanding, but implacable. "A simple act. Degrading to contemplate, but pleasurable in the end, I sincerely hope. I am not unknowledgeable in these matters, after all." His hands kneaded her shoulders, his fingers crept down to touch the swell of her breasts. "His life, your decision, Elizabeth. A coach to the coast, or a corpse wagon to Hell."

What must I do? Save? Destroy? Honor? Dishonor? This is his revenge, True. You would say resist, even if it meant

*death, I know. But can I? Can I live without you? I would
rather die than hurt you, and I would rather endure the
horrors of this night than see you die.*

"One night with me or a lifetime without him," O'Shannon
said, evidently reading her mind. He took her left hand from
her lap, raised it to his lips and kissed her fingertips. "Is the
choice that difficult, Elizabeth?"

"He'll be set free? In the morning?"

"You have my word."

"The word of a pirate and a brigand. That isn't good
enough."

"I swear it on my son's life, then. Is that good enough?
Emilio!"

A thin, ferret-faced little man entered the room. O'Shannon
spoke to him in rapid Spanish, then waited until he left before
translating for Elizabeth. "I told him to go to the Ciudadela
and bring Señor Paxton here, to see that a coach and fresh
horses are waiting in the morning, and to be ready to leave
for Veracruz at any moment after sunrise. Is that better?"

Elizabeth had recognized some of the words, was reason-
ably confident he had told her the truth. It was all she could
do not to snatch her hand out of his, but she didn't. She was
less successful in controlling the tears that welled in her eyes
and ran down her cheeks. Somehow, she willed her tongue
and lips to form the words she prayed True might never learn
she said. "The coach," she whispered, barely audible. "I
choose . . . his life."

An iron door banged open and a lantern blinded the inmates.
A murmur of suspicion greeted the guards who entered. Eyes
squinting against the unaccustomed light, wide pupils narrowing, the prisoners woke and shuffled rapidly out of the way of
the tramping boots and the prodding bayonets. There had
been no executions for almost a month. No one wanted to be
stood against the pocked, bullet-riddled wall at the north end
of the compound just for calling attention to himself.

One of the guards grabbed a ragged man with a withered
arm dangling at his side before the prisoner could scuttle out
of harm's way. "The North American. Where is he?"

"In the corner," the prisoner bleated, terrified. He pointed.
"In that corner. He is very sick, I think."

True heard the commotion without comprehending what it
was all about. He pressed the palms of his hands against the

floor, but the tremors would not go away. The sickness was on him again. He had been unable to eat for three days and had taken only a few sips of water, and that at Juan's insistence. He was suffering the heat of the desert, the chill of a blue norther. Only when he was grabbed and savagely hauled to his feet did he realize that they had come for him. He tried to struggle, but was too weak to do more than twist about and mumble in delirium. A musket stock to his barely healed ribs wrapped him in ribbons of fiery agony and he collapsed, dead weight in the arms of his captors. What was left of his boots made a rasping sound on the stone floor as the guards dragged him from the cell.

The room was quiet and warm, the bed turned down. The flames above the candles danced like living jewels. Elizabeth had eaten very little, only a bite here and there when she told herself she had to keep up her strength. Now, as she stood in the doorway, she could feel each breath searing her lungs with a cold she had not believed existed. It was, she thought, the icy breath of the grave that waited for that part of her that was doomed, that she would sacrifice in order that the man she loved might be saved. Only two things kept her going. First, that True's life was worth the sacrifice. And second, that if Luther O'Shannon did not keep his word, she would kill him. Somehow, some way, he would die.

"Close the door. I am waiting."

She did as ordered, walked across the room to the balcony doors, heavy oak panels inlaid with glass, and started to draw the curtains.

"Leave them open."

Her hand fluttered from the cord.

"Sit next to me."

Each step was agony. Each move required its own command. The moment she came within his reach, O'Shannon grabbed her wrist and forced her down onto the covers. Elizabeth fought the urge, the impulse, the *need* to scream, to fight back, to scratch his eyes, and instead permitted him to kiss her. Suddenly, he swept her skirts to her waist and, with a single jerk of his hand, freed himself and was atop her and brutally entering her. She could not help screaming. At each raw thrust, she cried out. And when his seed spilled from him, she thought she would choke with revulsion.

O'Shannon moaned, let his weight rest upon her for a

moment, then stood. Quickly, he shed his trousers, coat, and shirt. "An excellent appetizer," he said, his voice thick and languid. "Now for the main course." He reached down and helped her to stand. "Out of the dress, there's a fine girl. And be quick. We've only one night, you know."

Elizabeth cursed her tears, hated the sound of her sobs. Her knees almost buckled. Her fingers fumbled at the gown. What she couldn't unfasten neatly, she tore.

"You've a need of manners, my dove. That was an expensive gown." He flopped down on the bed, rolled over onto his back. "Now, let me look at you."

Her head held high, she stood naked before him. The tears had stopped and she was filled with the same ice cold loathing she had felt when her father had touched her. O'Shannon, she swore, might take her, but he would never have her. Never. She looked past him to the candle. The flame seemed to spread, to envelop her until all she saw was a heart of fire and all she felt was the purgative flame. There was no other world, no pain, no shame, no awful bruising thrusts, no sickening carnal grunts, no humiliation, no submission to the even more obscene demands. Her soul was flying free across the open prairie, alone in the happy solitude of the forest, atuned to the delicate, gracious music of the stream. Even as she permitted the domination of her body, she remained unblemished and inviolate, and survived untouched.

At last, how much later she didn't know, O'Shannon rolled off her and lay spent and panting. "My son . . ." he said, his voice trembling with grief even as it surged with triumph. "He was headstrong, too wild perhaps, too much like me. But he was all that I had. And now I have all . . . *all* of what his murderer held dear and treasured. No mere slash of a saber could give me that."

He began to laugh. Elizabeth covered herself and, unable to look at him any longer, turned aside. Only then did the full measure of Luther O'Shannon's revenge strike home, filling her with horror. For framed in one of the window panels of the balcony door was the fevered, tortured face of her husband.

True had seen.

He had watched . . . everything.

Chapter XXXI

The creak of wood and hemp line. The sharp double ring of the bell from the quarterdeck. Ding-ding. Ding-ding. Ding-ding. Six bells. Three o'clock. The afternoon sun in the Gulf of Mexico was hot in spite of the breeze that slid over the deck, caught the sails, and sent the schooner northward, back toward Texas.

True lay in his bunk below and stared at the wood and past the wood to an empty realm devoid of answers. "Remember me," O'Shannon had said, leaning into the coach. Unwillingly huddled in Elizabeth's arms, burning with fever and tormented by the nightmare he had been forced to watch, True had heard the Irishman's final, mocking words: "Remember me." He would have given all he had to forget.

The sound of Elizabeth's knock, soft on the door, mingled with the other ship sounds. When there was no answer, she pushed the door open, tiptoed into the cabin and, trying to judge if True was awake, stood quietly against the bulkhead. "True?" There was no answer, and fearfully—for his fever had not yet broken and he was still terribly ill—she hurried to his side. But then she saw the blanket covering him rise gently with each breath, and her brief panic, felt too often the last few days, faded. Sighing with relief, she stood and looked down at him.

The ship rose and fell over the long swells, rocked easily against the slow force of the wind. The cabin smelled of sea spray and old maps and worn pewter and damp hemp and tarred wood. They were good smells. "Are you asleep?" she asked him.

He did not open his eyes or acknowledge her presence.

"The captain expects to reach Corpus Christi in three days. After that, we'll be home before long."

He might as well have been deaf for all the response she received.

"Hogjaw can't wait," she went on, trying to sound cheerful. "He says that little squall we had last night reminded him why he quit the sea in the first place."

The grain of the wood in the bulkhead, seen from only inches away, reminded True of a plowed field. The crops had barely been planted when he had left. He wondered how they were doing. Had insects eaten them? Had there been enough rain? There would be a great deal of work to do when he got home.

Home. Returning home as if nothing had happened. Home. Would it ever be home again?

"Damn it, True! Say *some*thing!" Elizabeth hissed, the tension and accumulated guilt threatening to destroy her self-control. "Do you think I *wanted* to? *Say* something!"

His head felt weighted. The muscles in his neck didn't want to work, but he willed them to. Only slowly did his head turn away from the wall and drop in her direction. "I don't have anything *to* say," he whispered, and closed his eyes again.

Elizabeth glared helplessly at him, at last whirled around and ran from the cabin. Her footsteps faded and became indistinguishable from the ship sounds. Behind her, the door to the cabin swung back and forth with the motion of the schooner. True clamped his hands to the side of his head but the ache remained no matter how forcefully he pressed. And always, no matter what, the voice of Luther O'Shannon rang in his ears.

"Remember me. Remember me. Remember me. . . ."

True slammed his fist against the bulkhead. "I will," he whispered between clenched teeth. "I will. I will. I swear I will!"

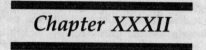

Chapter XXXII

There had been little difference between night and day at sea. True's fever was raging the day they sailed across Corpus Christi Bay and tied up at the docks in the Nueces River. He had a vague recollection of being carried onto land, of a cool room and the weight of blankets. He thought he recalled being placed in a wagon he later learned had been rented. He seemed to remember hearing interminable discussions held over the cold towels placed on his forehead, and wondering why they bothered when he only wanted them to leave him alone. The jolting had started sometime later. There had been heat and dust to torture him. His thirst had been unquenchable. And then one day he had opened his eyes and realized he was back in the cabin they had built. The first thing he remembered seeing was Elizabeth's eyes. They were wet with tears, but he was strangely unmoved.

If he had not been beaten so badly, if he had been more used to the food, he would never have wasted away so terribly in prison. Nor would his recovery have been so difficult. The process was slow and painful. His stomach would not hold solid food for the first month. His teeth hurt. Just when he thought he was recovering, diarrhea would sap his strength again. The length of time between the ravaging bouts gradually increased, though. He spent many hours in bed, almost as many more sitting in a small bower Hogjaw had built for him down by the river or, on cooler days, in the sun by the front door. He climbed on a horse for the first time in the middle of August, and by October, after starting slowly a month earlier, was splitting wood for the winter. One morning in December, he woke to the realization that he had become virtually a hermit. Vast changes were in the offing, but he had neither listened nor watched nor cared. One thing, though, had not changed: "Remember me," dwelled within him and ate at his soul.

Elizabeth would certainly have gone mad had it not been for Lottie and Joan and the others. The first two months were easy enough for she told herself that True was simply sick. It was easy to lose herself in nursing him and caring for the house and farm. As the days went by, though, and as he recovered his strength but still didn't respond to her, she began to worry. She made little treats for him. She sent to San Antonio for expensive white flour so she could make the white bread, hot and crusty, that she knew he loved so much. She stayed up late at night to make extra batches of crab apple jelly that he had once said he liked as a child. One afternoon she tore three fingernails building a ladder that was ugly but serviceable, carted it down to the riverbank, and propped it by an old cottonwood tree. She knew he used it because she spied him sitting in the tree one day, but he never thanked her for it. When he got well enough to do some work, she fashioned a special girdle for his ribs, which had not healed properly and which became very tender if he tried to do too much. He wore it for three days, and then left it off and put up with the pain. And always, no matter how he filled out, how he healed, how he tanned and ate and strengthened, his eyes remained empty. Worst of all, she knew that he watched her when she got ready for bed at night, and remembered.

The world had been going about its business. Stephen Austin had been released from his Mexican prison as a rare conciliatory gesture and he, Travis, Sam Houston, and a host of other self-ordained patriots had been busy fomenting revolution. The settlers and colonists had become impatient, and momentum toward creating an independent republic had gathered. The Revolution for Independence began in the waning months of 1835 in Gonzales, when the colonists rose and drove the Mexican soldiers from their midst. By the end of the year, the whole territory south of the Rio Grande had been emptied of Mexican troops. There was great rejoicing tempered with a calm fatalism: no one believed that Mexico would give up that easily. Santa Anna's soldiers would be back, and one day the Texians would have the war—and freedom—they had sought for so long.

True had heard the stories, had listened when Hogjaw or Joseph or one of the other men brought back the news, and had decided that, all in all, he'd had enough of Mexico. If anyone wanted a war it was fine with him as long as they marched around his land and fought somewhere else. It was early February by the time he got around to going into San Antonio to see and hear for himself. What he saw and heard was a state of confusion beggaring description. Most of those present wanted revolution and freedom, but beyond that certainty, gossip and speculation were the order of the day. The legendary Davy Crockett had arrived from Tennessee with a group of volunteers and was spoiling for a fight. Austin had assigned William Travis to command what army he could muster in the Alamo. Travis hadn't wanted the job—San Antonio had too few soldiers and was too poorly provisioned to make a good place to fight, he thought—but he took it anyway. Jim Bowie had showed up, and the Revolution was such a badly managed affair that he too had been given command. Sam Houston, commander-in-chief of what was loosely called the Texas Army, had sent word that the Alamo was indefensible and should be blown up; Bowie declared that he and his men would die to the last man defending it. Travis and Bowie, both in command, were at odds with each other and issuing contradictory orders. By eight in the evening, True lost the tangled skeins and said the hell with trying to understand any of it. Exhausted, he begged off attending a big get-together in General Cos's former headquarters and retired to Mama Flores's to get some sleep, leaving Elizabeth to go to the gathering alone.

The meeting wasn't the first of its kind. All across the state, spontaneous meetings had been held for months. Views had been exchanged, great oaths sworn. In settlement and city alike, the talk was always the same: of independence, of a new nation, of freedom.

"We hold," Reverend Kania thundered, concluding his reading to the throng packing the ballroom, "that we are a sovereign nation, and that the bonds of independence from the oppression of the government in Mexico City must at last be broken. And remain so broken, if need be, through force of arms!"

The rhetoric from the latest draft of the proposed declaration from the leaders of the rebellion was what everyone had come to hear. Their souls stirred, the colonists roared their approval with a great cheer that filled the room, set the candles trembling, and jiggled the lamp chimneys in their holders. William Barrett Travis stepped onto the speaker's platform as Kania stepped down. "Talk of war becomes you, Reverend," he shouted, raising a clay mug of *tequila* in a toast.

The room pulsed with laughter and good-natured catcalls. "The Lord never forbade conflict in the course of justice, Mr. Travis," Kania replied.

"And justice is our cause," Travis agreed to general tumult. He raised his hands for silence. "The dancing and drinking will commence as soon as I shut up and step down from here. But I don't want you to forget that the main reason we're here lies on that table." He pointed to the rear of the room. "Sometime during the evening, stop by to sign the petitions and tell the folks what you can give—a pair of fighting hands and a rifle, a horse or two if you have extra, money, clothing, tack, provisions . . . we want everything we can get our hands on and we need to know how much more we can count on and from whom. Any questions, I'll try to answer. And now, if the fiddler isn't drunk already—"

"Don't say that. Hell, if Jake was sober, that's when we'd be in trouble!"

The fiddler took a bow amid more shouts and catcalls.

"—we'll start the dancing!"

Jake hit the first chords and swung into a two-step. The crowd milled, separated, and headed for the bar, the dance floor, and the tables at the rear. Mila Kania put her arms around Buckland and kissed him in front of everyone, much to the delight and applause of the onlookers. Padre Salva, one of the many Mexicans anxious to be rid of Santa Anna's capricious authority, joined the applause and shook Buckland's hand. "I'm glad there's one thing we can agree upon after all, Reverend," he said, beaming his approval.

"Some Reverend," Buckland demurred, a little embarrassed by all the fuss. "I have yet to finish building my church."

"It appears," Salva said, "that God has called you to help build a republic instead."

The children had long ago been trundled off to bed to leave the remaining hours of the evening to the adults. Earlier, Elizabeth had tried to talk True into coming, but when he insisted on going to their room, had left alone in a fit of pique. Now she knew it was time to leave, but not wanting to face True just yet, she stayed and watched from her vantage point against the back wall with the others who weren't dancing. A small mountain of pies and cobblers, *tortillas* and *frijoles*, and barbecued chicken and goat had been consumed. Off to one side, an argument was raging over which was best for the liver, corn whiskey or *tequila*. A swirl of dancers filled the center of the room, shouted requests at Jake the fiddler and his two cohorts on guitar and accordian. Across the floor, Joseph swung Lottie around and sent her spinning into another couple. Buckland and Mila Kania were sipping punch and engaging in a lively debate with Jack and Helen Kemper. Helen kept her pointed chin tucked against her chest and peered at Mila over her glasses. The good Reverend might succeed in bringing Jack into the fold of humanity, but Elizabeth doubted he would ever extract the milk of human kindness, as Hogjaw put it, from the likes of Helen.

Kevin and Mildred Thatche came by to say goodnight. Kevin was carrying Kevin, Jr., who had fallen asleep upstairs in the nursery set up in General Cos's deserted office. Kevin had grown taller and added weight, especially in his shoulders and chest, which were broad and manly beneath his home-spun shirt. At sixteen, Mildred had already lost the first bloom of youth, for frontier life was difficult at best. Elizabeth tried not to think too much about the new lines she saw on her own face in the mirror each day.

A hand touched her elbow. "May I have the honor of this dance?" William Travis asked.

"The floor is crowded," Elizabeth answered flatly, her mood as gloomy as the winter night.

"The street isn't." His face was slightly florid from too much drink. "We'll dance there."

"It's too cold."

Travis raised one eyebrow. "A beautiful woman can always find a reason not to be alone with a man. It's one of the first things they learn how to do." He uncorked a bottle of *tequila*, poured some into his punch, and tasted. "That is awful."

"Why do you drink it, then?"

"It's a soldier's lot to make do."

"Soldiers," Elizabeth scoffed. "I'm sick of the word."

"But it's a necessary one in these troubled times. It's soldiers who'll give us a country of our own, free of Mexican domination."

"And widows and fatherless children in the same breath. Don't forget them."

Travis shrugged, apparently unconcerned. "I haven't. But as has been pointed out, we all die sooner or later. Better to do so for a cause instead of accidentally, from disease, or in a senseless barroom altercation."

That hit home. Elizabeth closed her eyes and, against her will, saw an image of her father, his skull crushed, his mouth agape. "Still," she said, shuddering, "too many will die."

"On the contrary. Some, to be sure—perhaps even myself— but not *too* many. There are never too many in the name of freedom. Besides, we have the march on them. Sam Houston's army is forming. Mine will grow. Mexico is riddled with warring factions, and Mexico City is a long way from here. I doubt Santa Anna will be able to muster more than a couple thousand men, and even if he does the coast is being watched and we'll have plenty of warning. He'll need an advantage of at least three to one if he hopes to beat us. Of course, if he tries . . ." Travis's eyes lit up with a secret fire. "A small war will help our cause, for it will settle the question once and for all."

Elizabeth stared at him in horror. "You *want* war, don't you? You'll be disappointed if Santa Anna doesn't march, if you don't get your bloodshed and glory."

Travis looked uncomfortable for the first time. He ran a hand through his neatly combed black hair. "I wouldn't say—"

"You're the first man I've ever met who *wanted* a war. It's indecent!" Elizabeth hissed.

"I think you're beginning to sound hysterical, Mrs. Paxton," Travis said, trying not to show his growing anger.

"No," Elizabeth said. "That's not being hysterical. It's being honest. We should fear you more than Santa Anna."

Travis's voice was cold and haughty. "Our cause is just, Mrs. Paxton. A great many people believe in it and are convinced our way is the only way. I am sorry I cannot convince you—or your husband, evidently."

"I'm not sorry at all. I'm sick of causes. And the only thing I'm convinced of is that spring will bring more than yellow roses to my door." She set down the cup she held and, eyes flashing, stepped back from him. "And now, if you'll excuse me . . ." Angry and frightened at the same time, she threaded her way through the knot of colonists who had gathered to listen, narrowly avoided a collision with Mackenzie Campbell who, arm in arm with a laughing señorita, was leaping and kicking out his heels, and fled out the door into the silence of the winter night.

The north wind pressed against her, chilling flesh and bone. Elizabeth hurried up the street to Mama Flores's *Casa del Rio* and, shivering uncontrollably, burst into the main room. It was warm inside and uncharacteristically quiet except for the subdued interchange of voices coming from the little *cantina* off the lobby. Curious, she crossed the lobby, pushed open the door, and found Scott and Joan Campbell sitting at one of the tables. The stolid, squarejawed blacksmith waved her in. "I thought we were the only ones here," he said, pulling out a chair for her.

"I didn't mean to intrude."

"Nonsense, dear," Joan said with a laugh. She poured a glass of cider from a clay pitcher and slid it across the table to Elizabeth. "We've been toasting February. With the last of the cider we brought with us." Joan hiccuped and giggled. "It's only fair you should have some."

Elizabeth had never seen the woman's cheeks so red. "What on earth, Joan . . ." She tried not to stare. "I believe you're—"

"I am not!" Joan interrupted, squaring her shoulders and correcting a slight list to the starboard. "I am undertaking a very important mission. I am determined to outlast the gentleman across the table from me."

"I can't believe it."

"Now, now. I will be the same pillar of earthly wisdom and kindness tomorrow as I have always been. You young people think you're the only ones who are young. Well—" She blinked, considered the last sentence, and decided it was close enough to what she meant. "It's not true. Ruthie and Dianne are asleep. The gentleman and I are alone, and if we want to be young again, we will."

It was impolite to laugh, perhaps, but Elizabeth couldn't help it. "Joan," she said, giving her a hug, "you will always be young. Always."

Joan nodded solemnly. "That's right. Keep your youth, I always said." Her good cheer faded suddenly and she stared into her glass. "Hmmmph! Might as well take an oath to foolishness. Like my boys traipsing after Travis and Bowie. Ready to whip a whole army, they are. Think their skins are made of iron. Foolishness."

"The hell you say," Scott roared, slamming his fist on the table.

"Graveyards are full of boys like ours," Joan snapped over the rim of her glass. "Good boys."

"And people like Santa Anna are going to keep sending them there if nobody does anything about it. Right?" he asked Elizabeth.

Elizabeth didn't agree, but didn't want to contradict him, either. "Well . . ."

"Scott! You promised."

Scott's anger faded as quickly as it had flared, and a sly, drunken look came over his face. "If you don't want me to talk, then why did you make eyes at me and call me in here?"

"For shame!" Joan exclaimed. "I never—"

"Made eyes at me, she did," Scott said to Elizabeth, and winked so his wife couldn't see. "Sashayed over as pretty as you please. And the things she whispered in my ear? Lordie and Saint James, they'd sprout hair on a bald man! Even Leakey, God bless him. Fill my tankard, woman. Fill it, I say."

"It's still full from the last pouring," Joan said dryly.

"Oh," Scott replied sheepishly. Suddenly, his cheeks puffed out, he swallowed a belch, and groaned. "Ah, but I love this woman. You know that, don't you, Joanie? That I love you?" He blinked, arched his eyebrows, and looked at Elizabeth. "If you tell this to a soul, I'll deny it," he said. The words were no sooner out than his head dropped forward and he slumped over onto the table, sound asleep.

The room was quiet while Joan moved Scott's drink out of the way and arranged his head more comfortably on his hands. "Four for him and and four for me," she said with a triumphant grin. "Even Stephen. After all these years."

Scott began to snore.

"You mean you? . . ."

Joan nodded. "Every few years. Last time it was with bergen—bourbon, that is. I beat him that time, too." She raised her glass in Elizabeth's direction. "Here's to February, my dear."

"To February," Elizabeth toasted, stifling a laugh and then drinking.

"And something else, Elizabeth." Joan looked entirely serious, now. She pushed her hair back from her face, sat with her elbows on the table, her hands around her glass. "I'm an old woman with too much cider sloshing around in me for my own good. It gives me a loose tongue, so you'll have to forgive me if I talk about something that's none of my concern."

Elizabeth's smile faded and she could feel her shoulders tense. "I don't think,—"

"It's plain to see that things haven't been right between you and True since you came back from Mexico." Elizabeth started to protest, but Joan ignored her and plunged on. "Let me say only this. Love isn't enough. No matter how sweet and airy things are at first, you find out that love isn't enough. Like with me and Scott, and the business of the boys and this stupid war. If all we had was love, we'd've gone our own ways a long time ago. But there's such things as understanding and patience—to help you over the rough spots, so to speak. It's like a three-legged stool. Without patience and understanding, love can't hold you up. It takes all three. . . ."

Joan sighed, put her hand over Elizabeth's. "Well now, here I am in my cups and running all over your feelings like I had the right to." She touched Elizabeth's chin, turned her head so they were looking into each other's eyes. "I'm sorry, Elizabeth, but it's the truth." A gentle smile warmed her face. "And sometimes the truth is worth a hurt feeling or two."

"I—"

"No," Joan said, shaking her head. She stood, helped Elizabeth to her feet, and kept a firm grip on her wrists. "You don't have to say anything. Just give me a little hug so I'll know I'm forgiven for speaking out of turn, and then, off with you. I want to revel in my glory, because sure as the sun rises, this man of mine will deny everything in the morning. A Scotsman hates to be bested by his wife even if it is good for him every once in a while."

Elizabeth's throat felt uncommonly warm. There was something wrong with her eyes, too, and she was forced to blink away the tears. Suddenly, she was holding onto Joan and crying as she had cried in her mother's arms when she was a little girl.

"There, there," Joan whispered, remembering the difficult years that she, Scott, and everyone else she knew had gone through. "There, there. You'll be fine. He'll be fine. You'll work it out some way."

"The world needs a few more like you," Elizabeth whispered in Joan's ear, and giving her a peck on the cheek, ran from the *cantina*.

The lobby was as empty as before. Elizabeth's shoes were the only sound on the stairway. The upstairs hall lanterns had not been lit, but she knew the way and found their door by touch. Inside the room, the wan glow of a half-moon gave enough light to see by. True was there where she had left him, in bed.

Maybe tonight. Maybe at last after nine months. Nine long months.

The fire had died down to coals. Elizabeth undressed quickly and, forgoing her nightgown, slipped into bed next to True. "I'm cold," she said, her breath in his ear.

He didn't move, didn't answer her, but she felt him tense as she touched him. She moved closer, felt her nipples tighten when they brushed against his arm and chest. She slid her leg across his groin. Her hand stroked his chest and her lips traced a line of delicate kisses in the hollow of his neck. "True?" she whispered. "Darling?"

He tried. He squeezed his eyes so tightly shut that the lids ached. He concentrated on her hand, on the pressure of her thigh against him, on the touch of her breasts.

O'Shannon kneeling over her. Her legs spread, opening to him. O'Shannon plunging into her. Elizabeth lying there, not fighting while he took her and took her and took her.

He threw back the covers and stood, naked. Elizabeth sat up. True spun, forced her down on the bed, his mouth covering hers in a savage kiss that hurt her, then shoved himself away and began to dress.

"True? . . ."

"Leave me alone."

"True . . ."

"No one asked you to come to Mexico. I could have escaped. Would have."

"You would have died."

"No." His voice was choked, as if the words poisoned him. "Maybe. What do you think *this* is? What am I now?"

"You're my husband and I love you. Nothing else matters."

True's laugh was strained, a hoarse parody. "To be . . . like this . . . like I am . . . doesn't matter?"

"No," she said, meaning it, wondering how she would

feel if she had seen him in bed with another woman. "It won't last forever. We are safe, True. Free."

"I am *not* free, goddamn it! I never will be. He's here in this room, taunting me, taking his revenge."

"He is not in this room," Elizabeth said. "If he is, it's because you invited him in."

"Bullshit!" The poison spilling from him, uncontrollably spilling. "You're the one who gave him the revenge he wanted. You, goddamn it! You!"

"Me?" Her face was white with fury. "How dare you? You act as if I liked what was happening. As if—"

"You weren't fighting him, were you?"

"What!"

"Fighting, goddamn it. Biting, scratching, kicking, hitting. Fighting! You were just lying there! Just . . . goddamn . . . lying there!"

"Stop it!" Elizabeth shrieked. "Just stop it!" Wild, she found herself on her knees, pounding the mattress with clenched fists. "Just stop it!"

"It's a little late for stopping, isn't it? You should've thought of that—"

"No!" She was too stunned, too shocked to cry. She could barely breathe. "You think . . . you think . . . My God, True, how could you think I wanted . . . I let . . ." And at last tears scalded her eyes and face as great sobs wracked her body. "It was your life, True. Your *life!* My body for your life. It was all I had to give!"

True hadn't moved. He stood on one foot, the other foot halfway into his boot. How long he stood that way he didn't know, but at last he shuddered as if awakening. "You should've stayed in Texas," he finally said, his voice emptied of emotion. "Where you belonged."

Elizabeth lay back with her head on the pillow and stared at the ceiling. "You should never have left Texas in the first place," she countered, as bitter as she was sad. "Your place was with me, True. I should have been more important to you than everybody else in all Texas."

True jammed his feet into his boots. Elizabeth drew up her knees, wrapped her arms around them and lowered her face into the blanketed peak. "Oh, True," she sighed wearily. "Listen to us. Just listen to us. I don't think I can stand this. I love you, True. I need you. We need each other." Tears streaming down her face, she pleaded with him. "He took one hour of my life, True. One hour I couldn't stop him from taking and that he didn't deserve. Don't let him take the rest of our life. Don't let this destroy us, True. Hold on to me, please?''

Creak of leather belt, click of bootheel on wooden flooring. True walked to the window and leaned on the sill. The moonlight, hardened by the frost on the glass, made his face look bone white. ''Questions . . . are all I have left, Elizabeth. Questions.'' He turned from the window, paused by the coatrack, and headed for the door. ''No answers. None at all.''

''Where are you going?'' she asked faintly.

''Out.'' The door creaked open. ''Out to look. For answers.''

''Don't leave me, True. Please?''

''I have to look. I have to.''

''Plea—''

The door closed and she was alone in the darkness. She lay back on the bed and imagined a three-legged stool. Its legs were splintered and spiders had cast webs around and through the ruined wood. ''Love, patience, understanding,'' she whispered to herself. And closed her eyes to shut out the image.

True left by the rear exit and, burrowing into his coat, walked quickly to the stable. Firetail's distinctive whinny directed him to the rear stall. The stallion nuzzled his hand, butted him in the chest with his head. True scratched behind Firetail's ears in return, then moved to saddle him.

''True?''

Lantern light spilled over him as he turned around to see Andrew entering from a side tack room. ''Thought you'd be at the party,'' True said.

''Was and will be,'' Andrew said with a grin. ''Found out that Kemper received a load of gunpowder the other day and hasn't moved it to Agradecido yet. He was going to blow stumps with it, but Travis and Bowie figure we can put it to better use in rifles.'' He laughed shortly. ''That's one thing they agree on, at least.''

''What's Kemper think about it?'' True asked.

Andrew pulled one of the draught horses out of a stall and began hooking it up to a wagon. ''Doesn't know, yet.

''He will,'' True drawled. He tightened the cinch, dropped the stirrup, and led Firetail out of his stall. ''So will Helen.''

''No problem at all,'' Andrew explained. ''We're giving

him a receipt. Here. Hold this idiot animal. 'Sides, they're patriots, aren't they?''

"Sure. But storekeepers first. Helen will tell you that—and a few other things the minute she learns what you're up to.''

"Which I'll let Travis take care of, thank you." Andrew disappeared in the darkness, then came back with the other draught horse. "Won't matter, anyway. It'll all be in the Alamo by the time they find out, and it'll be too late to do anything.''

True held the second horse while Andrew harnessed him. "I still think the Alamo's a bad idea. Hell, you can walk into it through two of the damn walls, such as they are. You better hope Santa Anna can't find it—if he comes this way.''

"Yeah, that is a problem," Andrew admitted. "Actually, I'd rather be with Sam Houston. He'll probably be the one who sees all the action. Back up, damn your hide! C'mon. Back, back! You ever see such a dadblamed obstreperous animal?''

"Sure have," True said, mounting Firetail. "I just helped one harness a team, and there's a whole bunch more all ready to trail along behind your friend, Travis. Not to speak of Houston and Bowie. See you. Have fun with your gunpowder.''

Andrew stepped out from between the horses. "It's not too late to join us, True. You won't be sorry, once we're a Republic.''

"That's just what you don't understand," True said, looking down at Andrew. "I've already given everything I care to for the cause." He nudged Firetail's flanks with his heels. "And I'm already sorry.''

"Where you going?''

"For a ride.''

"In this cold? Hardly makes sense.''

"Neither do a lot of other things, little brother. If you'll get the door for me?''

The wind was fiercer, if anything. Wetter, too, True decided as he cut down an alley and headed south. The stallion's breath was a ghostly wisp that lasted but a second. When he came out from between the buildings, the wind grabbed at him. True rose in the saddle and pushed his coat tails underneath him, pulled up his collar, and settled in for the ride.

Ten minutes later, he was quit of town. Overhead, translucent clouds skimmed the scimitar curve of the moon. Andrew had told him that the Coushattas called the wind the breath of the Great Spirit, and as that breath altered the cloud pictures in the sky, so too did it change the fortunes of men. The path they were taking had not changed, though. The trail steepened, turned left to follow the looping arc south of the city. Higher up, and broadside to the wind, True felt the temperature drop even lower.

Boulders loomed ahead but horse and rider did not slow. They had come this way before, a little over a year earlier. The path was etched clearly in their minds, as was the twisting, flat place ahead, where Firetail shied back from the edge of the cliff. True dismounted, led the stallion into a cul de sac out of the wind, and walked to the edge. Far below and in the distance, San Antonio was a collection of twinkling, amber jewels set in a shadowed valley.

Lean forward. Lean. Perhaps the answer lies below.

There Ramez swerved the white stallion, there a little farther along the two animals collided, and there . . .

Lean forward. Is that dark spot on the boulder blood?

So easy to end the torment. No one knows how easy. Just one more step. An end to revenge.

The wind seemed to suck him into its arms. The shadows below danced like demons at play among the jutting rocks.

Cannot undo what has been done. The past is written. How simple to compose a future free of trouble, to think no more. Dead anyway, so what is the loss?

His body wavered, wavered like a reed caught in a spring flood.

Just one more step.

The ghostly glow of moonshine on rocks made them look like bones, like bars.

Iron bars, Pain. Hands stretching through bars, cheekbones slamming into metal.

The rocks were crumbly underfoot. One slipped over the edge. He heard it tumble and start a small slide.

O'shannon watching from the rocks, waiting for the final act. Is that him? No, a cactus. There? No, a boulder. Or shadow play or dust stirred from a crevice by the wind.

Her body for his life. Oh, but Christ, he hurt!

"Aaaaaahhhhh!"

A cry in the hills, snatched away by the north wind, spread over the land like a distillation of pain. A man kneeling on the edge of a precipice, a broken man in a broken land.

But a man, nonetheless, and like a man, struggling to rise.
There were no answers, at least no easy or quick ones.

True stumbled toward Firetail, climbed the boulders behind
him and stood at the top of the heights to look toward the
south. The wind pressed against his back now, but he no
longer felt the cold. Let Santa Anna come, he thought. And
let the others fight for Texas, if that's what they wanted. He'd
be waiting for the man who came with Santa Anna, for
Luther O'Shannon.

And he would remember.

Chapter XXXIII

"Enough," Elizabeth said, dropping the tamping tool and wiping the sweat from her forehead.

True looked at the sun, decided it was close enough to noon to call it a morning. He counted silently. Since sunup they had set the four corner posts and the two gates posts for the garden fence, plus eight of the regular posts. "Only eighteen to go," he said. "You ready for some lunch?"

He had worked without a shirt for the past two hours. Already he was tanning, and the sweat ran down his face and chest, over the smooth, corded muscles. Elizabeth felt hollow, almost sick to her stomach with desire. "There's stew and biscuits left over from last night," she said, making herself think of more practical matters. "You can build up the fire and put them on if you want. I'm going down to the river first."

They'd worked hard, True digging and Elizabeth setting the posts and tamping the earth around them. There had been neither time nor inclination for talk—which wasn't at all out of the ordinary, Elizabeth thought sourly as she headed for the house to get a change of clothes. Some days they barely spoke at all, and then only when necessary. It wasn't a situation that pleased her, but she simply found little to say in the face of True's silence.

More and more she held to Joan's image of the three-legged stool. Love, patience, and understanding, she kept telling herself. The love part was easy enough—God knew she loved True—but the patience and understanding aspects of the prescription were difficult to remember, much less follow.

A more beautiful day couldn't have been imagined. An early spring sandwiched between cold snaps had turned the meadow green and coaxed a light green haze from the willows by the river. A hint of a south breeze eased the heat of the sun. Elizabeth stripped under the watchful eye of a redtail hawk that had taken up residence in the top of a dead cottonwood on the far bank, and plunged into what they'd come to call the bathing pool. The water was icy cold, and a second later she stumbled, shivering, into the shallows to give herself a quick scrub before getting out.

If True had only come with her, she thought, moving the bench they kept by the river into a patch of sunlight. What a perfect way to spend the noon, lying together in the sweet grass in the warm sun. . . . How long had it been? The night before he left for San Antonio to collect signatures for the petitions he would carry to Mexico. Nine months? Ten? Lord, how she ached for him, wanted him with her and in her. And how she plagued herself, she scolded silently, toweling her hair dry. It would happen when it happened, when he was ready, when he had exorcised the devils that haunted him. She stood and bent forward at the waist, let her hair fall over her head so she could brush it out. Only one thing to do, she thought, even then fantasizing him emerging from the water, wet and aroused, coming to her and not even waiting for her to lie down. . . .

"I have to stop this!" she said aloud, straightening and slapping the back of the brush against her thigh until she could no longer stand the stinging. "It's stupid and silly . . . depraved!" It wasn't though, she knew. Any normal, healthy woman would feel the same way. What, after all, was more normal than wanting your husband to make love to you? If she could just talk to True, make him understand how she felt, he might . . . But she had, in a hundred ways. A look, a touch, a tender word.

Quickly, not able to bear the soft touch of the air on her skin any longer, she pulled on her clothes. The sun seemed a little duller, the green of the grass less vibrant as she walked back to the cabin. She could see True driving the wagon back from the spring, and went inside without waiting for him or saying anything. The stove was hot, the coffee pot and stewpot both steaming. Working mechanically, she set out plates, forks, and cups, took the biscuits out of the warming oven and put them on the table. "Damn harness. The cruppers broke. I'll fix 'em before I leave. Ought to be enough water to last until we get back, though,'' True said, coming in the front door and going directly to the table.

"Back?'' Elizabeth asked. "Oh. Yes.'' She had forgotten that Hogjaw was due to come by that afternoon and that he and True were leaving that night to go hunting. She was about to ask him not to go when she noticed him studying her with an intensity she hadn't seen recently. "What is it?'' she asked, a shade defensively.

"You. What you're wearing. Exactly the same as the first day we met.'' He smiled without realizing it. "Only then you had a pistol pointed at me.''

Elizabeth almost answered sarcastically, then realized this show of humor was the healthiest sign she had seen in him in months. "Lucky for the likes of you, Mr. Paxton, that your name wasn't Holton . . . whatever it was.''

"Bagget,'' True remembered. "Luckier for him I was there.'' He handed her his plate, watched silently while she poured a dipperful of stew over his biscuits. "Life was simpler then, I think.''

"Not for me,'' Elizabeth said. She fixed her own plate, sat across from him. "Nor for you, either, really.''

"At least I was sure of myself. Knew where I was going, what I wanted, more or less what I was going to do.''

"And now?'' Elizabeth asked.

True's eyes dropped and he concentrated on his stew. The veins in his neck stood out. The muscles in his forearms bulged and his hands balled into fists. At last, with great effort, he forced himself to relax, and picked up his fork. "And now I'm going to eat. And then split some kindling. You're about out. I'll make sure you have enough for three or four days. We should be back by then. I still wish you'd stay with Lottie.''

"That's no answer,'' Elizabeth replied.

The cabin seemed still and close. True cut a chunk of gristle out of his stew, took another mouthful.

"What you wanted to do was be with me,'' Elizabeth finally said. She felt faint, but couldn't stop, had to go on and ask. "Has that changed?''

He couldn't look her in the eye. The stew had lost its taste. *Has it? Has it changed? Have I stopped wanting her?*

"I can't think anymore, Elizabeth. I'm tired of trying.'' He put down his fork, shoved his plate away from him. "Let's just let the minutes come and go. Maybe time will bring me answers.''

"And I'm supposed to sit here and wait?'' Elizabeth demanded more shrilly than she intended. "Is that it?''

"You do what you have to do. That's all anyone can expect of another.'' He pushed away from the table and stood. "What's certain is that there's kindling to be split and harness to mend.''

"And our lives? Who will mend our lives, True?''

True paused in the doorway. Who would mend their lives? Not him, evidently. God knew he'd tried, but every time he thought he had it licked, he saw O'Shannon having his way with Elizabeth and the sickness returned. He'd told himself a thousand times it wasn't her fault, blamed himself for making life hell for her. Nothing worked, though. He felt himself less the man for having to admit it, but he could find no way out: his only hope was to confront O'Shannon. And the only way he was going to see O'Shannon was if Travis and three quarters of the rest of the people in Texas got their wish. "With a little bit of luck,'' he finally answered with a short, bitter laugh, "maybe Santa Anna.''

Elizabeth watched him go, listened to his boots hard on the porch, then soft in the dirt. Santa Anna, she thought, no less bitterly than True. She stared into her coffee, found herself wishing she had some milk to put in it. Here she was, her face sun and wind burned, her hands calloused, her finger-nails broken, her hair tangled, and her whole body aching from hard work. All of which she would have endured gladly if he were returning her love. He wasn't, though. He was making bad jokes. And all Elizabeth wanted to do was rage.

She ate a biscuit instead.

New harness was out of the question, given the money spent to effect True's release from Mexico. The old had been mended one more time and hung ready for use again. True headed for the woodpile. He didn't mind splitting cordwood, but kindling was a chore he disliked. Disgruntled, he pulled a half dozen larger, dry oak logs from the pile and tossed them next to the chopping block. He had left the ax sunk deep in the block so the edge wouldn't rust, and he had to jerk it three or four times to free it before he set to work. With one hand holding the log, the other wielding the ax, he split piece after thin piece until they piled up around his feet and he had to kick them aside.

Long ago on the Mississippi. In Natchez Under the Hill. Lucky for you your name wasn't Holton whatever it was.

God, but she was pretty. Angry, but pretty. And later, the next morning, by the campfire . . .

"This is Elizabeth Michaelson."

Look at the way her hair flashes. Her eyes, open, frank, full of fire and ice. This is the girl I want. This is the woman I will marry.

"We've met. . . ."

The drumming of hooves intruded on his thoughts. *Hogjaw? From that way? Should be coming from . . .*

He looked up in time to save his life. A Mexican soldier wielding a long, iron-tipped lance, was thundering down on him. Dust exploded from the hooves of the charging horse. The soldier's mouth was a crescent of teeth, lips curled back in a roar of triumph. True yelled and threw himself to one side. The tip of the lance missed him by a fraction of an inch, dug a furrow in the soft earth as the horseman rode past.

"Hey!" True leaped to his feet and swung around as a second lancer, eyes wide with battle lust, bore in for the kill. On reflex, True grabbed and swung the ax. The heavy blade drove the wooden lance upward before biting into the soldier's side. The lancer shrieked and toppled from his horse, jerking the ax from True's grasp. True whirled to see the first rider charging him again. Weaponless, he dove over the pile of kindling and out of lance range. Just as he hit the ground, he heard the crack of a rifle. The soldier dropped his lance as he was blown out of the saddle and rolled to a grotesque stop, lying dead and bleeding on the earth.

True grabbed a billet and came to his feet. Elizabeth was standing in the house, framed by the window. Black smoke curled from the rifle she held. "Watch the door!" he yelled at her, hearing the commotion of a third horseman at the front of the house. Moving fast, he snatched up the second rider's lance and rounded the cabin in time to see Hogjaw reining in Mama.

"What the hell's going on?"

"Soldiers! Around there!" True yelled, pointing. "Maybe more. Keep an eye out. Elizabeth!" he yelled, heading for the door. "It's me coming in. Don't shoot!"

He found her still staring out the window at the man she

had killed. "Oh, my God," she was saying, over and over. "Oh, my God. Oh, my God. . . ."

"No time for that," True said, taking the rifle from her and running to the fireplace to reload immediately.

"Oh, my God. . . ."

There were no other soldiers in sight. Hogjaw left the one Elizabeth had shot and moved toward the other soldier, who was still alive. True grabbed Elizabeth, spun her away from the window. He ripped aside the curtain that separated their bedroom from the rest of the cabin and shoved her toward the chifforobe. "Get together what you can. Some warm clothes, a little food. Don't take long. I'll saddle Firetail and the bay mare. Hurry."

"I killed him," Elizabeth said, dazed. Suddenly, she doubled over and began to vomit.

True held her while the spasms tore at her and then led her outside to the porch. "Hogjaw?"

"Right here," the mountain man said, coming around the corner.

"Well?"

"They're both dead. One said something about a whole army before he passed on. We better get movin'."

The second lancer's horse ambled around the side of the house, and stopped to look at them. Elizabeth was sitting on the steps. " 'Lizabeth," Hogjaw said, dropping to one knee in front of her. "Come on. We got to get outa here."

"I killed him," Elizabeth whispered, staring at her hands.

"Yes, ma'am. A good shot, too."

"I never . . . have . . ."

"I know. It ain't easy the first time. Ain't something a person ought to have to do or see."

"Oh, my God!"

"Call on Him all you like, 'Lizabeth. Just remember, though, He could have made you miss if'n He'd wanted you to." He took her by the hand, helped her to her feet. "C'mon, now. Let's get ready. There's more where them first two came from."

True rode out of the barn on Firetail, detoured past the lancer he had wounded. A fresh stain of blood from his throat wetted the ground. Hogjaw had been swift and merciless. Whatever the lancer had said about more soldiers coming had been the last words he had spoken. Elizabeth and Hogjaw were just emerging from the house as he came around the corner.

"Some warm clothes and enough food to last a few days," Hogjaw said, throwing a pair of saddle bags over Firetail and another over Elizabeth's bay.

"Good," True said. "Mount up and let's ride, then. We have to warn the others."

Hogjaw helped Elizabeth onto her horse and caught up Mama. "Best get a better idea of what we're gonna warn 'em against, first," he said, nodding toward the ridge on the far side of the river. "We'll take a look from up there. Keep to the trees and it won't take us that much longer." He booted his mule in the ribs and started off. "Let's go, Mama."

Elizabeth didn't move. True sidled Firetail up to her, touched her on the arm. "Elizabeth?" he asked.

"I'm . . . I'm on my way," she said grimly, and rode after Hogjaw.

True took up the rear, turning in his saddle for one last look. The first flies were already gathering around the dead men. The cabin, only a few minutes ago a symbol of safety, a haven, looked small and vulnerable. Suddenly, he wasn't at all sure he wanted to leave it. Certainly not for Santa Anna, and maybe not even for the Irishman who was sure to ride at his side.

The lancers had come from almost due west. Hogjaw, Elizabeth, and True rode south across the meadow, forded the river, crossed the south quarter section of bottom land, and started the climb up the cedar-choked slope. Once out of the open, not wishing to overtax their mounts, they slowed the pace to little more than a walk. Within twenty minutes, they reached the rounded summit of the ridge, where they dismounted and tied their horses before crawling through the final few yards of cover.

Below, the land rolled away to the south, and across it, like a giant, poisonous slug, danger marched through the bright spring sun. "What day is it?" Hogjaw asked, his voice hushed, almost reverent.

"The twenty-first of February. Why?" True asked, his eyes riveted to the mirrorlike flashes of sunshine on metal.

"I got a feeling folks are gonna remember it," the mountain man replied. "Well, I seen enough. Best get out of here."

They crawled backward until they were sure they couldn't be seen, then rose and ran for the horses. "Down the hill the same way we came," True said, helping Elizabeth up, "then due east until we come to Cutter Creek. That'll put us a mile and a half south of Joseph's place."

"I'll go first," Hogjaw said, already moving. "There's gonna be more o' them scouts out. Keep your eyes peeled."

The trail dropped rapidly. When it turned left, into the sun, Elizabeth shaded her eyes and remembered she'd forgotten her bonnet. Stupid, she thought to herself, thinking of a bonnet when . . . The fear struck, crept up her spine, turned her heart cold. She concentrated on the path and her riding. If she had an accident now . . . Her ears were ringing, her mouth tasted like copper. If there were only some way she could take back what she had seen. Soldiers, cannon, cavalry. A low dust cloud rising above the horizon.

They were off the ridge, riding abreast at an easy gallop across the bottom land. "I ain't seen so many men in one place since eighteen-twelve," Hogjaw called to True. "That whippersnapper Travis reckoned Santy Anna wouldn't be able to gather much more than a couple thousand men. Hell, we seen that many ourselves, 'less I miss my guess, and that don't count neither their advance or what's making that dust cloud to its rear."

"How many doesn't matter," True answered. "What's important is, Travis has his war." He pointed down the trail. "We turn left just past that grove of pecans. Kind of narrow and boggy there. I'll go first."

They headed north and within fifteen minutes had intersected the trail on the top of the low ridge that ran below Joseph's. True reined in to give the horses and Mama a chance to blow. "The Alamo has to be warned," he said. "As big a mess as they had there a couple of weeks ago, they'll need every minute they can get. There's nothing between them and that army except empty land."

"I'll do that," Hogjaw said. "You an' 'Lizabeth warn the others, then get yourselves on into San Antone. Hole up in the Alamo with the rest of us."

True shook his head. "No. That's where they're heading. The Alamo's the worst place we could pick. You two gather up everyone around here. I'll holler at the Kempers when I ride past their place, so they'll be ready when you get there. You can cut cross country due east, camp out overnight, and get to Sutherland's Ford sometime tomorrow. Meanwhile, I'll tell Travis and Bowie what they're in for, and then ride out in the morning and meet you at Sutherland's.''

"The hell you say," Hogjaw argued. "I'm goin' to San Antone. You stay with 'Lizabeth, where you oughta be.''

"That isn't the point," True said bluntly. "Mama's fine, but she can't run as fast as Firetail can. Besides, you know a hell of a lot more about keeping alive than I do. Stay with her, Hogjaw. Will you do that for me?''

"Well . . .''

True swung Firetail around, met Elizabeth's worried look. "Do what he says, Elizabeth. Listen to him." He took the saddlebags off Firetail and slung them across her bay, then steadied her as she leaned across the empty space between them. Suddenly, his arm was around her, holding her in an awkward embrace. "Don't worry," he whispered hoarsely. "You'll be fine and so will I. We'll see each other at Sutherland's tomorrow." There wasn't time for more. He glanced at Hogjaw over her shoulder and silently mouthed, "Take care of her." A second later, he had let her go and was racing away from them toward San Antonio.

"I reckon we'd better . . .'' The sentence faded and Hogjaw slumped in his saddle. "Well, hell and damn!''

Elizabeth followed his line of sight, then sat motionless, staring at the coiling smudge of smoke that must mark her and True's cabin and outbuildings. Numbly, she pictured all the possessions she held dear consumed in the flames. A letter from her grandfather, the family Bible, the furniture she and True had built, the daily menial implements of life valued as treasures to no one but herself. Most precious of all, their leaves just budding green, two rosebushes, yellow roses, by now surely curling into embers in the fury of the engulfing flames.

Chapter XXXIV

"Are we ever coming back?" Ruthie Campbell asked, watching her parents disappear inside the cabin. Her eyes were wide and, like her sister Dianne's, showed fear.

"Of course we are, silly," Dianne replied archly. She stepped over a sack of potatoes and threw her winter coat into the back of the wagon. "Aren't we, 'Lizabeth?"

"Of course," Elizabeth assured her, keeping a nervous watch on the twin wagon ruts that marked the road leading away from the farm to the south.

In the buckboard sitting next to the Campbells' wagon, little Bethann Elaine Paxton squalled her displeasure with a world that had upset her pleasant routine of eating and sleeping. Lottie rearranged the baby's wrappings and, shielding herself from view, opened her blouse to nurse the indignant infant.

Joseph and Scott emerged from the house carrying a massive chest of drawers between them. At the same time, Hogjaw came riding up the road from where he'd been keeping watch from a small knoll. "Leave it!" he shouted to the two men. "There ain't time!"

"Damn it, Hogjaw," Scott exclaimed, "this has been in my family for years. Came over from England."

"I don't give a hoot in hell if it came from the king hisself. Joseph, the first smoke's comin' up from your place. You stay here and dinky dally with this damn chunk of wood and you'll see that babe of your spitted on a lance."

Joseph blanched, looked apologetically at Scott, and dropped his end of the load. "Sorry, Scott. Can't take the chance. My buckboard's empty too except for essentials." He turned and trotted to his wagon. "If you're smart, you'll do the same."

"Joseph's place fired already?" Scott asked, paling. Suddenly, as if it had just then dawned on him how serious the situation was, Scott dropped the other end of the trunk. "Joan!" he yelled, scooping up Dianne and putting her in the back of the wagon. "Out! Fast! Mackenzie! Let's move! What's taking so long?"

Mackenzie Campbell trotted his gelding around the corner of the house. "Right here, Pa." He rode up to the wagon, carefully set a heavy bag into the rear. "I split the powder and shot. Half for you and half for me." The gelding stopped again, this time at Scott's side. "I guess we'll find each other later when this is over with."

"Later, hell, lad," Hogjaw said, booting Mama toward Mackenzie. "Where you bound?"

"Dennis is in San Antone with Travis and the rest. I ain't about to miss the fun."

"It won't be fun, lad. And you're needed with your folks."

"No disrespect, Mr. Leakey, but I don't think so. I aim to fight." Mackenzie turned his back on Hogjaw and leaned down to shake his father's hand. "Don't worry, Pa. I'll look after Dennis. Coupla weeks when this is . . . Hey!"

Hogjaw had reached out, grabbed a fistful of shirt, and was pulling Mackenzie out of his saddle. The young man struggled, but it was too late. Before he was even fully aware of what had happened, Hogjaw had tapped him gently on the skull with the hilt of a knife.

"Leakey! . . ." Scott shouted.

"Relax, Scott. I've got an angel's touch." He turned Mama toward the Campbells' wagon and unceremoniously dumped Mackenzie in the back with Dianne and Ruthie. "You may thank me later. There's a time to die and a time to sleep, and a man needs to know the difference 'tween the two." The deep folds in his face settled into a grim mask. "Now get your woman out of here, man. I ain't gonna wait any longer."

He didn't have to ask twice. Laden with an armload of clothes, Joan emerged from the cabin. "This is most of it," she said, stopping when she saw the chest in the middle of the yard. "Whatever? . . ."

"Into the wagon, woman," Hogjaw said shortly.

Scott grabbed the clothes from her and carried them to the wagon.

"It'll slow us down, Joan," Elizabeth said. "We have to hurry. Please?"

"But it means so much to me!"

"As much as Ruthie and Dianne?" Elizabeth jerked her head toward the south. "Our house is on fire already. So is Lottie's."

"Let's go!" Hogjaw roared. He caught the reins of Mackenzie's horse and, riding close to Elizabeth, handed them to her. "Git, girl. Joseph, you too. Goddamn it, Scott, pick her up an' throw her in if you have to!"

His voice was like a slap that, along with the sight of Joseph and Lottie's buckboard leaving, brought Joan to her senses. She suddenly ran for the wagon, let Scott help her onto the seat. "Move back inside now, girls," she said, in turn giving Scott a hand up. "Find a safe place. We'll be driving fast."

"Mama, Mack looks so funny," Ruthie said.

Joan turned, gasped when she saw her unconscious son. "Oh, my God! Mackenzie!"

"Giiiaaa, horses!" Scott shouted, releasing the brake and slapping the reins over the team's back. "Move move move!"

The team bolted forward. Joan grabbed the seat to keep from falling into the back of the wagon. "What happened?" she shouted over the racket.

"An angel touched him," her husband said. "C'mon, horses. C'mon!"

"What?" Joan shrieked, incredulous.

"Hogjaw's way of telling him he ought to come with us. If I was you, I'd get back there and put something under his head so it won't bounce."

Joan disappeared in a tangle of shirts and legs. Scott glanced over his shoulder. Behind him, the sky was ominously black with smoke. "Move, horses, move!" he shouted again, wielding the whip. The last thing he wanted Joan and the girls to see was their house burning.

Mila Kania made one final, quick tour of the cabin she and the Reverend had called home. Hastily built shortly after the move to Agradecido, it was virtually identical to the others. Only the Campbells had had a larger cabin, and that because of the four children. There had been talk of putting up the church at the same time, but Buckland had refused any special favors or treatment. It was better, he had said, that everyone should have a roof over their heads first. He would be glad to accept their labor later on when there was time to spare. Fifty feet from the modest cabin, the church had, in fact, been started. Osage orange, or beau d'art, logs held the floor off the ground. Hand-hewn and pegged framing, gray from exposure to the weather, rose on all four sides. Six benches served as temporary pews. Buckland himself, with hands little suited for carpentry, had built the pulpit from scrap wood. Mila thought it was beautiful.

The skeleton of faith, she thought now, pausing at the window and imagining it complete, its white spire reaching for heaven. Only a few more months, another year perhaps . . . Her eyes filling with tears, she snatched the quilt from the bed and hurried out the door.

"Scott will ride one of your horses and you can sit with Joan," Elizabeth said. "Your food and clothes are already in the wagon."

"In other words, hurry up," Mila said, wishing with all her heart Buckland hadn't chosen this day to venture to San Antonio.

"Yes. In other words."

"May I say one thing, Elizabeth? You'll have to promise never to tell."

"Feel free. My lips are sealed," Elizabeth replied.

Mila glanced around guiltily, then reached up to whisper in Elizabeth's ear. "Goddamn this Santa Anna to Hell!"

"Mila!"

"There. I feel better." She stepped off the porch and headed for the waiting wagon. "Remember. You promised."

The half-completed shell of the church made a lovely fire too.

Nels and Eustacia Matlan weren't home. The Thatche cabin lay silent and empty. The fugitives did not tarry at either place.

"I'll tell you the same as I told True," Jack Kemper said. I'm not going." Hands on hips, his narrow jaw thrust out, he was a figure of intransigent determination as he stood on the front steps of his trading post.

"We're not going," Helen corrected from beside him. "We haven't done anything, and we intend to conduct business as usual. And if Santa Anna comes, so much the better. At least there'll be soldiers about to protect us from thieves," she added, referring to the gunpowder taken from them earlier that month.

"That was conscription," Hogjaw pointed out. "not thievery. Now get to your horses."

"You leave us alone. All of you!" Helen screeched.

Mama flapped her ears and backed a step. Hogjaw quieted her. "Damned mule has more sense than you do. You got a shovel, Miz Kemper?"

"What?"

"I surely hope so. 'Cause if you stay, you'll be buryin' your man here."

Jack looked at Helen. "Maybe—"

"We are *not* leaving, and that is that." Helen's mouth was pinched tight with anger. "Jack," she said, stalking up the steps and into the store, "your dinner will be ready in fifteen minutes."

"You see how it is," Jack said with a helpless shrug.

"Come with us, Mr. Kemper," Elizabeth pleaded, walking her mare forward. "Make her come."

"It's a fool's risk, Jack," Joseph said.

"I . . . I don't think so. I—we've talked it over and decided we'd be better off trying to live with the powers that be than getting involved in some vain opposition."

"Good Lord, man," Hogjaw exploded. "These folks ain't opposin'. They're runnin'. It's two different things."

"Maybe so," Jack said stubbornly in spite of whatever misgivings he had. He gestured to the trading post which he had built onto the front of his cabin. "But this is all we have in the world."

"That an' your lives," Hogjaw pointed out. "They tried to kill True without even askin' what he thought or whose side he was on. They'll do the same to you."

Jack shook his head. "I don't think so." He tried to smile, but failed. "You better go if you're going. I know we've never been good friends with the rest of you. It's just . . . our way, I guess and . . . well . . . I love my wife. My place is with her."

"Have it your own way, then," Hogjaw snorted. "Let's go, folks." He pulled Mama's head around and rode to join the wagons outside the gate. "No sense wastin' more time here, 'Lizabeth."

Elizabeth understood and, leaning forward, touched the

storekeeper on the shoulder. "Good luck," she whispered, and was gone in a cloud of dust.

Jack Kemper watched them go, watched the wagons move up the road, watched Hogjaw's mule ride into and out of the dust they raised. After a few minutes, they vanished behind a rise in the land, and all that was left was the dust. Then it too settled, and he was alone. The afternoon was still. The sun, as he faced it in the west, was warm on his skin. A slight breeze from the south worried the fruit trees he'd set out the spring before. In another year they'd have fruit of their own. Maybe even enough to make peach jam, he thought, or apple butter. Apple butter was best, cold and thickly spread on fresh bread.

Senseless, running like that. How far did you have to run? All the way to Louisiana? Jack walked to the well, lowered the bucket to the icy surface twenty feet down, retrieved it and set it on the stand. Never run away from sweet, cold water, someone had told him. Don't abandon a good well unless you know without a doubt where there's a better one for the having. He took a dipperful and savored each swallow.

"Jack!" Helen called from the doorway.

He hung the dipper on the hook by the crank and started toward the trading post. "Coming . . ." he said, and stopped short.

Helen had seen them through the window. A dozen Mexican lancers were riding in from the south. Sunlight glinted off their brass trappings. Their green and white uniforms looked almost festive in the distance. "Stay inside!" he shouted and walked toward the front of the trading post to wait in the open.

Their hoofbeats sounded like steady, rolling thunder. Their formation was precise, even rigid, three ranks of men riding four abreast, lances pointing toward the sky. *"Buenos dias!"* Jack shouted, holding out his hands to show he was unarmed and meant no harm.

Onward came the lancers.

"Jack?" Helen called again, concern at last coloring her voice.

"Be quiet," he yelled back, a little frightened now, himself, and edging toward the front porch. *"Buenos dias,"* he shouted again as they thundered into the yard without slowing their pace.

The lances dipped, pointed straight ahead. Jack spun, took two running steps. Suddenly, there was incredible pain as an iron point skewered him between the shoulder blades and popped, moist and horribly red, from his chest. Jack was lifted off his feet for a few seconds, to wriggle and die a few yards from his front porch.

The lancer yanked and twisted his weapon free of the *norteamericano's* corpse while his companions spread out to fire the buildings. Their *generalíssimo's* orders were explicit: drive the *norteamericano* settlers out, kill those who tried to stay, lay waste to their homes, and rendezvous in San Antonio.

The door to the trading post opened and Helen Kemper stepped outside. She appeared not to notice the soldiers. The lancers made way for her as she gingerly approached the rag doll body of her husband, watched quietly as she pointed at him and, rocking from side to side, began to giggle. It was a chilling sound, and several of the lancers blessed themselves with the sign of the cross. They did not kill the madwoman as they had been ordered, but left the house and trading post as they had all other buildings in their path.

Burning.

Chapter XXXV

Bowie had come down with pneumonia and Travis, who had assumed the mantle of sole authority, listened avidly, even raptly. He had waited for this news and now savored every word of it. His vision had become reality. Santa Anna was on the march, was less than twenty miles from San Antonio and the defenders of the Alamo, the ragtag army that would stop the Mexicans dead in their tracks and so settle the question of independence once and for all. Travis's earlier qualms about defending San Antonio had been forgotten, and he couldn't have been more pleased. The confrontation he had long sought was at hand. His moment in history was assured.

True did not waste time in the telling. He had pushed Firetail, run him hard all the way to town. Now, with the great roan being cared for in the courtyard outside, he stood in the commanding officer's headquarters, once the rectory of the mission, and gave a clipped, concise description of the army he had seen, its location, and the direction of travel. When he finished, Travis leaned back in his chair and closed his eyes. "Well?" True asked after a moment of silence.

"I'm thinking."

"Thinking!"

"Separates the men from the beasts."

"And the quick from the dead," True snapped sarcastically. He looked past Travis at Andrew and decided his little brother appeared perfectly ridiculous trying to play soldier without a uniform, and especially as Travis's adjutant. "Hell's bells, Andrew! *You* tell him. There isn't a thing between here and there to even slow them down."

Andrew gestured helplessly. "Colonel Travis is in command."

340

Travis still hadn't opened his eyes. True talked as if the man wasn't there. "Then why the hell doesn't he give a command, for Christ's sake. Wake him up and tell him to give the order to pull out."

"You are being insubordinate, Mr. Paxton."

"Insubordinate, my ass. Stow it, Travis," True said. "I'm not in your misbegotten army."

The eyes opened. True had his attention. "You may not know it," Travis said, "but yes you are. Every man here, native born or immigrant, if he's lived here, if he came to raise a family and make a home, is a Texian, and that includes you. If you've left your sweat on this land, which you have, then you're a soldier, and deep down you know it."

"Spare me the rhetoric, Travis, and give the order to get the hell out."

"I can't do that," Travis said, and seeing True's expression, amended his words. "Very well. I *won't* do that. Feel any better?"

True studied him, and decided with a sinking feeling that Travis meant exactly what he said. Getting him to change his mind would be about as easy as convincing an old longhorn bull that he ought to give up his masculinity, but True had to try. There was too much at stake. The settlers outside the walls needed protection, for one thing. And there was no way True could ever hope to find O'Shannon if he was stuck inside, for another. "In God's name, Travis," he said, making every effort to sound like the voice of reason itself, "this is no time to dance on your pride. You don't have a hundred able-bodied men to put up against—"

"I have almost a hundred and forty men I can count on right now," Travis corrected. "And more will come the closer Santa Anna gets to us. We'll hold 'til Hell freezes over."

"Fine. A hundred and fifty say. And what else? You call this a fort? How much food? What happens when they cut off your water? How much powder and shot? Enough to withstand an army that size, whatever that size is? Enough to protect God knows how many civilians, women and children, who are going to crowd in here the minute the first lancer rides into town? Are you willing to sacrifice them so the world will never say Buck Travis ran? Believe me, the world won't care one way or the other."

Eyes blazing, Travis jumped to his feet. The chair clattered to the floor behind him. "I'm not concerned about the world, Paxton," he said, spitting out True's name as if it had burned his mouth. "Texas is what worries me at the moment. If we stop Santa Anna here—" He slammed his hand on the desk. "—he's stopped, period. He's whipped. He'll tuck his tail between his legs and run." Fighting his own anger, he strode to the window. Outside, he could see men hurrying through the courtyard, others pacing sentry duty atop the crumbling walls. His temper under control, he returned to the desk and unrolled a stained and wrinkled map. "You're too good a man to fight with," he said calmly. "I'd rather have you on my side. Now, look here." His finger stabbed the map. "I accept the possibility we don't stop him. Very well. Here is your farm and, allowing for a few hours' progress, the probable position of Santa Anna's army right now." His finger moved east and south. "Over here somewhere, Sam Houston is trying to raise and train an army. A real army. But he needs time." The finger returned to San Antonio. "And here we are in the middle, metaphorically speaking. I intend to give Sam Houston as much time as I can by keeping Santa Anna busy here. We are entrenched. He can't afford to pass us by and have us harassing his rear. He'll have to take us by storm or siege, and I intend to make it as costly for him as I can. And that, my friend," Travis said, his eyes narrow and blazing, "will be costly, indeed."

True stared at the map, looked up to Travis and realized there was no sense in arguing further. "Well," he sighed, "it sounds like you have it pretty well thought out." He turned his back on Travis, stalked across the room, and picked up his rifle. "Good luck, I guess."

"You're leaving?" Travis asked.

"I told my wife and Hogjaw to tell the others I'd meet them tomorrow at Sutherland's Ford. You're damn right I'm leaving."

The map rolled itself up when Travis let it go. "We need every rifle we can get here in the Alamo."

"So do Elizabeth and Lottie and all the others," True said. "I told them I'd join them, and I will."

Travis's voice was soft and flat. "I'm sorry. I can't let you go. As of this minute, you're conscripted."

"Oh, really?" True seemed to grow an extra inch. His hands curled around his rifle, and his knuckles were white.

"You ought to know, Colonel, that it takes a lot more than one man's word to *conscript* a Paxton when he doesn't want to be conscripted. I'll tell you what, though." He pointed with his rifle to the door. "There's the door I'm going to walk out. You have until it closes behind me to try to stop me. Any questions?"

Someone outside shouted and a rifle fired, but none of the three men inside seemed to notice. Travis glanced at Andrew, who wore a pistol in his belt. "Lieutenant Paxton? If you please . . ."

Andrew looked from True to Travis. "Sorry, Colonel." His hand stayed well away from the pistol. "I see the sense of what you say and I'll be staying at this *fiesta* until the music stops. But True's my brother. He's never stopped me from doing what I thought was right, and I won't try to stop him. You'll have to find another man for that job."

True nodded to Andrew, slipped out the door, and hurried down the steps before the headstrong Travis could figure out another way to prevent his departure. Outside, Firetail waited at a hitching post. He'd been rubbed down and watered, but the boy True had promised to pay for taking care of him had disappeared. The horse had had a hard ride, but looked fit enough to make at least another five miles, True decided after a cursory examination. He had just swung into the saddle when the church bells in the center of town began to ring frantically. At the same moment, a trio of buckskin-clad, bearded men raced around the corner and headed for the front courtyard. True felt a quick catch of fear, a tightness in his throat. There was no way that Santa Anna's army could have marched that far that fast. An advance of mounted lancers or riflemen could have, though. And if they had . . .

Firetail could smell danger. Ears pricked, the stallion trotted across the compound, past a low wall that once might have been an aqueduct, then into the main courtyard and pandemonium. Men were racing for the walls, shouting to each other and to people outside. Gunfire spattered in the distance. The bells in town were ringing, and the mission bell answered. True wove Firetail through the running men, jumped him over a water trough, and aimed for the main gate. To his surprise, the gate swung open without his bidding. He put his heels to Firetail's ribs, and galloped through, swerving sharply to the right at the last minute to avoid a collision with a horse-drawn cart that was racing at full speed toward the safety of the mission walls.

The cart was the leading edge of what turned out to be a veritable stream of humanity. Behind it, the *Calle de la Mission* and the *Camino Real al Presidio* were packed with men and women and children afoot, on horseback, and in conveyances of all sorts. True wanted to go east, which meant he had to cross through the throng. At the same time, Firetail was excited and becoming unmanageable. The only way to get across was to walk him. True continued to where the road turned toward town, dismounted, and eased into the flow, working his way to the far side of the road as he went. Just as he broke through, he spotted Buckland Kania on horseback and managed to catch his attention.

"Bad as that?" True shouted over the noise of the crowd.

The Reverend was having trouble with his horse, too. "Worse," he said, waiting for True to mount. They stopped a half dozen yards away from the road. "Mexican cavalry, guns and lances. They're pouring into the city, arresting people, riding down others. It's a mess."

"You think this is a mess, wait until tomorrow. There's a whole army on the way. These are just the van!"

"Why didn't anyone warn us? What happened to the coast watchers?"

"Came by land, I guess. Lancers hit our place this afternoon. The main body of their advance must have gone on around us earlier. I sent Elizabeth east with Hogjaw and rode in as fast as I could."

"You see Mila?" Kania asked, trying to be heard above the noise. "Is she safe?"

True shook his head. "Don't know. Hogjaw and Elizabeth were going to collect everyone they could on their way out. I'm sure Mila will be with them. I told 'em I'd meet 'em at Sutherland's tomorrow." He looked up at the sky. It was getting dark and clouds were rolling in from the north. "What I thought I'd do is head out the Old Cart Road until I get into the hills, then cut south and east for a few more miles before I stop for the night. Firetail's pretty well worn out. Can't take much more than that."

"Sounds good to me," Kania shouted. "I'm right behind you."

Firetail leaped away. Kania swung his mare around and tried to keep pace. The east side of town, what there was of it, was strangely deserted. The horses swept across open lots, around the occasional adobe house, between the forlorn *jacalitos*. Just as they reached the Old Cart Road and turned left, a squad of riflemen in pursuit of a buckboard driven by none other than Kevin Thatche emerged from between two short rows of *jacalitos*. Mildred, sitting next to Kevin, clung to their little boy with one hand and to the edge of the seat with the other. The situation was immediately obvious. Trying desperately to reach the mission, Kevin had forsaken the refugee-choked road in favor of open ground. The only problem was the ground itself, which was littered with limestone rocks and riddled with ruts and erosion gullies. Before True could turn Firetail, the wagon hit one such gully, slammed down, bounced crazily to one side, and threw a wheel.

There wasn't time to think, only to curse and act as the Thatches spilled onto the ground. True on Firetail leaned precariously into the turn, charged across the dry land toward the sprawled and staggering family and the riflemen bearing down on them. Behind him, Kania hurried to the rescue too. One of the Thatches' horses was down and screaming. Crazed, the other reared and, trying to escape, trampled its companion. Kevin had grabbed Mildred and the baby and was pulling them between the team and the Mexican soldiers. True leveled his rifle and fired. His shot was low and took the lead horse in the chest. The animal continued on for a few paces and then went down, spilling the officer head first into a patch of prickly pear. Behind him, horses and riders tried to evade a collision, but the double row of *jacalitos* had bunched them too tightly and they were moving too fast. The horse behind the downed animal tripped. The one behind it broke both front legs and its rider's neck when it tried to clear the entanglement of kicking hooves and sprawled bodies.

True shoved his rifle into its scabbard, reached down, and swept the baby into his arms. "Mildred, too!" he shouted. "You ride with Buckland!"

Kevin grabbed Mildred and helped her onto Firetail. She clutched at True. "Duck!" Kevin yelled, immediately pulling her halfway off.

True looked behind him and saw a soldier aiming at him. He twisted away and heard a gunshot. When he didn't feel anything, he chanced another look. This time the soldier's mouth was open and he was sliding off the horse. Behind him, smoking pistol in hand, Buckland Kania stared in horror.

"Lord forgive me," the preacher said, still not moving.

"Time for that later," Kevin shouted, pulling Mildred upright again and slapping Firetail on the rump. "Get 'em out of here!"

"And bring this poor soul into heaven."

"No time! No time!" Kevin screamed, leaping on behind Kania. "Jesus Christ, go!"

What was left of the squad had regrouped and was preparing to charge again. More soldiers rode down the Old Cart Road toward them.

"Amen!" Kania shouted over his shoulder. "Git, horse! C'mon, c'mon, c'mon, c'mon!"

There was only one direction left: back to the mission. Mildred had her arms wrapped around True's waist. True held the baby in one arm, and guided the sweating, almost blown Firetail with the other. Kania's horse, fresher and wild with frenzy, overtook them. The baby was crying, Mildred sobbing. True heard the whine of bullets overhead and the pop of gunfire almost as loud as the heavier, thudding sound his heart made. He smelled powder smoke, acrid and sharp in his nostrils, and the sweat smell of fear. Vision blurred, became a sluggish progression of frozen images: of scared faces turning toward him, of farmers and storekeepers scattering out of his way, of a horse down, its neck twisted and its head out of sight beneath its body. And a gate that seemed to take forever to reach, but in reality took no more than a couple of minutes.

Suddenly he was through and in the middle of the compound, reining Firetail to a halt next to Kania. The Reverend's face was white from fright and he was fighting to keep his hands from shaking. "You look like you'd better get off that horse before you fall off, Buckland," True said.

Kania gulped and nodded, looked startled as if he'd forgotten he'd been carrying a passenger when Kevin slipped off his horse and ran to help Mildred from Firetail's back. "Think so," Kania gasped and, unable to sit his horse any longer, slipped off and buried his head in his arms on the saddle. "I killed a man, True," he sobbed. "Oh, God, I took a life. Sweet Jesus . . . Sweet Jesus! . . . ."

Not caring, the crowd of frightened refugees swirled around them. Kevin steadied Mildred with one arm and, his dust-streaked face radiating thanks too profound for words, he took the baby from True.

Gunfire rattled from the walls as the last of the stragglers from town raced through the gates, and then the gates closed. Firetail's chest was heaving, his breathing labored. True's legs were shaking so badly he didn't think he could stand, but he dismounted anyway and held onto the saddle for support. Slowly, dull comprehension seeped into his weary brain. He was inside, Elizabeth was somewhere to the east, and he wouldn't be able to join her. Not with Firetail in such bad shape. He was inside. Trapped inside. Elizabeth was . . .

First things first, he told himself. First things first. Moving carefully, keeping his mind on each step so he wouldn't think of Elizabeth, he removed Firetail's saddle and let it fall to the ground. Next, he untied his bedroll and, using his blanket, began the long, slow process of rubbing down. The horse's sides were heaving painfully, his muscles quivering with fatigue. *First things first. Save the horse so you can ride out later if you get the chance. Hogjaw will take care of Elizabeth.*

"Easy, boy," he crooned, as much to himself as to Firetail. "Easy, easy. Gonna get you all fixed up. Steady, boy, steady."

The gunfire subsided. The crowds had quieted. Torches stuck in cracks in the wall and here and there in the ground, gave a fitful light. Firetail stood with head down. Near exhaustion, True made himself stand, let Firetail have a few sips of water, and began to rub him down again. Only gradually did he become aware that he wasn't alone. His eyes bleary, he turned to see Colonel Travis standing behind him and watching him. "What do you want?" True asked wearily.

The shadow of his hand passed over his face and then was gone again as Travis saluted. "Not a thing. Just glad to see you're back after all." He started to walk away, then hesitated. A small, self-satisfied smile played across his face. "Welcome to the Alamo, Mr. Paxton."

Chapter XXXVI

Distant thunder woke her. Elizabeth lay flat on her back and looked up through the cedars to a clear sky, and only then realized the thunder was that of gunfire. Instantly alert, she rolled out of her blankets and stood, trying to discern the direction from which the sound came. It was impossible. The dull mutter seemed to surround her. A few feet away, Lottie sat upright and clutched Bethann Elaine to her breast. Scott and Mackenzie had already taken their rifles and moved away from the fire. Elizabeth picked up the rifle she had taken to carrying and joined them at the perimeter of the campsite, just inside the protecting thicket of cedars.

"Anything?" she asked, crawling between them.

The quiet was ominous. Bethann cried out, but was quickly hushed. It was barely light. Far off, a flock of crows discussed the morning in raucous, irreverent tones. Scott shook his head. "Don't know where the cannon fire came from. Someplace from the southwest, by the wind. There were five other shots, though. Hogjaw and Joseph, maybe. They're out there somewhere."

"We ought to go help," Mackenzie said, stifling a yawn.

"Where?" Scott asked. "They can take care of themselves. And if they can't, our place is here. We'll wait, see what we see."

They had already waited a full week. Driving their horses hard in headlong flight out of the path of the oncoming army that was cutting a swath through the land, they had arrived at Sutherland's the day after they had left their homes, and found it deserted. That night, not knowing what to do, they had camped in a creekbed where they could watch for True. The next afternoon, a rider brought them news of the events in San Antonio. The messenger had escaped the mission just before the arrival of the first elements of the main Mexican army, and was on his way to Goliad where he hoped to find Fannin and bring help. He didn't know True personally, but had talked to him briefly just before he'd left. True had asked him to keep an eye out for his people if he passed anywhere near Sutherland's place, and to tell that his horse was in bad shape but that he would join them in a few days if it was humanly possible. That night, Hogjaw scouted around and the next morning, before full light, they moved to their present position.

Hogjaw had chosen their hidey hole, as he called it, with great care. Situated a little more than halfway up a steep hill overlooking Sutherland's, it was invisible from below. Less than fifty yards away, a spring welled out of the rocks. The cold, clear water pooled briefly and trickled down the side of the hill and through the camp. The land had been logged some dozen or more years earlier, and was now covered with a copse of scrub cedar no taller than eight or ten feet. By the end of the day, they had cut an inconspicuous path through the brush, cleared a campsite and observation post, and sat down to watch and wait.

There had been no further word. No other riders passed through the cleared land below them. Hogjaw had gone out to scout each morning and evening. Twice he had brought meat—a goat once, three chickens the second time—but never any news. And it was the morning of the eighth day.

"Someone's coming," Mackenzie said, looking back toward the campsite.

He and Scott were up and moving with Elizabeth close behind. Ready to reload, Mila, Joan, and Lottie were already behind the Campbells' wagon, which was situated so that it faced the opening through the trees. Scott, Mackenzie, and Elizabeth threw themselves down behind the makeshift wall they had built under the wagon and took aim. "Two of 'em, sounds like," Scott whispered.

"Comin' awful fast and loud," Mackenzie added. "Don't make sense."

It didn't to Elizabeth either, and she was worried. Strangers wouldn't have ridden so boldly into what was surely a well-defended position. Hogjaw and Joseph always rode stealthily.

"Thank God," Lottie breathed from behind them as Hogjaw and Joseph burst into camp.

Elizabeth wasn't so reassured. Joseph looked worried and

Hogjaw's face was pale and twisted with pain. The mountain man was literally holding on to Mama for dear life. Scott and Mackenzie rolled out from under the wagon. Mackenzie grabbed Mamma's reins, and Scott helped Hogjaw from her back and eased him down by the fire. "What happened?" Mackenzie asked.

"Ran into a patrol. Five men. We killed two, the rest took off," Joseph gasped. Lottie handed him a canteen and he drank deeply. "How bad is it?"

Joan and Scott and Elizabeth were clustered around Hogjaw. Scott had already cut off the left leg of the mountain man's pants to reveal a ragged bullet hole in his thigh. "One of them rascals could shoot," Hogjaw groaned. "Oh, Jesus, that hurts. I think it's broke."

"Hush," Joan snapped. "Get rags, Elizabeth. One long one, some shorter ones. Scott, put your knife in the fire." She pressed the heel of her hand against the wound to stem the flow of blood. "The bullet's in there," she said when Hogjaw winced. "It'll have to come out."

"You ain't tellin' me nothin' I don't know," Hogjaw said weakly. "You know what you're doin'?"

"I've done it before, if that's what you mean," Joan said, turning to Mila. "Build up that fire and put on more water. I'll want it boiling. Just a little at first so it'll be quicker. Mackenzie, get these animals out of here. Where's those rags, Elizabeth?"

Hogjaw had lost blood, but seemed to be holding his own. Everyone but Mackenzie, who left to watch the entrance to the camp, worked quickly. Within minutes, the knife and tourniquet were ready, and in minutes more the water was boiling.

"Pour it back and forth between that and the coffee pot," Joan ordered. "It ought to be clean enough, and a little coffee won't hurt so long as we keep the grains out. Somebody get a stick for him to bite. Lottie, don't just stand there. Get a cleaning rod and stick it in the fire. I'll want it red hot."

A cold sweat had broken out on Hogjaw's forehead and his face was pale. Elizabeth got blankets from her wagon and covered him, then cradled his head in her lap. Joan's face was grim. "You ready?" she asked.

Hogjaw nodded weakly.

Joan washed the wound with the still warm water, then wadded up a rag and, holding it in place over the arteries, tightened the tourniquet around his leg. "Hold him, Scott. Don't let him kick while I'm cutting. Bite, Hogjaw!"

The knife plunged into the flesh just above the wound. Bright blood spurted. Hogjaw groaned and his jaws popped as he bit into the stick Elizabeth had given him. Mila turned her face away, and Lottie sat down weakly. Elizabeth thought she would faint, but took deep breaths until the dizziness passed.

"Get over here and help, Mila," Joan said between clenched teeth. "Bring that cleaning rod." Mila sobbed, but did as she was ordered. "Now hold it open with one hand and dab with the other," Joan said, handing Mila a rag. "Gimme that rod."

Hot metal hissed against flesh. Hogjaw jumped, but Elizabeth and Scott held him fast. "Last of that, I think," Joan said. "Dab, honey, don't rub. Oh, sweet Jesus. Lottie, put this back in the fire."

The ball had broken the bone. Her fingers slippery with blood, Joan picked out the ball and the three pieces of bone she could find. "It's the best I can do," she finally said. "Let me have more of that water, Lottie. And the rod again."

How Hogjaw stood the pain without passing out, Elizabeth couldn't imagine. He was breathing shallowly and pouring sweat. His face, ashen gray, looked worse than ever. Elizabeth winced at the smell of burning flesh as Joan cauterized another vessel.

"Ought to sew it," Joan said, pulling the edges of the wound together and pressing a rag over it. "But it might be better to let it stay open so it can drain if it wants. I wish I knew more. Here. Hold this, Mila." She added more rags and tied them snugly with a long strip torn off her petticoat. "I'm going to release the tourniquet now. There should be enough pressure on the bandage to keep it from bleeding too much."

Joan's hands hovered over the stick twisted into the tourniquet, at last reached down and undid it. As the pressure eased, Hogjaw sighed with relief. "It holdin'?" he asked, trying to look down over his chest.

"I think so," Joan said. She touched the edges of the bandage, peeked underneath the wrapping. "It looks like it."

Hogjaw smiled wanly, barely enough to move the folds of flesh that hung down from his jaw. "Good. I thank you, Joan."

"Don't be too quick. We'll know more in a few days. How do you feel?"

One hand raised slightly, fell back to his stomach. "I feel . . . fine," Hogjaw said, and passed out cold.

"Well?" Scott asked fifteen minutes later as they sat around the fire and drank coffee.

They had splinted Hogjaw's leg, moved him into the Campbells' wagon, and covered him well. He was sound asleep with Lottie watching him. The question hung on the air while Joan considered. "I just don't know," she finally said. "Pieces of bone broke off and all. At his age, I don't think he'll ever walk right again, even if he doesn't get blood poisoning."

"What about moving him?"

"It'll be hard on him. We shouldn't, for a few days at least."

Scott stared into the fire. "We can't stay here, though. The place is beginning to crawl with Mexicans. We're too close to San Antonio."

"He's in bad shape," Elizabeth said. "Besides, True expects us to wait and I think we ought to. If we leave . . . I vote that we stay."

"Like the Kempers?" Joan asked. "Lord knows what's happened to them."

"This is different."

"No, it isn't," Joseph interjected. "Those soldiers are going to pick up our trail sooner or later, and from what Hogjaw and I saw out there, it's gonna be sooner. The way I see it, we have to leave. Today."

Elizabeth had made up her mind. "You heard what that messenger said. True will be along. You go if you want. I'm staying right here."

"You know he'd want you to go," Mila said, speaking for the first time. "You're saying the same things I did when you came by my cabin. I wanted to wait for Buckland, but I left with you. Come with us, Elizabeth. It's the only right thing to do and you know it."

There was no more room for argument. They were right. Elizabeth stared around the circle of faces that waited for her answer, and dropped her eyes to her lap. "It all happens so fast," she whispered. "One day it's spring and the sun is shining, the next, our lives are seared by blood and death. We go to bed safe and wake up to danger. If only Hogjaw hadn't been shot . . ." The breeze, gentle and balmy, suddenly seemed cold and evil. The morning sun, yet to rise above the hill behind them, seemed to have forsaken her. True, her own True, seemed further away than ever, and she felt lost. She inhaled deeply, raised her head. "I'll leave with you," she said. "When do we go?"

The weather gave them an extra chance they hadn't counted on. By noon, it was evident that a late norther was bearing down on them. Joseph and Scott decided they should load up immediately and depart the minute the first winds hit. The idea was to put as many miles as possible between them and the nearby threat, at the same time that the soldiers were seeking shelter from the storm for the night. With luck, the soldiers would stay holed up for at least another day before they took to the trail again. By that time the refugees' tracks would be wiped out by the rain and they would have a creditable head start.

The wind hit a couple of hours before sundown, and the temperature plunged forty degrees by the time Scott and Joseph called a halt just as it was getting dark. They camped again in cedars, always the best place because the evergreens were plentiful and offered the most protection against the wind. The hastily arranged campsite was no more than six miles from where they'd started, but they chanced a fire anyway because Hogjaw desperately needed something warm to drink. It was a terrible night. The bitter cold affected them all. Hogjaw's splint was loose from the continual jouncing he had taken and he was in constant pain. Only when the splint had been tightened and he was laid in a small depression lined with warmed stones and grass and cedar did he finally sleep. Ruthie and Dianne were terrified and cold. They slept in the Campbells' wagon with the women. The men bedded down in whatever sheltered spot they could find to wait out the night.

The wind howled, and set the canvas slapping against the frame. The storm lantern that hung above their heads cast a pallid glow. Joan had taken the outside next to Ruthie, who lay in her mother's left arm. Next came Dianne, then Mila. Lottie huddled against Mila and cradled Bethann between herself and Elizabeth on the other end of the row of bodies. Sometime after everyone was asleep, Elizabeth woke to hear Bethann squawling. Before the others woke, she rolled onto her side and took the baby in her own arms. "Hush little lamb," she crooned, "do not tarry. Papa's gone a'hunting and you must marry. Your husband will love you, my dearest little one. Handsome and gentle, he is the King's son.''

Bethann stretched and burbled, then slowly relaxed. Elizabeth hugged her close. How she envied Lottie. Elizabeth tried to imagine what it would be like to have True's child. No, she thought. Children. Several of them. Oh, she wanted a family. She wanted to be surrounded with children. She wanted a house full of laughter and love.

But all that seemed so far away, so ultimately impossible. She had no idea where True was. He could have been trapped inside the fort or captured and killed trying to reach her. ''Oh, Bethann, Bethann,'' she whispered, chiding herself for flirting so outrageously with despair. She pulled the covers away from the child's face and gazed down at her. Deep in the shadows, Bethann stared back, her eyes shining with the timeless wisdom that fills the eyes of infants—the eyes of God.

To lose hope . . . is to lose . . . everything.

''I won't, baby,'' she promised. ''Neither will your Mommy or Daddy. You'll see. And when your Uncle True comes back, we'll all laugh and pretend we weren't so scared.''

She couldn't go on. Words were too difficult. Lulling herself as well as the child, her voice undercutting the whining north wind, she hummed the lilting ballad. Soon, Bethann's eyelids grew heavy and then closed. Elizabeth watched over her for a long moment before pulling the covers back over her. Watched over her as if she were her own.

Her very own.

They called a halt the next night at an unnamed creek some fifteen or so miles to the east. More clouds had followed the clearing norther, and though the weather was still cold, it wasn't as bad as the night before. The creek was a dry prairie gully dotted with pools of water and treacherous drifts of wet sand left over from the last rain. Since it looked like more might fall, they crossed and made camp on the far side. Mackenzie and Mila began collecting firewood. Lottie took care of Bethann and Ruthie and Dianne Campbell while she started a meager supper. Joseph rode out to scout the area, leaving Scott to guard the camp itself. Hogjaw had rallied a bit during the day, but was still wan and weak. Grateful to be stopped again and on solid ground, he lay docilely while Joan and Elizabeth removed the bandages and checked his leg. The area around the wound was red, but there were no telltale streaks as yet. Joan began to lave it with fresh, boiled water, and then placed a salt poultice over it. "I wish we had some whiskey to pour on it," she said, dribbling more of the salty water over the bandage.

"I'd die 'fore I'd be the cause of wastin' good whiskey," Hogjaw groaned. His voice wavered with the pain. " 'Specially just for a skeeter bite like this," he added.

Neither of the women were convinced, especially when, by the next morning, the first streak appeared. It was a worried Joan who replaced the dressings with fresh ones and retied the splint before Scott and Joseph loaded Hogjaw into Joseph and Lottie's buckboard and rigged a canvas cover over him. "This is the last time we move him, no matter how much he wants to sleep on the ground," she told them a few minutes later, out of his earshot. "I'm getting scared. We have to find help. Someone who knows more than I do."

They tried. Joseph rode out to the left, Scott to the right. The scattered farms they found were all deserted, though, and the one small settlement they skirted had been burned out. During the afternoon they heard shots in the distance behind them. An hour later, riding hard and low, Joseph caught up to them and announced that he had barely eluded what looked like a whole company of cavalry out sweeping the country-side. Whether the patrol was alone or part of a larger body, he could not say.

Whatever advantage the weather had given them, it now took back. The ground was soggy and hard to negotiate. That night they risked fording a fast-running, muddy-bottomed creek before camping. The fire they built, small and hidden as it was, did little to cheer them. Hogjaw's wound was actively festering. Puss seeped out of it and the red streak ran all the way up to his groin. Joan drained it as best she could and soaked it in salt water rags, but although she kept her voice carefully controlled, it was obvious she was pessimistic.

Used to the chore of making camp under adverse condi-tions, they settled in rapidly. Supper was ready before dark and the women went off to sleep shortly thereafter. Joseph, Scott and Mackenzie divided the night into three watches. While Mackenzie took the first, keeping an eye on the ford, the only reasonable place they had found to cross the creek, the other two found dry spots and fell asleep immediately. Elizabeth couldn't sleep, though. True was on her mind and she couldn't stop worrying about him. The Mexican lancer she had killed was haunting her. At last, she slipped out from under the covers, pulled on her coat, and dropped out of the wagon. The fire was down to coals banked under green wood for the night. Elizabeth hunkered down next to it, stirred it, and warmed her hands. A heated twig burst into flames, burned brightly for a moment, and fell. The wind brushed the coals, set them twinkling with a living, dancing, red and white life of their own.

"Girl . . . 'Liz'beth . . . That you?"

Elizabeth rose quickly, hurried to Joseph's buckboard, and climbed in. Hogjaw's poor ruined features looked especially ghostly in the light of the storm lantern they had rigged for him. "I couldn't sleep," she said, kneeling at his side. "You, too?"

Hogjaw nodded. "It hurts. I'm a strong man. Stronger than most, an' one who never did like to admit he was hurtin', but I got to now. Worse'n my head did 'cause it's goin' on longer, I guess. That an' the bouncin' around."

"The buckboard rides smoother than the Conestoga. We'll be able to stop in another day or two. Find a doctor and all."

"Maybe. Maybe not. But that ain't what I called you for." He pushed back the blankets and reached inside his shirt to pull out a buckskin pouch that hung around his neck on a leather thong. "Help me off with it."

Elizabeth raised his head and slipped the loop free. "What's this?"

"Somethin' I kept with me ever since I come through this part of the world the first time. That was seventeen, eighteen years ago, girl. A long time." He worked the bag open and removed a crumpled sheet cut from deerskin and worn smooth and shiny from handling. "Lookee," he said, handing it to her.

The writing had faded and was hard to see in the dim light. She made out a circle marked San Antonio, an assortment of markings indicating a generally western course and culminating in an "X" that lay between two scraggly lines—possibly hills on either side of a valley. "A map? Of what?"

"I done me a sight of trekkin' in them years and since. Seen the elephant an' bearded the critter in his den. Found gold and silver and passed it by after takin' enough to get along on for a while. Lived with an' fit Injuns. Best of all though, the one thing I never forgot, was the valley I found that first year. Good water, good grass, protected from the northers. Saw it in the fall when the grass was all gold, like your hair. Gold in the sun.'' He smiled, remembering. ''There was a *hacienda*, too. Lord knows when it was built or abandoned, but the Comanch' told me that them that lived there up an' left one day and never came back. I reckoned that since I found it, she was mine. Filed on it with the Mex government. If you're lucky enough, that was long enough ago that they didn't get around to erasin' it during the recent troubles.''

Hogjaw groaned, tried to shift his leg into a different position. ''Anyways, it's a mighty hard place to find. I stumbled onto it myself by following the river north. Place you come to looks like the river peters out, but it don't. Just sorta spreads out through a funny little flat place full of buckeye, cedar elm, live oak, willows and such. When I got through that, I knew I'd found one of them places the world's forgotten about an' lets be. Holed up there that winter, an' when I left in the spring, I figured that one day I'd come back an' light there, raise me some kids, have a family an' all. 'Course, that was before . . .''

He touched his face. His fingers moved to the top of his head and followed the edge of the leather skullpatch. ''A man who looks like Ol' Scratch hisself ain't about to latch on to a woman willin' to go along with him or be a wife an' mother. Hell, I get sick of seein' myself. Reckon other folks do, too.''

''That isn't so, Hogjaw,'' Elizabeth replied gently.

''Yes it is, dadgumit! Now hush an' let me finish.'' His eyes closed and his jaw muscles bunched under the loose skin as he fought the pain. ''Never had me no kids,'' he said, his voice plaintive. ''Got no one to pass what I own on to, 'cept you an' True. The two of you, the children the ol' gut eater never had the luck or woman to raise.''

Elizabeth tried to press the map back into his hands. ''All this talk of passing things on,'' she scoffed, trying to sound as if that was the last thing she could imagine. ''I won't hear it. You'll be up and around in no time.''

Hogjaw clamped his hands into fists. ''No, 'Liz'beth. You keep it. An' after all this is over, you an' True go there. See if what I said ain't the plumb by God truth.''

''We'll all go together, then,'' Elizabeth said. ''Otherwise—''

''I'm dyin', gal. Don't you see that?''

''No!'' Her voice was pinched and high. Elizabeth had to

clear her throat before she went on. "I won't let you carry on like this, Hogjaw. I won't," she said, and wrapped the thong around his hand.

"Stubborn from the day I met you," Hogjaw said, watching her. After a moment, he raised his hands and dropped the loop over her head, then gripped her arms with hands that had once been strong as steel. "Hear me out, gal. I don't have the time for you to carry on, you understand?"

Elizabeth bit her lower lip to keep from crying.

"Now, it's around your neck, so keep it there. An' listen up, 'cause this here's the hard part."

"I don't want—"

"When you head out tomorrow, I'm stayin' behind."

"No!"

"Yes. Joseph didn't want to worry any of you, but he saw more than he let on. That Mex cavalry is barely a mile off, there's a whole hell of a lot of 'em, an' we left a trail a blind man could follow. I aim to give them somethin' to think about while I still got the strength."

"But you can't—"

"There you go again, talkin' instead of listenin'. Now, I seen enough punctures in my time to know a bad one, an' that's what this'n here is. The bone's gone an' it's infected. Blood poisonin' is settin' in. Hell, give me a couple of days an' I'll be so damn delirious from fever I'll be worth about as much as cobbler's tacks to a Comanche. This way is better. I choose the time and the place, go out the way I wanta go, which is fast. I got my bugle, an' when you all are clear, I'll wait a spell and then play a tune them soldiers will flock to. Yessir, we'll have us quite a shindig."

"But that's suicide," Elizabeth said, incredulous.

"It's common sense."

"Hogjaw—" She leaned closer to him and took one of his hands. The tears streamed down her face. "Do you remember when we first got to San Antonio? We were at Mama Flores's, and you said you'd spent some fifty-odd years not bein' a damn fool. That's what you're doing now, don't you see? We can take care of you. Scott, Joseph, Mackenzie, me—that's four rifles."

The mountain man grinned and patted her hands. "Sometimes," he said gently, "a fella would be a damn fool *not* to be a damn fool. I know what I'm doin', gal. What I'm buyin' an' who I'm buyin' it for. A man can't ask for anything more. If I stayed with you, I'd just slow you all down an' get everybody captured. An' then die in a day or two anyway. No thankee." The grin disappeared. "I never held much truck with souls, but if I have one, I wouldn't want that on it. Don't you see, gal?"

Elizabeth's mind reeled. *Not Hogjaw. Not him too. Oh, please, Lord. How much must we lose? Haven't we paid enough?* "The others . . ."

"Will find out come mornin'," Hogjaw said, rubbing a hand across his face. " 'Cept now I'm tired of talkin'. Never did so much all at one time. Explainin' is the hardest thing a man is asked to do in this life. I'd as soon bear hug a porcupine."

"Hogjaw—"

"No, I'm done with gabbin' and bein' gabbed to. Said an' listened all I aim to. But set with me a spell, 'Lizabeth. Will you do that? Set with me a spell?"

Her mind was in chaos. She nodded in stupefied acceptance. He was wrong, but she could order no arguments to convince either him or herself. One did not argue with blood poisoning. The idea of watching Hogjaw Leakey thrashing in delirium as he died a slow, lingering, demeaning death made her cringe. And yet . . . And yet . . . Wrapped in a blanket, lying at his side, willing time to stop, she slept.

And woke to darkness buzzing with whispers. Joseph had roused the camp, explained what they were about, and started the hurried process of packing gear and harnessing and saddling stock. The eastern sky was graying when the fire was quenched and Hogjaw was taken for the last time from Joseph and Lottie's buckboard and carried on a makeshift stretcher to the spot he, Joseph, and Scott had chosen. There they propped him against a tree and, at his own insistence, loosely tied him there. If he did lose consciousness, he would still be sitting up when he came to. His field of fire commanded the entire ford and the narrow path rising from it. No man would cross the creek on horseback or with dry powder for many hundreds of yards in either direction. At his side, they placed his rifle and one other with a broken stock, good for one shot. On a flat stone within reach of his left hand, they left a brace of pistols, a small box of patches, a rod, two horns of powder, and a bag of shot. His armaments included a broken lance they had found in the burned-out settlement the day before, his Arkansas Toothpick, and a tomahawk.

"I seen a picture of a fella like this once," he said, gritting his teeth against the pain. "Looked pretty silly at the time. I guess I'm ready."

One by one, they paused to stop by the miniature fort, to say goodbye to the hero who would stay behind while they fled. Mila first, who brushed his forehead with a kiss. Mackenzie, who was too old to cry, and was glad the darkness hid his tears. Joan and Scott—

"I'm sorry, Hogjaw," Joan whispered, broken-hearted.

"You done good, Joan." He held her hand, the one that had cut him and picked the ball and broken pieces of bone from him. "Don't never blame yourself, girl. That's the only thing I'd ever hold against you. Scott?"

Scott hunkered down, moved the pistols an inch closer. "Yeah?"

"Them two little girls are the prettiest things. You take care of them."

Joseph and Lottie, weeping openly and holding Bethann so Hogjaw could touch her. "Worth it all for her alone," he said, laying his gnarled, calloused hand against her cheek. "Watch her in this weather, now. Don't let her take a chill."

"It took me a while," Joseph said, reaching down to shake Hogjaw's hand, "but I know now why Father counted himself lucky to have you for a friend."

"Poor ol' Thomas." Hogjaw grinned. "He'd've enjoyed this. Kind of foofaraw he liked. You see him, you tell him how it was, and that he won his bet."

"Bet?"

"Yeah. He always said I'd never die in bed. Well, he's won. Tell him I'll leave his winnin's with the Devil."

For sure.

Elizabeth waited on her horse until the others had left. When she was alone, she dismounted the kneeled by his side. "Hogjaw?" She held out the pouch, then placed it inside her shirt. "We'll go there."

Hogjaw squinted up at her, rubbed a scarred and hairy hand across his eyes. "Damn grit. Blinds a man."

"Hogjaw?"

"Maurice. My name is Maurice," he said.

He tapped his battered bugle against the butt of his rifle. "Yes. That's what makes it worth the doin'." He looked straight up, back to Elizabeth. "Gettin' lighter, gal. Best join the others. And fare thee well."

He turned from her. Elizabeth somehow found the strength of heart to stand, mount, and ride away.

Alone then, Maurice Leakey waited and watched the ford the enemy would cross. Somewhere behind him, he heard the creak of wagons and the soft drum of hooves. And then there was silence. "Fare thee well," he said again, and added, in a whisper, "daughter."

Chapter XXXVII

Mist, driven from the west by a backing wind. Soft and enveloping, steadily drenching them as they climbed the ridge and clung to the narrow, winding path that followed the hillside to the top.

Thunder, low and menacing, as if from the throat of a savage animal.

Thunder and a distant bugle, the notes carried on the wind, blaring defiance.

Thunder and perhaps, though hard to tell at that distance, the crackle of gunfire. And still the taunting bugle.

They paused on the crest. The mist shrouded the distance behind them in an impenetrable veil. "Hie up!" Joseph said, and the wagons began to move, to descend into the next valley.

Elizabeth hung back, scarcely breathing. Suddenly, there it was again, fading but unmistakable. The indomitable bugle.

She thought of True at that moment, and strangely, she knew she would find him and bear his son. At peace for the first time since those hours past when she was called from the fire, she touched her heels to the mare's sides, and rode off the crest. Behind her, thunder rolled again, and only thunder.

Nothing more.

Captain Hernandez rolled a cigarette around between his lips. A shred of tobacco stuck to his tongue. Three times he tried to spit it off and at last picked it off with his fingers, first wiping them on his tunic. By that time he had lost the taste for smoking and the cigarette was soaked from the rain anyway, so he threw away the butt. It was that kind of morning.

He heard the riders approach long before he saw them

come sloshing toward him through the rain. *"Madre de Dios,"* he muttered, and spat in a puddle, just barely missing the disintegrating cigarette. If he'd stayed in San Antonio, none of this would have happened. If he'd stayed in San Antonio . . . Pagh! If "ifs" were *centavos* he'd have a pocketful.

The general rode a magnificent gray stallion. The animal pawed at the mud and tossed his head, showed the whites of his eyes and flared his nostrils. He seemed to mirror his rider's irritation with the world in general and events in particular. The general returned the captain's salute and stared down at the running water and the rocky bank opposite their vantage point. "How many" he asked.

"Two were killed on this side, General, and another crossing the creekbed. One was drowned trying to cross lower down. Three were wounded going up the path. The bastard chose his place well. We had to storm his position, and the fighting was hand to hand even after he no longer had time to reload. Another three—no, four—died before our sabers and pistols finished him off."

"Him?" the general asked, hating the soft, lisping Castillian Spanish that Hernandez spoke. "Only one man?"

"Yes," the captain admitted. His smile was the sickly display of a man who has run out of excuses. "But one like a devil. A monster in truth, General."

"One?" the general repeated scornfully. Wearied of incompetence, he shook his head. Rainwater dripped from the brim of his chapeau and from the ends of his moustache. "Show me," he said. "Wait here," he told his entourage.

Captain Hernandez saluted and nudged his bootheels into his horse's flanks. The horse shied at the water, but crossed without incident and struggled up the mud-slippery bank, almost throwing his rider. The general's gray crossed and ascended easily. The stallion was sure-footed and well-trained, as coolly competent as his master. It was starting to rain again. The captain pointed to the rocks, to the splayed legs and massive torso of the defender. Rain had washed much of the blood from him, but his clothes were slashed and punctured in more than a dozen places. His face was bloodless, ashen gray. His skin hung in folds that nearly covered his eyes and dripped from his jowls as if it had melted briefly and then, running down, frozen in grotesque ripples. A battered bugle lay at his side next to his right hand, which was nearly severed from his body.

"So . . ." Luther O'Shannon said.

"As I said, General, a veritable devil."

"Yes. A devil." O'Shannon repeated. He peered into the gloom ahead. Somewhere out there was Elizabeth Paxton. And True Paxton also? Hard to say, but maybe . . . O'Shannon's lip twitched. If Paxton were there, they'd meet again. He stirred, straightened in the saddle. "You were lucky you lost only eight, Captain."

Hernandez's lips puckered. "General?"

"I want him buried with all honors, and his grave marked." O'Shannon turned his horse and started to ride back, but then stopped. "Where he lies, Captain," he said. "Where he lies. He deserves that much."

The captain looked perplexed. "I'm sorry, General," he said to O'Shannon's back. "I don't understand. You know this man?"

"No," O'Shannon said, his voice gentle with the obeisance one warrior pays another when they are no longer enemies. "But the face is familiar."

Chapter XXXVIII

"The hell you say," True snapped.

"That's right. The hell I say. Just after midnight," Travis barked in return. He circled the date on the hand-drawn calendar on his desk top. March third. The siege had been going on for nine days, counting from Santa Anna's arrival on the twenty-third of February. New units of the Mexican Army had been arriving daily, with more to come, according to the reports of the scouts who made it through the lines. The defenders were tired. Most of them had been wounded at least once. They were running short of food and the aqueduct that supplied them with water had been cut. "You wanted out and now you're getting your wish."

"That was before," True said, stepping out of the shadows and leaning toward Travis.

Cannons roared in the distance, followed by the concussion of iron shot falling into the Alamo. Chunks of adobe wall flew high into the night air. Men found holes into which to crawl or corners to crouch behind or remnants of walls to press against. The room shook. Dust settled like a brown snowfall on lamp, maps, desk, chairs, and the four men in the room: Colonel William Barrett Travis, Captain Dickinson, Lieutenant Andrew Paxton, and True.

"What's changed your mind?" Travis asked.

"My brother is here, my friends are here. I'll stand by them."

"Fine. You'll do that best by obeying my orders. With the extra thirty-two men who came in Tuesday night, we have over a hundred eighty men. Even if Fannin can't send help from Goliad, that should give us enough to hold. *If* we can find Houston and convince him to take some of the pressure off."

"It makes sense, True," Andrew said. "Even if Houston can only bring a couple hundred, their harassing Santa Anna every time he turns around would make all the difference in the world. You'd be more help than if you stayed. It's your rifle or Houston's army. And as good a shot as you are, we'll take the army. Let's face it. Firetail's the fastest horse in the compound, and no one can ride him but you."

"No one thinks you're getting off easy," Captain Dickinson added. Dickinson was a younger man with a clear, honest face topped by a blood-soaked bandage covering a wound made by a wood splinter. Only his wife had refused to leave when Santa Anna had allowed the other women and children to escape unmolested from the fortress mission, and because of this he was paid great respect by the men. "Look at it this way. If you make it past the sentries you'll only have an army of five or six thousand men to fight your way through. We're not doing you any favor."

"Since you put it that way, how can I refuse?" True grumbled.

"Good," Travis said. He handed True a leather dispatch pouch. "Another man, John Smith, will be going out on foot ten minutes ahead of you. He'll try to make it down the ravine east of here, so I want you to ride a little to the south of that. Your horse's speed gives you an edge, but the ruckus and diversion you create gives him an edge. Between you, one ought to get through. You are, by the way, carrying identical letters."

True took the pouch, slung it over his shoulder, and shook Travis's hand. "I don't like you, Colonel. Haven't since the day I met you. But I'm willing to say that maybe it's not you so much as it is the times. You do have my respect."

"Which I value, sir," Travis said, somewhat formally. "And if we've been at odds, I respect you too, and wish you the best of luck and Godspeed."

Andrew accompanied True. Together they paused at the top of the steps, from where they could see the courtyard and, beyond the walls, the campfires of the besiegers. The Alamo was a motley conglomerate of night-shaded shapes made ghostly by the flat light of the moon, dark houses in which exhausted men slept soundly in spite of the cold. The last of a herd of cattle had stampeded through the Mexican lines and through the main gates five days earlier. They saw the moving shadow of a man on an errand, the silhouettes of sentries.

Low battlements stood battered and precarious, along with walls made of dirt, stones, and overturned wagons, carts, and barrels. It was said that some of the cannons were loaded with crucifixes from the mission; brass crucifixes made excellent grapeshot to fire into massed ranks of attackers. Ironically, it was inside these same walls that General Cos and his men had holed up only three short months ago before being driven out of San Antonio by the aroused Texians. Ironically too, the Mexicans had been allowed to leave with their lives: Santa Anna was not so generous. He had promised no quarter—death to the last man for the Texian defenders.

The two brothers descended the steps and walked quickly to the stable. Inside it was warmer, and they found Firetail already saddled and ready. Kevin Thatche, Nels Matlan, Dennis Campbell, and Buckland Kania stepped out of the dark interior into the lantern light. "Heard you were going out," Matlan said.

Andrew shrugged innocently. "I had faith in Travis's persuasiveness," he replied to True's angry stare.

"We wanted to say . . . well . . . God bless you," Kania said, holding out a rifle.

True took it, checked his pistols and the saber scabbarded on Firetail's saddle.

"And don't forget to duck," Kevin added, forcing a grin.

A cannon boomed in the distance. Seconds later, fragments of adobe pattered like hail against the stable walls. "Close," Dennis said. "Wish Mack was here."

True glanced at his brother. They were a long way from the Carolinas. "Travis talks a good fight, but it looks like you've found your time and place, little brother."

"I'm not ready to give up yet," Andrew replied grimly. "But if so, I've got no complaints."

Forcing all emotion from their expressions, sensing the frightening finality of this parting, the brothers embraced. When they stepped back from each other, True looked at each of the faces around him. Nels Matlan, a kindly, simple man of education who found himself in a situation where the pen was not mightier than the sword, and had unhesitatingly buckled on the figurative armor of battle. Kevin Thatche, young father, now young patriot. Dennis Campbell, who had looked for a fight for eight hundred miles and two years, and finally found the granddaddy of them all. Reverend Buckland Kania, the Lord's shepherd who, in his faith, did not fear the shadow of the valley of death. They were etched in True's memory, as were the others. Three wives, two children, both sons.

"If Eustacia were here she'd give you a farewell kiss," Nels said, as if reading True's mind.

"Mildred too, I reckon," Kevin added.

True knew that was as close as they would come to mentioning their wives or children. He looked to Kania and saw the same concern. Silently, he swore he would find their families. And tell them of their husbands' and fathers' love and bravery, and help them get a new start. Not to embarass anyone with words, he nodded to show he understood. "A handshake will do from you boys," he said, taking their hands one by one. The tension seemed to lighten.

"Paxton!" a voice hissed from the doorway. "Smith's gone. Time for you."

"Right." True wrapped one arm around Andrew's neck, pulled him briefly to him. "That's it then, I guess. See you . . ."

Andrew led the way through the moonlight to a narrow gate. "Pass the word," he called out softly to the sentries. "Hold your fire. Man going out."

True listened, could hear the message repeated three times before the sound faded. The air reeked of powder smoke and sulfur. The night lay heavy on the land. The stars were bright—too bright—and the moon was only three days from being full. He would have to ride low and fast, and count heavily on surprise and luck. Dickinson had been right. They were doing him no favor. He shivered and hoped it was from the cold. "Hard to believe March is the month of spring," he said through chattering teeth.

"Let's just hope they're busy trying to keep warm instead of watching," Andrew said, swinging open the gate. "Take care, True."

True checked the cinch and saddle one last time, shifted the dispatch pouch so it hung on the back of his hip, then walked Firetail through the gate. When he looked around to say a final word to Andrew, the gate was already shut.

There hadn't been anything more to say. Nothing important, anyway. He stared at the dark ground, at the winking campfires in the distance, slowly mounted, and adjusted the reins. The temperature seemed to drop twenty degrees with the knowledge that he was in the open and alone. His hand moved to his chest. The pressure of the gold amulet against his skin gave him courage. He leaned forward to pat Firetail's neck. "One more race, boy," he whispered. "Just remember. Nothing out there but a whole goddamned army."

One more race. Only one more, and the prize—death or glory. Campfires, twinkling, drew closer, deadly jewels in the darkness. The shapes around them looked like wraiths of doom but became men, more dangerous than specters. Circling the Alamo, Santa Anna's army was a vast encampment of soldiers in fighting prime, men of conquest, used to victory. The Alamo seemed so small and beleaguered in comparison, but behind those battered, crumbling walls stood Texians—men from a dozen countries but now all Texians—with a cause and willing to barter their lives for the blood of their enemies.

Firetail had been born ugly, but fast enough to race the wind. The blood of pirates and warriors pounded in True's veins. Only an army? A vision of his father on a red-stained deck with his cutlass crimson to the hilt filled True's head. What? Only *one* army? Thomas Gunn Paxton's back was to the sea. He was besieged yet fighting on and reveling in the desperate odds he faced. So be it! Wild glee surged through True's breast and a demonic yell ripped from his throat as he fired at the nearest man and threw the rifle at a tent, then whipped the saber from its scabbard and guided Firetail straight toward the nearest campfire.

"*Madre!*" a voice shrieked as the unexpected horse and rider flew over the fire.

Bodies rose from the darkness. True leaned close to Firetail's neck. Gunfire erupted all around him as he galloped through the heart of the camp. Soldiers believing a whole troop of Texas riders was in their midst staggered from their tents and fired blindly into their equally startled companions who, seeing the muzzle blasts and hearing the whirr of musket balls, returned the fire. Among them, one man rode low, hard, and fast, straight at a wall of men armed with muskets directly in his path. "*Amigo!*" True shouted. "*Amigos!*"

Uncertain, the men held their fire and waited for the horseman to rein in. Seconds later, Firetail exploded through their ranks and there was time enough only for the men to dodge as they could from the hooves and slashing blade.

The saber struck something, stuck, and was jerked from his hand. True leaned dangerously far to his right and, feeling no pain as the flames blackened his hand, snatched a torch from one of the soldiers. A musket ball creased his thigh and jarred Firetail as it slammed into the saddle. True shifted his weight and dragged the flaming brand across the surface of a nearby tent, then another and another before he lost the brand, too.

Amid the fire, the noise, the shouts and screams of the wounded, Firetail balked, reared, and pivoted just in time for True to see the lancers. He didn't bother to try to count them. One would have been too many. Fighting Firetail, he brought the half-crazed stallion under a semblance of control and turned to his left, away from the merciless iron weapons, and then found himself in the air as one of the burning tents exploded.

Firetail went down. True sprawled in the dirt, rolled to his knees and fell backward as a second explosion rent the air. The lancers, just opposite the tents where black powder had been stored, took the full brunt of the explosion. Earth and wood and armor and flesh filled the air with grisly shrapnel. Ears ringing, vision doubling and shifting, True staggered to his feet and ran to Firetail in time to grab him as he heaved himself off the ground.

They had been forgotten, or lost momentarily, in the pandemonium. "Easy, boy, easy," True croaked, quickly checking the frightened beast. He was standing on all four legs, so no bones were broken. There was a small cut on his left front leg, a larger one on his withers, but neither was dangerous. More important was fear. A horse exposed to battle could never be fully trusted. Gingerly, True mounted, turned Firetail away from the gruesome carnage behind them, and gave him the chance to do what he did best: run.

Cool night air washed around him. Firetail swerved around a small clump of scrub cedar, and headed up a long, gentle slope. Behind them, the fires and commotion faded. The stinging scent of black powder eddied away. Every nerve alert, True could feel the sweat evaporating from his clothes, feel the driving power of Firetail's legs, smell the churned soil where an army had marched, hear the sound of hoof beats. . . . He looked over his shoulder, saw what looked like a whole company of dragoons angling toward him. Behind the dragoons he could see the fires where the ammunition tents had gone up and behind them, a dark squat shape beneath the canopy of stars, the Alamo.

The Alamo! And the men who surely peered into the

darkness and wished him through the flames. Each one of them. Andrew and Buckland and Kevin. Each grief and triumph, each hope, each past, each future. They were with him, him and the man named Smith who had gone out on foot. Identical messages. The diversion might have helped, but there was no way to know with certainty. True had to get through. Had to. Wishing he had the light racing tack he'd used so often in the past, he leaned forward. "Come on, Firetail. This is it, boy. Run!"

The hammerhead's ear flattened and his stride lengthened. It wasn't even a race.

The ground sloped down again and dark tree shapes along a creek bed loomed out of the starlight. The dragoons had given up and slowed their beaten mounts minutes ago. True had quit looking over his shoulder. He was not running to escape now, but out of a sense of urgency. As hopeless as the Alamo's predicament seemed, the men there might still have a chance if he could get to Houston and return with help.

Clear cold water erupted around him. Running by instinct, Firetail took the creek and scrambled onto the opposite bank, hind legs digging in the soft earth, breaking stride for only a few seconds before finding a semblance of a trail. True had enough presence of mind not to try to guide him, but to let him use his own eyes and instincts to fathom the night. Cautious now, though, he slowed to a fast lope and took stock; he must rest the great stallion for the long run ahead. His hand hurt where he had burned it, his right arm, too, where something had cut him. His right thigh was warm with blood, but the wound was slight and didn't need caring for immediately. The trick now was to relax, to save his strength for the days . . .

The limb stabbed out of the dark, plucked him from the saddle and hurled him savagely to earth. True at first thought he was still astride the horse, but then felt twigs and stones digging into his back. "Not too bad," he thought, sitting up, relieved that he wasn't hurt. "Lucky it wasn't too . . . Ahhhhh!"

A white-hot coal of pain exploded inside his skull. Eyes bulging, throat tight in a silent scream, True felt the world slip away from him, and he rolled over and lay as if dead.

Chapter XXXIX

Mila Kania listened to the sky rumble a warning.

Rain again. Please, no more rain.

"Our Father who art in heaven . . ."

Poor proud Buckland. Man of God. But which God? Lord of peace? Lord of wrath? Was this blasphemy?

". . . hallowed be Thy name. Thy kingdom come. . . ."

Here, now, forever. A kingdom of endless journeying. Of death close at hand, the hound of death bringing us to bay. A kingdom of mud and numbing chill. Of hope and despair . . .

". . . Thy will be done. . . ."

Try to believe that. Try to want it. What I want is my husband. . . .

"Oh, Buckland, Buckland! . . ."

A hand touched her. An arm embraced her. Unseen, Elizabeth had climbed into the wagon for a visit and to offer comfort. "Let's pretend we're not afraid," she said.

Mila was wrapped in a blanket. Only her eyes and nose showed. "That's easy to say." Her nose was bright red with the cold and her eyes were dark and hollow with fatigue. "How do we begin?"

Elizabeth sneezed, and wiped her nose with a rag she kept up her sleeve. "Excuse me. All this interminable wetness. Maybe we'd be better off pretending we were dry and warm."

The wagon jolted sharply to the left. Mila lifted a corner of the canvas. "We're off the trail, I think." Her eyes clouded with panic. "What's happening? Are they back there again? Why don't they leave us alone? Why don't they just go away . . . go away. . . ."

"Hush," Elizabeth crooned, wrapping her arms around Mila and rocking her as she would a child. "We're just heading south across country. Nothing to worry about. Joseph and Scott think we should have come across General Houston's camp by now. They think we're too far north.''

They could hear the wagon wheels sucking in the mud. The Conestoga bounced and rocked violently. Mila let Elizabeth hold her. ''I should have stayed,'' she finally said in a tiny, flat voice. ''Buckland might have come looking. He was so proud of his church.''

''We all were,'' Elizabeth said gently. ''He'll build another.''

''No he won't.''

''Of course he will.''

Mila suddenly pushed Elizabeth away from her, crawled on all fours as if trying to escape. When she reached the rear of the wagon, she turned like an animal at bay to face Elizabeth again. The blanket had fallen from her head. The tendons in her neck stood out like hemp cords strung taut, her eyes blazed with fury, and her mouth contorted in a gorgon's mask. ''He's dead, don't you see? He's dead, damn it! Dead!''

The blood left Elizabeth's face. She could feel goosebumps prickling her arms. Her skin tingled. ''What?'' she whispered, shocked.

''Buckland is dead,'' Mila repeated.

''Mila, you can't—''

''I can. He is!'' The fight suddenly left her voice and she sagged back onto her heels. Her hands lay open and lifeless on her lap. ''He is, Elizabeth. I've known for a couple of days.''

''You need to rest.''

''We all need to rest. Rest won't bring him back, though.'' Mila's hands started to move. Slowly, rhythmically, she rubbed them up and down her thighs. ''The funny thing is, I can't cry. Maybe I will later. I was sleeping, and then I was awake. I knew he was dead. How he died I don't know, but he was dead. At first I thought I was dreaming, but then I knew I wasn't. He stood there and watched me for the longest time. I saw him as clearly as I see you now.'' She seemed to become aware of the movement of her hands, and clasped them together. ''I'm not mad, Elizabeth, so don't be frightened. He was saying goodbye.''

''Mila . . .''

''He said I was to live.'' She twisted the gold band on her finger, saw in it an empty distorted vision of an uncertain future. ''Live for us both, and not to be afraid . . .''

Elizabeth sneezed again. Her throat felt raw. Water dripped through a hole in the canvas onto her shoulder. She was beginning to believe Mila, and belief worried her. If Buckland was dead, then what of True?

Mila had slumped forward. Elizabeth helped her back to the pallet, and pulled the cover over her again. A moment later, Mila was asleep. Still thinking of True, Elizabeth absent-mindedly pulled another quilt out of the trunk, tucked it around the sleeping woman, and crawled out the front to take her place beside Scott on the driver's seat.

Inside, Mila curled into a tight ball underneath the bright patchwork colors. Buckland was dead and she was alone. In her dreams, days passed and fragments of eternity spun into deep abysses. She did not know it, but she was crying.

Traveling east and south, they left the prairies and entered, once again, the deep woods of east Texas. The world behind the slate gray curtains of rain that preceded and followed them was a wagon-rutted trail closed in on either side by dense growths of rain-blackened trees, mostly pine but with a smattering of beech, magnolia, hickory, and oak. It was a world of wet, bitter winds and cheerless skies, of sodden red mud that clung to feet, horses' hooves, and wagon wheels alike, of cold meals uncaringly cooked over reluctant fires and consumed in the confines of the canvas-topped Conestoga prairie schooner.

Scott and Mackenzie rode rearguard in the buckboard. In the lead, the Conestoga carried Joseph, Lottie and Bethann, Mila, Joan and the girls, and Elizabeth. Tethered to the wagon gates were the horses, heads bowed like mules as they plodded forward on weary legs. No one talked. Energy was a precious commodity not to be wasted.

Joan, Ruthie, and Dianne sat in a line across the back of the wagon and stared dully out the rear. Elizabeth sat propped against a trunk of provisions and watched Lottie and Bethann sleep. Bethann stirred as the wagon jostled to one side, dipped precariously, and righted itself. Elizabeth leaned forward automatically to adjust the baby's blanket and let her hand linger to touch the tiny girl whose dark hair and broad, happy features resembled her father's. Bethann blew a little bubble at the corner of her mouth and snuggled up against her mother. Elizabeth sighed and pulled her hand away. When the wagon lurched again, she shifted to one side so the latch of the trunk wouldn't dig into her back, adjusted the blanket she had wrapped around her shoulders, and returned to her reverie.

She had been considering names, repeating to herself those she might choose for her own children. The world was full of names. More names than she could remember or had even heard or read. But children? There were never enough children. Without children and the joy they took and gave to balance the grief and harshness of the world, how dreary life would be. Even drearier than now, she mused, hearing the patter of the rain on the canvas increase to a dull roar. The temperature hadn't changed, but the change in the sound made her shiver. Her hands were shaking, her teeth chattering. Her forehead was beaded with perspiration that she repeatedly had to wipe away. Her throat was scratchy, her chest and joints ached dully. Her fever was worse, and she wondered how long she could hide it from the others.

Names. Think of names.

Joseph, Andrew, Mackenzie, Dennis, Scott. Buckland, Nels, Thomas or Tom, Kevin. Maurice, of course. Or True. True, Jr. Vance, of course, for her grandfather Vance Michaelson. Vance was a good name. And didn't True have an uncle named Stewart? Or Thomas, like his father. Thomas Gunn. A strange name, but somehow nice. And what about girls? Lottie, Ruth, Joan, Eustacia. Sarah? She liked the name Sarah. It was from the Bible. A pretty name, Sarah. "Sarah?" she called in a whisper. "Sarah, come to Mama, dear."

She willed her hands to stop shaking. They complied for a moment, but only so long as she watched them and held them clasped together. When she lifted one to wipe the perspiration from her forehead, she could feel it trembling. Outside, the heavy downpour slackened once again into its usual monotonous patter.

Sunshine would be nice. What she wouldn't give for sunshine! Or doing something different—anything. Wistfully, she remembered the day in November when all of Agradecido had gotten together to butcher and make soap and sausage. The day had been brisk but sunny. She had been in charge of the soapmaking, and could smell the sweet leaf fat as it rendered next to the vat of sharp smelling lye dripping from the trough filled with wood ashes. That had been nice. Hard work, to be sure, but better than just sitting and hurting.

She could stand the inactivity no longer. Groaning, she threw off the blanket and forced her arms into her slicker.

"Joseph," she said, shoving aside the canvas flap and poking out her head. Joseph was drenched to the bone. His clothes were plastered to his skin. His hat was a sodden, misshapen excuse for headcover. The brim dangled like a flap of paper over his ears and eyes. It appeared not to matter, for the mules held to the muddy trail without direction. When Joseph gave a start, Elizabeth realized he'd been dozing. "Sorry," she said contritely.

" 'S'all right," he mumbled, managing a smile. "I thought for a moment it was one of the mules. I've spent enough time talking to them that it made sense they were starting to talk back."

"Come on in and rest. It's terrible out here."

"I'm fine," he insisted.

"You're asleep on your feet—or whatever."

Joseph straightened and shook his head. Water flew from his hat and sprayed Elizabeth. "Not now. Wide awake."

"Don't be stubborn, Joseph. You've already ridden out here more than your share of the time." Elizabeth crawled out, and arranged the slicker underneath her before she sat. "C'mon. Give me the reins."

"Can't get any wetter, the way I see it." He pushed his face close. "You look like hell. Get back inside. A few extra hours don't matter."

"They do to me," Elizabeth said, taking the reins from him. "Besides, I don't look any worse than you do." The reins were icy cold except where his hands had warmed them. "Go on, now. There are dry clothes inside."

"And you call me stubborn," Joseph said, suddenly yawning widely. "Well, suit yourself. Just a few minutes, though." He crawled over the seat, turned to shake the water from his hat before taking it inside. A moment later his head reappeared. "One little thing," he said, stifling another yawn, and kissed her on the cheek. "That's for bein' game."

Alone again, Elizabeth turned up the collar of her slicker, and lowered her head. *Names. Think of names. Matthew, Mark, Luke, John. Peter. Paul . . . Jesus. The Mexicans use Jesus a lot, only they pronounce it "Hay-soos." Don't think it would sound right for True and me. . . . True . . . True . . .*

She had no idea how long she'd been sitting there when the squat, squarish shape swam out of the misty gloom. Blinking to clear her vision, Elizabeth realized she had been staring at it for several minutes before actually seeing it. The mules paid no attention, slogged on without a break in rhythm. Dappled patterns became walls and the outline of a roof became a cabin. Elizabeth pulled back on the reins and kicked on the brake. Behind her there was a startled grunt as the change woke Joseph. The wagon rocked slightly as he jumped to his feet, grabbed his rifle, and poked his head out the flap. "What's wrong?" he hissed in her ear.

Elizabeth pointed to the cabin, and heard Joseph's rifle click onto cock, just in case.

"Any movement?" Joseph asked.

"Nothing." Together they peered at it, searched the surrounding forest for signs of life. "No smoke, no horses."

"Looks like home to me." Joseph sounded pleased, then wary. "If we're lucky. Let's take a closer look."

Elizabeth eased off the brake and clucked to the mules. Only when they had come closer and rounded the side wall did they see that the cabin was nothing but two walls roofed with a handful of charred timbers. A mule snorted to her left. Elizabeth looked over and saw the buckboard move past her. Scott held up a restraining hand. A moment later he waved her forward and then to a stop in front of the remains of the cabin.

A clump of mounded earth lay just outside the stone front stoop. Elizabeth squinted and rubbed the water out of her eyes. She jumped from the wagon when she heard a muffled curse from Scott, and started toward him. "Go on back. It's nothing you need see."

She should have, but the words didn't register until too late. By the time her brain comprehended and her feet obeyed, she was standing at Scott's side and looking down at a pair of bodies, one tossed on top of the other, both riddled with torn holes, some of which sprouted broken-off arrow shafts. They had been man and woman, probably husband and wife. Both were naked and had been scalped. Both showed signs of hideous savagery, had been repeatedly slashed and mutilated. Bloodless, their skin was a dull gray white covered with an ever-changing pattern as the rain alternately splattered them with mud and washed them clean.

Elizabeth moaned. Her stomach heaved, then contracted violently when she heard the sound of vomiting.

Mackenzie was leaning out of the buckboard. "Pa. Pa!" he sobbed.

Why Elizabeth followed Scott she didn't know, but her feet

and legs moved automatically. A third mound, what had been a little girl of four or five years, was lying next to the fence. Her skull had been crushed against a post. She had not been mutilated, but left crumpled and lifeless by the gate.

"Dear God!" Joan gasped, pulling Ruthie and Dianne to her and holding them so they couldn't see. "Why? Why?"

"Comanches," Scott said to everyone and no one in particular. "They picked the right time, with everything else going on. Let's get out of here."

"No."

They all turned to see Mila standing over the bodies in front of the door. As they watched, she took off her cloak and draped it over the corpses. "It's plain to see we'll be safe for a while. We won't leave until we bury them." Her face was bloodless and tears streamed from her eyes, but her shoulders were straight and rigidly set. "Mackenzie. Stop blubbering. There's a shed back there. See if you can find a shovel. We'll put them—" She pointed to a small knoll. "—there."

Joseph, Scott, and Mackenzie were too embarrassed not to do her bidding. The women sat in the cover of the wagon while the men took turns digging. The job took over an hour, but at last was done, including a cross hacked out of the burned wood from the house.

"All of us in our lives have lost someone," Mila said when they had assembled around the muddy mounds of earth that held the unknown family. She closed her eyes and saw Buckland, hale and strong, standing in the sunlight. The image was so strong she wanted to run to him, but knew she couldn't. Her voice caught but she went on. "We don't know who they were, God. We don't know if they believed in You, what they thought, or anything really, except that they were here and they died and . . . and . . ." Her throat was swollen and burned. *Oh, Buckland, Buckland. Did you die this way too? Was it painful? Dear God, watch over him for me, please. I loved him so. . . .*

Scott left Joan's side, wrapped his arms around Mila and pulled her to him. Deep sobs wracked her body, and her cries were muffled against his chest. He looked around the small group, down at the fresh earth, up to the weeping sky. "We're going now, God. And if it's true that You look over every sparrow that falls, we know You'll look over these poor folks, and—" One great hand patted Mila's back, and he let his cheek rest for a moment on the top of her head. "—others . . . who have been taken too. Amen."

The charred cross was out of sight before they left the yard. Fighting back tears, Elizabeth stood and slashed the whip across the rumps of the mules. The wagon lunged forward. Joseph rode ahead to scout. Scott rode far to the rear for the same reason. Mackenzie followed in the buckboard.

Mud caught at the wheels, sloshed and spattered and smeared the canvas. The mules' feet sucked out of the mire with small plops almost lost in the creak of the wagon and the patter of rain on canvas. Rain lashed at her cheeks, stung her flesh like darting wasps. Rain drove away the images, washed her clean, drove her past and through the fever. A shape materialized on the trail ahead. Elizabeth sawed the reins, felt the wagon slide and lurch to one side as it stopped.

"All clear ahead as far as I can see," Joseph said. He got off his horse, tied the animal to the rear of the wagon, and climbed onto the driver's seat next to Elizabeth. "Let me have the reins. You go back in and dry off."

Elizabeth nodded, but instead of getting in back, climbed down from the wagon and stumbled toward the her horse. "Elizabeth?" Joseph called.

"I need to be alone for a minute," she answered, mounting.

"That trail is dangerous, damn it. You'd best . . ." He watched her ride past him, laid the reins to the mules. "Well, shit! Elizabeth!"

Elizabeth whipped the mare, put a gap between her and the Conestoga, then let the little bay slow to a walk. How much more, she asked herself, her brain buzzing. God was blind, God was deaf. God watched humankind and took no notice of its entreaties. Incensed, the dead lay in muddy graves with no one to cry out against the atrocities inflicted on them. Bewildered, the living begged for answers even as they stumbled through the maze laid down for them, turned the corners, encountered blank walls, turned and turned and turned until they were dizzy with confusion.

Lost. That's what we are. Moving around blind corners and in circles while death nips at our heels and pulls us down one by one. How much more before the price is paid? Another death? And another?

She sneezed, shivered so violently she almost fell off the horse. How could she be cold when her face burned so? Time passed unreckoned. The wagons behind her were forgotten, family and friends too. She was the sacrifice, and sacrifices could not afford attachments.

Lost, and the price of deliverance another death. One death more? Take me then. Will that be enough for a little while? One more death so the others can go free. Lottie has a child. The child is all that is left. I have none to leave behind. No one. So I will give her life. My life for hers. My life for hers.

Lightning was a mere flicker, barely perceived. Thunder in the clouds. Thunder speaks, is God's own angry utterance.

"Mine for hers!" Elizabeth shouted.

Bethann would be next, then all of them. Bethann, her skull shattered, pieces dripping from a fence post. It had to be stopped. Had to be.

"Mine for hers!" Her head was tilted to the lowering heavens. Her body swayed precariously in the saddle. Words pushed themselves up from her aching chest through her ravaged throat. "Mine for hers!"

"Who goes there?"

Elizabeth pulled on the reins. The mare danced skittishly before stopping.

"It's a woman," a second voice said.

Two men in homespun clothes and ragged slickers stepped warily from the safety of the trees. "You're 'sposed to ask for a password, idjet," the tall one said.

"Hell with the password, Lem. She ain't no goddamn Mex soldier."

"Looks crazed. What was she a'sayin'? Watch yerself, Harry."

The man named Harry gingerly approached the bay mare with the woman rider. His voice soothed the horse even as he caught her bridle. "Easy, now, girl. Easy, now. Whoa, whoa."

Elizabeth tried to think, tried to react. She shivered again, blinking her eyes. If only the hammering in her head would stop. Who was she looking for? Her husband, of course. "True?" she croaked. "Is that you?"

"What the hell, Lem?"

"Colonel Travis . . . he knows," she mumbled. "Take me to Colonel Travis."

Harry shot Lem a glance, signaled for him to take the far side of the mare. "Travis, ma'am?" he asked. "We're sentries, ma'am. Guardin' the camp over yonder." He jabbed a thumb over his shoulder. "Army of the by God independent Ree-public of Texas, Gen'ral Sam Houston commandin'. I'll take you over if you want."

Elizabeth shook her head doggedly. "Travis," she gasped. "My husband is with him. My husband, True . . ."

"Lord!" Lem said, his eyes widening. "She don't know."

"Shut up, Lem," Harry said. His narrow, scruffily bearded face glistened in the rain. "And help her down. This lady's sick."

"Know what?" Elizabeth asked, the world reeling. "Know what!?"

"Sure don't, ma'am. Now you let us help you down. . . . What the hell?" He peered back up the trail. "Christ, but it's more of 'em. A whole wagonload, I'll bet. What the hell we gonna do with more refugees?"

"Travis . . . True . . ."

"Travis is dead, ma'am," Harry said, his voice gently sympathetic. "More'n a week ago. Santa Anna stormed the Alamo. I'm sorry, ma'am, but there weren't no survivors. They died to a man. Now why don't you jest let us help you down. . . ."

He kept talking but Elizabeth only stared uncomprehendingly at him. *Dead? True? The others? All dead?*

"No," she moaned, protesting weakly. "No. . . ." Her hands were numb. She could feel them slipping from the saddlehorn but couldn't make them hold on. "No," she breathed. "No," and felt herself falling.

Rough hands caught her, cradled her with tender strength.

Elizabeth heard the storm, heard a voice hail the approaching wagon. Her head fell back and the world turned upside down. A raindrop hit her nose and she saw her father's eyes staring up at her.

And then she heard and felt nothing.

Chapter XL

She saw Joseph and Lottie.

Her chest ached terribly, and then felt as if someone had driven a nail into it.

She saw the Campbells.

Her eyes burned and she could barely swallow the warm broth they made her drink.

She saw Mila.

The buzzing sound in her head wouldn't go away. Her arms felt like lead.

She knew she was dreaming because she saw True, too.

Dreaming? Dying.

Death was the only reason. Fear for a moment, then calm and expectancy. True was waiting for her. He had come to stand at her side and wait for her. She would join him in a little while.

Soon, my beloved. Soon . . .

The cave was cold. The walls were wet with seepage and stone white, like skull fragments. She was on something soft, and covered heavily with blankets. There was a strange glow on the white walls. It looked like firelight reflected from water, and she concluded that she was surrounded by a pool at the base of a limestone column. A face peered at her from the shadows. It was her angel of death, it was her husband.

Soon, beloved . . .

The cave dissolved. Or did the pool expand? The shimmering surface lapped beneath her, lulled her insistently, until only the pool existed. Like the cave, the waters of the pool were cold. She could feel them where she lay. So cold.

Never been so cold.

The cave was gone but the waters remained. A blurred face

skimmed across her vision. Next to it, a flower. A rose as yellow as the sun. Then it became a candle. Then the face again. True! Closer than ever before. She felt his hands under the covers, his fingers fumbling with her gown and stripping it from her. The burning in her eyes wasn't important. She opened them in time to see the blanket pulled back. True was naked! Deep inside herself, she shivered as he lay down next to her and pulled the covers over them both. His flesh was warm against hers. His arms felt like hot bands around her.

Death was warm!

That was a surprise, to find warmth in death. Not the stygian iciness of silent sleep, but warmth! His arms were warm. His kisses were warm. His chest, his belly, his legs, all were warm. She could feel the heat passing from him to her, entering her body, seeking the cold and thwarting it.

Hold close sweet death angel. Hold me while I sleep.

And now heat! Heat! Was she awake? Awake, asleep . . . it didn't matter. She was hot. Hot! Burning! Wildly, she kicked at the covers, tried to throw them off but his hands restrained her, calmed her. His lips touched hers. Cool, now, they comforted her. His hands were cool too now, draining the maddening heat from her neck, her breasts, her stomach. She was drenched. Her eyes burned again, salt burn from sweat. A weight pressed against her chest. She was in a giant vise that pinched her with poker-hot steel fingers.

And now he was gone! Her angel of death was gone! In terror she fought the blankets, fought the cool hands and towels pressed to her body. Someone lifted her, placed her on coolness which quickly became as hot as her body. Voices murmured worriedly. Faces appeared and disappeared with a rapidity she didn't understand. She wanted her angel of death. Why had he left her? If the others would only go away and leave her alone, perhaps he would come back to lie with her with his warm hands and his cool hands and his gentle kisses. She tried to tell them this but they wouldn't listen. Suddenly, she was weeping bitterly, bitterly. It was too much. The strength drained from her and an enervating lassitude stole through her. She felt herself slipping, slipping into sleep. Sleep so deep . . .

Metal rang on metal, the unmistakable rhythm of a hammer on a horseshoe. Slowly, Elizabeth woke and found herself staring at row upon row of branches laced with vines. She was lying in a lean-to. Flames danced in a fire pit to her left. A blanket covered the broad opening. A plate of beans and cornbread sat on a board placed next to her pallet. A cup of coffee, still steaming, was at its side. Slowly, she took stock of herself. Her eyes no longer burned. She was dry, not too hot, not too cold. She wore a gown, her own from the look of the sleeve, though she didn't remember putting it on. She felt weak, and but for a dull ache in her chest, well enough.

She was alive. Strangely detached, mildly curious. Where was she? What had happened? How long had . . . ? The dream. Frowning slightly, she worked to recall the dream. As she did, a great sadness swept through her. True had been there at her side. She had asked him to wait for her, told him she would be along in a little while. He had been so near, but then to survive and wake . . .

Light flooded the lean-to. Elizabeth let her head fall to the side in time to see a man, his face obscured in shadow, duck under the blanket and enter. Scott? Joseph? She closed her eyes again. It didn't matter. It wasn't her angel, the one and only one she wanted.

"Your eyes were open. Are you awake?"

It isn't! It can't be!

Her joints felt as if they had turned to molasses. She could hear her heartbeat in her ears. She didn't dare look . . . was terrified . . . couldn't help looking. . . .

He was kneeling by the pallet and staring at her. Except for a new white scar on his forehead, he looked much the same. Leaner, perhaps. A little older, maybe.

"True? . . ." She felt the tears filling her eyes. Felt the weight of the blanket against her body. The smoke from the fire was sharp in her nose, the beans and coffee smelled like ambrosia. She could sense the air filling her lungs, the blood pounding in her veins. She blinked to clear her vision, but everything was blurred. She blinked again, and when she opened her eyes his face was closer, coming closer, blotting out everything else, filling the world with love. "Oh, True," she whispered. "Oh, True . . ."

And then his lips were against hers, and there was nothing more she needed or wanted to say. He was there, he was real. Nothing more was necessary.

She woke to darkness and the sound of insects. For a while she lay without moving, just savoring being alive. That afternoon she had eaten ravenously and then fallen asleep immediately. Now she opened her eyes to see True sitting crosslegged beside the pallet and dozing. The second she moved her hand, his head snapped up and he was staring intently at her. "Awake?" he asked.

"Mmm-hmm," Elizabeth said, watching him.

"Something wrong?"

"No." She found herself smiling. "I'm still afraid, I guess."

"Of what?"

"That it isn't really you."

True grinned, shifted to a kneeling position, and poured a tin cup full of water. "It's me. Here. Drink."

She drank slowly, enjoying the taste of the water and the feel of his hand steadying hers. "Tastes good," she said when she'd finished. She lay back and looked at the ceiling. "Did it stop raining?"

"For a little while. Wouldn't surprise me if it started again any minute."

How long was I . . . sick?"

True started to answer, then stopped. A faraway look came into his eyes and he wet his lips. "Not as long as I was."

Elizabeth tensed, had enough presence of mind to give him time.

"It's not something I want to talk about again, maybe ever, but I have to say it, Elizabeth." His eyes closed and he swallowed hard. Tears squeezed out the corners of his eyes and ran down his cheeks, and he could barely speak. "I knew you didn't enjoy it, Elizabeth. I knew all along, but seeing you there, and him, I . . . I . . ."

A lump burned in his throat and he had to fight to get out the words. "But there's knowing, and there's knowing. It had to be worse for you, him . . . doing . . . that. . . . But you got to understand . . ."

She was holding his hand, cupping it to her face, filling his palm with tears.

". . . that for a man . . ."

"Shhh, love, shhh . . ."

". . . for a man to see that . . ."

"Shhh. Oh, True, True. You've said enough. . . ."

"I love you, Elizabeth. I love you more than anything in this world, I love you."

"True, True, True . . ."

A thousand repetitions. She could have sung his name a million times. Each heartbeat, each breath! Never such wild—such strangely soft and tender—exhilaration! She kissed his hair, raised his face to hers and kissed his lips and cheeks and eyes, kissed away his tears—his tears! Kissing and laughing. Laughing outrageously. Too much happiness for one person! "Oh, True," she gasped at last, lying back and looking up at him watching her, at the curious, puzzled, faintly comic look on his face.

"Oh, True, True." The laughter stopped, and in its place was more love than she thought any one woman could ever bear to hold at once. "Do you have any idea," she asked, barely able to speak, "how happy it makes me to be your wife and friend and lover?"

The fire had burned down, but it didn't matter. Together they lay, almost like children, her head on his shoulder, his arms around her. "True?" she asked.

"Mmm?"

"You never answered my question."

He sat up groggily, slid off the pallet, and stirred the fire to a bright blaze. "What question?"

"How long was I sick?"

"Oh. That question. Well, today's the twenty-third of March. You and the others ran into us a little west of here on the seventeenth. You've been pretty well out of it since then. We, ah—" He took her hand and held it. "We had to take you along with us. You gave me quite a scare. I was pretty worried there for awhile."

"Pneumonia?"

True nodded.

"When I was fourteen, a lady two farms away died of pneumonia. There wasn't anything anyone could do. Are the others okay?"

"Everyone is fine. Bethann had a little cold, but she got over it."

"Thank God. I remember worrying about Bethann, thinking she would be . . ." She trailed off, found another subject. "You have a scar."

"My wound." True laughed. "Which, my lady—" He laid her hand on the covers and took the lid off the pot he'd carried in earlier. "—I will tell you about while you eat. Part of the Mex army is right across the river from us. You need to build up your strength. No telling when we'll be moving again.'' He ladled something onto a plate, set it by the pallet, and helped her into a sitting position. "This is stew. Joan fixed it and I promised her you'd eat every bite." He placed a board on her lap, set the bowl of stew on it, and handed her a spoon.

"I got to San Antonio about a half hour before Santa Anna's advance did. They'd gone right past our place, I guess, without us or anyone else knowing the difference." The story unfolded; the attack, saving the Thatches, Firetail so winded True had feared for the stallion's life. Elizabeth finished the stew, handed him the bowl, and received a cup of honey-sweetened tea in its place.

"At any rate, Travis sent me and another man out on the night of the third with messages for Houston and others. I was worried about Firetail but we made it through the lines. It didn't take long, but that ride was holy hell. I almost made it, though."

He pointed to a scar on his forehead. "The last thing I remember is riding along a creek, and then I came to sometime before morning and didn't have any idea of where I was or what I was doing. My head hurt like blazes and I was too sick to do anything but hole up for a day and a night. The next morning I was trying to figure out what to do next when darned if that stallion didn't come back looking for me. A beautiful sight to see, especially since the place was crawling with Mexicans. We stayed there another two days. On Sunday the sixth, all hell broke loose. I could hear cannon, see a lot of smoke. Ran out of food that night, too. By Tuesday morning I figured I had to do something, so I tossed a blanket around me for disguise and rode into San Antonio."

He paused and poured himself some coffee. "It was all over with. Had been Sunday afternoon. Mama Flores put me up in a back room and told me what happened. Then Wednesday afternoon I went to the mission, what was left of it, for a look."

Eyes unblinking, face expressionless, True stared into the fire. "All that was left . . . was bones. . . . The Mexicans had built a pyre of alternating stacks of logs and bodies and set it afire. It was still smoldering. The stench made me throw up. Nothing but blackened skulls and bones like broken sticks. Travis in all his glory. Nels, Kevin, Dennis, Buckland . . . I found Buckland's Bible. Mila has it now. There was a letter to her in it. . . ."

"The only survivors, the only ones they hadn't slaughtered, were Captain Dickinson's wife—all the other women had left earlier, but she'd stayed—and a slave. Everyone else was dead. Every last soul. No quarter, they said. I knew then what that bugle call meant. Worst of all was Andrew. So young, part of that pyre. So full of life . . . that way he had of grinning like the world had been created for his amusement . . . Christ! Kind of takes the wind out of your sails, finding out that your little brother is dead. Like the order of things had gotten fouled up somehow. Anyway . . ." He poured the dregs of his coffee on a smoldering log, watched them boil away. "There was nothing else to do but try to find Houston's army. I had a map Travis had given me. It made the going a little easier. Ran into some Mexican families along the way. They were fugitives too. I brought them with me." His eyes found hers. "I joined Houston the day before you did."

Elizabeth waited, but he seemed to be finished. She set aside the board she had been using as a tray and lay back down. "They . . . You heard about Hogjaw?" she asked.

True nodded. The firelight played on his face, shifted its planes and angles and curves. "That old man," he said in a low, soft voice. "Joseph told me. When he did, the map you were carrying made sense." His face hardened. "Another debt to be accounted for."

"Debt?" Elizabeth asked, worried. There had been a dangerously disconcerting timbre to his voice, one she had hoped not to hear again. "I don't want to lose you, True. When I thought you were dead, part of me died. Now you're here and we're together again. I don't think I could stand . . ." She turned away and blinked rapidly, trying not to cry.

"I meant what I said earlier, Elizabeth, but that was between you and me. This other is between me and them. I can't let it rest where it is. I can't let it go at that, Elizabeth."

"Of course you can! There's no need to . . ."

He was staring at her. His face was divided, one eye in firelight, the other in darkness. It might have been the sickness that gave her such clarity, but she was seeing True—and herself—as she hadn't been able to before. The darkness was stubbornness, the stubbornness that had sent him to Mexico. The darkness was that malignant, base part of him that lurked in every man no matter how noble. The division of light and dark was the division of themselves that she dreaded even more than physical separation. Mila and Buckland were an example of that. Buckland was dead and Mila alive, but they were still together in a very real sense: much more than True and Elizabeth had been for the last months.

It was up to her. The choice was hers. A man and a woman came together. They married, made love, bore and raised children. They grew, became part of one another, or shrank into themselves and lived mean and petty lives of dissatisfaction and regret. Outside of running away or death itself, there were no other choices, and in that one moment, she knew she had to make hers.

She loved True. No other man she had met fit her so well. He was strong, he was capable, he was intelligent. She had seen him play with and teach Tommy Matlan and the Campbell girls: she knew she wanted no other man to raise her children. He was a hard worker, a good provider. He stood ready to defend her, his friends, and what he believed in, and would never shrink from doing so, no matter the danger. And she? In her heart, she knew she was worthy of him as he was of her. She had traveled the long road from Pennsylvania. She had risen above the ugliness with her father, not fallen prey to the weaknesses of her mother. She too was strong and capable and intelligent. She was tough, a good worker, a good housekeeper. It was not unseemly pride, but confidence and surety that told her he would never find a better woman to bear and raise his children. She too stood ready to defend, and would never shrink back. Life was not meant to be easy. It never had been, and most certainly not in toubled times or in untamed lands. Life demanded that one struggle to survive and build in the face of the ultimate realities one must finally accept. Life demanded joy in the process. Life demanded not a slavish condoning, but a reasoned compromise. Two people did not become one person. They remained individuals who saw past each others' frailties, ghosts, and hobgoblins without rancor, and gave of themselves withal. If this was a dark and troubled time for True, her own such time would come, and she did not doubt that he would stand by her.

All this was love. Without it, life would be a fruitless search through a succession of mates. Without it, the trembling in her loins, the fire in her veins, the tears in her eyes when he came to her, was a petty charade any two people could play. With it, a third entity composed of two singular individuals was born. With it, loneliness was held at bay and defeated. With it was life in the deepest, absolute meaning of life.

The choice was hers.

"Listen to me, will you," she said. The tension in her voice was gone and she was at peace with herself. "Oh, True. I love you so much. Tomorrow you will do what you have to do, and I will face it with you. Tonight, True, come to me, please . . . now. . . ."

Only slowly did the anger in his eyes abate, and his face soften. He seemed hesitant, unsure of himself. "Are you sure you're . . . ready?" he asked, more of himself than of her, though not admitting it.

Elizabeth held out one hand to him, pulled back the covers with her other. Her gown was open at the top to reveal one breast, and had ridden in a tantalizing manner to her waist. "I have never felt more ready," she said, with a strength he found surprising. "And you?"

True stared at her. For a moment, a slight frown creased his forehead, but then he felt a smile spread over his face. Slowly, he stood and stripped off his shirt, kicked off his boots, and stepped out of his trousers. Life stirred in him, and he knew he was whole again. "Never more ready in my life," he said at last, his voice husky with love and desire. "In my whole life."

Chapter XLI

They were tired, they were wet, they were hungry, they were angry. Part of Santa Anna's army—some of the self-same men who had massacred the patriots in the Alamo—sat a mile away from them across the Colorado River, and they itched to fight. When their general refused, they whispered of mutiny and dubbed their campaign the Runaway Scrape, for running was what they seemed to do best. Not two days after Elizabeth's fever broke and she began to recuperate, word came that Colonel James Walker Fannin's forces had been defeated at Coleto. General Sam Houston, a mountain of a man and rugged as stone, held firm against the hotheads who wanted instant revenge. His ragtag army was all that stood between Santa Anna and the Republic of Texas, so he gave the order to retreat that they might fight another day when the odds were better. That night, they decamped and struck out across country thirty miles to the Brazos River. Hundreds of terrified and suddenly unprotected settlers, white and Mexican alike, struggled through the mud and rain in their wake.

Even then the running wasn't over. They were on the move again a day later, this time north along the flooding Brazos. The army was in a state of near mutiny. Houston's fourteen hundred shrank to less than nine hundred as soldiers deserted to save their families. Wagons had to be unloaded and half driven, half floated across swollen streams and gullies. Livestock drowned in fierce currents. Wagons by the dozen were abandoned in quagmires. Food was scarce: what could be found and half cooked was cold and unpalatable. On the morning of the first of April, they were camped on high ground at Groce's Crossing, twenty miles north of San Felipe, and surrounded by water that had risen during the night. It was apparent they would be there for some time, but if anyone had thought about rest, he was sadly disillusioned. The rain persisted. An epidemic of measles broke out. Colds, influenza, and diarrhea affected everyone to one degree or another. Only Houston had any idea of what Santa Anna was doing or where his scattered armies were, and Houston wasn't saying.

What Houston was doing was buying time and organizing. Jared Groce's plantation supplied food. His house was stripped of lead pipes which were turned into shot. What was left of the once magnificent structure became a hospital for those stricken with measles. Many of the women helped there, along with a Medical Corps Houston shaped out of the two or three doctors he found and the men who weren't fit to fight but could help in other ways. At the same time, the army began to grow again as new blood joined it. Houston was tireless. New units were formed, new lines of command instituted. The army grumbled but settled down to work in earnest when grim news reached them: after Fannin's defeat at Coleto, he and virtually all his men had been massacred at Goliad and burned. The debt was growing. The men lived for revenge. Santa Anna's soldiers were perfidious heathens and needed killing.

Life became a succession of dull, rainy, muddy days. The women established their own camp, spent the majority of their time cooking, making bullets or bandages, and helping out in the hospital. The men drilled incessantly. Scott and Joseph were made sergeants, True a lieutenant. They saw their wives long enough to stare at them over a bowl of stew or gruel before falling into a stuporous sleep.

And then, suddenly, they were moving again. Two days were spent crossing the flooded Brazos, two more slowly moving south along refugee-crowded roads that were ankle-deep in mud. An air of expectancy raced through the mud-caked camp on Saturday night. Before morning, everyone knew. One of Santa Anna's aides had sent a derisive message to Houston in which he revealed that Santa Anna himself was on his way to Harrisburg in an attempt to capture the provisional government of the newly formed Texas Republic. The letter was undoubtedly meant to draw them hither, but no one cared. Trap or no, the men smelled blood. And any one of them would have walked willingly into a cage full of wildcats for a chance to strike at Santa Anna.

Not often, in the annals of military history, has the march

that followed been equaled. Everyone helped—men, women, and children. Animals died of fatigue, fell and drowned in mud. Men literally lifted cannons out of the mud and carried them to the next solid stretch of road. Creeks, bayous, streams, gullies, and ravines all deep in water, blocked their way. They crossed each one with little more than raw courage and the strength of the driven. When it was over, they had marched fifty-five miles in two and a half days under impossible conditions. And only then, as if in recognition of their effort, did the rain stop. Few noticed. They were too exhausted.

The rest had done him good, the solitary walk even more. True stood high in a cottonwood that grew on the edge of Buffalo Bayou across from the town of Harrisburg. Across a hundred yards of open water, campfires winked and flared. The campfires of the Mexicans. Much the same as he had seen another night not long before. Not as vast as the army encircling the Alamo, but awesome all the same, for it was the cream of Major General Antonio Lopez de Santa Anna's army, the ones in whose number he hoped to find the man he sought, Luther O'Shannon. Four weeks had passed. Four weeks of running and hiding. Four weeks of retreat, and always retreat with no visible end in sight. Now there would be no more running, no more retreat, no more humiliation. They would fight. Houston had been right after all. The time was right, the place was right. The men were hardened and angry as hornets. They would fight with a ferocity that would overcome thrice their number. True would fight with one added incentive: Luther O'Shannon.

O'Shannon was there. True could feel his presence in his bones. The sensation struck him like a bolt of lightning. The skin on his arms and neck grew flush. His hair stood on end. O'Shannon was there. He had to be. How many yards away? Watching the dark woods, perhaps, at this very moment? Feeling True as True felt him? He hoped so.

The bark of the cottonwood was cool against his cheek. Frogs set up a din from the darkness below. Slowly, True climbed down from the tree and walked back through the woods, stole past the sentries using tricks Hogjaw had taught him, and found his way to the fire around which sat their little group, the Campbells, Joseph and Lottie and the baby, Mila with Buckland's Bible held close, and Elizabeth.

"Well?" Mackenzie asked as True materialized at Elizabeth's side.

"They're out there. You can see their fires."

"He'll have to let us get our licks in now," Scott said. "No way a lousy hundred yards of water are gonna keep us off their backs."

Elizabeth glanced from True to Joan, who shook her head in agreement. "I just wish I could be with you when it comes," the older woman said, thinking of Dennis.

"Changed your tune, haven't you?" Scott asked.

"You're damned right I have," Joan said. "Killing all those boys in cold blood . . . He deserves whatever he gets. Serve him right to have a woman shoot him, too."

"Maybe we'll just go over there and bring him back so you can," Mackenzie said. "If," he added with a sneer, "our Runaway General will give us leave."

"Mighty brave talk, son. For a boy," a deep voice rumbled from the darkness outside the light of the fire.

Mackenzie gulped, and choked on a swallow of coffee. "Oh, shit," he wheezed, jumping to his feet with the others.

A tall, buckskin-clad man, whose lot it was to lead the glorious, mud-caked remnant of the Texas army, stepped into the light. Sam Houston was making his rounds, as he did almost every night. Rarely did he stop by the individual encampments to seek the fellowship of his men. Rather he kept to himself and, behind those stony features that hid his thoughts, he evaluated the heart and soul of each man he beheld, as if gauging whether this one would stand and fight, this one run from powder smoke or bayonet. "Ladies," he said deferentially, touching his hat brim. "Hope you got some rest. And vittles."

"Yes, thank you," came the chorus of agreement.

Houston nodded to True. "Saw you come in. Reckon I'd better have a word with the sentries. It was my Cherokee blood that spotted you. Who taught you?"

"Hogjaw Leakey."

"Ah." Houston's head nodded up and down. "That makes you Paxton, then. Heard of you. Knew Hogjaw, these years past. Damned shame. A good man gone under."

"The best."

"He died fighting at least," Mackenzie snapped, bent on showing he wasn't afraid of Houston.

Steel-gray eyes hooked into Mackenzie like a barb in a

bluegill. "You'll get your chance to do the same, boy," the general growled. "But when it counts. Not before."

Mackenzie's insolence melted and he hung his head.

"His brother's death weighs heavy on him, General," Scott interceded.

"On us all," Joan added. She sat with her hands folded around a cup of coffee. The veins on the backs of her hands were dark scribbles underneath the skin. "It's hard, General, to know they're dead and not do anything about it."

Houston pursed his lips, sighed softly. "Not a man nor woman here but feels a loss, ma'am. We have to be strong enough to pick our time, though. There never was any sense in running off half-cocked."

"Nor was there ever sense in never going off at all," Joseph interjected, jabbing his thumb over his shoulder in the direction of Santa Anna's army.

"No, I reckon not." Houston locked eyes with Joseph, the only man around the fire who matched his height. A slow secretive smile played over his face. "But I wouldn't worry on that account, if I was you."

Bethann interrupted with a squawl. Lottie reached down quickly, picked her up, and began to jiggle her. After a loud burp, the squawl became a soft cooing sound and then a pleased giggle.

"That's the sweetest sound in this whole big ugly world," Houston finally said, his voice rumbling deep in his throat. A second later, he was gone as abruptly as he had appeared.

Houston's words never went unremarked. Every comment he made or was reported to make was grist for the rumor mill. The small group sat around the fire and eagerly dissected and analyzed everything he had said to them until, at last, Lottie yawned and took herself and Bethann off to bed. A moment later, Joseph followed. Joan and Scott soon said goodnight and went off to their wagon, which they had, miraculously, managed to keep through the long journey. Mackenzie slipped away at the same time to join some companions his own age and regale them with his recent confrontation with General Sam himself. True and Elizabeth sat chatting quietly across the fire from Mila, who was reading her Bible. The night was quiet and peaceful. Horses stirred, and nickered to one another. Frogs and insects chorused the coming of spring. Soft laughter and the voices of men at ease drifted across the open ground. Once, Mila turned a page and the hastily scrawled letter from Buckland fell out. She hurriedly picked it up and wiped it off before putting it back.

"He was a fine man," True said, reading her anguished thoughts. "But then, I'm not telling you anything you don't already know."

"It's nice to hear it," Mila said. "He loved you both. He loved God. And he loved Texas. Too much, perhaps."

"I don't think so," Elizabeth said, reaching to touch her arm.

Mila placed her hand over Elizabeth's and gave it a little squeeze. "Neither do I. Although I wish . . ." Her eyes misty, she closed the Bible and held it to her breast. "Someday," she finally said in a small voice, "when I'm . . . When I can . . . Someday I'd like to read you his letter. Right now, I think I'd like to try to sleep." Mila's voice broke and failed her. Weeping softly, she ran from the fire and, a moment later, crawled out of sight into the tiny tent they had found for her.

True and Elizabeth sat without touching each other, as if somehow embarrassed at being together when Mila was alone. Somewhere across the camp a voice swelled in a gentle, lilting ballad. Elizabeth hummed along quietly.

Love is the one you are silent with. Love is the silent moving stream that moves unhurriedly—there is time enough, always time enough—to reach the sea.

True's arm crept around her waist, drew her to him. "Yellow Rose," he said, his voice husky with emotion. "You are my Yellow Rose, Elizabeth."

Elizabeth craned her neck to look at him. "What did you see out there? You looked different. Less . . . I don't know what to call it. . . . less angry?"

"Maybe." He sounded lazy, half-asleep. "Calmer, I guess. Not less angry." A muscle in his arm twitched. "Because I know it'll be soon. So the waiting doesn't bother me any more. I can even enjoy it. You about ready for some sleep?"

"I guess."

Their house was a half-shelter pitched over a ground cloth, their pillows rolls of clothes, their bed three wool blankets they had managed to salvage. One by one, careful not to knock down the flimsy poles that held the shelter erect, they crawled in and arranged themselves. The blankets were warm after the moist night air, and Elizabeth was soon dozing, then sound asleep and dreaming of a rose bush consumed in flames, of thorns, spindly branches, green leaves, yellow blossoms turned black and charred. She woke with a violent jerk, lay trembling and breathing heavily.

True held her in the crook of his arm. "Nightmare?"

Elizabeth nodded. "I don't want to be alone like Mila," she finally said. "I don't, True. I don't."

"You won't be."

"Hold me, True? Just hold me?"

He turned onto his side, caught her hip with his free hand and pulled her to him. Their lovemaking was ardent and demanding, a fierce union, as consuming as love's first joining.

Or last.

Chapter XLII

Elizabeth woke to empty bedding. Sensing activity before she saw it, she hurriedly arranged her clothes and ran from the tent just in time to collide with True. Over his shoulder she could see the camp in an uproar, men clasping their wives close and hugging sleepy children. Her heartbeat quickened. "What's happening? Are we leaving?"

"Not you. Me."

"I don't understand."

"There was an early morning meeting. The women and children are to remain here. Houston's leading us to Santa Anna. This time we're not running."

Elizabeth had suspected as much from the very first. She could hear the weeping and the frightened moans of some of the women. She too wanted to hold her man, to keep him safely with her, to have him close. But pride and a sense of duty—and more, love—would not let her make a fuss. "You've forgotten the pistol," she said as calmly as she could, assessing his armament. She disappeared into their tent and came out with the weapon.

"I need three days' rations," True said. "I'll be drying powder while you get the food ready."

Two hours passed. The cannon had already been taken away to allow for a head start. The unmarried men, those who had nobody to say goodbye to, were beginning to form a rough marching order. Elizabeth stood by True and looked around, as if memorizing all she could see to tell those who came after her the price that was paid for the land they called Texas. Scott held a daughter in each arm and could not receive enough of their kisses. Mackenzie suffered embarrassment in his mother's embrace and tried to hide the emotion he felt as deeply as any man. Lottie cradled Bethann and wept against Joseph's chest. When he let her go and turned to leave, she followed him for three steps and then, cheeks streaked with tears, retreated to their tent. True held out his arms and folded Elizabeth in the cocoon of his embrace. "God, how I love you," he whispered.

Elizabeth could feel his pistol against her ribs, the scabbarded Arkansas Toothpick against her left hip. His rifle hung over his shoulder and knocked against the back of her hand when he bent to kiss her. "There will be coffee and a meal waiting for you when you return," she said, her lips numb from the pressure of his kiss. "No matter the time, no matter how long it takes, they will be waiting. You come back to me, True Paxton."

An hour later, when she could no longer make him out among the crowd of men that marched down the road along the side of Buffalo Bayou, she turned to the fire and put on the coffee. It was Wednesday, the nineteenth day of April.

General Luther O'Shannon rode at a distance of half a horse's length to the rear and three aides away from Santa Anna, and mused on the quality of intelligence *el Presidente* was forced to rely on. Earlier that morning they had thought Houston's army was headed for the United States border. The plan of action had been to capture the provisional government of the so-called Republic of Texas, then move quickly to cut off what was left of the rebel army. And now they found out that that same army was behind them! It was unconscionable. If he had his way, heads would roll.

A sour thought. Flush from victories at the Alamo and Coleto, prideful of his roughshod advance over practically all of the rebellion-wracked territory, Santa Anna had become his own expert. He had never said as much in so many words, of course, but O'Shannon could tell when his services were no longer needed. The process had been painstakingly simple. As Santa Anna's generals brought him more and more good news, he had listened less and less to O'Shannon. The next step was obvious. The other Mexican generals had always been jealous of the Irishman. Now that they were in the ascendancy they would drape the first failure they could find or manufacture over O'Shannon's shoulders. There was only one solution to that problem: to slip quietly away with what gold he could carry before he lost his head.

* * *

They'd had a rough night, but not a man complained. Marching along Buffalo Bayou through the afternoon, they'd crossed two and a half miles below Harrisburg, then turned back in the face of a norther and slogged through the cold, wet night. Midnight saw them wading Sims's Bayou, two o'clock picking their way over the bridge that spanned Vince's Bayou. By daybreak, they were encamped almost directly across from where they had started. They had spent half an afternoon and a whole night to make little more than a hundred yards that, in dryer times, they could have waded in half an hour.

Still, no one complained. Instead they laughed, joked, and bragged. They checked their powder and flints, swabbed out their rifles. They slaughtered a half dozen beefs and prepared a hearty breakfast. They listened with pricked-up ears and wide grins when the word was passed through the ranks: Santa Anna was coming to them.

By the time they finished eating, a scout came riding hard into camp. One and all, they ran out of the trees to the edge of the meadow and saw the sight they had been waiting for for nearly two months. Barely three hundred yards across the meadow, the short, squat Santa Anna sat his horse and looked back at them. Behind him, in battle array, his army waited his command.

True returned from reconnoitering and strode toward his brother's campfire. He noticed Joseph, Scott, and Mackenzie digging an embankment for themselves. "What the hell are you doing?" he asked, astonished. "I thought we were going to fight."

"Digging in," Joseph explained.

Mackenzie wiped a dirty forearm across his face. "Houston's orders," the youth said, almost in tears from frustration.

"What orders?"

"The word's been passed," Joseph said, angrily throwing a spadeful of earth. "We wait."

True rubbed the back of his neck and looked around in disbelief.

Wait . . . for what? No. Not now. Not so close.

The men continued to dig in the dark earth.

O'Shannon kept his face neutral, saluted smartly, wheeled about, and marched out of Santa Anna's tent. "We will wait

for General Cos,'' he snapped to an aide. ''Tell the men to
prepare a barricade along the edge of the meadow and then
eat. You!'' he barked at a diminutive figure who carried *el
Presidente's* opium pouch. ''He wants you. Now.''

The damned fool! O'Shannon withdrew to his own tent to
fume. There was no better time. The rebels were a misbegotten
outfit with no discipline. Ill-fed so-called soldiers with back-
bone but no training. The time to attack was that moment.
The hell with Cos. They didn't need Cos. What they needed
was a general willing to take a chance or two. The more
O'Shannon thought about it, the more he was sure. The first
opportunity he got, he was leaving. By sundown the next
day, he'd be gone.

''Bloody sit around with our fingers up our asses. What the
hell!''

''Heard that question a lot of late, 'what the hell.' ''

''Couple of boys drew blood this afternoon.''

''Not enough, goddamn it. Hell, that was just a skirmish. I
don't want no Mex scout. Santa Anna's the one I'll roast.''

''Stand in line, boyo.''

''Line, hell. We'll run again. You wait and see.''

''Bullshit.''

''A gold Eagle against the pimple on your ass says we will.
Any takers?''

''Wait, hell. Can't wait much longer.''

''Don't hear no one offering to take the pimple.''

''None of us. But I'll take half of that gold Eagle.''

True listened to the voices, the easy banter and never
ending grumbling that always accompanied an army. He closed
his eyes and tried to sleep, but the phrase echoed in his skull
and kept him awake.

Can't wait much longer. Can't wait much longer.

Noon. Afternoon, by the sun. Better if the rain had kept up.
They wouldn't be sleeping so soundly.

O'Shannon paced, kept a wary eye on the empty meadow.
Jesus, was he the only one in the whole damned camp with
sense enough to worry? It looked like it. *El Presidente* had
kept his men up all night waiting for an attack that never
came. O'Shannon had tried to tell him that all that riding
around out in the meadow and on their flanks was a rebel ruse
to keep them awake, but would he listen? Of course not. And

now his men were exhausted and he'd given them leave to rest along with Cos's five hundred who had arrived an hour earlier. While Santa Anna himself dreamed after his daily pipe of opium, to boot. Well, the hell with it. Let them sleep. He was going to pack while nobody was looking. There were always wars. He'd have no trouble finding work. A shame to leave Mexico, though. He had hoped to put down roots there. Had tried, even with a son.

The bitterness welled in his throat. The son who had been taken from him by True Paxton. Voices returned to haunt him with faint echoes. His eyes played tricks with his mind. The vision pulsed and cleared. Suspended in the air, Ramez was staring at him. Glistening red and white entrails spilled from his poor, broken abdomen and his shattered arm hung straight down to point at his father. Horror-stricken, O'Shannon shrank from the sight. "Not me," he breathed under the accusatory pointing fingers. "Not me. It wasn't my fault."

Miraculously, the hand moved, swung like a slow pendulum, and stopped at the rebel camp across the meadow. O'Shannon turned and stared across the open ground. Was that it? Could he believe the sign he'd been given? Of course. Paxton was there! It was improbable to be sure, but he was there, waiting, and would come to him.

Come to him to be killed, this time. His face grim, O'Shannon returned to his tent and entered. He could wait one more day, he thought, buckling on his saber. Meticulous, now, he removed his pistol from its case and began to check it thoroughly.

One more day. Not too long to wait to see a man sent to Hell.

Nothing. A few shots the afternoon before, but then nothing. Thick stands of trees on either side of the bayou obscured the view. Firetail whinnied and pulled at his ground tether. He sensed it too, Elizabeth thought. The sun was warm and dulled her senses, but she had promised to have hot coffee and a meal when he returned. She added water to the beans and stirred them. She moved the coffee pot a little further from the fire. And then, since there was nothing else to do, she sat back and waited.

"Bullshit."

"Too strong, my ass!"

The word had passed like wildfire. The men's faces turned red with anger. They cursed Santa Anna and the Mexicans, but mostly their own Runaway General. His orders stood. Santa Anna's army was too strong, especially with the arrival of its reinforcements. They were going to retreat. Again. True listened as the orders were explained, and then did a peculiar thing. He picked up his rifle and started to walk. "Now's as good a time as any," he said aloud.

He walked along the line of men lying behind the low earthworks they'd thrown up the morning before. "Going for a little walk," he told each of them. "You're welcome to come along if you want."

That word passed, too, as fast or faster than Houston's. By the time True had gone fifty yards, he met Joseph coming his way. "You really going?" Joseph asked.

"I am."

"Alone?"

"If need be."

Joseph thought about that and nodded. "Maybe I'll walk with you."

"Glad for the company."

"Wish Andrew was along."

"He is."

Joseph shouldered his rifle and stepped onto the earthworks next to True.

"Paxton," a man called from their rear. "Lieutenant Paxton. Gen'ral Sam wants to see you in his tent. *Pronto, amigo.*"

"Tell him to come to me."

"Huh? Where'll he find you?"

"Across the meadow. In Santa Anna's camp."

True and Joseph started. Before they'd gone three steps, men began to join them at the edge of the line of trees that had sheltered them. Two men became four, and in like manner became ten, twenty, a hundred, eight hundred.

The line paused just in the shade of the trees. Before them lay three hundred yards of open ground, then a barricade of wagons and logs behind which rested the Mexican army enjoying its *siesta*.

"How the hell do we cross it?" someone whispered.

"One step at a time," came the answer. It was Sam Houston on his white charger. The General had a sly look on his face.

Still they waited. To True's left, the cannon crews were

wheeling out their weapons. Past them, the line kept moving
for a moment before it stopped. True stared at the Mexican
camp, saw in his mind Luther O'Shannon's humiliating, sneer-
ing face just out of reach. He stared at the camp and saw
Andrew and Buckland, saw Kevin and Nels and Dennis and
all the others, all the others become a mound of charred
bones.

"Go on, boy," he heard a voice say, and swore it was
Hogjaw. He glanced up, saw a hawk circling far overhead.
He stared at the camp.

"Remember the Alamo! Remember Goliad!"

Ten yards crossed, now twenty. A murmuring force, eight
hundred strong. All the pent-up frustration and bitterness and
anger and rage had been unleashed at last and now walked
through the sun across the flower-flecked meadow.

"Remember the Alamo!" Louder now. No power on earth
could stop them now.

Fifty yards, now a hundred. Still not seen! Almost to a
man, they were suddenly running forward, a storm of vengeance and hatred breaking over the land. They were seen.
The alarm was raised. Halfway there! The sentries began to
panic and run!

"Remember . . ."

Almost, now. They could see the enemy's faces, drawn
and haggard. See them stumble and run.

". . . the . . ."

Almost, almost! Rifles were leveled. Knives unsheathed.
Now! Now!

". . . Alamo!!"

A roar erupted from eight hundred throats. A wild, hideous, bloodthirsty warcry and the rippling explosion of rifle
fire rent the afternoon.

The horde poured over and through the barricade. Dazed
sentries died rubbing sleep from their eyes. Men scrambled
from under blankets and out of tents. Half-dressed, in stocking feet, weapons stacked out of reach, the foot soldiers
watched in horror and then ran in terror from the flashing
guns and knives and axes as the rebels charged into the
slumbering, peaceful Mexican camp. Lancers died reaching
for their lances. Cavalrymen raced for their horses, slashed
the tethers, mounted bareback, and then fought their plunging
beasts as they tried desperately to control the animals.

Filled with his own bloodlust, True leaped a barrel and a

stack of saddles. A man loomed up in front of him and leveled his musket. True shot him, paused to reload. Texians swarmed him. The gunfire and shouting was deafening. A lancer ran at him. True sidestepped, parried the thrust with his rifle, twisted his hands, and drove the butt into the man's throat. A rifle ball plucked at his sleeve. He fired at a naked soldier standing awestruck in the door of a tent, then quit trying to reload and used his gun like a club.

All sense of order was lost. Pandemonium ruled. The Mexican officers barked commands to stand, to form lines, to fight, but the soldiers ran.

True's rifle broke. He threw it away and used his pistol, fired, loaded, fired again on the run.

"Me no Alamo! Me no Goliad!" came the screams, the pleas for mercy.

A soldier charged True. Another rebel shoved True aside, caught the soldier's bayonet in the chest, and fired his own pistol. The two men collapsed in a embrace of death. On his knees, True caught a glimpse of Houston leaping from his dying horse and onto a loose pony. Barely pausing, the general wielded his bloody saber, hacking from side to side, felling soldiers whether they stood and fought or turned to run.

The battle passed him by. True ran to catch up, stopped to help a fellow Texian surrounded by three Mexicans and fighting for his life. A tremendous roar deafened him, almost knocked him off his feet again. He turned to see one of the Mexican cannons that had been swiveled about and fired into a compact group of Mexican regulars trying to form a skirmish line. Grapeshot ripped through the troops, shredding arms, legs, and torsos.

A musket ball carved a furrow in True's left forearm. He aimed and killed his attacker with a shot to the head. The dead man tumbled into a cook fire. A cauldron of chili tipped over and spread its greasy contents over ground already moist with blood.

The battle had disintegrated into small fights involving a half dozen men at most. True evaded one encounter, avoided a second by ducking through an open tent. No more than five minutes had passed, and already the Texians had won the day. It was time to search for the one man he knew had to be there. For Luther O'Shannon.

The Irishman had seen the handwriting on the wall by the

time the initial charge had carried the barricade. Single-mindedly, he had fought his way back to his tent. The rebels were mad, of course, attacking in broad daylight, but he had to admit there was purpose to their madness and further, that they were going to win. Already, a melee swirled around his tent. He hacked his way through, and ducked inside to get his saddlebags. No sooner had he pulled them from under his bedroll than the tent flap ripped open and a Mexican in an officer's uniform stumbled in. The front of the officer's uniform was stained crimson. His throat had been slashed. Dying, he fell forward onto O'Shannon, who thrust the corpse aside just as a rough-and-tumble Indian fighter leaped into the tent.

"Remember the Alamo!" the Texian yelled. His eyes wild, his beard matted with gore, his dagger red to the hilt, he charged.

O'Shannon dodged the man's knife thrust and shot him in the face. Before the rebel hit the floor, the Irishman was crawling under the back of his tent, and looking for his horse.

True staggered through the dust and stumbled over corpses. The stench of death filled his nose, the awful sounds his ears. Rifle fire and tearing flesh. The dull thudding sounds of axes and tomahawks cleaving bones. War cries and screams. He was sick of killing, of the charnal work that surrounded him. It was a bad time to see O'Shannon.

The Irishman galloped past not ten feet away. True snapped off a shot with his pistol and missed, snatched up a musket from a dead Mexican and threw it away when he realized it was broken. A riderless horse galloped past. He caught the trailing reins and somehow managed to slow the frenzied beast and bring it under control. It was already almost too late. O'Shannon's horse had reached the edge of the camp and would be gone within another few seconds. But in that same instant, his stallion took two leaping jumps and dropped in its tracks. O'Shannon fell clear, rolled, scrambled to his feet, and disappeared in the heavy undergrowth that bordered Vince's Bayou.

The rest of the battle might as well not have been taking place. O'Shannon was the only thing that counted. True dodged his mount around and over obstacles, then pulled up at the edge of the trees and dismounted. The woods were murky and quiet, choked with vines and underbrush. The ground was soft and spongy underfoot. The sound of battle faded to a hush broken by the warning call of a jay. The air was heavy and fetid, tainted with the reek of powder. True reloaded his pistol, and began to follow the tracks that lay before him like a map.

"Here," a voice said. "Over here."

True turned.

Luther O'Shannon stood alone in a clearing. "I saw you. Could hardly believe my good fortune. And you brought me a horse."

True hesitated, then pushed through a stand of blackberries into the open. He was tired. He was sick of butchery. He felt no elation in this confrontation. He only wanted it to end.

"That's it. Come closer," O'Shannon chuckled. He held out his saber and cut a swath through the air. The blade, an extension of himself, leaped and darted with alarming dexterity. "I hoped we'd meet again. I owe you this one favor: to put you out of your misery."

"You're a dead man, O'Shannon."

"Really? Aren't we all?" He beckoned with the saber, and took a step sideways to more solid ground. "More to the point, how is your lovely wife, Elizabeth? Fine, I trust. She was when I left her. You *do* remember how that was, don't you," he added in a mocking voice. "In a state of . . . disarray, shall we say?"

True did not launch a wild attack to put an end to the mockery. Instead, he stood and stared at O'Shannon and saw in him all the sickness and useless waste of hatred and depravity.

"Come, my young enemy. My saber against your knife. You bragged on it once. Let's test your merit and skill. I'll wager . . . why, my life! And yours, too." O'Shannon sliced the air once more, then held his blade ready. "Be quick, then. En garde!"

True didn't move. Twenty feet away, he simply stood and raised his pistol.

O'Shannon paled. What about the duel, he thought, beginning to panic. This wasn't how it was supposed to go. The duel. A matter of honor. The final contest!

"Wait!" he exclaimed.

"I didn't come to fight you," True intoned. "I came to kill you."

And he fired.

EPILOGUE

The valley was as beautiful and secluded as Hogjaw had described, the promised grass as green, the water as sweet. Together, hand in hand, True and Elizabeth stood in the heavily loaded wagon and looked to the north along its length. "Any regrets?" True asked, pulling her to him.

It had been a long journey from the bayous of east Texas where Santa Anna's army had been broken and *el Presidente* himself, a beaten man, had been dragged before Houston to surrender all claims to Texas. Time and money had been spent collecting Eustacia and Tommy Matlan, Mildred Thatche and Kevin, Jr., and seeing that everyone returned to Agradecido with the wherewithal to take up their lives in the free and sovereign nation they proudly called the Republic of Texas.

"Except that those who died aren't here now to see it with us," Elizabeth said.

"Andrew and Hogjaw are," True said. A hot lump burned in his throat. "I swear they are. As long as we are here, they will be too."

The morning was awash with the fragrance of cedar and wild clover crushed beneath the wagon wheels. The hills swelled gently to either side, then swept up to become rippled, amber bluffs. The river cutting through the center of the valley was the color of liquid sapphire, and matched the cloud-decked sky. Ahead was the *hacienda* Hogjaw had told Elizabeth about. Cream tinted walls, red tile roof. Abandoned, needing repair, waiting for life.

They stopped in front of the *hacienda* and climbed down from the wagon. Firetail nickered questioningly. "It's all yours," True said, untying him and removing his bridle. "Go see what it's like, boy. Have a run!"

Elizabeth pulled off her bonnet. Her hair, gold as the sun,

gold as the amulet that glinted at her breast, floated on the light breeze. A spirit of joy welled in her and she opened her arms, spread them wide as if to encompass all she looked upon.

"Yes!" she shouted, and then louder, loud as she could, "Yes!"

The echo played among the bluffs, returned, darted out once more to find its way through distant valleys and meadows and hidden hollows.

"Welcome home," True said, at her side.

"Yes," Elizabeth said, "home." His arms came around her, her head rested against his chest. "Welcome home."

The wind touched them. The wind passed by and danced across the land to dally with the tall grasses and, wild and free and waiting to be discovered. a single, perfect yellow rose.

Turn back the pages of history...
and discover

Romance

as it once was!